Oedipus
at
Stalingrad

GREGOR VON REZZORI

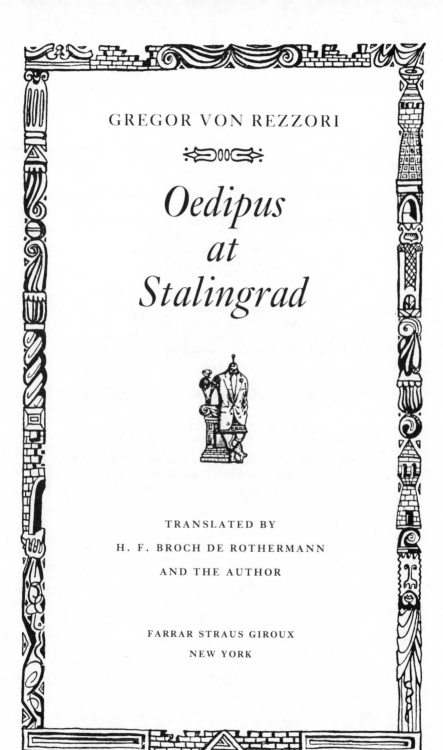

Oedipus
at
Stalingrad

TRANSLATED BY

H. F. BROCH DE ROTHERMANN

AND THE AUTHOR

FARRAR STRAUS GIROUX
NEW YORK

Translation copyright © 1994 by Farrar, Straus and Giroux
All rights reserved
Originally published in German as *Oedipus siegt bei Stalingrad* by
Rowohlt Verlag GmbH, Hamburg
Printed in the United States of America
First edition, 1994

LIBRARY OF CONGRESS CATALOGING-IN-PUBLICATION DATA
Rezzori, Gregor von.
[Oedipus siegt bei Stalingrad. English]
Oedipus at Stalingrad / Gregor von Rezzori ; translated by H. F.
Broch de Rothermann and the author.—1st ed.
p.   cm.
I. Title.
PT2635.E98O3713   1994   833'.912—dc20   94-9800 CIP

The title-page and chapter-opening decorations
are from the original German edition, and were drawn by the author.

The publisher gratefully acknowledges the assistance of Jefferson Chase
in the preparation of this volume.

AUTHOR'S NOTE

This novel was written more than forty years ago, at a time when West Germany was still pockmarked by bomb craters and bristling with skeletons of burned-out cities, when thanks to the magic of hard currency the German Economic Miracle—the *Wirtschaftswunder*—occurred, when the Eastertide ringing of cocktail shakers and the resurrection of fashion magazines and class spirit compelled me to look back into Germany's recent past.

G.v.R.
New York, 1994

A day is a blank sheet of paper.
Bound up over a year, these sheets make a book
which bears the title The Past *and contains*
no lessons for the future.

CEDRIC VON HALACZ,
an explosives terrorist,
in a psychological test

Oedipus
at
Stalingrad

Qu'as-tu fait, ô toi, que voilà pleurant sans cesse,
dis, qu'as-tu fait, toi que voilà, de ta jeunesse?
VERLAINE

O YOU REMEMBER THE PEOPLE YOU ALWAYS ran into at Charley's Bar? I admit it's been quite a while since then, since those prewar days when they were the regulars, the ones who came mostly in the late afternoon and degraded that venerable pub to a gossipmongering den. But it's them I want to speak of, not the sunny playboys of the Roaring Twenties whose caricatures adorned the wall behind the bar, that gallery of happy gnomes who conjured up the supreme spirit of blissful carousing. As far as *they* were concerned, hardly anyone of our belated generation had ever seen them in the flesh, and Charley himself, even when he wasn't drunk, spoke of them only with a certain forbidding reserve and austerity, as witnesses to an illustrious past with whom young rowdies like us could hardly aspire to identify. Every sphere, my good man, has its own kings and courtiers. You can tell where we fit in by the scant respect our clumsy familiarities and miscalculated tips commanded from people like Charley Schulz.

Oh well. More than once have I struggled with Charley's aristocratic, monosyllabic reserve, for I was fascinated by those legendary gentlemen and would have loved to learn everything about them. Even the cartoons of them stirred my fantasies: they had that special ghostly vitality of routinely mediocre caricatures which, once you've seen them somewhere, can haunt you for days. Of course, the fellow who drew them back then could never have suspected how well he had succeeded in capturing his subjects. No doubt his intentions, insofar as his limited talent allowed him to express them, had been malicious. But not even the purest malevolence could have achieved so strong an effect without some divine intervention. Dear heaven, how much time—measured in the dry martinis whose proper dosages

3

Tom knew so well (Tom the Mixer, not Tom Mix, as he wittily insisted)—did I spend staring at those stupendously universal heads on that wall, strangely sprouting from their dwarfish bodies in disregard of normal proportion, wondrously giant, blown up like bubbles, tinted with delicate watercolor washes, exotic flowers of human magnificence. And the enviably correct tailoring of these little people! What devilish exactitude in the details! Their handkerchiefs, the carnations in their lapels, their pearl stickpins revealed an entire world! What is Hebbel's criterion for a work of art? That it depict the whole by means of the parts, I believe. Well, there you are. What's more, a large wall mirror between the panels meant that if you leaned forward you could even see yourself amidst the menagerie.

Incidentally: haven't you ever asked yourself where those types vanished to? They were simply never seen again. Gone. Disintegrated. Never have I seen even one of them roaming about in the wild. So where the devil had they all withdrawn to? They couldn't very well have all died and rotted away, could they? Why didn't they come back anymore to Charley's Bar? What had driven them away? Had they in the meantime chosen some other secret lair as an arena for their celebrations—or had they simply retired, become fat and middle-class, living off cherished memories and tending their prostates? All these questions are of some importance, dear sir. What we're faced with here is a serious problem: the passing of pub generations in all its sociological and metaphysical aspects. Personally, I'm inclined to believe that one fine day (or better yet, one fine night) they were all shipped off by the supreme spirit of carefree pleasure to some suitable Valhalla: a glittering grotto deep beneath the earth's surface, with stalactites and stalagmites covered in a shimmering mosaic inlaid with shards of *fraise-* and amaranth-colored mirrors. There they sit, dressed in silver dinner jackets, bathed in the magical rays of flashing neon lights, on a revolving circular dais supporting a concentric, counterrotating bar of sheer Plexiglas, an endless conveyor belt for their fizzes, flips, and cobblers; a thousand alert bartenders shake their tumblers without pause, a thousand naked girls dance before them on the freely rotating pentagonally mirrored dodecahedrons, and a thousand saxophones and Negro minstrels shout Hallelujah!—the good old Hallelujah of the Jazz Age, needless to say, not that tired stuff you hear nowadays in every church.

As I said, I hadn't meant to tell you about the old playboys. I'm speaking of a later decade. The table in the rear of Charley's, in the left-hand corner next to the sofa, if you remember, was occupied nearly every evening by the same patrons. Its nucleus, the intellectual pole around which the various particles were ordered, was a dead-beat doctor—you know the one I mean: tall, stooped, gray-haired, and fairly seedy, a stereotypical tubercular intellectual from Berlin's miraculous Weimar Republic decadence, a great sarcastic wit. Okay. Do you also remember the blonde with the marvelous figure who was usually at that table? She was a girl with a bad reputation.

She came from a really solid background, Rhenish munitions or something of that sort, but her parents lived in Berlin. These were highly respectable people who had been well along in years when their belated little bundle of joy arrived, like a trial imposed on them by the hand of God himself—her father, now prematurely blind and deaf, a pathetic little man of euphoric senility; her mother, by now in her sixties but still in full sap, rumored to be a lady with a somewhat turbulent past. Like mother, like daughter. Their offspring made her debut, not quite sixteen, at the *thés dansants* on the roof garden of the Hotel Eden, and it soon got around that the young lady was not only fast but downright hasty.

I can't help it: I always liked her very much. There was something grand, something brisk and luxurious about her—as well as humorous and scurrilous. As I said, a splendid physique, an amazon of most plausible dimensions. Long thighs, small in the hips (but with hips, mind you), tits good, everything else good. Moreover: regular features, strong and fine, with a superb carmine-painted Marlene Dietrich mouth, though fuller, lazier, and more lascivious than the hard lips of that insatiable lady. And violet eyes, albeit a bit lacking in lashes. Quite often she wore large horn-rimmed glasses—not with dark lenses, of course, as has latterly become fashionable even among office temps, but regular clear ones, optically ground, three and a half diopters. When she took them off, she had the enticingly helpless look of all nearsighted women. Exceptionally good teeth, which she liked to show off, and sleek, if large, pampered hands. She was excellently maintained, as fresh as a meadow—as one expects of people who are raised in spacious, well-ventilated nurseries. She dressed with chic, rather country-clubbish, yet given her physical assets nonetheless startling, like an aurora borealis. I can well imagine whole herds of little girls in plaid skirts and knee socks having the wind knocked out of them when she passed by— Super Sex Symbol, Goddess, and Queen of Titmice. The most conspicuous part of her whole breathtaking appearance was her hair: a true lioness's mane, a platinum-blond shock of such fullness and body that it would have been the envy of any Merovingian king. It resembled the tail of Mazeppa's horse, Falada—and indeed it was the banner of a horsepowered nature endowed with a savagely exuberant and triumphant physicality. And, as even the mildest of tongues readily acknowledged, the thought of reining in the slightest of the impulses imparted by that physicality never once occurred to her. *She* had known the noble chaps of Charley's Bar personally, known them well and some of them especially well, and after their unearthly disappearance she had immediately joined up with the new crowd and became a *rocher de bronze* at Ciro's, the Jockey Club, the Quartier Latin, and at cocktail parties given by attachés from the Yugoslavian, Moldovlachian, Peruvian, and other Third World embassies.

And yet, as the years went by, this poodle of a girl no longer felt content inside her own notorious skin. It may have been the times in general, a certain frostiness in the air with a tendency toward *völkisch* heroism that arose in the late thirties, but for whatever reason, she began to show signs of a more tempered way of life. She never showed up at Charley's before seven and then only for two or three drinks and to be amused by the witty doctor's spirited monologues.

Around the same time another character surfaced at Charley's, a certain Jassilkowski—Mr. *von* Jassilkowski, please, crest of Topor, from one of the roughly thirty thousand families who, on the occasion of a victory over the Voivode of Czernowitz, had been raised, right there on the field of battle, into the hereditary nobility, simultaneously receiving a coat of arms bearing gules à mace argent.

6

I no longer remember exactly how the story went, but I believe the vanquished Voivode responded to his defeat by impaling all those who had managed to return home on pointed spikes and by preparing a retributive expedition, following which he conferred the coat of arms of the house of Kwilcz (argent à gules mace) to thirty thousand of his vassals. But, as I said, I may be mistaken about this.

Unfortunately, for specific reasons, I have to relate the life story of Knight Jassilkowski in greater detail, though it is rather tangled and complicated.

His first name was not anything like Zbignjew or Mdzjiszlaw, but simply and stirringly Traugott (a Christian name with Teutonic echoes meaning "trust in God"). For Mamá's maiden name was Bremse (a perfectly good name, if you can overlook the fact that the word means both "brake" and "horsefly"), but unfortunately not *von* Bremse, and you will see of what importance this was for our hero's fate. She came from Allenstein, East Prussia, left, right, left, right, forward march! Papá (the clear stress on the second syllable of both the paternal and maternal titles had a particular evolution, having originally fallen on the first syllables of each) was a crew chief—excuse me, estate manager—of one of the estates of Count Lehnhoff or maybe it was Döndorff, anyway, an estate in the Pillkallen district. Or Gumbinnen. Of course, Gumbinnen. Though it could equally well have been Eydtkuhnen. Okay. Lieutenant during the Great War with the Cuirassiers or the Dragoons, or the Uhlans, the Hussars, the Light Brigade, whatever strikes your fancy. Cavalry, anyhow. As you can well imagine, he knew a thing or two about domestic animals, including horses. He was a gentleman of medium height, robust, and of masculine comportment, with a thick, black nightwatchman's mustache, waxed up into two points, a round head with stubbly hair cut to military length, and a scalp that would reticulate in wormlike folds whenever he was called upon to exert himself, especially in thought. According to a saying he often repeated, he put less stock in theories and fancy notions than in practice. In a word, he was the prototypical *Junker*—you know, blood and soil—and in his case more soil than blood. Please keep in mind that a good deal of time had passed since the battles against the Voivode of Czernowitz; the heroes had dispersed and lost their captured booty in reversals of fortune; some of their descendants had emigrated; documents had been burned and had otherwise disappeared (just consider the devastations wrought by the Thirty Years War)—in short: Papá Jassilkowski could look back on a line of ancestors consisting of exactly two (read: two) true-blue Prussians. One of them had been awarded the Iron Cross at Sedan in 1870—in the enlisted ranks, which meant something. Both had been crop inspectors on rural estates. There you have it: tradition.

Papá Jassilkowski, to his credit, didn't care about genealogies and their implications for social status. He was—though it is really quite irrelevant what he was or what he was like—a crop inspector through and through: conscientious, sweaty, narrow-minded, choleric, and tied to the land. But Mamá, née Bremse, whose cradle had stood in the house of a chief district veterinarian, could not rid herself of the gnawing suspicion that somehow she had married below her station.

I regret not being in a position to give you precise information about the intellectual and physical attributes of the former Miss Bremse. I suspect that even young Traugott, to whose existence, after all, she had contributed a not entirely insignificant part (on the contrary!), would also have found it difficult. She was—how should I put it?—so utterly amorphous, colorless, and washed out . . . We live in an age, dear God, which has already supplanted the Biedermeier ideal of the maternal woman with the curvaceous females of the Belle Epoque and which today tends toward the hot-blooded thoroughbred Hollywood type. I'm sad to say that Allenstein, East Prussia—especially at that time of golden-braided grain-harvesting maidens—was hardly a place capable of producing this type, nor Pillkallen a region that could preserve it. In any case, Mamá was an excellent housewife and, as we know, of higher (if actually rather mediocre) birth. A certain familiarity, based on shared interest in women's matters, arose between her and the Countess, the latter having come over on several occasions, after Mamá had finished cutting a new suit for her boy, whom she always kept immaculately neat and taught all the proper manners, in order to borrow patterns for her own children.

In any case, at least in those early phases of his development,

Mamá was for little Traugott something like what the ether seems to have been for Hölderlin. Because of this, he hated Papá all the more passionately.

As the beneficiary of the insights of Bruno Bettelheim and Lady Seidel, you will surely know what a profound and full vessel the soul of a child is. Regarding the case at hand, it may be enough to consider what the squire Jassilkowski, reflecting on it later, would term "the tensions resulting from differences in genotype," to wit: Faustian excitability (presumably from the Bremse gene) paired with the dull brooding melancholy of Sarmatian herdsmen blowing their panpipes (Papá's heritage). Then there was the class difference between his parents, you understand: the nobility-bourgeoisie conflict. To illustrate this with an example: Mamá, sitting in the dusk of the inspector's quarters, pours all of her conflicting emotions into a rendition of Sinding's "Rustles of Spring" on the piano of the former chief district veterinarian; and Papá, coming home from the fields, vexed by the poor work habits of the Polacks, hoarse from screaming, and exhausted from having to stand around and do nothing himself, with the hot blood of a people who had conquered the Voivode of Czernowitz boiling irrepressibly in his veins, thrashes his wife and child with his inspector's rod. Add to this a certain weakness in the boy's chest, and there you have, in a few broad strokes, a psychological profile of the young Mr. von Jassilkowski —something like Philipp Otto Runge with a dash of Hieronymus Bosch. And don't forget the atmosphere of Gumbinnen.

The inspector's rod was a knotty oak stick, ending not with the usual metal tip, but with a tiny rectangular shovel designed for probing and examining topsoil. Be that as it may, allow me the following question: is Sinding's "Rustles of Spring" a fair weapon in the class struggle? Nor was the lady, née Bremse, otherwise unarmed. Papá possessed, if I may say so, a rather strongly erotic disposition. On many nights, extremely tumultuous scenes of courtship and obstinate resistance were enacted in the Jassilkowski bedroom—resistance no doubt made all the more stubborn because Mamá's sense of social self-esteem (God knows) stood in internal contradiction to a certain willingness in principle on her part. But who may presume, I ask you, to distinguish between right and wrong,

9

between cause and effect in the tangled web of human relations?

Oh well. In any case, the spatial dimensions of the inspector's quarters were rather tight, and more than once, young Traugott, sleeping in a dark adjacent room, was awakened by the heated, incantatory, and increasingly angry mutterings of Papá and the alternately brusque and scornful, always nakedly contemptuous rejections of the former Miss Bremse, which, after loud and prolonged rumblings and crashes of furniture, the clattering fall of bedside lamps, et cetera, gradually subsided into wounded lamentations and other woeful sounds that occasionally lent themselves to alternative interpretation. In the darkness, Jassilkowski Junior first experienced the typical sensations of classical tragedy—fear and pity—which, as you know from reading Nietzsche attentively, arise from the spirit of music.

The boy's impressions must have been all the more frightening as his imagination lacked the appropriate pictorial images that would have allowed him to understand that what was transpiring on the other side of the door was, if I may say so, harmless and natural. Quaking in terror, his heart pounding, plagued by dark suspicions and vague surmises about monstrous and despicable acts which, as far as he could see, or better yet hear, the participants strangely seemed to value highly, he followed with avid ear the noises from behind the door until his inability to translate them into actual images became unbearable torture. The single vision that dominated his fantasy, in almost tactile clarity, was that of the naked and gnarled figure of Papá, which he knew from his morning wash at the water tap in his room (during which Papá always stood unabashedly naked before him): his disgustingly white body sharply distinguished at the neckline from his reddish sunburned head, with a pronounced masculinity that simultaneously repelled and excited him and also humiliated him by making him aware of his own physical weakness.

You will surely be astonished by my knowledge of such intimate details, all the more so because they crassly contradict the impression that anyone who ever met Jassilkowski was bound to have formed of his background. I am convinced that even Charley, for instance, despite his keen eye (a quality developed by all people who practice a high level of hospitality), never suspected such dire circumstances as the aforementioned use of the water tap in the child's bedroom. Not that Knight Traugott had anything of the show-off self-inflatedness, the complacent fussiness, or the calculated ennui of the typical baron. His manner, my dear fellow, was cool, elegant, discreet, measured, restrained, most finely polished in all the formalities—oh, what can I say: light on the reins and firm in the saddle, the whole in perfect equilibrium, a real Prussian; the hard snap and the tough streak both left to the imagination, nothing obvious, you understand, a monocle of the soul, so to speak. And what's more, excellent morals, Potsdam garrison church on Sunday mornings, entirely free of intellectual additives, pure biodynamic breeding. And a hint—but only a hint!—of rusticity in his overall appearance, ethically fortified and aesthetically transparent . . . You see, venerable friend, in the grueling struggle for personal acknowledgment, which requires so much energy and circumspection that it consumes most of our abilities and time, sublime alternatives exist to the popular forms of stupidly aggressive showing-off, and the most sophisticated of these relies on a strategy of distinction, conservation, and omission (in this sense, it's almost an art form, isn't it?). Such a strategy disdains the trumped-up pose and selects instead the soberly convincing gesture—but only if skillfully executed, please! You understand? Its effect relies on the spaces it opens for and assigns to the play of the imagination: it is the refined way of showing-off, which disdains showing-off. But don't go imagining, my good man, that either you or I could master it if we wanted to. Certain intellectual limits are required for that sort of creativity, too, and even though I'm prepared in principle to grant them to anyone, in this case we are talking about divinely inspired limits of genius, and I doubt whether mere industriousness can be a substitute. No, my friend, it's no good simply to pursue it. It has to be *lived* in every fiber of your body and the deepest recesses of your soul. For who can say whether all true greatness does not ultimately derive from immeasurable self-deception, from an illusion that has been believably believed. So, therefore, be so good as to show proper respect for what it takes to become a Jassilkowski—and *last, not least*: don't underestimate the importance of sheer luck, which at times had to smile on him as well.

Witness the following: I have no idea what outlook you, not being of the landed gentry, might represent—no matter. It is a truism that expert milking, starting with the flirtatious and playful preparation of the udder, from the tenderly arousing and fortifying massage of the teat all the way to the actual draining of all four, is as much the starting point for a future understanding of how to raise a halfway decent herd of registered cattle as the latter is an important element in the creation of a young nobleman, regardless of what inclinations he may later choose to follow. However, as you might well surmise by now, it may not have been exactly this train of thought that led Papá, shortly before Squire Traugott was to be sent away to the academy in Königsberg, to intervene in his development in a way that was rich in consequences. For various reasons—in order to ensure that practice had its proper place in the boy's education, and because of his weak chest, that is, mainly because the boy's doctor, following the same train of thought, had issued dire warnings against it, and above all, because Mamá objected on social grounds—he sent the boy to work in the cow barns for a while. Thus, little Traugott spent one long summer on the one-legged milking stool, which was attached to his trousers, battling against swarms of flies and dung-heavy cow tails, laboring amidst biting manure fumes, which east of the river Elbe are believed to be as edifying for the spirit as they are salutary for the lungs.

But it so happened that Mother Bremse nurtured fears of an entirely different sort. It's possible that she was not pleased by her son's overfluent use of terms like "dry mounting" and "vaginal prolepsis," although they were as familiar to her from the professional vocabulary of her father, the chief district veterinarian, as they were to Papá Jassilkowski, full-blooded descendant of trans-Carpathian scimitar nobility. But surely, above all else, she feared that the commentary of the herdsmen, elaborating on scenes that occur every day in stables, would be guided more by their own coarse sense of humor than by thoughtful consideration for the fragile mental welfare of an inquisitive young man. In order to protect little Traugott from any possible harm to his psyche (knowledge is power!), she decided to enlighten him in decent language about sexual matters.

She proceeded with an extreme delicacy, made all the more touching because the Count's children had long since helped the lad understand certain activities common to the henhouse and the parental bedroom—not to mention practice them. But the good lady could hardly have suspected this.

She selected a Sunday, when Papá was away in Pillkallen, to spend the day with her son. Earlier than usual, she played Sinding's "Rustles of Spring" and then, as if following a sudden impulse, informed him they were going on a walk. Arm in arm, they walked along the cart path through the fields, punctuated by red patches of wild poppies, leaving behind the farm buildings shadowed by oaks, elms, and chestnuts, a dark island in the golden wheat fields, and then continued, under high drifting clouds, through the swaying grain. Finally, far away, in front of a big field barn, she picked some arnica, marigolds, and buttercups—or whatever the devil else may have been in season in the furrows of East Prussia—and began to explain to the boy the process of pollination, with the help of stamen, pistil, and pollen. Mother Bremse in the role of Maya the Bee, if you will! What to him had taken on the dimensions of a sexual homicide committed two or three times a week, she wanted to illustrate here with the examples of liverworts and forget-me-nots! It was true, as she freely admitted, that in the case of human beings and other vertebrates, mild breezes and butterflies were uncommon as means of conveyance, but, she hastened to add, this was of course regrettable. She went on in some detail and did not fail to provide both aesthetic and ethical rationales for her opinion.

Little Traugott was dumbfounded. As far as he could grasp, the whole thing was obviously screwed up from the start; it was, so to speak, the cloven hoof of creation. (See the Bible, Part One, Genesis, as well as countless other relevant passages. This also came up in the fine arts, opined Mamá, with which he would soon become intimately acquainted at Königsberg—you need think no further than someone like Karin Michaelis . . .) But that was all useless theory. In practice, this much was certain: it simply was what it was, horrible, violent, brutal, humiliating. And dirty, most of all dirty. Chickens trampled into the dust, cattle bellowing out, dripping blood and straining against their ropes, dogs in heat unable to separate from one another, showered by a hail of stones from the village youngsters—that's how it was, that's how it had always been, in his parents' bedroom as well as the Lady Countess's. And that's how it would be later in his own bed. Yes, you could understand why it was the most venal of the sins.

The blue, oh so blue summer sky spread majestically over the earth, and large clouds sailed by like ships, without a sound; the grain had grown high and flies buzzed in the grass; a swarm of pigeons circled over the distant mansion and descended on it with rigidly spread wings, shining in the sunlight, almost touching the roof in bold arcs of flight. Then they flapped their wings and ascended again. Cattle grazed peacefully in their enclosures. Little Traugott walked alongside his mother, downcast, suffused with a vague feeling of tenderness for her, full also of guilty conscience and, at the same time, of anguished fear that she might touch him. She talked on and on, but he did not understand much of what she said; it was always the same thing, and only when she spoke of *purity* did he listen attentively. Purity was the magic word. Purity could absolve the sinfulness that had come over the world; it was the beginning and the end, the secret formula of salvation in the metaphysics of sexuality. It makes us forget that our children are born amidst blood, filth, and tears, that they are not delivered to us fully processed at home by Mrs. Sulamith Wülfing. Purity here, purity there, purity *über alles*—little Traugott listened devoutly. As for the joys of love, they were—to put it succinctly—nothing but a load of crap. He, Traugott, decided then and there, because it was the right thing to do but also because he felt a vague and embarrassed sense of affection for Mamá, that he would inscribe the motto "Purity" on his shield once and for all.

Don't weep or fret, dear mother mine!
What matter that the cupboard's bare.
I'm your blond child and of noble line,
Crowned by your blood, which I too share.
RILKE, "ADVENT"

 CERTAINLY SHALL NOT TEST YOUR PATIENCE with a severe *Bildungsroman* à la *Emile*. I'm almost through with the preamble to this story. Little Traugott was sent to Königsberg and, once there, dutifully dozed through his school years. For a little while, the memory of that summer day with its premature revelations and noble intentions hovered over him like a guiding star, but then it gradually faded, grew remote, and finally—as usually happens—sank below the horizon of consciousness into his unconscious, where it persisted, together with other such rubbish, in its own shadowy and obdurate half-life. Otherwise, he developed normally; the young squire came somewhat early to that vice whose deceived deceivers are, according to Rilke, lean, hard boyish hands—incidentally the only activity in which he empirically benefited from his apprenticeship on the milking stool. One hard winter, Papá, while shouting excessively at the beaters during a hare hunt, inhaled a bit too much of the icy east wind and, within a few days, passed on peacefully. With her small widow's pension, granted to her by the Count in recognition of the services rendered by her very regrettably deceased husband (all things considered, the hunt had gone quite well), Mamá moved to Allenstein. Of course, there could be no question of Traugott's continuing his studies in Königsberg. But her little son spared the old lady the necessity of worrying over his continued education. One fine day, barely seventeen, he disappeared for Berlin.

Despite my good intentions, I can't tell you what he did there, in the Berlin of those days—dear Christ in heaven!—I hardly need paint you a picture of the rich asphalt pastures that grew even then for young blades all the way from the Lützow canal to Halensee.

Trust me, that young product of Pillkallen was indeed made of the best material; no working student he with trousers tucked into his boots, eager to absorb life's miracles like blotting paper; no backwoods savage or prehistoric horse, *Equus przewalskii*, pounding the pavements of Babylon; but, on the contrary, a spiritual thoroughbred, the pedigreed result of a special high-performance breeding: Traugott von Jassilkowski out of Bremse-without-a-von—mark the powerful tension!—favored to win the Blue Ribbon of the Kurfürstendamm.

Enough. The years passed swiftly, and another fine day, Mamá Bremse's doorbell rang in Allenstein, and when she opened the door (she hadn't expected anyone and was wearing her apron), who should stand there but her long-lost son. And in truth, the young falcon had grown fine new feathers! She was so stunned at first by his appearance that it was only toward evening that she calmed down a bit and could scrutinize him. Hadn't he grown tall and handsome and imposing! And elegant—a real fashion plate! He had a small mustache, pitch black and melancholy, like a Cuban guitar player's, almost troublesomely handsome—and he wore a silk-lined hat and fine suede leather gloves, which he dropped without noticing where, and his shoes were new, pointed and polished to a mirror finish. It's true: this was not what the reigning zeitgeist proclaimed as the model of young manhood. Germany's admirable network of highways, for example, could not have been achieved with the labor of such a type. But it corresponded to the German soul: the desire to expand beyond the border of a determinate existence. *Volk ohne Raum*—people deprived of space—means also space-seeking soul, and space was symbolized by the image of the cosmopolite. Young Traugott brought with him a whiff of the wide world, and he carried with him a heavy expensive alligator suitcase. He had just come over from Zoppot to visit for a few days.

And stay he did. He was surprisingly domestic—never went out at all. He almost got angry when she urged him to look around town a bit. "Oh, leave me alone—these people here . . . I've come to spend time with *you*, Mamá, not with Allenstein!" Mamá—do you hear? Mamá—it sounded like something from a French boarding school. In any case, the former Miss Bremse had to suppress a smile of embarrassed pride. But she collected herself and asked him soberly whether perhaps he had any socks she could darn for him. No, he didn't. His underwear was fully intact—all silk from head to toe, what can I tell you, each individual piece artfully monogrammed with arabesque intertwined initials, T.J., surmounted by a five-pointed crown the diameter of a saucer.

So she cooked his old favorites, sweet-and-sour pork stews and semolina pudding with raspberry sauce, and she was in seventh heaven, though a bit puzzled. He slept until noon, sat around in his bathrobe, yawned, smoked cigarettes, and leafed through some old issues of the *Illustrated Weekly* she had borrowed from an acquaintance, yawned again, looked out the window, and then attentively examined the room at some length. Her grown-up son. The prodigal son returned from the big city.

"Are these your parents, Mamá, in that photograph on the wall?"

"Why, of course, dear boy—Grandpappy Bremse—don't you remember him?"

"He was a doctor, wasn't he? But his wife was already dead by the time I was born?"

"Granny passed away a bit before you turned two. We took you along to the funeral, but you were probably too small to remember."

"What was her family?"

"She was a Kohn."

Traugott winced.

"One of the East Prussian Kohns, of course, with a *K*, the Aryan ones," Mamá hastened to add. He nodded distractedly, silent and brooding.

You understand: a man turned in on himself. Long silent hours, caught in the ghostly web of the past. Dark voices in his blood, just like the turn of the tide, when strange portentous things are uncovered on previously flooded ground.

And so one evening went by, and then a second and a third . . . The little lamp with the fringed silk shade, on which were glued a ring of silhouettes, chubby-cheeked children in Biedermeier costume, the boys in tails with droll starched collars and curved top hats, the little girls in crinolines and poke bonnets—that old lamp, whose wire frame had been bent here and there by occasional falls, vividly bringing Papá to mind, shed its mild and somewhat gloomy light. Fair Traugott looked down on Mamá's graying hair as she sat and darned her stockings, and then for a long time he contemplated her dress and her hands. Finally, staring at the ground, he whistled the tango "Yira, Yira" silently, barely exhaling it over his lips, and, lost in thought, fiddled with her spare reading glasses, which lay on a pile of Weeklys—a thoroughly ordinary pair of glasses, whose steel bow she had wrapped with a bit of chamois so that it wouldn't dig into her nose.

Why didn't he tell her anything about Berlin? How did he live? What precisely did he do?

He was doing fine, thank you very much. Living at a frightfully nice lady's, a Mrs. von Schrader. Not a great name, admittedly, but she, too, was highborn: née Countess Rumpfburg-Schottenfels; only the misfortunes of the Great War's aftermath had forced her to run a boardinghouse, the Pension Bunsen, Knesebeckstrasse—anyway, Mamá surely knew the address.

And what did he live on? What business had called him to Zoppot?

Oh, nothing really: just a few days' vacation. But apropos Zoppot: he had run into a Count Zapieha there—"you know, one of those Zapiehas who also belong to the house of Topor or, at least, are close to it—in any case, relatives, so to speak. And can you imagine? This arrogant bloke thought he could snub me. He simply cut me down. These Poles with all their delusions of grandeur don't know which way is up."

It should be acknowledged that this was the first time that Mamá, secretly astonished, had heard the Counts Zapieha spoken of as relatives. On the other hand, what he was saying about Poles was only too true. The Führer, after all, thought the same. What did either of them really know about the other, after all those years of estrangement? . . . Why was it that little Traugott wrote only seldom to her, she who had only him and nothing else in the whole wide world, a lonely mother's heart . . .

Much abashed, little Traugott defended himself: hadn't she received his letter thanking her for the money?

Yes, of course, both times. She would have liked nothing better than to have helped him more, but surely he knew how tight her circumstances were . . .

"For God's sake, Mamá, don't mention it. It was merely a temporary difficulty, before my articles came out in the paper."

You are flabbergasted—what? You think that you might not have heard correctly: articles in the paper. But it was a fact. Articles in the paper. And don't try to convince me that you'd been expecting it, that ever since you'd heard about his childhood, you had, in fact, been waiting for something of this sort. No dice, my dear man! Art is the expression of surplus energy, so says Mr. Houston Stewart Chamberlain, created by unresolved inner conflict, but that hardly makes it one of the foundations of the twentieth century. Nowadays, you can walk around with as many unresolved conflicts as you want, but it won't make you a poet any time soon. Not in this day and age, my venerable friend.

I'll tell you exactly what it's about, and you can call it whatever you want, but let's not kid ourselves: put simply, this is the century of the closet. The apotheosis of clothing confection. Stendhal maintained that one should sell the shirt off one's back in order to see Raphael's Loggias or, if one had already seen them, to see them again. Today we would gladly auction off Raphael's Loggias piecemeal to America in order to buy more shirts. What stirs our passions, dear sir, is not the turmoil of the soul in urgent conversation with the universe, but rather the question of whether to order our next glen-check suit double-breasted or single with three buttons. If we are already talking about predestination, then in the case of Jassilkowski, let it be via his magazine articles—which bore the following headlines: "The Jacket with Side Vents: A Classical Style?" or "The Renaissance of the Short Raglan: The Above-the-Knee, Fingertip-Length *All-Round* Overcoat for Mild Weather"—appearing to general acclaim in Baron von Aalquist's *Gentleman's Monthly*.

Incidentally, this has as little to do with a true calling as with a profession. Profession—who nowadays still has a real profession? You have a *job*, in order to keep your head an inch or two above water. But a regular profession? A fellow sucker in the grip of contemporary history. An extra in some set piece with an unknown ending. Half a dozen directors, five billion prompters. Meanwhile, as something of a special cameo, you get to playact yourself for a while. *C'est tout.*

But try to explain that to the former Miss Bremse!

As I said, the days went by until it was time for him to go. Shortly before they went to the train station, Traugott found a cane in some corner or another.

"What kind of a cane is this, Mamá?"

"Why, don't you recognize it, m'boy? Father's inspector's rod. I dunno why I brought it along. Probably slipped in with the rest of the things when I moved."

Her boy examined the rustic instrument. "May I keep it, Mamá? I don't have anything at all to remind me of Papá."

Mamá gladly handed it over. "You sure won't be able to use it much in the city. Have it fitted with a regular tip instead of the little shovel."

Then they walked to the train station and Squire Traugott thoughtfully scratched along the rails with the Papá Jassilkowski Memorial Rod. "You should get away from here, too, from time to time, Mamá. This Allenstein, with the years you've picked up the whole accent . . ."

And then the train came, and he boarded, and the train left, and she stood and waved goodbye to him for a long, long time, blinded by tears, the good-natured former Miss Bremse-without-a-von— tears of proud bereavement.

Oh well. Done with the preamble. In any case, in early '38, sometime around Easter, the young Baron von Jassilkowski was first seen in Charley's Bar.

Sero te amavi, pulchritudo tam antiqua
et tam nova—sero te amavi!

AURELIUS AUGUSTINUS

938—YOU'RE NOT BY ANY CHANCE WRIN-
kling your nose at my mention of the date? I should
hope not, venerable reader. For if you are, you only
prove that you don't understand the crux of the
matter. Therefore, let me explain in advance: 1938
was a magic year. Great Germany became an even
Greater Germany. The Austrians found themselves
back in the womb of the Reich and enlarged and
enriched it with a touch of their legendary elegance. Famous Alpine
resorts were again open to patrons who had missed them for years.
The Salzburg Festival was cleansed of Jews. Furtwängler triumphed
with *Die Meistersinger*. Frau Ulla von Haniel let her horses run
in Baden Baden, Frau Emma Göring-Sonnenmann held court in
Berlin—and yet, and yet . . . something in the air made all this
appear as if it weren't quite real, an abstract reality, if I may say so:
a present without a link to either past or future. The days floated
like loose balloons in a summer sky. Everybody seemed to wait
for something that never happened; what happened didn't happen
really; it was a time of expectation, and actually nobody cared about
what they were expecting. You know what waiting for someone or
something means: it means that you feel the flow of time, that by
growing impatient you feel time and nothing but time, time in which
nothing happens or in which what happens is of no weight, of no
importance whatsoever in relation to what is going to happen. Only
by considering this will you be able to appreciate the adventure of
Baron Traugott's social career.

It's child's play to succeed in a blossoming society. In seventeen
hundred and whatever, for example, it sufficed to lean up against
some mantelpiece in an ambitious lady's salon, casually scattering
a few well-honed and healthily cynical aphorisms, to be accepted

as a wit and social lion. In 1928, all you had to do was stuff your pockets with a bundle of Krupp shares and the next day you would find yourself sitting at the Königin Bar between the Baroness Goldschmied-Rothschild and Dr. Flechtheim. But in times of expectation, when time has no other notion than flowing ahead, no weight to carry on the happening of things, things freeze in their actual state; the social mass coagulates into little groups, and each little social group is complete within itself. That means that each social group becomes a sort of aristocracy. *Then* go and try to graft yourself onto the priceless patinated embellishments of a closed caste—now that's a work of art, worthy of emulation!

Give me another minute to differentiate. As you surely recall, aristocracy literally means domination by the beautiful and the good. Very well, that may have indeed been the case in ancient Thessaly or somewhere down in the Balkans, but our kind understands something quite different by the term. To be truly distinguished in this sweat-drenched era of ours, something has to be totally useless. The aristocracy, according to our conception of it, is that exquisite class of people who long ago cleansed themselves of any sort of meaningful, everyday social function (especially something that has become as commonly vulgar as domination!). Thus, this class exists in and of itself but also in seemingly direct defiance of all extant physical laws, for even the law of inertia fails to explain adequately its continuing existence, priceless though it may be, as a kind of Kohinoor diamond whose very contradictions make it sparkle. The aristocracy is not what it is but what it has been. On the other hand, in order to be what it is, it is not allowed to be what it was . . . It would be superfluous to cite further examples of the value of an outdated value system. Only Jews pay nothing for heirlooms: Justus Perthes of the *Almanach de Gotha* thinks otherwise and—*hélas*—the rest of the Occident with him. And consider, if you will, that even in A.D. 1928 the regular roundtable gatherings at the Romanische Café were aristocracies in the sense delineated above. Let alone the crumbling world of the Prussian Junkers.

Now you can appreciate that it takes a truly refined taste to seek one's field of play in such a lost territory—a sensitivity having nothing in common with a run-of-the-mill upstart's vulgar pushiness.

Just consider the inherent difficulties: a caste complete in itself, closed on all sides. Its exclusivity is—to express myself in today's jargon —ontologically predetermined. One cannot arrive in it: one either belongs to it or not. No tricks or open sesames are of any use. Nor ducats, nor a good little head on one's shoulders. Money? Money is vulgar. Anyone can have money nowadays. And intellect—big deal! No matter what you understand by the term, it's simply disreputable. Intellect has always been the capital of Thersites and Co.

Now please grasp what finesse it took to choose Charley's Bar at precisely that moment in time. Was it not still a storied nightspot, as it always had been, if also a bit moth-eaten, vegetating at the mercy of its daytime customers, a first-class establishment available at a discount—something of a Grand Dame O.B.E. among call girls? As if following some organic instinct, all the cliques of the local *jeunesse dorée* congregated there, and with their *haut goût*, they gave the upper Kurfürstendamm a racy tint, all those fresh vegetables with roots sunk in the mother earth of golf links, sharply seasoned with olives and garlic cloves from various southeastern embassies, musclemen usually seen auto racing at the Avus or on the tennis courts, and, as goes without saying, the cream of the intelligentsia: well-camouflaged dissident columnists forced to write for Dr. Goebbels' media, plus the tatty film elite from the studios in Neubabelsberg—in short, everyone who knew that the best fashion ever invented was to follow whatever had just gone out of fashion. All of this, well measured and mixed into a rich stuffing for our turkey, dear friend, was something for a gourmet, just the right thing to fill up the old oven, particularly when topped off, as with a few pistachios, by a handful of beautiful young men, like Greek ephebes, who had somehow managed to slip through the patiently tended meshes of the law.

No, my good man, you can see that it was no simple matter. *Miles* Jassilkowski knew what he was doing. He had chosen the right place to play in. And, of course, you mustn't imagine him making an entrance under the concentrated glare of spotlights and to an extended drumroll and an excited "Ah!" from the audience. No. One evening he was simply there as if he had always been part of the team. He was sitting at the bar, throwing dice with Charley for martinis. Personally, I only noticed him a while later, after he had begun coming regularly every day around seven.

Gracious heavens!—Charley's Bar! Don't you think it's a crying shame what Lord Zebaoth has done to our old stomping grounds! It's just gone all to hell, now . . . I can still tell you the exact position of every nail in the place: the bar here, Charley behind it (drunk, of course) together with Tom (the Mixer, not Tom Mix, as you well know), the gallery of grand playboys hanging on the brown-paneled wall behind them; over there Jassilkowski; and kitty-corner behind us, next to the sofa, the regulars' table with the witty doctor and that blond thoroughbred. And all the other people who came to Charley's back then . . .

Incidentally, speaking of that convincing blonde, something peculiar seemed to happen to her around that time: she dressed even more provocatively than usual, if that was possible, and seemed more excessively lively and effervescent. She arrived every day very punctually—and she had fun at Charley's, it's hard to believe how much! She greeted even the doctor's most vapid jokes with peals of laughter, and every time she laughed she would glance over at the bar, her eyes myopically blurred, teeth sparkling and lips opened up like a sweet, ripe fruit . . . And meanwhile Baron Traugott . . . I haven't neglected to provide a detailed description of him, have I? Well, the butterfly had emerged from the chrysalis, his metamorphosis complete: no more thin mustache, no more "Southern Cross in the black velvet of a tropical night"—instead, Mayfair. How should I put it? No more silk—instead, linen and wool, though despite his sober English haircut there was still something of the pitch-black waviness of his grandfather's curls, and beneath the sporty tan from afternoons on the shore of the Wannsee, still the rose-petal blush of the former Miss Bremse's skin: "you seem to be your mother's mirror, giving her back the fair May of her bygone days," isn't that the case? Thus Baron Traugott sat at the bar with his back to the blond thoroughbred and stared ahead off to his right, with the hint of a skeptical yet philanderous smile on his lips, one eyebrow raised diabolically, sipping portentously from time to time at his drink. It was sheer accident that I discovered the deeper meaning of the reciprocal expressions he was making: between the caricatures of the playboys hung that large mirror where they could see each other at an acute angle.

Oh well. Finally, one fine evening, a simultaneous urge to refresh themselves prompted them to disappear to the rest rooms through the door at the rear of the bar, where the gentleman gallantly let the lady go before him.

So far, so good. The natural course of things. After a little while, they reappeared, needless to say separately, as required by decorum, and assumed their respective seats. While Baron Traugott allowed himself a double cognac, she carefully redrew her lips. And a few days later, on a more suitable occasion, they introduced themselves. No fault there. But after a week or two, the story took an unexpected turn.

 HAPPEN TO BE IN A POSITION TO PROVIDE
you with firsthand details of great subtlety and fate-
ful significance on the strength of personal observation, to wit, as an actual eyewitness. Be so good
as to admire therein the fine hand of providence,
for here, too, it is not that occurrences themselves
determine destiny, but rather that the mysterious
echo of seemingly meaningless circumstances turns
an everyday happenstance into a significant event. Goethe himself
—as you no doubt remember—using the example of Napoleon,
asserted that in modern times fate is determined by politics. I take
the liberty to question the truth of this maxim. As if politics were
still in the hands of outstanding personalities! Hush, papá Tolstoy!
These days, politics is a term used to describe the more or less
effective management of the masses, and I leave open not only the
question whether the managers of *our* day have enough personality
to influence the trends that the masses follow, but also the question
whether a concept such as fate can be applied to entities like mi-
grating termites or schooling herring. If you insist on it, I am willing
to concede at most the marginal case of the rats of Hameln following
the Pied Piper, whose surprising musicality would support such a
claim, but that's as far as I'm willing to go.

That notwithstanding, as far as the destiny of the individual is
concerned, the hand of God is still clearly at work. Supernatural
forces direct and influence the course of our lives. And in the days
of expectancy, when anything that happened was of no weight at
all, things happened behind our backs, so to say. If, for instance,
we were to examine the fate of Baron Traugott von Jassilkowski,
we would find him—as you shall hear shortly—ensnared in a
decision-making quandary, a tragic either-or, which can be postu-

26

lated, if at all, only in symbolic and geopolitical terms. On the one hand, the inherited hero complex burdened the descendants of the victors over the Voivode of Czernowitz (this may be summed up in a narrow sense by the word "Potsdam"), and on the other hand, there was Charley's Bar (in its full metaphoric significance, of course). Where lay the golden mean? And was he, standing now at a crossroads, truly a Hercules? Or some other symbolic figure, one more closely wedded to that *unio mystica* of blood and soil—an Antaeus of the Kurfürstendamm, so to speak, who would forfeit all his powers as soon as the soles of his feet no longer touched that familiar pavement? Just so we don't get ahead of ourselves in the story, permit me to leave this question open for the time being. The events that I am now going to relate are in any case only a preamble and introduction, the impetus to the impetus—and yet at the same time, like the tree contained in the acorn (entelechy!), this whole conflict was already present.

In the beginning, it was an evening like any other, but for some unfathomable reason everybody at Charley's had drunk themselves halfway under the table. The regulars at the corner table near the sofa were going a hundred miles an hour; one sharp witticism from the clever doctor led to another, accompanied by ever louder and more uninhibited choruses of laughter, topped by the peals of the blond thoroughbred. Similarly high spirits ruled at the other tables. The ephebes were twittering and chirping in their remote corner as from a birdcage. Elsewhere a group of Balkans or Moldovlachians or whatever—almond-eyed blokes with helmet-shaped haircuts and inch-thick lips, diamonds and rubber heels—was celebrating some high national holiday (the Benediction of the Ram, no doubt), and there was even an additional surprise visit—God only knows how they ever found the place—from a few young ladies unmistakably of Lower Silesian nobility, who somehow had been enticed to come to Berlin from their turnip fields for a ball of the former Mounted Guards or some other matrimonial market and who, together with their escorts, were indulging in carefree revelries. Bubbly was being drunk all around. The bar itself was in high gear. Baron Traugott sat there on his usual stool (he assiduously avoided the witty doctor's table of regulars because of a violent and poisonously reciprocated aversion to them; when all was said and done, he had no binding commitment, now, did he?)—very well: he sat there at the bar with the other epigones and in view of the old playboys, his back to the blond thoroughbred, throwing dice, betting for drinks, and boozing it up. Charley, his old barkeep's eyes totally glassed over in diffident solitude, observing the goings-on of the world with tragically clear-headed drunkenness, and Tom the Mixer, his hands a blur of juggled bottles . . . To make a long story short: hustle and bustle, high spirits, as in the good old days. All this coming out of nowhere, you understand. And yet (though this may be only my personal impression) there was a strange tension running through it all, an excited, almost cheerfully nervous undertone, as if something special were about to happen.

And indeed, suddenly, around midnight, there was a commotion in the checkroom, a babble of voices, people poked their heads in, and the swinging doors allowed a momentary glimpse of some festively entwined figures. Finally, both doors flew open, and with swelling emotions a kind of procession of the Holy Grail swept into Charley's. At its head was an agitated little man with glasses, busy hands, and, in spite of the Nuremberg Laws, a Jewish manner of intense concentration and haste, along with a gangly young man with a provincial, secretarial mien—these two dubious confidants immediately demanded two tables, allegedly reserved in advance, in the imperious tones of people who are used to giving orders. There followed several sporty squires in plaid jackets with rounded shoulders and droopy mustaches, one of them even wearing a sloppy leather waistcoat. Then, to everyone's surprise, some pretty young things appeared with apricot-painted faces, violet lips, and blue-green-shadowed, belladonna eyes (at the sight of which the ephebes emitted cackles of delight like parakeets), followed by the upper half of a chauffeur, who, along with Charley's doorman, held the doors wide open for, at long last: the Grail herself. The guardian of this Holiest of Holies was a small, stocky, somewhat Mongolian-looking gentleman in a dinner jacket, silk-shirted and slick-haired, absorbed to the point of distraction in the chivalrous task of escorting *The Miracle* at his side. She floated in on a cloud of white fox and silver lamé, carrying a gigantic bouquet of long-stemmed white roses, her hair artfully sprinkled with three matching buds. It was quickly apparent that she was not quite *so* miraculously beautiful as she had seemed at first, but she carried the burden of her beauty with the tragic reserve and womanly forbearance with which, as you can read in Wildgans, queens endure their fate, and which is in fact the exclusive characteristic of pure-blooded Viennese porters' daughters. Indeed, the two waiters at Charley's rushed forward to attend and pay court to her—and waiters, dear friend, are the kingmakers of today. Charley himself zigzagged out from behind the bar like a somnambulist and greeted her reverently.

As was whispered soon enough among everyone present, these people were, of course, notables from the film world. The Miracle was a star (not immediately recognized by all because she seemed on the one hand even more improbable and on the other so much more commonplace *in natura* than they had imagined). The Mongolian pony at her side, the Oberon of this procession of the Faerie Queene, was a famous director, Aladar or Elemer de something or other—I'm sure you know all about him: Magyar of ancient lineage, former Imperial and Royal captain in the mounted hussars, and so on, twelve times condemned to death by Béla Kun and today at the pinnacle of German filmmaking—in short, a big deal. Among his retinue a second starlet of somewhat lesser intensity could be made out, more the Vamp type, eclipsed of course by the long-suffering Beauty. Anyway, the entire hierarchy of Neubabelsberg was introduced by name and title, starting with the producer down through the cameraman and editors and whomever else all the way down to the scriptwriter. Someone made it known that they had just finished shooting their latest oeuvre and, following a sudden whim, had up and come to Charley's.

Lovely. They congregated around the free tables in the middle of the place, the star carefully enshrined, and Charley fiddled knowingly with the roses until they were arranged in a vase—all things considered, it was no great sensation, but it was stimulating, no? And if the earlier cheerful din had been dampened a bit by general astonishment, it now returned in a new key and twice as loud, as if it had been artificially constrained before. Everybody tried to act as if nothing had happened, but the whole scene was a notch more fashionable. The Lower Silesians especially took pains to appear casual, but everything soon perked up. For a change, people didn't stick muleheadedly to their own crowds: the ephebes spread out, the plaid squires swarmed forth, and the Vamp was kidnapped away to the bar. It was only then that things really began to get lively.

If I'm not mistaken, it was Kierkegaard who described music as the expression of unmediated Eros. If you grant that there is a certain musical quality in a breathy Danubian accent (as most people do), Kierkegaard's statement would have been confirmed (at least in the short term) by the aforementioned Vamp, who, baring her baby teeth, availed herself of a synthetic dialect reminiscent of a Hungarian pig farmer with a great deal of "Yoys!," "paprikas," and "tamprrament"—behind which (for good reason, as you shall soon hear) hints of even more primitive possibilities could be detected. Soon a pack began to form around her, as you can imagine. A certain underhanded spirit of community seemed to take hold of the team gathered at Charley's brass rail, and streams of extravagantly offered highballs and manhattans began to disappear down her gullet. Finally, she admitted with girlish brashness that she might be "a leetle beet teepsy," but this was quite obviously only a polite exaggeration, for it was plain to see that she had developed a professional capacity for holding her liquor. Nonetheless, the collective expectations of her admirers were approaching the moment of fruition. An artful game of subterfuge developed between deceivers, themselves deceived, and while she simulated being just "a leetle beet teepsy" to further her own divine scam, she gradually got fantastically loaded.

As I said before, the evening had built up its own momentum. As early as 2 a.m., touching scenes came to pass in the men's room; the Silesians saw to it that corks were popped, and an extensive brotherhood spread throughout the place even to the remote corners of the room. Only the star remained glacial, suffering in splendid isolation behind her roses, and the Mongolian pony next to her stared somberly into them. At the regulars' table by the sofa, the witty doctor fired off his tepid aperçus with a cynical bite—but by then the outbursts of laughter that followed lacked the melodic line that usually carried them. The blond thoroughbred, you see, had withdrawn her attention from the circle and, somehow distracted from the effervescent mood all around her, had been for quite some time absently playing with her pearls. Slowly she let the cool, silky beads run through her slim fingers, then, still lost in thought, she selected one at random and brought it to her pursed carmine lips, pressed it to them with one of her scarlet nails until they parted, whereupon it was given a swift and playful bite. With the matte pearl lodged between her much whiter teeth, she would then pull a bit on the string—all the while keeping her head down and glancing only occasionally toward the bar, her eyebrows steeply arched above the frames of her glasses. Over there, everything was one big lumpy mass. The crowd at the brass rail filled every last square inch of the mirror. Baron Traugott's impeccable shoulders were buried in a thick tangle of ostentatiously friendly male arms, and right next to him in the confusion gleamed the bare back of the Vamp.

Then two things happened, both with serious consequences. First of all, you must know that the Mongolian pony, Elemer the Director, having sat there for some time like a study in dark Cumaean brooding, had let his speedy buttonhole eyes wander around the room until they came to rest upon a certain blond thoroughbred. Isn't it the truth: "my glance shall come to rest upon your golden shining hair . . ." The star at his side went on suffering in isolation, although also with increasing displeasure, but having gotten up his nerve, he continued his ogling, at first blindly as if under the spell of a momentary muse and then with fully conscious concentration and the appraising eye of two generations of horse-trading gypsies. Suddenly, around a quarter past two (the Vamp was smashing her first glasses of the evening against the bar), he signaled to the zealous little man with thick glasses and whispered something in his ear, while directing significant glances from time to time at the corner table by the sofa. The little man went right over to the regulars and bowed importantly and with irritating sophistication to the witty doctor, whom he asked to join them for a minute at the VIP table. In turn, the doctor expressed his gratitude, rose, graying and self-important, and marched over to bow before Elemer the Director. He was introduced to the star (Neubabelsberg was a stickler for etiquette), and then he sat down for a while, listening politely to Elemer's lively carrying-on. Afterward he returned to his own table to inform a certain blond thoroughbred, not without a touch of humorous malice, that the director, Mr. von Elemer, had taken an interest in her cinematic potential and would be greatly honored if she would join his table. As you can well imagine, something like this could hardly pass unnoticed. The Lower Silesians giggled heatedly, and all eyes turned to the thoroughbred in breathless anticipation. She smiled briefly with amusement, once again glancing at the bar, and then took off her glasses—a gesture of both defeat and victorious charm, which also shrouded her in a veil of myopia. She folded them up and tucked them away in her handbag. As the doctor gallantly pushed back the table, she rose in all her impressive corporeality and, brushing her blond mane majestically from her brow with a lazy hand and gracefully swinging her luxurious hips, strutted over to the celebrities. As chance would have it, she had to pass by the bar on her way, and, again as chance would have it, she happened to bump rather hard against the back of the Vamp just as she was raising her glass to her lips. A somewhat uncontrolled reflex sent most of her sidecar into her décolletage instead of her mouth. Baron Traugott immediately offered his handkerchief.

This was the first thing that happened. The second was the result of the fact that God has sown the seed of enmity among the various peoples of Southeastern Europe. As you may be good enough to recall, the table in the other corner was occupied by gentlemen from the Moldovlachian embassy. These young democrats had been celebrating their holiday, swapping jokes and making merry, ogling those present and trading lewd comments about them. But shortly after the entrance of the Magyar Elemer and his retinue—though no one else seemed to notice this at the time—they had fallen silent and had stuck their woolly heads together. Smoky guttural sounds rose occasionally from their whispered conversation. As the blond thoroughbred (a frequent guest at diplomatic parties) now rose in the full splendor of her ample figure, they turned around as one and, glowering silently, observed her movements, including the little incident with the Vamp. When Elemer the Director greeted her with the gloomy obsequiousness characteristic of a hussar of the old school and introduced her to the long-suffering and by now mortally offended star, a single word was clearly heard from one of the Moldovlachians, a single word, but obviously one that carried a great weight. Elemer changed colors to a shade halfway between antique silver and olive green but restrained himself with Asiatic discipline until the blond thoroughbred had taken her seat. Then he too sat down, but before he did, he glared venomously at the hostile diplomats with his melon-seed eyes and hurled in their direction a single but quite fundamental word in Magyar.

What followed can only be described in expressionistic swatches: a hoarse roar, six bared fangs, magnified as in some nightmare by a tigerish leap, the table and some chairs flipped over, six pairs of brownish-yellow eyeballs bulging from their sockets, as well as six fleshy cyclamen-colored tongues searching in vain for consonants. Already Elemer the Fearless Knight had jumped up and grabbed handfuls of the star's roses, which he now whipped at the faces of his oncoming attackers. Petals showered down on the ladies, and the thorny stems, soon coated with hair ointment, whistled through the air, leaving broad, bloody streaks wherever they found their mark. Shattering glass, bedlam, and shrieks. The Vamp at the bar toppled over backward but was lucky enough to be caught in midair. In their efforts to stand her upright again, two dozen helpful hands met in the confines of her lingerie. Charley and the two waiters threw themselves into the fray and managed to separate the warring factions.

You know how things like this are wont to end: a hue and cry, pushing and pulling, negotiations animated by violent threats and flickering flare-ups, handkerchiefs to wipe liquor stains from clothing and blood from mouths and noses, waiters efficiently restoring order, agitated ladies. Behind the ruins of the VIP table stood Knight Elemer, his hair in oily strands and his black bow tie hanging limply, surrounded by his page boys and satellites, who, although excited themselves, were trying to calm him down. He concluded the contest of honor by issuing an order to the zealous little man with thick glasses: "Dr. Mayer, you're in charge of settling this!" The dean of the Moldovlachians shouted over the shoulder of the waiter who was dragging him away that he would not be intimidated and that an army stood ready at the border with bayonets fixed. His diplomatic colleagues drowned him out, promising that they personally would roast every last Magyar on sticks and serve them up as kebabs;

however, they then began to get in each other's curly hair over this subject (perhaps because of some culinary controversy) and to flagellate each other with the remnants of the rose stems. All of them were successfully evicted, and on Charley's orders the doorman locked up the place.

A lamentable pall fell over the general mood. The star, now in a heretofore unprecedented condition of affront, demanded to be taken home, but when the zealous Dr. Mayer represented this wish to Elemer, he received the morose reply: "Let her go to hell, that stupid cow!" She swept out, a tragic figure. But I don't have to tell you that she was immediately followed by Elemer, after he had taken formal leave of a certain blond thoroughbred (for etiquette is the rule in Neubabelsberg), and most of his satellites departed with him. Only the regulars remained: the thoroughbred and the witty doctor, as well as an insatiable Lower Silesian couple, some of the ephebes, and a few of the plaid squires together with some random females, plus a sizable crowd at the bar who were within immediate handling distance of the Vamp—among them Baron Traugott, needless to say.

And as Charley's door was shut behind the last of those departing, one of the Moldovlachians, still kicking up a row outside in the street, managed to insert the tip of his rubber-soled shoe in the narrow slit of the closing door. Doggedly, he overcame all interdictions and obstacles and finally landed at the bar, where he declared to the intimates—his lips all cracked and gory—that his diplomatic colleagues were truly a bunch of drunken swine, and that the whole incident should be excused as patriotic excess on the part of youthful and overeager attachés. Finally, overcome by his own exuberant rhetoric, he began to weep over the empty vase, sobbing so as to break your heart, and after he had been consoled, he finished by clapping his hands and ordering champagne for the whole bar. However, Charley obstinately refused to serve any more alcohol, so right there on the spot, the Moldovlachian invited the whole party back to his home. This invitation was accepted out of curiosity, inebriation, and existentialism. Two of the ephebes went along out of sheer wantonness. The Vamp led the horde. There was some crowding in the coatroom, but then everybody was out in the open. Charley's gold neon signature over the door was switched off.

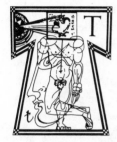HE NIGHT WAS COOL AND STARRY. A BIT farther up Wielandstrasse, the Moldovlachians were still beating each other up. Everybody piled into cars and took off, cutting corners perilously close. In the cones of headlights monstrous residential blocks materialized like spooks and rushed by, city squares sprang up suddenly, and then somewhere next to one of those red-brick Gründerjahre churches whose architecture always seems to blend in piously with the adjacent public toilets, the procession was halted. Yet another quarrel broke out, this time with the building super on the landing, and then everyone was inside an apartment replete with carpets, heavily shaded hanging lamps, cozy nooks, and a large sparkling chrome bar. Everyone collapsed onto couches, someone turned on a phonograph, and the next round of drinks, a sharp oily slug of something, helped to blur the line between things and events.

The blond thoroughbred was dancing. She had gotten hold of one of the squires and was swaying loosely with him, he dangling in front of her like a marionette. The step was an abruptly syncopated rumba. A shock of her blond mane fell in front of her glasses. Behind their lenses, her violet eyes were half shut, and her red lips were parted lasciviously, yet also with a kind of childlike guilelessness. She kept her arms pressed close to her body, her hands gracefully angled outward, fingers slightly curved, white blossoms terminating in blood-colored, almond-shaped, shieldlike nails. Her breasts bobbed provocatively under the thin black silk dress, and her feet traced a meagerly choreographed arabesque on the parquet, the rhythm of the music barely indicated by the full sway of her hips, and every time the husky rattling of maracas interrupted the melody, she thrust her pelvis forward like a snake.

The guests settled down into picturesque groups. The host broke up a lump of ice into small cubes with his teeth and spat them into a cocktail shaker. Dubiously shrouded in the aura of his sparkling remarks and the cloud of his tubercles, the witty doctor lounged in a deep armchair, silently smoked, and from time to time coughed out his bottomless contempt for the world with a cynicism emanating from the depths of his pulmonary cavities. The squires were boozing it up. Like shadows melting into the background, a few couples danced, already close to mutual accord. The Lower Silesian couple stood off to one side with expressions of somewhat puzzled zoo visitors, not wanting to miss anything: the young lady had an inbred lankiness, a mere pencil sketch, fashionably attired, with saber-curved legs and wolfish teeth that grinned hungrily; the precociously tall young man, in a suit he had already outgrown, had the bold, recklessly slanted hooked nose of a pirate, grandly protruding ears and no chin at all (he actually appeared to be nibbling on his Adam's apple with his front teeth)—in other words, people of the upper crust. Next to them, the Vamp was rolling around with five men on a couch.

And as the wild rumba on the phonograph mechanically filled the room with sounds of tropical excess, the tragic adventure of a beautiful soul was being shaped by a drama of the most subtle opposites.

It is part of the tragedy of the Occident, dear friend, but also if I may say so, part of its late beauty, that the twilight of dusk enveloping it has blurred the old categories. You have to admit that variety is the spice of life. Thanks to modern psychology and its art of illumination, the robust plasticity of concepts like good and evil, beauty and ugliness, intelligence and stupidity has metamorphosed into a kind of ballet, a kind of private clearinghouse in which masks and attitudes may be constantly exchanged—although it can happen that, if you are a bit clumsy at the game, you can end up with your head growing between your legs. Even in the revaluation of values, you need to know that you can go too far, eminent reader.

Be that as it may: things began to get a bit wild on the Vamp's couch. The company had begun a massed assault, and the young lady, remembering that the power of women lies in the free choice between resistance and voluntary surrender, opted to defend herself with increasing determination. Like Laocoön, she tried to free herself from the coils that entrapped her, but in so doing she slipped not only out of the halters of her evening gown but out of the dear white, red, and green gingham dialect which she had been wearing as a costume and which had earned her this sort of blunt treatment from rank amateurs. The latter costume yielded to the more soberly colored and therefore far brisker idiom of Berlin's Hasenheide. Nonetheless, a determined grip managed to bare her breasts: greeted jubilantly, they sprang from their brocaded restraint into the light and jutted out, full, alabaster, and rosy-tipped, toward the appreciative gazes of the experts. The Vamp hastily concealed them with her arms. At the same time, she opened her mouth to release a flood of artfully polished folk expressions over the visibly aroused gentlemen, a wave of curses that nipped their responses in the bud.

But behold, something strange happened then: Baron Traugott freed himself from the reluctantly flagging scuffle and said most forcefully, "Stop! That won't do! It's unseemly!"

You have to admit: a confusing sentiment. Everyone present looked surprised and uncomprehending.

"It is ugly," elaborated Baron Traugott, thereby further increasing the conceptual difficulty. No one could muster a reply.

But a spark flew somewhere in the Vamp: "Wot don't ya like?!" she asked, overly loud and menacingly, her head aslant and her eyes narrowed to slits. "You're sayin' my tits're ugly?" Enraged, she opened her arms and stuck the insulted organs in his face like a pair of close-combat weapons. "If they ain't to yer likin'," she screamed at him mockingly, "then ya better run back to Momma in Ass Prussia—mebbe she's got sumpin' better to show ya!"

Stormy acclaim and shouts of bravo greeted her from all sides. Baron Traugott did not join in. For a moment, the helpless grief of someone sadly misunderstood was reflected in his face. Then he turned with an expression of stale satiety from the enemy nipples. As he straightened up, he was the object of a knowing look exchanged by the Lower Silesians.

We have touched here on so delicate a point that you must allow me the liberty of devoting further thoughts to it. What we're dealing with here is nothing less than the ultimate failure of language. Surely,

Locke should have written more than a single chapter on the inadequacy of words: all the exalted platitudes that have been uttered in the course of the past five thousand years should have convinced us by now that what is most profound cannot be articulated. If Gautama Buddha and Lao-tse had ever met, they wouldn't have said a word.

Do I really need to tell you about the heartbreaking effort it takes to express oneself—about the agony of being incapable of making oneself understood? Language—how did Humboldt define it?—the eternally repeated labor of the human mind to make articulated sound express thought; truth be told, it's a Sisyphean task. Why don't you try it once and show me: round up a flock of words as a sheep dog does, circling close and ever closer around the mavericks trying to escape; there's one that entices you; you imagine it might be just the right one—try to grab hold of it in the midst of the teeming throng! Try to pull it out, try to push away all the others surrounding it, one by one—try to grasp it in all its thousand meanings, nuances, qualities, and shadings! Alas, your herd consists of nothing but creatures of legend, my dear friend. All in a row on Shirley Temple's little plate, wolf and lion, bear and lamb. I am talking about words. The poets! The poets and their ecstatic circumlocutions, their beggar's cups always ready to collect everyone's feelings so that they can drink from the stale and tepid remains! We are all deaf-mutes, I assure you, linguistic Neanderthals at best! Our vocabulary consists of nothing more than a hodgepodge of celts, flints, and pebbles that shatter at the slightest impact. Go ahead and talk: there's always a genuine and inarticulate conversation going on behind the veil of words. And there, behind language, so to speak, things are oh so much more unspeakably fabulous, so much more colorful and adventuresome! And not only that: they are also more just. In the dialogue of sensoria, there's no such thing as a lie. The unblurred categories of divine origin reign there, and all objects yield up pure answers. But thick veils hang down in front, making everything distorted, blurry and indistinct, as though you were standing behind a waterfall. And it is solely through all of this and together with it that whatever you want to say—whatever you *are* at that very instant!—can be expressed. You have to go down a path as complex and intricate as a knight's move on a chessboard, forced to detour by all the barricades of convention, contorted by so-called experience, shackled by obsessive imaginings, all in the wink of an eye, and whatever you may be able to rescue from this will be compressed into some clumsy verbal mold, ultimately allowing no more than a cataract of rough sounds to bring to light mere rubble from the sublime. Hence, the inhuman torment in the human gaze, whenever we undertake that labor of making articulated sound express thought.

You may well note, my venerable brother-in-arms, that mature cultures therefore allow their languages to wither away. Civilized races, such as the Anglo-Saxons, file down their vocabularies to mere stumps, over which communication can glide, so to speak, as over ball bearings. And between human beings of great sensitivity, words ultimately become entirely superfluous. Martyrs, sages, lovers— human beings of the highest order—can all make themselves understood through their gaze.

Thus you will readily comprehend what an effect the glance between the two young Lower Silesians was bound to have on Baron Traugott. It was the manifestation of a higher level of life, an invitation back to his spiritual homeland—an instantaneously revealed expression of a sublimated, multilayered, and symphonically harmonized capacity for shared experience, reserved for a privileged species, quite unlike the instinctual impetuous utterances of the amorphous, if linguistically colorful, masses. And yet, this glance had been exchanged above his head.

Very well! It is obvious that you are not yet fully acquainted with our hero. The Baron got up—you should have seen *how*! That was an experience: like someone who has been excluded, certainly, but also like someone whose status as one of the chosen few places him beyond the realm of profanity. He rose as if on sumptuous display, a peacock's fan of human dignity, wearing the classical dandy's expression of divine calling, that totally empty countenance in which dull eyes are lazily held open by raised eyebrows while the nose, permanently stuffed up from abundance, requires the lips to be kept open as well. Thus did the Baron walk between the two Lower Silesians and over to the phonograph.

The thoroughbred was dancing. Another squire was weaving sinuously in front of her and mimicking her stylized pelvic convulsions like an erotic shadowboxer. She favored him from time to time with a conventionally lascivious smile, and yet behind her half-shut eyelids she was keeping track of the events on the couch.

Meanwhile even the most inveterate devotees of promiscuity had let go of the Vamp. She sat alone in the numbness of her total victory and glumly concealed her breasts once more within their brocade; with malevolent compassion, someone offered her something to drink, and she drained the glass into her gaping red maw in a single swallow, still sitting in the same position, disheveled and lipstick-smeared, leering ahead glassy-eyed, as if searching for some half-forgotten memory—irksomely interrupted by the tail end of persistent hiccups. Slowly her eyes took in the circle of individuals in front of her, the dancing thoroughbred and the two Lower Silesians, who were watching her in turn with their enthralled zoo-visitor gaze, from there to the eager faces of the squires and the washed-out, drink-bloated visages of the women, to the Moldovlachian host, who had fastened his violet lips on some willing girl's shoulder, from the cooing ephebes and the couples already entwined in the shadows to the witty doctor: he hung in disjointed boniness deep in his armchair and stared back at her, straight into her eyes, and as he continued with his unbroken gaze, he brought a cigarette to his lipless mouth, sucked on it avidly, his cheeks wrinkling with the effort, let the smoke rise from his jutting lower jaw into his nostrils like two gray snakes, and then finally inhaled it deeply into his corroded lungs. This brought on convulsions of coughing that choked, strangled, and tortured him, shaking his shoulder blades, before releasing him, breathless, his eyes brimming with tears. He drew a handkerchief from his pocket, wiped the bitter-tasting corners of his mouth, and slapped away the ashes from his clothing—all the while not letting his eyes waver from the Vamp for even a single heartbeat. The Vamp closed her lids. She stayed like that for a second or two, her eyelashes lowered in pain and shame, but then one of her hiccups shook her once more, and she opened her eyes, as someone sentenced to death might look out in unbelieving hope for the last time at the light of this world. But nothing could be done: the witty doctor had turned away in disdain. As if drawn by invisible wires, she tumbled to her feet and wandered, with the face of a sleepwalker, toward the phonograph, where Baron Traugott stood, doing nothing. Taking his arm, she turned him toward her and said sharply, "You're the best."

With that, she put her arms around his neck and kissed him.

You could clearly see how the resistance of his hard lips melted in her mouth like a ripe pear, and as her fingers dug into the back of his head, his teeth parted in an incompletely repressed moan. You could feel it, this was one kiss that went all the way down to the tonsils. His legs twitched from oxygen deprivation. When he finally managed to wrestle free, gasping for breath, he almost bumped heads with the Lower Silesians, who had closed in to study the phenomenon as though performing a scientific experiment. A short dialogue ensued:

The Lower Silesian gentleman (in unmasked admiration): "For Chrissakes, that's what I call clearing your throat." (Poking his young lady in the ribs): "Juttel, girl, you could learn a thing or two! Do it again, fellows!"

Baron Traugott hastily demurred. Automatically, his tongue checked the soundness of his fillings.

The Lower Silesian: "Come on! Do it again! What kind of a man are you? Another one of those movie pansies, I bet."

This was where the Vamp came in.

The Vamp: "Dat's no movie pansy, you idiot, dat's a real baron, ya unnerstan'? Here!" And before Baron Traugott could stop her, she pulled open his jacket and, with an uncertain finger still shaking from the last eruption within her diaphragm, she pointed toward the finely embroidered monogram, surmounted by a seven-pointed crown, on his shirt. "There! You see! A genuine baron!"

The Lower Silesians perked up and exchanged a glance.

The Lower Silesian: "What's that? A baron? From whereabouts?"

Baron Traugott (with dignified reserve): "East Prussia."

The Lower Silesian: "East Prussia? Where?"

Baron Traugott: "District of Pillkallen." (Or Gumbinnen; might also have been Eydtkuhnen.)

The Lower Silesian: "Pillkallen? You know the Döndorffs over that way?"

Baron Traugott: "I certainly do." (He also knew the Lehnhoffs.)

The Lower Silesian: "Bodo? Natango?"

Baron Traugott also knew Weidewud.

The Lower Silesian (highly agitated): "Man, Weidewud! I was at the Academy in Brandenburg with Weidewud. In fact, we must know each other. What's the name?"

Baron Traugott (tersely but with precision): "Jassilkowski."

A perplexed glance between the young couple.

The Lower Silesian (as if hard of hearing): "How's that? Come again!"

Baron Traugott (firmly): "Jassilkowski."

Perfunctory glance between the couple. A tiny pause.

The Lower Silesian (with decreased interest): "Well, then: cheers!"

Baron Traugott (with cheerful control): "Mud in your eye!"

(Note the subtlety!)

Since the young couple made no further effort to exchange polite greetings, Baron Traugott—from head to toe the nobleman and representative of chivalry—pushed aside the Vamp with the back of his hand and bowed to the young lady from Lower Silesia. With polished nonchalance, he said, "Shall we dance?"

She exchanged one last significant look with her escort and then stood ready. Baron Traugott placed his arm around her.

It was the grip of an expert. You can believe me: this was how a Yehudi takes up a violin, in one single motion, weightlessly, each fiber drawn to the edge of intonation, between his chin and collarbone. It was the masterful, strong, and yet forgiving gesture, a hand's width above the waistline, which draws the lady snugly to the gentleman's double-breasted jacket—and surprise! her bust was by no means as underdeveloped as one might have thought at first glance. While the Baron, his face an unmovable mask, took the initial graceful step, she looked at him inquisitively and somewhat prematurely, baring her wolfish teeth, hungry for life. An elegant turn took them past the thoroughbred and into the romantically muted lights of the adjoining room. In high spirits, the young gentleman from Lower Silesia hastened to the phonograph and placed the needle at the beginning of the record.

The thoroughbred was herself an enthusiastic dancer and *this*, as she well knew, was not something to be dismissed with a shrug. She kept on dancing with a glassy smile, raised eyebrows, and her full lower lip sucked in below her teeth and the tip of her tongue. The other couple reappeared unperturbed once more from the shadows and danced a victory lap around the room, the Baron still stony-faced and the young lady still with an insatiable grin and a high blush on her cheeks. Then the darkness reclaimed them, and they remained hidden for a good while.

Lipstick-smeared and leering glumly ahead, the Vamp remained alone by the phonograph. Once more, her gaze made the rounds, this time skipping the witty doctor and fixing on the blond thoroughbred, dumbly following her charming gyrations. The frequency of the spasms in her diaphragm had subsided, but they had become all the more implacable, each time, it seemed, rudely cutting the thread of some ephemeral but doggedly pursued remembrance. Nevertheless, she went on stubbornly retying those tenuous threads, even though they quite patently had no logical connection, until suddenly, as if under the effect of some surprising revelation, she stumbled to the center of the room, swept away the other dancers with an irately uncertain gesture, and began to dance all by herself.

Oh well. Her performance could hardly be called a carefully executed work of rhythmic art. What could be discerned at first was a vague combination of a czardas with an only superficially mastered tap-dance routine, during which she got caught up in the hem of her long evening gown, stumbled dangerously but caught her balance with some adventurous contortions, as if riding the crests of imaginary waves, and then came to rest in a state of perplexed immobility. Eventually, she figured out the problem and, with an admirable display of *desinvoltura*, gathered her skirt to her hips and tucked the hem into her décolletage. Since apparently she still felt hampered by the stiletto heels of her silver sandals, she kicked them off acrobatically into a corner. Now bare of the shackling drapery and in her stocking feet, she came into her own, and awakened, so to speak, to the blood flowing in her veins . . . You are no doubt familiar with the theory that the origin of dance is to be sought in the daily rhythms of labor: her eyes ecstatically closed to glittering slits and her lower jaw protruding lasciviously, she threw her rump this way and that, grinding her thighs together in a lewd belly dance.

43

Among the aroused spectators, the young gentleman from Lower Silesia stared in total fascination. Then, unable to restrain himself, he clapped his hands and called out: "Take it off!" The demand was promptly adopted on all sides. The Vamp raised her arms and immediately one of the ephebes helped her draw her gown over her head. She still wore a camisole, but the audience claimed that last covering too, and in no time she had stripped it off and thrown it away, a fragrant floating cloud. With the dexterity of a magician, the eager ephebe swiftly unhooked her garter belt. She now danced quite naked, her stockings having fallen in wrinkles around her ankles, and she writhed passionately to the rhythms of the maracas, licking her lips, clawing at her breasts, and tousling her disheveled locks in front of her face.

What can I say?—it was quite boring. After some initial coarse encouragement and salty commentary, the general interest began to flag. The banality of nudity had its paralyzing effect. Even if, as Schiller writes, the living human figure is the appropriate object of man's play drive, no one there seemed much drawn to it. Someone let out an impolitely loud yawn. The plaid squires scratched their heads and openly consulted their wristwatches. Moreover, there was an uproar in the background, for the shrill apartment bell had sounded, and in the anteroom the building superintendent had appeared, white-hot mad: the remaining Moldovlachians had massed on the staircase and were loudly demanding admission. With a smacking sound, the host tore his yellow-purple lips from the girl's shoulder, armed himself with a ladle, and ran outside. The muffled sounds of an exchange could be heard. Someone slammed a door shut, causing a nerve-racking shudder. All of a sudden the witty doctor rose from his armchair and went to the adjoining room, only to recoil at the door with a hasty "Pardon me!" A moment later, Baron Traugott appeared at the threshold, his face stony, and behind him the young lady from Lower Silesia, still exhibiting her earlier hungry grin. All innocence, she slunk over to the phonograph and began to study the record covers. Baron Traugott leaned against the wall, his arms folded, and watched the dancing of the nude Vamp with utter revulsion.

A soul forged by fire, dear reader, obeys its own laws. The network of alternatives, the management of which is the very definition of existence, is woven much more subtly for that kind of soul than for unrefined, dime-a-dozen creatures. For such a soul, every mere episode can become a decisive event. As to what may have occurred in the dusky shadows of that adjoining room, not only the rules governing gentlemanly conduct but also a rough estimate of the time elapsed prevents us from concluding that it was a fait accompli. For those who storm through the landscape of the soul like Napoleon under the demonic obsession of some majestically conceived strategy, tactical implementation will always remain the province of the lower organs. All the same, kindly imagine the following: he darkly perusing the battlefield from some hilltop, in the vacuum of momentous events triggered by his own will, secretly longing for the naive and divinely inspired deed of his most junior lieutenant, while at this very instant—let's say at Marengo—that same lieutenant utters the words of someone blighted by imagination: "Is that all?"

You understand now why, ever since we ate the worm-infested apple of knowledge, all our victories have necessarily turned into defeats. Baron Traugott leaned against the wall, and the artful emptiness in the dandyish mien of this Julien Sorel of the district of Pillkallen had turned into the dolorous void of total satiety: a King Midas who sees himself cheated of his daily bread by fantasy gold, a Brillat-Savarin of the soul faced with life's field kitchen.

The eternally repeated rumba was trite and unbearably long. While the tumult of the battle among the Moldovlachians slowly ebbed down into the street, the Vamp brought her dance to a close amidst general sobriety.

Only the young gentleman from Lower Silesia still had some spirit left in him. While the Vamp was tapping out the last beats of the song, he, assisted by some of the ephebes, threw himself upon the next-best female—a plain, rather elderly person of whom, up to then, no one had taken notice—and screamed in her ear, in a voice well trained by Academy drills: "Take it off! Take it off!" The old maid balked somewhat, vainly bashful, giggling foolishly and heatedly, and finally eluded his coarse grasp by announcing that she would strip alone in the next room.

Again the shrill doorbell rang, urgently and persistently, and someone went and opened the door. The host stormed in and breathlessly exchanged the ladle for a coal scoop and hastened out again. This time, he was followed by some valiant gentlemen who managed to drag him back from the stairs. As he uttered blasphemous oaths and cooled a black eye with the remaining ice from the cocktail shaker, the aging female coquettishly stuck her head through the gap in the door and requested a tango. Someone started the record. With the first schmaltzy accordion phrases, she finally gamboled out of the darkness, without her clothes, but draped like a fantastic gypsy with a tablecloth diagonally wound around her shoulders and meager chest and a bedside rug over her loins. Jerking her head in sulky yet bold motions above her gaunt shoulder blades, she lumbered around the room imitating the romantic postures and rump-contorting scissor steps of a Sevillana. General silence. One of the squires attempted a witty remark, quickly stifled by Baron Traugott's terse "Shut up!" When the tango concluded, the gypsy sank mortified into the folds of the bed rug and fled, red with shame, into the next room.

All of a sudden everybody realized that it was five o'clock. You could feel the dank morning cold in your marrow. Even the young Lower Silesian refrained from repeating his demand—the sad fate of the categorical imperative being simply that at no one time does everybody obey it. The thoroughbred looked for her handbag and inquired after the witty doctor, but the latter had slipped away in the meantime. She got up. The party was over.

Stark naked, her hair in total disarray, the Vamp sat on the edge of the couch. Nauseated, Baron Traugott pushed her clothes, lying in a bundle, toward her with the point of his shoe. Following some great urge from the depths of her subconscious, she gathered her clothes inadequately in front of her breasts and asked in a menacing voice: "Who said I was a slut?"

No one remembered having publicly drawn such a superfluous conclusion, but the Vamp screamed in uncontrolled rage: "Who's the slut here?" And now, as she turned straight toward the blond thoroughbred, her voice skipped into a treble: "Wot gives ya the right to call me a slut?"

The thoroughbred moved away with a dismissive shrug.

"Where do ya get off sayin' I'm a slut?" the Vamp raged on, tears pouring down her cheeks, attacking with claws bared.

But once more the unexpected happened: with a single step, Baron Traugott was at the side of the thoroughbred. He swept away the Vamp and said loudly and unequivocally, "Come on, it's time. I'll take you home."

And while the Moldovlachian tried to calm down the Vamp by promising her comfortable quarters for the night, the Baron escorted the blond thoroughbred past the females, squires, and ephebes, past the aristocratic young lady from Lower Silesia as well, and out of the room, without so much as a goodbye.

Outside, in the anteroom, she drew close to him with an inquisitive cuddly motion, pleasantly surprised by her victory, but the Baron retreated with determined reserve. Silently he donned his overcoat and followed her down the stairs. Then they were out in the open and walked in silence next to each other.

*Pray tell! What great ill is there
in taking the night's fresh air?*
MOLIÈRE, GEORGES DANDIN

 N THE STREETS IT WAS STILL FOGGY. FAR
beyond the edge of the city, there was a hint of the
coming dawn, but here it was still dark, the darkness of the hollow hours in which the dim light
from streetlamps swims as if dissolving into the
mist. All at once, the night had become an immense
hole, you understand: terrifyingly empty. Every
night was a yawning hole in the midst of life; the
colorful garlands of day hung ruffled and papery over a deep abyss
of black. Loneliness, huge, horrifying, and overpowering, stood waiting within that nothingness, and the thin confidence of daytime, that
hastily riveted together vessel of anxiety, smashed to pitiful smith-
ereens. It broke open like an ark containing nothing but freaks and
monsters, so that all your fears and apprehensions, large and small,
wild and tame, clever and wise, perfidious and candid, swarmed
from the wreckage, teeming in panic and hysterically fastening their
claws onto your poor soul, dragging it down to its final terror. And
then it came, magnanimously: that great solitude came with a maternal gesture.

There was frost in the fog. Baron Traugott, his throat soured from
all the drinks and his heart sated with excess, turned up his collar.
With a shy motion, the thoroughbred grasped his arm and timidly
put her hand in his coat pocket; he tolerated it there and, charitably,
clenched her cold fingers in his. She pressed against him, seeking his
nearness, and he felt her warmth through the fur coat against his
shoulder and let her press against him, magnanimous in his great
loneliness. They looked for a cab and made a detour to find one,
but the stand was empty, so they continued on foot through the
dead streets, their matching footsteps muffled by the fog. Haltingly,
as if torn here and there from the turgid night by errant insomniacs,

the city awoke. Elevated trams thundered by, empty and brightly lit along the overpasses, and far-off locomotive whistles could be heard. Near the zoo station, a sausage vendor with a cheese-colored face stood freezing in the acrid light of a carbide lamp. Newspaper carriers, raffishly muffled, swished around corners on their bikes and almost silently threw down their heavy bundles in front of the closed kiosks. Across from the Gedächtniskirche, workers were welding rails. They had lit a small basket fire that festered dimly in the haze. Next to it, the welding irons intermittently flared, coldly and mechanically, red sparks shooting from their blinding fiery core, giving off a lurid, almost tactile light which haunted the square and touched the surrounding buildings, momentarily extracting them from the ashen darkness and scaring up hordes of scurrilous shadows in front of them, instantaneous apparitions emanating from extinguished façades, dream-pale ornate cornices, and phantasmagoric configurations, petrified as if in sudden fear, above exotic portals. Behind this ghostly foreground, dark Berlin stood black and enormous, a monstrous honeycomb built by troglodytes, confusingly interlocked, pressed upward into towering ramparts of merlons, crenellations, and chimneys, chaotic structures, fissured into labyrinths, crisscrossed by empty roadways, blind beams leading out into nothingness.

Baron Traugott bravely walked ahead. Was this still their city? His, Traugott Jassilkowski's, and the blond thoroughbred's? The brisk, sober, generous, lighthearted Berlin we all know and love? Were these still the same streets, Tauentzien, the Ku-damm, Kant- and Rankestrasse, and so on? Maybe they were nothing but an illusion. Can we ever be sure of anything? Who can warrant us that it was really like that, once? Who can assure us that the Romanische Café actually stood there—*had* stood, mind you, had stood there of its own free will, year in and year out, day and night—even nights, for example, when neither you nor I nor Baron Traugott nor anyone else was there? Who, dear God in heaven, can convince us that we're not really blind, that the whole stuff and nonsense is not just taking place internally, a reflection within us, somewhere way in the back inside our blind eyes—deception, betrayal, and appearance, all those things, familiar things, beloved things, hated things, indifferent things—dearly hated, beloved, indifferent things . . . Who can convince us that they truly exist? You, perhaps? The Romanische Café! Where is it, then? Show it to me! Go there and look for it! There you will be able to experience philosophy, be it Parmenides, Kant, Traugott Jassilkowski, or whoever you please.

The night was dark, hollow, and without end, filled with terrifying visions, and Baron Traugott marched through the hazy cold nothingness with the thoroughbred hanging on his arm, lost, swept away in the pathos of his great fear. The world had come out of joint, you understand, busted at the seams, dissolved into a misty chimera, a nothingness, an insect swarm of will-o'-the-wisp atoms. Adieu reality, adieu beloved firm actuality; the time had come to take leave. Leave, do you hear that? Never again—what a dreadful phrase: never again! Never again will a house stand ready for us, never again will a tree with green leaves grow for us, nevermore shall we hold another human being, warm and alive, in our arms. Nevermore for all eternity. Eternity—nothingness. Doesn't everything get absorbed into that nothingness? Aren't you always taking leave of things, every moment of your life? Weren't there already thousands of things which had been, which had pretended to be, dense and warm and alive—all of them vanished? Away, no longer here, dissolved into nothingness . . . oh, for Sinding's "Rustles of Spring"! It may be kitsch, kitsch from here to eternity, but well-loved kitsch, composed with the heart's own blood and tears, much-longed-for, nostalgically thick, warm kitsch for us to wallow in. Don't come back at me now with nihilism and other such bugaboos. What's nihilism, after all? The gentleman's disease of the century. The clap, experienced internally. And as for its mother, literary aesthetics, that old bitch, dear sir, you can't get rid of her so easily with a few injections of Christian penicillin.

As I said, the night was large and without end, and oh, how very fed up Baron Traugott was with himself! *Horror vacui.* In folksier terminology, he was sick and tired of everything—most of all his own self. This dreadful evening. The night. The day that had been and the one to follow. Every day, one like the other. And in between them, nights. And again and again another day and Baron von Aalquist's *Gentleman's Monthly* and the Café Kranzler and the movies and Mampe's pub and Charley's Bar and boozing and females, the more the merrier. That girl at his side—what did she want from him? What could he do with her? Woman, what am I to do with you? And the saber-legged tadpole from Lower Silesia—they were all made of the same stuff. Her young Lothario had been dead wrong: there was nothing for her to learn. "Well, then: cheers!" Very well, cheers, then! And it made him want to puke, all of it, thoroughly and with absolute finality. He despised it—and himself, most of all. Himself and his dirty tricks of the trade and his vulgar pragmatism. Oh, good thing the night was large enough to conceal the shame reddening his cheeks, good thing there was nothing but nothingness all around, good thing one could be alone in that nothingness.

But then a voice within him spoke up (don't bother to rack your brains how I have come to reveal to you the contents of Baron Traugott's whispered inner monologue: that's just the way it is, by virtue of necessity and my narratorial omnipotence)—an inner voice spoke to him: "Not at all! You are hardly alone, Brother Traugott, fiery soul, knight-in-arms, and life-artist—for *I* am here with you, I, too, am here, your other self. Don't you go believing Nietzsche: no one who seriously reflects on himself can miscalculate the number of souls within him, for, alas, since Goethe's Werther there are two and only two who inhabit your breast: you and I. Not Ormuzd and Ahriman, darkness and light, but you and I, a pair of brethren, simply and rather touchingly *frère et cochon*—you, the dwarf, the actor, the swollen-headed dime-a-dozen braggart, and I your cynical conscience and secret pride, your support and your hope, your obscenely magnified self-complacency, your narcissistic mirror image in a puddle. How greatly I resemble you! How I appreciate all your adolescent philosophy of nothingness! Night, darkness, and loneliness—what a cozy corner this makes up, a *buen retiro* with hot and cold running water when compared with true Nothingness. Do you know what that is? The day, my friend, the clear, visible revelation of general purposelessness and senselessness. The eternal sameness of senseless tomorrows: Kranzler, Mampe, Baron von Aalquist's *Gentleman's Monthly*, the movies, Charley's Bar, and females, the more the merrier. That is the great loneliness, the great terror. Not bashful or shifty, but open and undisguised, embarrassingly exhibitionist, the finality of eternally identical repetition, of absolute monotony—*that* is true nothingness. What would you be in its midst, you worm, without me: scornful, courageous, penetrating, and clever! You little shit! Where would you be without me, recording everything, keeping tabs on you, getting a good chuckle in the process—you pitiful creature, with your fears and pious lies, you flat-footed high-wire artist of the soul! Where would you be if I did not bestow upon you the secret nobility of knowing your lowliness? If I weren't standing beside you, upright in your abasement, if I didn't hold it in front of your eyes? For this is what I am: the truth within you. The angel who casts you out of the paradise of self-deceit. The great power which renders you powerless. Thus we coexist in equilibrium, you and I, feeding each other in reciprocal surfeit. That is true nothingness."

Thus spoke Baron Traugott's whispering inner voice.

And with that, they had happily arrived at the thoroughbred's house on the shore of the Lützow canal. She stopped and looked up at him and for a moment was deeply moved by his expression. His face was so very handsome in that instant, pale and distorted by pain, totally human, you understand: *ecce homo.*

"I can't take you upstairs with me, *darling*," she said quickly, filled with pity and confusion. "I live here with my parents."

He merely nodded. He closed his eyes briefly and nodded, an understanding smile playing weakly over his mouth. And even before she could raise her arms to him, he had bent down and delicately brushed her forehead with lips that were pure and chaste. "Good night," he said softly, and walked away into the fog.

Mechanically she unlocked the door but turned once more, still holding the handle. *"Darling!"* she called in a low voice after him (for she did not even know his first name). *"Darling!"*

But his footsteps had already faded away in the gray mist.

She opened the door and, slowly and full of a strange sense of wonder, ascended the stairs, considerably frightened but also strangely happy.

 EVERAL HOURS LATER WHEN SHE AWOKE IN
her four-poster (I owe my knowledge of these de-
tails to a fortuitous combination of circumstances
that need hardly concern you)—now, when she,
as I said, awoke after a few hours of sound and
healthy sleep in her four-poster—word of honor,
it was a genuine canopied four-poster bed, straight
out of childhood dreams, and no fairy-tale princess could have had one more magnificent: downy, plump, and
droll on hobbled mahogany legs, covered by a ballooning canopy
of flowered chintz, right in the middle of her light and airy teenager's
room, flanked by all her old dolls in a row on top of her wardrobe
and fairy-tale pictures on the walls (a languishing page carrying the
train of a queen, Peter Cornelius or Schnorr von Carolsfeld or some
blather of the "they couldn't be together and yet loved each other
so much" variety, you know?). Lovely. In the left corner of the room,
a low lacquer table with some books, Huysmans' *A rebours, Les
Fleurs du mal*, a couple of trash novels by Cronin or Bromfield or
whoever those jokers were, and an attractive deluxe edition of
Dickens' *A Christmas Carol* illustrated by Rackham. In addition,
a set of red-ringed shot glasses stood on a tray, and a portable
phonograph with some records, next to which lay her fox coat,
carelessly thrown over a chair upon coming home, as well as her
half-open handbag, out of which had slipped her eyeglasses, a
lipstick-smeared handkerchief, and her key chain. On the vanity
table, in front of the mirror, there was a row of fluffy powder puffs,
red, purple, and poison green, a big pot of Pond's Almond Cream,
spit-moistened mascara tissues, and countless Elizabeth Arden cosmetic jars, also an ashtray filled with lipstick-reddened cigarette
butts, and behind a tall Chinese screen water trickled slowly from

53

the faucet over a bottle of vodka and drained away with a deep gurgle . . . Anyway, as I said, when she opened her eyes, after a few hours, in the floor-polish-scented safety of her parents' house, it was noon and the February sun over the zoo was shining through her windows. She hadn't bothered to take off all her clothes and lay still half covered by a black silk slip with a broad lace inset, wrapped in goose down, voluptuously spread out in the full ripeness of her ample figure. The dollhouse bedroom of this particular princess was filled with the sensual heavy fragrance of Chanel No. 5. Hung over, she drew the covers to her ears, wrinkled her nose, and blinked into the light from the mass of surrounding pillows, trying to put together a halfway coherent reconstruction of the preceding evening out of swatches of faded images and vestiges of atmosphere. One thing at least seemed certain: this time, thank God, she had worn her sexy lingerie for naught. But then she suddenly remembered everything, most clearly the parting scene in the gray dawn, and behold: once more, surprise and sweet terror, bliss and tenderness flooded her heart. She awoke fully, threw back the covers in one fell swoop of delight, stood and let the black lace slip slide from her priceless limbs, went behind the screen, removed the bottle of vodka from the washbasin, and, filled with happy thoughts, brushed her teeth. She then sat down at the vanity and put up her platinum lion's mane, smeared a generous pat of cream on one of the Elizabeth Arden cleansing tissues, and with practiced wiping motions cleaned the somewhat faded spectrum of colors from her façade: the shadows on her eyelids, the demonic arched eyebrows, and the lascivious Marlene Dietrich lips. And thus, naked and touchingly bereft of color, myopic and with some reddish spots here and there, with a child's pale mouth, she gazed into the mirror and smiled. She was in love. Tenderly she appraised the rosy nipples of her breasts in the mirror. Finally, she stood up happily, put on a bathrobe, grabbed a bar of soap, a brush, and a large sponge under her arm, and in her straw slippers shuffled with joyous disregard through the noonday silence of her parents' home to the bathroom.

She was in love, and as behooves the rosy blond daughter of a floor-wax-scented household, she immediately thought about how to cement this great happiness with a bright, well-aired, and carefully maintained home.

Oh, bliss! You realize of course that this sleek bird was basically as square as they come. She was no longer the youngest of the young, no longer had those proverbial ants in her pants, and for quite some time already her whole priceless free-floating existence had lost much of its allure. In the final analysis, what it came down to was nothing more than meandering through bullshit.

Very well—she proceeded with a thorough and objective examination of her latest prey, and behold: the more she scrutinized him, the more she found him to her liking. Wasn't he custom-made for her? To begin with, he was obviously a no-good playboy, that much was certain, that much even a blind man could have sensed with his cane. But he had all the witty breeziness, all the human qualities, if I may say so, which unfortunately (or fortunately, depending on your perspective) only no-good playboys can possess. At the same time, he was also something of a decent chap. More than that: the fellow had character. There ran, through everything and despite everything he did, a streak of cleanliness—a streak of purity, she was tempted to call it.

What's more, he seemed to come from a more or less solid background. That is to say, she couldn't believe his story was on the up-and-up. There was something fishy about it, that much she could smell herself—for, after all, she herself was the product of a solid background, one could almost say a good stable. But what more did she want? Surely, he was the son of decent people—not the kind where you have to count the silver after they leave. And anyway: von Jassilkowski—there wasn't a special Eastern Section in the Register of Nobility where you could check it, but anyway he seemed not to have invented his "von." No one could take that away from him, for that's what his papers said; she had seen his call-up order: in the end he, too, had to do his duty and prepare himself to defend the fatherland. That tiny particle of a name made all the difference, if you please; it was nothing to sneeze at. My friend, the magic of this little preposition is not to be underestimated. I wonder whether schoolchildren throughout the Greater German Empire don't automatically prefer the Bay *of* Biscay to the stolidly bourgeois Hudson Bay.

Well—be that as it may. In any case and last but certainly not least, wonder boy also dressed like a dream. His suits, sir—why, the cut of the shoulders alone! And the materials, both the quality and the design! This was much more than faddish dandyism, believe me, this was true class! And what subtle combinations he chose: a dark blue saxony, for instance, with a sky-blue chalk stripe, six buttons in the most classic cut, high lapels, and discreet side vents: with it, a conservative shirt and tie, decent and respectable design, a black Anthony Eden hat and—you'll laugh—a very sloppy, worn fur walking coat, ending above the knee, rustic in style, made of loden or some such material—something to wear shooting rabbits, you understand, crusted over with the best sort of shabbiness. That was quite a combination, let me tell you! And what's more, an old oak cane with a tiny shovel instead of the usual metal tip! When he walked so attired on Sunday mornings past the Gedächtniskirche on his way to the Romanische Café—how could any passerby's heart resist him? That was aristocracy in its purest form, my dear sir, *noblesse de robe* in the most literal sense, translated into the Junker style. A cherub from another world amidst legions of jackboot louts, a witness and emissary of the quickly fading glory of bygone times.

In any case, he was a good catch, indeed, one of a kind. You can't find something like that nowadays with a divining rod. On the spot, the thoroughbred decided she would get this young sprat into the frying pan without further delay. She did not hesitate to reveal her intentions to her parents, in order to start her bidding with a well-rounded figure, nicely in keeping with the age of her dear old father.

However, Baron Traugott . . . things with him, you know, were never so simple. Of course, both of them were stuck with each other—and for us at Charley's, it was quite funny to see the old play revived by none other than these two. All of a sudden, they sat together at the bar, were seen everywhere only as a couple, and if one did happen to come upon one or the other of them alone, they were distracted and unsociable. They disappeared for days on end, neglected their friends and acquaintances—in short, exhibited all those asocial symptoms of the first stages of conjugal relations, symptoms that recede only gradually under the vaccination of legitimate marriage. Winter came and went and spring arrived, a typical Berlin spring of silence burdened with desire in the provincial side streets and the occasional warble of a thrush heard through the evening traffic—and then summer followed. It was not so simple, you know—Baron Traugott, you understand, his considerations weren't quite so hearty, healthy, and blandly uncomplicated as might have been expected. He recognized the opportunity, no doubt, even fore-saw the almost breathtaking possibilities whenever he weighed certain figures and listened joyfully to the zeros as they rolled, one after the other, over the sounding board of his soul. But things, as I said, weren't so clear-cut, hell no! This was a highly pitched instrument, the Baron's soul. It vibrated to the tones of much more tuneful melodies. Well now, our Hercules stood at a crossroads and had to cast a glance backward.

You see, quite some time had passed since that first visit home to Mamá in Allenstein. A lot of water had flowed down the Spree, many a pebble had been polished and many things had become smooth and round. At that point, after Zoppot and the meeting with cousin Zapieha, there had been a break in the action, a thoughtful pause to catch his breath and begin again, so to speak—and if you thought about it, all in all he, Baron Traugott, had managed quite well and come quite far.

We understand each other, I hope: we're not talking here about accumulating heaps of money or a position with a pension. Can it be that you, too, maintain such petit bourgeois ideals? Truly, I assure you: hard work doesn't ennoble—in other words, it doesn't set free, as was written later over the gates of Auschwitz and Buchenwald and Treblinka. Yet aristocrats know that in order to be spiritually free they have to work. In our day, true nobility has to combine stamina with speed—sticking to tradition, never failing in its duty toward class and fatherland, but also racing against the forerunners of today's dreary liberalism to secure the first social rank. Now as to the latter, we know that Baron Traugott had already done the best he could do. More difficult seemed to be Part One: to place Traugott von Jassilkowski, son of an obscure manager of Polish descent and the former Miss Bremse-without-a-von, in line with those whose names decorated the glorious history of Prussia. Charley's Bar, dear sir, was but one of the playfully conquered bastions over which he hoisted his pennon. With the conquest of the blond thoroughbred, the decisive skirmishes would be fought within the castle walls, around the citadel itself.

In order to pay tribute to a higher truth, I shouldn't neglect to advise you that, in his case, as in the destiny of every real man, a noble lady had been his initial sponsor. For, in fact, the transition from rear vassal of the Counts Döndorff into tenant of the Pension Bunsen had been one of the most significant parts of his unusual career: Frau von Schrader (née Countess Rumpfburg-Schottenfels, as you must know) was a full-blooded woman in her late thirties and—in spite, or let us rather say because, of the fact that once upon a time she had seen better days—possessed of great social enterprise. Her establishment was not only a favorite overnight accommodation of many of her social peers, but also the home of a bridge circle. We shall refrain from scrutinizing more closely the motives that may have led this lady to fancy her youthful tenant (since, between us, he played a terrible game of bridge). In any case, she had elevated him just like that from nothing more than a late bud on the trunk of Topor into an apparition whom a Zapieha would not snub, and under cover of discrepancies between the Culbertson and d'Albaran conventions, smuggled him into the circles of established—if like herself, alas, impoverished—aristocracy. Yes indeed, there he sat, little Traugott Jassilkowski, and without so much as a blink of an eye he was finessing the queen of some tatty Highness or brazenly doubling the three-no-trump contract of a disinherited Knight of the Golden Fleece on the strength of nothing more than a four-card suit up to the jack of diamonds.

Thus Mrs. von Schrader advised and guided all his steps, his visits, his church attendances and country outings, and, with her knowledge of tradition and of the commanding officers' wives, even selected the regiment for his military service. I'm telling you, things looked up. There even came a day when a somewhat absentminded general, retired, thought he remembered a Lieutenant von Jassilkowski with the dragoons number so-and-so (a high number, of course). The glory of those who had tactfully withdrawn into the mists of the past! A minute of silence for Papá!

But what am I saying! What good is the most loving support of even such a tender hand, what good are skills? "If our eye weren't of the sun, could it see the sun?" asks Goethe . . . You may be able to call the whole roll of regiments of the Old Guard without a hitch, you may let your conversation, spiced by racing jargon and hunting esoterica, bubble playfully over Gotha's Register of Counts, you may, as a proof of your noble rusticity, be just as qualified to hold forth expertly and politely on the Bang bacillus—what good is good fortune itself! You may be able to claim twenty heroes' graves at Ypres and Sedan—*you* remain the one, my dear sir, who has to embody the spirit of your caste. The metaphysics of his class alone creates the laws and guidelines according to which the individual crystallizes.

Naturally, anyone who takes a wholesale view of these things, judging them only from their glittering surface, will botch it all up like the dilettante he is. His imagination will be haunted by mixed-up terms like chivalry, nobility, gentlemanly behavior, and all that crap. The strict meanings of such concepts must be clearly distinguished. If you hope to get anywhere, you have to proceed scientifically. Witness: a cavalier, a gentleman, and a nobleman are three totally separate phenomena, differentiated both chronologically and etymologically.

Let's go over them one at a time. The cavalier, a French invention, represents the aesthetic variety of aristocrat. He is a direct descendant of the courtly knights with their bellicose conception of humanity —which puts him on horseback both literally and metaphorically: bombastically high-stepping, yet, if you will, also reined in by self-control, everything about him prancing brilliance. Above all, a being of the highest individuality. If he is called into action, it is always because of his own initiative, manifesting itself as a personality oriented around beautiful gestures; *le beau geste* causes him to unfold and blossom.

Quite another matter is the gentleman (the moral variety): for some time now he has conformed to a well-defined type. His actions are guided by formulae (formulae of injunction, as is usual in the moral sphere). There still may be a remnant of individuality, but moderated and rudimentary, a collective individuality, one might say, of an Anglo-Saxon stamp. His form is perfectly realized when he differentiates himself as little as possible from his peers. He is, approximately, a cavalier who has dismounted and joined the infantry's more democratic ranks.

Now finally, as regards the nobility of the Prussian Junker: neither

French revanchist feelings nor British envy can obscure the fact that he personifies the pure ethicist. His entire personality is subsumed under the idea of his caste. He is a liege man and, thus, an officer: a small screw in the machinery of state, a single link in an ancestral chain of lineage. His honor is his duty; he earns his dignity in service. He belongs to a race of termites, purebred for a Hegelian state (and if we had only succeeded in reproducing this variety on a broad popular scale, it might have enabled us finally to achieve a dynamic synthesis of the age-old dichotomy in the German soul between collectivism and individualism—to give Mr. Marx and Mr. Hegel a good spin, so to speak, on the gyro-wheel of history). You may now understand what breeding means: it links you to a chain of ancestors even if your own ancestral line is not long. Reverse history! Keep an eye on the future! Be Chinese: ennoble your ancestors by your own noble achievements, particularly by sticking to the rules of breeding you have studied so attentively in the cow barn.

Please do not take this as an idle digression: at that very moment, no considerations were more important to our hero. As I said, he stood at a crossroads: in front of him, but already also stretching out for some distance behind him, lay the dour path of duty, of well-bred moderation, of self-sacrifice in everything including his haircut, the renunciation of all too stylish dress, a restriction on the all too frequent visits to Charley's Bar. All the more promising did the ramparts of the Grail Castle shine! Good riddance to the milking stool, the bridge circle, and the glory of discreetly dead people! A few more steps—a few deft pushes by Mrs. von Schrader's knowledgeable hand—and he's there! The only thing still lacking was the seal of birth he could forward to his offspring: marriage to a young lady of station, a Potsdam officer's nobility or something of that kind, and the scion would be fully grafted. After that, a lieutenancy and some occasional happy-go-lucky fighting shoulder to shoulder with comrades of equal rank—bridging the gulf between Grandpapa's Iron Cross of 1870 through 1914–18 to the present generation—and the von Jassilkowskis finally belonged as equals to the caste of the Döndorfs, Lehnhofs, and Zapiehas.

Over here, however, on the well-paved side path, the lure of the yellowhammer warbling delicate flute notes from the bourgeois-liberal hazel bush, and it sounded so damn easy and comfortable, so classy and independent. Ultimately, as long as you had enough spare change to throw around, it would lead to the same end, isn't that so?

Fine. When the matter had ripened, so to speak, to the point of decision, Baron Traugott took a morning off for a meditative walk and strolled by way of Halensee out into the Grunewald, along the Bismarck-Allee and so on—alas, once upon that time there stood on both sides imposing villas of diverse architecture, trees blossomed in well-tended gardens, automobiles drove by, shiny, on swiftly humming silent rubber tires, and ladies in silk stockings took their dogs for walks—alas, it was a remote, beloved, and cruelly bygone world . . . And he walked and walked straight through the woods, all the way to Paulsborn, where the lake waters blinked like sun-gilded scales and peaceful philistines aired their underwear on the beach —but he had no eye for any of it, our young Jassilkowski, for he was deep in thought and overcome with melancholy, as often happens to people who stand on the threshold of fulfilling a long-cherished dream and are about to sense the disappointment reality always brings. And everything, all of it, arose once more before him—Papá and Mamá and Sinding's "Rustles of Spring" and the inspector's rod, his life in Berlin, the Pension Bunsen, Mamá's parlor in Allenstein, and a certain upper floor in Potsdam, Neue König-strasse, and Charley's Bar—trivial instances of quotidian reality and miraculous shining images of desire. And once again he loved and hated it all, but behold: hate and love were reversed, for now he hated what he had formerly loved and loved with a passionately jealous heart what he used to hate.

You see, much had changed: there was a childhood, chock-full of images, a colorful mosaic of memories; but time had dissolved them like magic Japanese flowers in a glass of water, and they floated around, transmuted, their respective weights quite different from before, some large and brightly blooming against the clear surface, others sunken, dark, and heavy, at the bottom. There was Papá— no longer a brutal, dull, sweat-soaked estate inspector, but forceful and pithy, a rustic nobleman with the crest of Topor and a lieutenant in the so-and-so cuirassiers, decorated with the Iron Cross First Class

61

in the Great War, hunter and horseman and trusty drinking companion, weather-beaten and basking in the golden aura of his voice happily thundering away. He stood in front of a background of innumerable fields of plump, healthy cattle, his boots planted firmly in the fertile soil, surrounded by the merry crackling of shots from a nearby hunt—life, dear sir, lusty life itself. And in his glance also some of the gravity and nobility imparted by duty: to be a bearer, a pillar among that class of people who feed and defend the nation. And quiet distinction: a link in a long chain of ancestors.

But then there was Mamá . . . oh, you know: "Rustles of Spring" and the fecundation of flowers and purity and everything fine and delicate: she was alive, reality, flesh and bone, solid vulgar reality. She was the weight that dragged him down to earth time and time again from the flights of his illusion, the abrupt yell that brings the sleepwalker down from the edge of the roof, as if with buckshot . . . She was—what more can I tell you?—a born Bremse, a real brake on his ambition.

It didn't help any to revert to the fairy-tale land of childhood: she was in the here and now and could not be denied, a frumpy old woman with a horrible accent who was busy darning stockings in some shabby little room in Allenstein. The very personification of amorphously washed-out, faceless, and low-class philistinism, a genealogical blemish incarnate, the perfect embodiment of all his burning shame at the all too customary question: "And your dear mother, tell me, by the way, what was she born as?"

Bremse-without-a-von—turn, forward march!

It is at this point that we take off on the grand adventure (the tears, the tears of Herzeloyde!), the great adventure of self-realization, the adventure that alone can transform a human being into a human being—what good are bravery, passion, and lofty sensibilities if the performance that society demands from us has already been ruined by the unfortunate nuptials of a hapless ancestor? For, in fact, she was precisely what she always had been: a brake. Some other mother (oh, something plain, nothing exalted, God knows— weren't there plenty on the list of simple patented nobility, more than adequate for an estate manager's household!)—some other mother, as I said, would have given him from the very first that predicate of pure breeding, and then adieu to Mrs. von Schrader and all her pimpish maneuverings, adieu to the bridge table and the whole godforsaken Knesebeckstrasse, and adieu and good riddance to all the moth-eaten Potsdam officers' nobility, a brisk kick in their rotten asses. Oh, to begin all over again and live in divine independence.

Well, then. Mamá was there. In Allenstein, East Prussia. Darning egg and wire-rimmed glasses, early-Biedermeier fringed lampshades and Sinding's "Rustles of Spring." Papá, on the other hand—though of course he had been the world's worst brute—at least had had the tact to pass on early. But Mamá was there. Achilles is dead, but— alas!—Thersites lives!

You are familiar with the path leading off to the left from the Paulsborn hunting lodge: you went straight through the woods and, if you were a passably good walker, emerged after about half an hour near Uncle Tom's Cabin. This, then, is where young Traugott strolled through the trees and brooded and brooded some more. Somewhere, discreetly hidden behind some bushes and a bit of barbed wire, was a shooting range, and you could hear bangs at irregular intervals, and because of this, he thought of his regiment in Ludwigslust and of the fact that he needed only one more training exercise to become a reserve NCO . . . You see, life can be rich, but it offers its wealth in such a low-down way: for every inch, it places you at a crossroads of decisions and bids you choose—one single, and never more than one single, possibility, forcing you to turn down all the others forever and ever . . .

You probably can't sympathize with the turbulent pros and cons of feelings that have such complex ramifications and at the same time are so lumpy and massive. You don't realize what it's like to wrestle with angels offering barely nibbled temptations—but please, there's something serious hidden in all this. At the very bottom of it all lies a dream of humanity: the venerable wish for ennoblement, the alchemistic desire to achieve transubstantiation—with flesh instead of lead. You'll admit that, ever since Plato, Christ, and Miss Annie Besant, this has been tried mainly via the spiritual-ethical route, with no other result than the revolt of the masses. So why not try it the other way around? Breeding, eugenics. Follow Mendel and develop yourself, not linearly, but in ascension! There's something to this, I tell you, a thought of Promethean temerity: the lofty goal of the perfect, synthetically produced human being. Planned economy and control of free-floating chromosomes. Assembly-line production of the purebred aristo-termite. Proletheus unbound.

As I said, here was a chance to correct all the blunders, all the mésalliances à la Bremse made by previous generations: namely, the young lady of rank he envisioned. And between the two of us, with this goal in mind our young friend had performed his courtship rituals quite cheerfully . . . You're not invited to Potsdam merely because you play a good game of bridge or can lay claim to an old title. Although nothing had been discussed overtly yet, Mrs. von Schrader could be relied on to wangle the deal very well; she certainly knew how to manage such matters. And at the same time, this would tie her personally to him (Mrs. von Schrader, I mean), for nothing establishes stronger bonds than allowing someone to render you a service of that nature. Spouse plus relations plus Mrs. von Schrader and her following, the whole thing interwoven and tangled up through familial relatedness—you see, that would be quite a solid edifice. A few more crossbeams and trusses running back and forth, slap on the cement of habit and let dry. All done. And that would afford him a pretty solid seat in the higher spheres of the world he craved to belong to.

On the other hand, Mademoiselle Blond Thoroughbred: she was not nobility, as we know, but she sailed under the full rigging of the most fashionable bourgeoisie—oh so much more impressive and convincing than the irritatingly presumptuous, tougher-than-leather, weed-infested Protestant blockheadedness of the whole overbearing Krautjunker from the Brandenburg marches. The girl was fresh air, streamlined, deluxe, independent suspension, and cosmopolitan styling. She would never sit darning stockings in fusty retirement in some back room in Allenstein, you could bet on that!

No. This female was cut along grander lines. Take her body alone: perfect for breeding! With a feeling of triumph not entirely free of a slightly lascivious tickling in the nether regions (a maliciously suppressed giggle of schadenfreude), the Baron reminisced about the almost showy elegance of her figure: those long, lazy, and voluptuously slim limbs, bathed in shameless awareness of their own blinding flawlessness; the lithe soft quality of her joints, her flowerlike, agile, and delicate fingers and toes with their oxblood lacquered nails—not to mention whatever else there was—her perfect teeth and her truly devastating, full blond mane . . . Dear sir, all this together was simply and exceedingly valuable; it had to do with money, lots of good money, for you can shop at Mother Nature's if you can afford the prices. Believe me, my venerable friend, that sort of milky golden sheen to the skin, that elasticity of flesh, is not simply embedded in your protoplasm. It's radiation. Money is radioactive. And she was fat where it counted, that blond thoroughbred, with an amount as obese as a round carp hung with the spawn of zeros. More than enough to give the shield of Topor a fresh polish. What am I saying!? Enough to sit as master in his own castle—you understand?

You apparently don't realize how stimulating the atmosphere of a summer walk through the woods can be. Even in the sandy marches of Brandenburg it is not merely the hussar Hans Joachim von Zieten who lies in wait behind the bushes, but also occasionally Pan himself with his retinue of nymphs and fauns, ready at all times to engage in mischief. It is also possible that the Baron's visions had been all too inspiring—I mean the visions of his escrow account: mark my word, money has erotic force! Fair Traugott, in any case, suddenly felt a lump in his throat. Imaginary insect swarms danced in front of his eyes, and the pines of Grunewald swam in a Chanel-doused golden mist of female aroma. But from the enigmatic depths of his soul there arose at the same instant an entirely different emotion, which caused all those delightful delusions to tumble down and shatter to the accompaniment of satanic laughter. He, Traugott von Jassilkowski, had not been the only man to possess this pricelessly enticing, this expansively currency-flaunting example of femininia.

Alas, she was a girl with a bad reputation. Unfortunately, my dear friend, there could be no doubt of its cause. All too readily had she yielded to his wooing, and in the process, all too skillful had she proved.

My friend, your dirty grin can't do justice to this matter. It's quite out of place, as regards the Baron, the young lady, and even yourself. Try to remember what we're dealing with here: the lofty goals of eugenics. And we're concerned with the question of whether you could make "*someone like that*" your wife and the mother of your children. Wife and mother, do you hear me? Doesn't your German philistine soul bubble like porridge at the sound of it? Admit it: quite spontaneously, Thusnelda appears in your mind's eye. "As a rule, the Germans honored their women," writes someone as early as Tacitus. You can make a virtue of necessity if you must, but don't act so superior toward others on account of your own emancipation. Everything goes with a little girlfriend, but when it comes to a wife and mother—thanks but no thanks.

Just think of the child's upbringing: its emotional life is determined by tension between the parents, so claimed Mr. Oscar Wilde. And consider this: wife and mother in the arms of other men—isn't it, so to speak, an archetrauma, an absolutely penetrating graphic image, which all of us have learned by heart from novels and which unleashes an emotional maelstrom in the deepest abysses of our souls!? Scraps of imagery, spit out at random, swirl in its wake: naked, whitish, blue-veined crumbly ripe breasts; armpit-sucking kisses; cigars; underwear; leering headwaiters; opera hats; the acrid stale odor of hotel nightstands; white kid gloves; and dueling pistols. These last ones, I admit, are usually swept away in a skeptical eddy as being far too ridiculous. What remains is scummy residue, saturated with a tired, dark-rings-around-the-eyes, cavalier eroticism with an aftertaste of hair and celluloid, something like what traveling salesmen are accustomed to, a slimy sediment of vicarious sexual desires, trembling with hysterical alarm caused by conventional concepts like *faithfulness, honor, duty, purity* . . . Would you want to lay the cornerstones for a lineage to come under stimuli of this sort?

Baron Traugott, in any case, felt the urgent wish to avoid such a contingency. But how? He was caught between two alternatives: either a little girlfriend, welcome tutelage in lower-body exercise, happy hunting, and amen—but also adieu to the millions and the breeding stock; or wife and mother, castle and shares of stock, blond hair and noble equine nature—in which case her whole lamentable past, shimmering in luxurious and iridescent colors, would trail behind her like a peacock's fan. Surely not the most appropriate train for a wedding gown, you have to admit . . .

But the millions, my dear friend! the backdrop of wishful dreams, poplar avenues, stud farms! Domestics! Herds of registered cattle!

You tell me: wasn't that common? Wasn't that the usual drop of bile added to precisely the most delicious morsel of them all? How liberating and simple, how conciliatory, purifying, indeed how good and basic, everything could have been! He could have loved the girl—what am I saying!—he could have respected her. Wife and mother, happiness and the blessing of children, peaceful silver years with the face of a senator, hands folded in pious thanks. But as things stood now? Providence was to blame. Eternal damnation into perfidy and baseness! Join in his lament, venerable friend, it applies to thee as well.

Thinking is an act of desperation. Right here was the blue of the lake, the light of the sun, the red of the pines, the green of the spruces, cushions of moss, and the scrabbling of bugs—none of it overly impressive, all mixed together, hardly Stifter's forest, even a bit mangy and sickly perhaps, but what more could you want? Airy damp clouds of early summer glided across the heavens, and all around was Berlin, the Berlin of 1938 . . . Hell's bells, it had seen better days, of course, but just think of the great potential it seemed to hold for the future . . . In any case, it was all around him, a glimmer and a distant roar. And this was where fair Traugott strolled through the trees, torn by the empty grief of indecision, and all that time, a second individual was walking beside him, mute and mild —oh no, my friend, not that other one from a certain earlier night, not the sneering archangel of nothingness, but rather the gloomy Jassilkowski, you understand, the noble parvenu in all of us, who has been following the whole sorry business from Day One and who silently weeps over it. Very well, he walked along with him, and all his frailties and everything he had failed to attain intermingled with all that he had longed for or sadly suspected behind these longings: Allenstein and Sinding's "Rustles of Spring," the blue of the lake, the rusty red of the pines and the green of the spruces, Kranzler and the airiness of the poplars, cushions of moss, movie theaters, Charley's Bar, and females, the more the merrier, and purity. Thus his escort raised his voice and spoke:

"It is not, brother of my heart, that all of life is nothing but endless self-denial, that we, forever standing at a crossroads between decisions, in choosing lose out on all those other wonderful alternatives; rather, it is that all those other possibilities would not change anything about our inherent desolation, that we continue to repeat the gestures and posturing of an age-old pantomime, which has become empty and stale, this age-old game—and despite everything we go on playing it—*that*, my dear brother, is the cause of our great sorrow. For while man may believe that his decisions are made in the context of almost boundless variety, in truth they are nothing more than vacillations between repulsion and desire, both of which aim ultimately at death."

Thus spoke the internal whisper of Baron Traugott.

And then it happened that a worm crossed his path.

The worm crawled right across in front of Baron Traugott's feet. It was an ordinary earthworm, *Lumbricus agricola*, of the annelidian species and of the oligochaete order, if this means anything to you, and it was a rather repulsive sight, blind and encrusted with sand, for it had crawled dumbly along the well-worn path in the blazing sun, easy prey for all its natural enemies, sparrows, hedgehogs, toads, shrews, millipedes, and ground beetles. It crawled, apparently endeavoring to reach the crumbly earth on the other side of the path, but it had been diverted from this objective time and again by various obstacles. The sight of it was so piteously repellent that Baron Traugott stopped in order to take it in more fully.

As I said, the worm failed in its aspirations. It dragged itself through the sand in sluggish yet hysterically convulsive motions by means of cramplike waves in its ring segments, quite literally the incarnation of an intestinal colic. Its front end, conically pointed, which in its naked obtrusiveness was reminiscent of nothing so much as a suppository, was raised during these endeavors to probe its surroundings, blind and overly sensitive, like a skinned finger. It somehow sensed the moist humus and the grassy shadow not more than six inches away and turned toward them. This hermaphroditic creature strove in that direction, wriggling in shameless humility. Its own lowly mechanisms for self-preservation were the cause of its failure. For no matter what it touched, whether a pine needle or a pebble, it recoiled in terror and detoured around the suspected peril in a widely circuitous curve. Thus, it came to pass that, instead of crossing the open ground, it crawled the length of it. A strangely convoluted dragged trail, no longer glittering with slime, told of its odyssey, for by then, the creature was parched, desiccated, and worn out. Its rear end wriggled, a powerless snaky tip, in tortured impatience.

Baron Traugott, moved by the symbolic power of the scene, leaned on the Papá Jassilkowski Memorial Cane as Parsifal did once on his lance and observed it musingly. "And where then is HE?" he asked himself. "HE not only allows this to occur, but observes it with satisfaction. HE observes this proof of HIS own power with scientific gratification. For as everyone knows, HE loves those whom HE punishes. And HIS love is immeasurable. It does not overlook even an ordinary earthworm. HE loves this creature and therefore grants him an existence on derisive terms. But," the Baron mused on, "I am not HE. And that is why, for once, in spite of HIS immeasurable love, the fate of one individual creature shall be determined differently, even if it is only that of this nakedly repellent thing."

And as he pondered this, the Baron took a branch from the ground and bent over the *Lumbricus agricola* in great disgust, intending to sweep it from the sandy path onto the cool lawn. But as soon as he touched the reptilian snail, it contracted suddenly in great fright. Baron Traugott reacted with a horrified reflex motion: the brittle branch broke and cut the earthworm into two equal, desperately wriggling parts. Shaken by revulsion, the Baron stamped the remains of the allegory into the earth with his heel and erased its traces with the sand of the Brandenburg march. Greatly frustrated, he continued on his walk.

Thinking, my dear friend, is an act of desperation, *ultima ratio*. The philosopher Bacon of Verulam derides those people who, like owls, are able to see only in the twilight of their own logical deductions and who, blinded by the light of deeds, lose the ability to discover what lies closest to them. One way or the other: the solution was obvious. *Bella gerant alii, tu felix* (or rather: Traugott) Jassilkowski *nube*. Mr. von Jassilkowski gave himself a manly prod and decided to travel to Potsdam that coming Sunday and have a look at a young lady of station in her paddock so that he might come to a clear and final decision. With that he had reached Uncle Tom's Cabin, whence he returned by subway to the city. That evening the Baron was seen in Charley's Bar.

*But you, Son of Man, behold. They
shall bind you with ropes so that
you shall no longer escape them.*

EZEKIEL 3:25

UNDAY CAME. IT CAME, SO TO SPEAK, DRESSED
in its Sunday best, pulling out all the stops with
that splendid azure-blue sky, which would stretch
especially over the western districts of Berlin, de-
serted for the weekend, in a heartrendingly luminous, remote, and untouchable way (made entirely
of air, the whole sky consisting of nothing but wide,
free, deliciously windswept air, if can you imag-
ine!), and accompanied by organ music: from one of the neighboring
houses a radio could be heard through an open window; a fugue
building its complexities with ambitiously pious zeal in the reticent
silence of Knesebeckstrasse. Baron Traugott, about to finish dressing,
with a net tightly drawn over his stylishly cut hair, stood indecisively
before the open door of his wardrobe and poked his finger absent-
mindedly among the silky colors of his ties hanging on the inside of
the door. The Pension Bunsen was shadowy and deathly silent. Apparently Mrs. von Schrader had not yet returned from church, and
the maids were busy in the kitchen somewhere in the back, so that
not a sound could be heard. The rather musty silence of the establishment, maintained by numerous admonitions and restrictions, was
almost palpably thick. Because of the height of the opposing houses,
no sun could penetrate the rooms facing the street, but a bit of sky
could be seen above the roofs, a bit of that wide, free, deliciously
windswept summer sky, far above the city. The organ hooted and
droned and thundered, sounding hollow and cracked in the tinny
radio; the fugue artfully rose and then artfully descended and was
finally brought to a triumphant close. For a few moments the air
continued to vibrate, then the sticky-dumpling announcer's voice
was heard, and Bavarian zither music began with the same blithely
mechanical zeal of the preceding organ: "I'm seeing my girl tonight,
everything will be all right . . ."

Baron Traugott—refreshed by his morning bath and subsequent cold shower, with the taste of minty toothpaste still in his mouth, closely shaven, the skin of his cheeks taut thanks to some strong aftershave—nonetheless brooded languidly and listlessly over his neckties. True, he had been able to solve the problem of the right suit with his characteristic skill (particularly for matters of fashion)—for nothing is more ridiculous than to throw on the same solemnly citified holiday costume every Sunday, as philistines typically do; on the other hand, it would have smacked of youthfully poor taste to pay a visit to Potsdam in an outfit that was too emphatically sporty and informal (especially since he intended to lunch at the Eden Hotel). He had settled on a summery lightweight gabardine in conservative stone-green, not in the least racy, equally suitable for a possible walk along the golf links and for the bridge table of the general's widow, while at the same time comfortable enough to wear in the hot weather that was forecast. Although the malleable softness of the suit's material (firm enough nonetheless to hold its well-pressed cut), the fluffy airiness of his cream-colored muslin shirt, and the solid fit of his elegant dark brown oxfords gave him a feeling of enjoyable well-being and of secure social superiority, a stale and dissatisfied irresolution refused to leave him. After all, only the tie could put this neutral—in the best sense of the word—suit into its musical key, its proper pitch, so to speak. It was the tie that indicated the subtle interplay between the event and one's own whims, between social convention and personal inclination, between one's connections and character; it was the finishing touch of what was *up-to-date*, the discreet but essential accentuation of one's own personality, the harmonizing compromise between the occasion and one's mood. But what would this day be like? What was his mood? The shadings of his soul seemed to shimmer, iridescent and chameleonlike in the cascade of silks and foulards. Were he, for instance, to select that rather obvious slender silk one, vertically striped in green and terra-cotta, which he could combine with a broadbrimmed panama straw hat, it would convey the happy lightheartedness of this summer day in a most gentlemanly way, though it might appear a trifle too foppish—the drone of the organ's bass, still resonating within him, issued subterranean warnings and made him penitently renounce overly sophisticated effects. The hint of summer airiness could, of course, be expressed as well by the diagonal stripes of a club tie, best matched with a brown Christie snap-brim, but this would also commit him to a sophomoric freshness of spirit to which he felt unequal. Best to limit himself to the tasteful economy of solids, something like a deep blue or, better still, that warm dark rust: they allowed equally well for a light panama hat or a felt fedora (if the summery accent was not to be played up). On the other hand, this combination lacked the unplanned nonchalance that seemed to him advisable for a visit to Potsdam: anything too well-mannered and subdued would be bound to attract suspicion in the sharp eyes of the general's widow. Polka dots, on the other hand, represented a challenging militancy. And a Jassilkowski simply could not bring himself to swallow the banality of a Scotch plaid or even a Prince of Wales double plaid. Secretly he longed for the demonstrative and naively asserted aggression of outright bad taste—an energetic, dismissive final stroke drawn under his personality: that's who I am, and you must accept me for better or worse! *Basta!* The latest American models in tiger- or zebra-striped or even salamander-spotted patterns certainly had the requisite tastelessness, but they were devoid of individual stamp—in fact, they were the opposite of the principle *d'épater le bourgeois* in that their very ugliness canceled out the distance separating them from their surroundings, thus also annihilating personality.

Oh well. The zither music from the radio started on the fourteenth stanza: I'm seeing my girl tonight, everything will be all right . . . Melody of excruciating stickiness, reinforced on all sides, so to speak, by obstinately iterating and reciprocally contrapuntal second, third, and fourth voices, in the Alpine fashion, each pursuing the others in primitive rustic polyphony. Unnoticed, this refrain had nestled deeply in Baron Traugott's unconscious, whence, nowhere and everywhere, it continued chirping throughout the day with the persistence of a lost house cricket. In line with the philosophical insight elaborated above, Mr. von Jassilkowski ruled out all the multicolored *embarras de richesse* and all other possible patterns, Oriental figures, geometric ornaments, cross-hatchings, bold waves, and fancy patterns imitating microscopic images of bacterial cultures, and, in a desperately sudden decision, pulled out from the whole lot a simple, black, woven silk ribbon, which his fingers hastily arranged. Putting it on in front of the mirror, he tied an expert Windsor knot and, fastening down the corners of his shirt collar, experienced the sublime process of a personality metamorphosing under sartorial influence. The selection proved a happy one in every respect: it was a bold venture to the borders of taste, where the effects of triviality meet with those of the most sophisticated experimentation and cancel each other out. This is the one area in which true stylistic innovation can still occur within the limits of convention. At the same time, lip service was paid to the Lord's Day. The material of the tie, a crunchy heavy woven silk, was sporty yet retained a certain sobriety, severe enough for the conventional Sabbath, but also original. The psychological advantages of this Proteus among ties could hardly be overestimated: his choice could be interpreted equally as the indifference of an absentminded professor and as a man of the world's confidence in the abilities of his valet (and his tendency toward subdued fashion). Plus, its austere blackness might lead others to surmise a death in the family, a supremely human occasion that both arouses sympathy and largely obviates the need for further personal disclosure.

As Baron Traugott assured himself of all these advantages with a final glance in the mirror—I'm seeing my girl tonight, everything will be all right—a clock somewhere in the house struck ten. The torrent of time to kill inundated the Baron. With exaggerated care, he once more filed his nails, but then, try as he might, nothing more could be done to improve his appearance. Still wearing his hair net, he sat down in a chair with a cigarette and a book, carefully minding the neat crease of his trousers. Mrs. von Schrader returned from church; he heard her full, slightly nasal voice in the corridor, and a slight click in his room's telephone extension told him that she was beginning her habitual Sunday-morning calls. The radio next door might have stopped or continued—it had slipped from his consciousness, having deposited its acoustic egg in his inner ear like some parasitic wasp: I'm seeing my girl tonight, everything will be all right . . . Far away, above the roofs, the sky could be seen, the wide, free, deliciously windswept summer sky.

Then somehow it was noon, and he took off the hair net, combed out the short curls, which were hard to tame, and put on his jacket. A soft brown felt hat and tobacco-colored, already slightly faded kid leather gloves completed his attire. For a moment, he wondered whether to take along a furled umbrella but rejected this idea as much too anglophile for Potsdam and instead ruefully grabbed the Papá Jassilkowski Memorial Cane. He then followed the instructions of his always fashion-conscious colleague Henri Beyle, according to whom the perfect dandy, the moment his toilette is finished, forgets his suit. As he was about to leave the room, his telephone rang, but certain it could only be the thoroughbred at this hour, he ran on tiptoe to the kitchen and asked the maid in a whisper to say that he had already left, destination unknown. He then recommended himself to Mrs. von Schrader by kissing her hand and informing her that he was on his way to the general's widow in Potsdam and would dine either there or in the city. On the staircase he glimpsed his own blurred silhouette in the multicolored panes of the windows of the landing and was rather pleased with its high degree of elegance. Involuntarily, he thought of his Zoppot period and what Mamá would say if she could see him today—I'm seeing my girl tonight, everything will be all right, cheers . . . And almost against his will, he felt a sudden surge of desperate love. All at once, everything came back clearly: the long, long afternoons, the peaceful evenings in the inspector's quarters, Mamá, still youthful in figure, how she would loosen the buckles of his Sunday shoes and put on his soft house slippers (his tiny child's feet in her gentle hands!) and how he would then sit on the rather narrow and uncomfortable, yet so proudly patrician red-velvet divan next to the piano, the tassels of which he always played with secretly, despite Mamá's gentle admonitions not to. (Princely saddlecloths were decorated with tassels like these: the violet cavalrymen from his halma game, three of which had already been lost, should have had Andalusian mounts with richly braided saddlecloths and tassels when he arranged them in solemn procession: flanked by the six yellow and the six blue runners and heralds, and followed by black, green, and red courtiers, then the tin camel, bearing a colorful bird's feather, some small black glass rods from one of Granny's dresses, and a tiny cinnamon stick—the gifts of the

Magi, followed by a solitary black rook from Papá's long-vanished chess set, the hangman in his courtly pageant.) Mamá would stroke his hair, which she allowed him to grow in long rich locks and which always rekindled Papá's rage, but right now she and he would be alone together, thank God, and thanks too to the inspection of breeding bulls or mounting stallions out there beyond the wide-open fields (watch-chain-proud, whip-cracking, booze-guzzling agricultural pomp and circumstance!). Mamá would cut the cake and put out a magnificent piece for him on one of the dessert plates from the good china and talk to him in a gentle voice, and finally she would sit at the piano, and under her suddenly excited and agitated fingers the sounds would come purling forth, at times in confusion and hesitation, but then smoothly again after a few harsh repeated notes—the sweet painful anguish of Sinding's "Rustles of Spring," drowning him in uneasy bliss, sometimes even startling him with the revelation of strange and unexpected sensations, a sudden greatness that he could not grasp and that left him with a nameless and unfocused frustration. The huge, high, limpid summer sky slowly darkened over the land. Her tenderness and self-sacrificing love, her mother's pride and humility, which had made him into a secret prince, her unfulfilled longing, sorrow over her powerlessness, her hidden passion in general . . . and the tears, oh, the tears of Herzeloyde!

Strangely enough, the image of the blond thoroughbred somehow worked its way into this memory, as if some weird connection or mystic relatedness existed between the two. He found an expression for it whose equivocal and nebulous ambiguity put him in a pensive mood: "The possibility of discovering oneself in the depths . . ." The street was empty when he reached it, spanned by an empty sky.

He turned into the Kurfürstendamm. A sparse flow of loiterers, mostly of working-class, Moabit-district origin, was already ebbing away. It was Sunday noon: for a few short hours, they had been permitted to mingle in the now empty playgrounds of professional idlers, strolling between the backdrops of the great play, past Kranzler, Mampe, and Venezia, past the couturiers and the photographers' shops, and now were going back to their tenements, disappointed and depressed by the emptiness of it all, like visitors to a seaside resort in September who seek to compensate for the chilly boardwalk with bacon and roast potatoes. Nothing came to life until Budapesterstrasse; despite the fine weather, there were only a few cars with diplomatic plates in the Eden Hotel parking lot. Baron Traugott sat in the lobby and inspected the public comings and goings. He recognized isolated individuals whose names he knew. He also knew intimate details about their lives thanks to Mrs. von Schrader's bridge tea parties—without, however, ever having had to submit to their personal acquaintance. He smoked a cigarette in a leisurely way, then rose and took the elevator to the roof garden restaurant. He enjoyed a light meal, smoked another cigarette with his coffee and cognac, paid the bill, and was back on the street. The clock on the Gedächtniskirche stood at half past one.

The Kurfürstendamm stretched out before him, broad and empty in the sunlight, extending all the way to Halensee, all the way to the remote pale horizon where the wide, free, and deliciously wind-swept sky rose over the shimmering city—I'm seeing my girl tonight, everything will be all right . . . Charley's Bar was forbiddingly closed, the bold signature over the door no longer a feverishly pulsing and flaming script but merely a banal and milky rigid glass tube. All the side streets, Fasanen-, Grolmann-, Knesebeckstrasse, and so on, whatever they were called, lay in shadows and were familiarly pro-vincial at this empty midday hour. The streetcars hummed along, empty, and from time to time automobiles sped impatiently past toward that far-off, blue, deliciously windswept horizon. Unfortu-nately Baron Traugott did not own a car to sweep him toward his destination, so he strolled the length of the Kurfürstendamm, his steps echoing at that empty hour, past Mampe, Kranzler, and Ve-nezia, past the Roxy and the Alhambra, the auto dealerships and the photographers' studios, and Emma Bette, Bud & Lachmann—good gracious, where have they all gone?! . . . And he crossed Bleibtreu-, Schlüter-, Wieland-, and all the other streets until he had finally reached the other end of the Kurfürstendamm at Halensee. He glanced up at the radio tower—I'm seeing my girl tonight—and down at the rails under the bridge, leading into the wide-open, into the wide-open . . . And above it all hung the sadness of a summer afternoon with nostalgic longing and anguished foreboding, the bit-tersweet melancholy of promise never to be fulfilled.

And the Baron continued to wander—past villas and gardens and water towers—and finally he reached the suburban streetcar stop in Grunewald. It was a quarter to three, and he could take the train to Potsdam. The carriages were empty, the wheels turned rhythmically—I'm seeing my girl tonight, everything will be all right—red pine trunks flew by the windows and green shadows flitted over his face: the blue of the lake, summer sky, cars and sailboats, an empty promise never to be fulfilled in his sorrowful heart. Cheers.

But thou, contracted to thine own bright eyes,
Feed'st thy light's flame with self-substantial fuel,
Making a famine where abundance lies,
Thyself thy foe, to thy sweet self too cruel.
SHAKESPEARE, SONNET

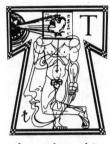 HE GENERAL'S WIDOW, TOGETHER WITH HER
young daughter, lived on one floor of a resi-
dential building in Neue Königstrasse. His Excellency had served with the colonial troops—
on great safaris, surrounded by faithful askaris,
you understand—and thus the apartment's anteroom resembled the armory of a Masai kraal,
bristling with lances and spears, quivers made
of monkey skins, teakwood cudgels, shields of buffalo hide, and
threateningly teeth-barbed arrows. This martial hodgepodge was
arranged symmetrically around some Menzel prints of Frederick the
Great's generals. Even the drawing room, which one entered through
a doorway hung with twin Moorish pearl curtains, bore the mark
of fidelity to tradition: the black, richly carved furniture in Old
German style afforded an impressive context for well-polished silver
racing trophies, while the walls were decorated with fragmentary
genealogical trees, certificates of commendation from various officers' associations, a reproduction of Michelangelo's creation of
Adam, and several photographs of the launching of the cruiser
Seagull in the presence of His Majesty. But also pieces of mem-
orabilia—ashtrays made of silver-plated hoofs of dear departed riding horses and cavalry sabers of fallen regimental comrades. The
center of the room was reserved for a table, surrounded by chairs
with zebra-skin covers and armrests fashioned from the crossed
horns of wildebeests. The cards for the bridge game were already
set out. The tea service stood off to the side. Broad French doors,
opening onto Neue Königstrasse, led to a balcony and, across from
it, a second French door also stood open, allowing the adjoining
rooms to be seen.

Baron Traugott left his hat, gloves, and cane in the cloakroom,

79

and while the elderly servant held back the pearl curtains to an-' nounce him, he made a studious effort to gather in his free-ranging Sunday thoughts on a shorter leash and to gird himself for an encounter with the general's widow. Her Excellency was a wiry lady in her fifties, of casual elegance and agility, née von Vorneweg (her mother a von Poppersloth-Tarputschen—in other words, true aristocracy; her father, a commanding officer in the Guard Uhlans), whose widespread experience gained in various garrisons, together with her iron-gray, rather dashing bobbed hairdo, always cut rather too short, and her dark-brown-stained fingertips—she was a passionate smoker of cigarillos despite her modest means—predestined her to act as the trusty, comradely confidante of younger people. For example, her earthy sense of humor was splendidly epitomized by her arrangement of the house facilities, or whatever you want to call the can: there, one of her cousins, crazy as a loon, had installed (with her tacit and amused consent, of course) the coin-operated box of a public toilet, so that you could only enter said convenience by dropping a coin in the slot—needless to say, a small saucer full of shiny nickels had been placed next to the door. Once inside, you found affixed to the door an enamel sign, taken from a public telephone booth, with the familiar slogan: "Make it short!" That's an example of why young and old alike agreed that she was "a real treasure."

She stood next to the tea cart, while her daughter slouched on one of the zebra chairs and doodled on a bridge notepad. As Baron Traugott entered—I'm seeing my girl tonight—the young lady rose, her eyes full of bored lassitude, gave her mother a suggestive glance, and came forward to meet him in two indolent strides. Baron Traugott, with hardly noticeable irritation, respectfully bent over the nicotine-stained fingers of Madame General. He then took the daughter's soft hand, somewhat moist in the palm, and squeezed it a bit too familiarly. The girl blushed and directed another suggestive and yet also pleading glance at her mother. After a tiny disconcerted pause, the social skill of the general's widow kicked in automatically, and without further ado she offered him a cup of tea. It was drunk standing, while waiting for the fourth, Colonel (ret.) von der Hecke. Soon enough the pearl curtains were parted once more, and Mr. von der Hecke, in his retirement civvies, joined the small group. After some exchange of greetings and the latest news from Cäcilienhof (the Colonel was close to the ex–Crown Prince's circle), everyone sat down for the game. The draw paired youth against the older generation. Madame General dealt.

The tea was thin and hot. They took up their hands, and quite soon the conversation coagulated into a crumblike commentary on the game, unspeakably worn-out witticisms swimming in a tepid whey of mindless semi-pleasure. In leaps and bounds, retracted several times because of mistaken interpretations of the Culbertson conventions, the bid climbed to four clubs, where it froze in blank terror at its own temerity. Then followed the richly accidental playing out of hands.

The smoke of cigarettes and cigarillos rose in blue swirls and lingered by the ceiling. It filled the room with a weathered, slightly dusty atmosphere of coziness, which even the ugly competitiveness of Colonel von der Hecke could not wholly destroy. Across from Baron Traugott, in the background of the sunless interior, the remote, blue, deliciously windswept summer sky visible through the open balcony doors towered over the Neue Garten—seeing my girl tonight, everything will be all right. And while our young suitor with patient subservience endured the retired colonel's long-winded and much-vexed speeches regarding his numerous errors in bidding and leading, his thoughts surreptitiously wandered to that melancholy promise outside, never to be fulfilled, lying in those far-off blue reaches.

Oh, summer! Oh, Attic blue of the lofty heavens! Oh, longing and anguished intimation of what has been lost forever—"emeralda and rubinia and the valleys of turquoise," as friend Rilke put it. Would someone please tell me who it was who put under our shirt that mawkish little man who always wants to weep? Why is it that we behave like simple enraptured goatherds, blowing on our panpipes the refrain of eerie moaning for what cannot be attained?! Billowing banners during a clear morning hunt, Böcklin and Sinding's "Rustles of Spring," a Victorian Sunday on the Thames, and last but not least a zeppelin floating in the sky . . . Oh, for a sky on which one might gaze without thinking anything but: heavens. Better yet: bugger it all to hell!

Somewhere behind the Moorish pearl curtains, a grandfather clock struck five with a typical Old Franconian rattle, the strokes fading away between the portraits of Generals von Schwerin and von Zieten, between the racing trophies and the Masai spears, and still the rubber was not yet over (youth had been able to register a huge head of points thanks to the colonel's stubborn rambunctiousness); the smoke of cigarettes and cigarillos curled up to the ceiling, and the Sunday sky above the Neue Garten was high and wide and deliciously windswept . . . Far away, from over the waters of the Jungfernsee, came the sound of many voices rejoicing, and Mr. von der Hecke finessed his queen the wrong way, which irked him so much that he forgot to draw trumps; Madame General rang for the elderly servant and ordered fresh water for tea. Baron Traugott raised his eyes from his thrice-protected jack of diamonds and fixed them valiantly and steadily on the daughter of the house.

She was a dark-haired girl. The Gotha register of Families of Old Nobility gave her age as twenty-four, and the glaze of an overly ripe female adolescence, perhaps already fermenting a bit, which found outlets, as mentioned, in the palms of her hands and her armpits, endowed her whole person with a strange appeal. She wore the traditional black silk dress favored by young ladies of birth for Sunday-afternoon teas, but with a surprising amount of rich heirloom jewelry. Her eyes were blue and slightly protruding, thereby giving her gaze at times that strenuously suggestive look which could be interpreted as that of someone either in the process of drowning or on the verge of an uncontrollable attack of laughter. At the moment, she fastened her gaze, which almost seemed to cry out, on Baron Traugott, while remaining absolutely motionless in voluptuously lazy silence, a faded smile on her red lips. Her short upper lip lifted in the form of a heart to disclose two sharp and shimmering incisors, and the shadow of dark down above her mouth, together with her eyebrows, which swept upward from near the base of her nose, readily suggested to the knowing observer some arousing associations. Her small, very comely, and exceedingly white hands held the fan of cards with aristocratic nonchalance. Above them, her girlish ripe breasts, rising with the easy motion of her breath, filled the tight silk of her dress.

Baron Traugott drank in this pleasant sight, while the girl's eyes strained toward his own, and the associations began to arise in him, like a swarm of dark birds beating purple wings. But all of a sudden, an arrow of irate reprimand cut their flight short: with broken wings, they plummeted and fluttered away like blind bats into the grottoes of his soul. Purity took over.

What do we know of the origin and power of illusion? Of the most innate human urge to indulge in beautiful fiction? Can your knowledge of endocrinology, of the balance between bases and acids and the influence of the anterior lobe of the pituitary gland on the psyche explain this exhortation to moral responsibility, which by itself had planted the seeds of love in Baron Traugott's heart? For it so happened that he appraised her with the disciplined eyes of the suitor, and behold: he saw her as pure, as pure as the pennant blue of the perfect-hunting-weather sky beyond the balcony doors, pure as the tints of her coat of arms, silver and blue, chaste and maternal. And his heart was heavy with sweetness like a honeycomb: in the azure frame of the balcony doors, a lovely fantasy image revealed itself. She was walking down a staircase, worthy of Schinkel himself in its formal severity, her countenance half hidden by a wisp of a veil. As she sought to find the next step with a light probing foot, she supported herself on the shoulders of two earnest young boys: wife and mother—everything will be all right—including a decent pollination.

Yet at the same time a slight tremor seemed to run through this lovely vision, a subtle rippling of the atmosphere, which soon multiplied and increased in density. Faint waves began to reach their ears as well. Even Colonel von der Hecke raised his sharp profile with a sudden jerk and listened sideways, while Her Excellency the general's widow sat wiry and ramrod straight, her stained fingers holding her cigarillo suspended halfway between her mouth and the ashtray. Even the lethargic eyes of her daughter darted away from Baron Traugott and rolled suggestively toward her mother. For a few moments, time held its breath. But then a kind of invigorating liberation came over the little circle: from far off, hardly audible but becoming clearer with each rhythmically syncopated beat, the sound of drums approached. As the rattle broke into a full roll, the party could no longer be held by the card table, and everybody rushed to the balcony. But who could describe their comic disappointment? Down there in Neue Königstrasse marched a procession of Hitler Youth. The older ones, eleven-year-olds, beat with grim expertise on the skins of enormous janissary drums painted with black-and-white flames, while a handful of smaller boys, cutely precocious in their starched brown shirts, tried hard to keep in step with the vanguard.

"Oh, goodness me!" exclaimed Her Excellency as she looked down on them with amusement. "The poor little squirts! Weren't they rather small for all that noise?"

Amused, everyone returned to the bridge table. Colonel von der Hecke examined his hand and the table with eagle eyes and then and there decided to bring about a decision *one way or the other*: "As birds in slow flight, thus looks ahead the prince, cool in his heart he takes in all events." But since the prince, or rather the colonel had, as you know, forgotten to draw trumps, his attempt to win the leg failed miserably, once more with four tricks down doubled.

The grandfather clock behind the pearl curtains struck six clattering strokes, and Baron Traugott once again immersed himself in the Frederician blue of the young noblewoman's eyes, which probed his own so strenuously as to suggest an impending rupture of her bladder. Without a word, they continued to play. Finally, around half past six, the elder partners made a game with minus nineteen hundred points, and it was decided to finish the rubber some other day. With some hesitation, Baron Traugott prepared to leave, and what do you know? The daughter gave her mother a suggestive look and announced lethargically that she felt like an evening stroll and might as well keep Mr. von Jassilkowski company on his way to the station. The general's widow amiably agreed. While the Baron signed his name in the guest book (a formality that had almost been overlooked), the young lady donned a light jacket and was ready. Colonel von der Hecke stayed on a bit longer, so as to report in fuller detail on the happenings at Cäcilienhof. The Baron bent over Her Excellency's browned fingers, careful to avoid the knock of her knuckles on his teeth, a danger he had learned to fear from his previous effort to kiss her hand. Then he and her little daughter descended the stairs and went out into Neue Königstrasse.

ID-LATE AFTERNOON. LAZY, SMALL-TOWN weekend celebratory atmosphere; leafy shadows in small gardens, classical architectural moldings, the dullness of an army town and fresh breezes from the Havel, rolled-up shades and blue flags, flute concerts and Schellenbaum . . . In silence they strolled together, reading matchmaking pleasure in the eyes of the petits bourgeois who admired how gracefully they walked; secure in their social standing, both of them felt rather childishly grown-up, conscious of their responsibility to be on display, to personify class, decorum, and grace . . . And since this long day was still far from over, they decided to stroll a bit longer through the Neue Garten.

They walked along the broad lanes almost as far as the dairy; the trees were tall and stately in their exclusive task of being on display and the green lawns awaited imminent mowing like virgins, untouched and pure—they strolled in that direction, their steps jointly crunched on the gravel, one with measured ease and one with well-bred delicacy. And a whispering voice, to which they paid no attention among the many different murmurings of the things around them (which spoke only of themselves), tried in vain to warn them not to disturb the evanescence of that hour, not to tear at its delicate veil with either a word or a gesture that might reveal and denude it, divest it forever of its magical promise. In vain the innate wisdom of their hearts advised them to preserve their illusions: they spied a half-hidden bench and sat down, both agreeing callously on what was to come. They had barely spoken on the way, and their voices were hoarse as they, tight-lipped, sought one another's verbal assent: sudden, constraining self-consciousness came between them so that their breath trembled under their pounding hearts. Silent again, they sat for some minutes side by side, their gaze lost in the summery green, which had an almost toxic glow in the impending dusk, but then Baron Traugott, with infinite gentleness, placed his arm around her, and when she leaned toward him, sighing, he hid his face in her hair in silent joy.

Behold the lovers: how they blindly fall into each other's arms, how they latch on, hold on for dear life in the overwhelming need of their abandonment! How they conceal their heads, their eyes in each other's bosoms, their pain in their hearts—what is it that makes them so desperate? What drives them together so inescapably, people who had previously seemed so indifferent and sure of themselves?

Much as I'd like to, I cannot tell you, my dear friend. Love, so says Chamfort (or Vauvenargues or Rivarol—one of those chaps, you can look it up in Bartlett's), love is the touching of two kinds of skin and the exchange of two kinds of fantasy. Exchange? I beg to differ. Alas, it's the exchange of blissful fantasy for merciless reality, the bartering of your firstborn for a dish of lentils and bacon!

Baron Traugott sheltered his face in the young noblewoman's hair and whispered: "My darling!" But his whisper died under her experienced and skillful kiss, his heart paused at the purposefulness of her hands, and finally and in dismay, he let her have her way.

The color of the sky above the Jungfernsee began to dull to that of a pigeon's breast. Baron Traugott caressed her hair and, in absentminded gratitude, her bosom as well, momentarily blinded by a monstrous revelation, almost cheerful, like a man about to die— yet remaining on guard for any strollers coming by. The evening breeze rustled in the crowns of the trees. Blood seeped from the pigeon's breast and condensed on the dark horizon, where far-off clouds were massing and silent bolts of lightning could be seen. And he was great and mighty, his stricken heart empty, closer and at the same time farther away than ever before from fulfillment. Without any remorse, he recognized the curse and the distinction of his unappeasable longing, and painlessly he let the unrest he felt from that sense of promise bleed out of him, all the bittersweet constraint, all the bliss and the anguished needs and hurts, and he felt richer for this great loss. As she straightened up, he kissed her on the lips, which were very soft and tasted somewhat stale, and on guard against approaching strollers, he continued to cuddle for some time in distracted gratitude. Then according to a custom they both despised, they went back the long way they had come, arm in arm.

E HAD FALLEN ASLEEP, AND WHEN THE ELE-
vated train reached the zoo station, he opened his
eyes, saw the city lights, and walked down to the
street as if in a dream, out into the hazy warm big-
city summer night. He let the crowds push him
through Joachimstalerstrasse and found himself on
the Kurfürstendamm under a starry sky, amidst
humming voices and night-wind-gasoline-perfume
aromas. As in some Oriental fairy tale, Kupferberg's champagne
glass was filled to the brim with ghostly glittering bubbles; they
spilled over and were transformed into a green grape, while next to
it, the Sarotti mooring blinked and vanished; Kranzler's fairy palace
floated like a dream ship in the dark current; crowds of diligent
pleasure seekers streamed from Mampe's pub, the movie houses
were bathed in the glare of their marquees, and over there on the
corner, Charley's dashing signature pulsated crocus gold in the indigo night . . . And he was great and mighty and enriched by his
loss. He beheld the sparkling and glistening pageantry of the fair
and the colorful lightbulb sky. "The stars of your destiny are found
in your own heart," isn't it so? He opened the door to Charley's,
and there they all were, all of them: Charley (drunk, of course),
Tom (the Mixer, not Tom Mix), the gallery of grand old playboys
against the stained English wood paneling, the regulars' corner table
with the witty doctor, and all the rest. And there was of course the
blond thoroughbred, five foot eight in open clearance, dressed like
a *Vogue* magazine cover, a fountain of light, luxurious in the glory
of her voluptuous figure, crowned by her shining peroxide-blond
mane . . . And when she saw him, her carmine lips parted in a radiant
smile, and her moist teeth shimmered at him.

She was a girl with a bad reputation, but so uniquely persuasive, so divinely assertive in her unencumbered carnal presence! He drank two Bacardis with her at the bar, then they went to the movies and afterward just for a moment to Ciro's, after which they were together for a bit longer, and all of it was refreshingly lighthearted, palpable and tactile, so well broken in . . . And after that he lay there alone silently, enriched by his great loss, alone with his thoughts in his own bed, and the great endless unresolved Sunday sank away, dissolved into the indigo of the night, while the lights over the Kurfürstendamm went out one after another, and only the Sarotti mooring still continued to blink and vanish, blink and vanish, for a long time. The sky, which earlier had been so remote and blue and deliciously windswept, now looked black and gorged with stars, and somewhere above, somewhere near the Alhambra, the Moldovlachians kept on pummeling and kissing, kissing and pummeling each other. And then it got to be Monday, with open shops and skittering buses, the local morning paper and the frantic Tauentzienstrasse, and everything so refreshingly palpable and tactile and so well broken in. The weather was fine and clear, a rose is a rose and work is work, and damn it all, a million or even something a bit short of it, sir, is nothing to sneeze at.

All well and good: in the course of repeated and thorough deliberation, Baron Traugott arrived at an unusually perspicacious line of reasoning. (For even if the mighty wings of moral determination cannot always free us from the shackles of irksome convention, the caged rodent always manages to gnaw his way to freedom, and analysis is the chisel tooth of any rational animal in the prison of constricting concepts.)

Dogmatic insistence on one's principles, said Mr. von Jassilkowski to himself, even insistence on purity, is a characteristic of petit bourgeois philistinism. The bride's unsullied virginity is an imperative that originated in legal claims regulating hereditary succession, as a guarantee of the genuineness of the breeding object. In patrician communities, the lack of such a guarantee is bound to be treated tolerantly, since it is almost certain that any indiscretion has been committed with another member of one's own caste. As a pure matter of breeding, then, such a blemish carried little relevant weight.

Moreover, even the most severe and old-fashioned bourgeois viewpoint allows for latitude. Room is left for a single indiscretion: a lover falls victim to a pardonable passion, the folly of youth, a dazzled infatuation, star-crossed crush, whatever. A single lapse, maybe two at worst. Anything in excess is not worth discussing. Between three and—well, let's say—five to seven, more or less, it runs into sheer smuttiness, the precocious erotic heat of salesgirls, puberty symptoms still in turgid ferment—in a word, unforgivable. It's quite another matter if the number reaches something like a dozen: that has something swashbuckling about it, a merry unbridled and hard-to-bridle affirmation of life, live and let live, perhaps even the good of the many before the good of the one. Such arguments hold up to eighteen or twenty, beyond which it begins to get nasty. Then either it's a case of scornful disregard for any and all social convention or it enters the realm of pathology. All control has slipped away and issues of motivation become incomprehensible. Levels in the mid-twenties to mid-thirties are to be rejected out of hand.

This notwithstanding, around the half-hundred mark one enters the territory of truly great personalities. It is here one finds—please forgive me the paradox—*the lady of stature*. Needless to say, she is entirely beyond your ken: not within your reach, my friend. In dealing with such a type, should you happen to encounter her, you would be best advised to use your most formal manners so as not to betray (perhaps by some winking familiarism) your clear inferiority.

You may determine these numbers quite differently. I grant you they vary by as much as five to seven points depending on location, social class, and religious affiliation. Nonetheless, their schematic order is correct. That's what counts, my esteemed friend, and we are greatly indebted to Baron Jassilkowski's quantum theory for finally bringing some order to the subject.

The Baron himself at that point was concerned exclusively with a single question: anything falling into the category "pardonably high-spirited lapse" (one to three in all) didn't count. And so he prayed with an ardent heart that kind providence might have left him this eye of a needle as a way out.

This is why, that very evening, as he was again sitting cozily with the blond thoroughbred, and she, as usual, was turning to the subject of marriage, he first brooded dourly and soberly on the whole matter and then, when pressed with questions, countered with acerbic rough allusions, which she in turn, caution awakening, managed to obviate by resorting to innocuous generalities. But then, he surprised her by springing the trap.

They were sitting in the apartment of an acquaintance (wisely he had not yet introduced her at Mrs. von Schrader's), he in a deep club armchair and she perched sidesaddle on the armrest, her arm around his neck and her impeccable torso snuggled against his shoulder, so that her blond mane cascaded over both their heads like a foamy platinum bell—a bell strongly scented with warm and captivating femininity, capable of disabling a man's will, to which he had wisely capitulated a priori. After a gloomy silence of sufficient length, he suddenly asked in a soft voice, his question poised between anguish and generosity: "Did you love *him* that much, then?"

There followed a hardly noticeable pause. Then he felt the cool tip of her nose on his temple, and as she tenderly took his earlobe between her lips, she whispered, "Let's never mention it again."

He looked up and saw tears in her eyes. The trap snapped shut.

Freed from the depths of his agony, Baron Traugott took a breath. The decision had been made. Any suspicion of exactly whom he had caught in his trap foundered in the golden Chanel-scented visions of jodhpurs descending the double curved staircase of a castle.

Never mind. What followed went swimmingly. Thanks to the onset of vehement activity by the thoroughbred, our good Traugott was spared the necessity of further effort on his part. A scant few days later, he was already being trotted out for her parents.

*I now live on the island of Ajax,
the highly treasured Salamis.*
HÖLDERLIN, HYPERION

T WAS AN INTIMATE DINNER BUT WITH ALL
the trappings, the heavy silver and the center-
piece, all very la-de-da yet emphatically matter-of-
fact, as if this were the everyday routine, with a
young hired servant who was far too smart-alecky
and who murmured the names of the expensive
wines in sudsy flippant Berlin slang into what he
presumed were the ignorant ears of the guests.
("Twentywon Rüsselslaara Veltscha 'n' Sack, Trocknbeernauslesooh
—aurom potabilee.") Mama, very imposing and somewhat *fanée* in
a mink stole and hung with clanking jewelry like one of August the
Strong's sleigh horses, dominated the table with the majestically
broad mannerisms of the most disgusting mega-bourgeoisie, and
delivered an uninterrupted lecture on the harmless topic of the pe-
rennial problems one has with domestics, the possible insidiousness
of which speech was suspected by our young friend (to play it safe,
he could not entirely discount it). The situation was made all the
trickier by her use of terms indicating shared social station, such as
"our class" and "*assiette*," her insistence on including him in these
pretensions, and her apparent call for his rhetorical endorsement.
Nevertheless, thanks mainly to his impeccable dinner suit, he managed to maintain a fairly decent posture.

The blond thoroughbred, for her part, remained entirely uncon-
cerned about the outcome of this maternal inspection, relishing as
she did the self-satisfied contentment of a job *eo ipso* well done,
devoting herself to the opulent meal with her usual hearty appetite
and only occasionally adding an impudent aperçu to the old lady's
long-winded elaborations. Without a doubt the happiest of those in
attendance was Papa, who in babbling senility had grasped only that
there was something festive taking place and who had already had

a few on the sly before the arrival of the guests: "German hunters stalk with ruse, in the evening after booze," isn't that so? Already pissed at the beginning of the meal, merrily dribbling mayonnaise over the front of his shirt, he chomped delightedly through it all and, after the first two or three glasses of wine, was completely inebriated.

So as not to have the occasion be too familial, one additional guest had been asked, a dashing bon vivant from the remnants of Mama's circle of admirers, a friend of the family for decades and a fraternity brother of the old gentleman. He was one of those stout monocle wearers of the albino, tight-collared type with froglike bulging eyes and somewhat fanglike teeth; he had the chummy, grandly dashing, and yet icy joviality typical of gentry from the right bank of the Rhine; he was a heavy cigar smoker with a dueling scar on his upper lip and a slight speech impediment. On the whole, he was somewhat the worse for wear—a shabby, slightly suspect, and quite moth-eaten old scoundrel. "The poor man has a slight imperfection in the weave," whispered the blond thoroughbred to Baron Traugott by way of introduction, "grandmother an Oppenheimer."

Jassilkowski the Knight immediately assumed a grave, understanding, and openly sympathetic posture.

That was a mistake. Remember that as you go along through life: such a reaction is always wrong. You've been told, no doubt, that tact, consideration, solicitude, and the rest of that rubbish from etiquette manuals are what you need to gain social prestige. That's old hat, let me assure you! Our nannies read too much Dostoyevsky. Anyone who takes as his social example the highly impressive but also seriously disheveled nobility of soul of a Prince Myshkin should not be surprised when every snot-nosed brat who comes along rides roughshod over him. Don't be overwhelmed by mob opinions. The relation between elites and masses has fundamentally changed. Once the elites gave the masses examples of how to behave; today, the masses are always hounding the elites. Followers become persecutors. Nothing is more natural than hunted animals doubling back now and again—although the masses, driven by the law of inertia, usually continue in one direction, giving elites at least a moment to gasp for breath. Another example of how demonstrating too good an upbringing is a sign of a bad one. A man of caliber stands unencumbered, above it all.

Begin with the sober assumption that every human encounter, regardless of what sort, is at bottom always a struggle for power. Even the most delicate engagement remains a duel of personalities. You will realize immediately why in Germany we pattern our social customs on military models. Even the introduction is, so to speak, a first exchange of fire: the behavior of the opponent is reserved and cool, your opening bow is kept to a minimum, anatomically speaking no more than a slight bending of the uppermost vertebra of the neck. Hands meet with probing firm grip. Names are pronounced tautly and precisely, with a cutting glance: name and heel click coincide like a detonation and the impact of a shot. Meyer—ping! Then the adversaries take cover. Let the other fellow come at you first. Wage a war of strategic attrition. Let him first reveal his secret location within society; no less a thinker than Schopenhauer discovered this truth: *We respect all those who despise us.* Therefore give your opponent the coldest shoulder you can muster. He is nothing but air to you—and bad air at that. Not Dostoyevsky, Clausewitz!

Unfortunately our little Traugott had not yet come far enough to realize that war is indeed the father of all things. Armed since childhood with a cardboard shield made by Mother Bremse on which the motto "Protect the Weak" was scrawled—as a cry for help rather than as a noble device—he approached Mrs. Oppenheimer's grandson with a fawning lack of guile. Consequently, the toothy bon vivant dealt with him mercilessly, running him through a classic drill consisting of all the basic exercises of social engagement. Having thus ridden his spirit into the ground, he added insult to injury by forcing him, by a deceitfully cordial address, sprung like a surprise assault, to reply in an overreaching way, with a clumsy eagerness that the bon vivant then let run aground in miserable awkwardness.

As I said, the gentleman in question had a speech impediment; specifically, each time he pronounced a consonant involving the tip of his tongue, he made a hissing and foaming sound, something between *sh* and *l*, in the corner of his mouth, which was pulled down by his dueling scar.

"Your family halsh itsh eshtlate in Ealsht Prulshia, Mr. von Jash-

95

ilkovlshki?" he demanded sharply, his monocle reflecting light into the face of the addressee. "Where?"

Baron Traugott, confused, protested in an overly correct manner against the flattering but regrettably erroneous phrase "family estate" and started out on an elaborate explanation of this situation, delving deep into the early history of the victors over the Voivode of Czernowitz. But a dismissive "Aha," short and biting like a whiplash, cut him short, and while he was describing the eve of the battle of Czernowitz, the bon vivant had already turned toward the host with another totally unrelated question. Baron Traugott, so as not to bog down in his rhetorical refresher course, tried other listeners, but since the hostess was still enmeshed in her treatise on the question of domestics and the host, hard of hearing, was busy with the bon vivant, he could discharge this all too familiar tale of the Topor tribe only by addressing it to the blond thoroughbred. Overcome by nervous awkwardness, he became insistent on its details, and its conclusion was greeted by a disconcerting general silence. Pale with embarrassment, he looked around the table as if to challenge his dinner companions but encountered only lowered eyes.

All right. Finally the old lady tactfully resumed the interrupted thread of conversation: her words buzzed in thick swarms around the corpses of her thoughts, while phrases and fragments of sentences escaped from the bon vivant, like the eruptions of geysers, hissing and bubbling, at irregular intervals. Brazenly using his deaf host as a kind of sound reflector toward the other table partners, he indulged his extensively cultivated culinary expertise in drawn-out dithyrambs—as an epicurean may harvest the cucumber of sophistication from the compost of late civilization, so to speak. He finally had a chance to showcase his articulate wit in all its grace: when Mama's logorrhea had led her to a hopeless tangle of social claims and assertions, the bon vivant took over. "Our glacioush holshtesh," he began, "dealsh with sheh queshtion of domeshtic help ash a shlplolem. I pershonally alwaysh have shlolved it with a shtrict divishon of labor: each tashk ish dlividled into itsh sheparatle shectionsh. For egzample, exershlize one: tshlake a bottle, ushe a corlkshcrew and dishposhe of the corlk. Exershlize two: tschlake a bottle anld drain. Exershlize three: tshlake a shlecond bottle, ushe corlkshcrew anld dishposle of the corlk. Exershlize fourl: tshlake the shlecond bottle anld shuck it drly. And shlo on. In a ligid dlivishion of labor, I have asshigned exershlizes one, thlee, five, shleven, nine, anld sho on to my valets and exershlizes choo, four, shix, anld eight, I reshlerve for myshlelf. Worksh out fine, anld in thish shpirit: cheersh, my dearl hoshtelssh, anld here'sh mud in your eyle, dearl flaternitshy blotherl!"

Cheerful applause from the ladies and the hired waiter greeted this jest. Since the host had not been able to follow it, being deaf, it was once more screamed into his good ear, and the geriatric's helpless, nonsensical bleating further heightened the general merriment. Devil only knows what came over our young Traugott— suddenly he felt pity for the old wind-sucker. Sympathy, pure and simple, made him close his eyes and in an irrepressible longing for love, understanding, and reconciliation, he raised his glass to him. Not for nothing has psychoanalysis taught us to watch out for such so-called Freudian slips: as he was about to bring the glass to his lips, while opening his eyes in something like tender rapture, he was met by the fang-toothed frozen stare of the bon vivant; as if struck down by the fist of fate itself, he bowed to him. In a barely perceptible motion, Mrs. Oppenheimer's grandson raised his eyebrows, then slowly took his own glass in his fingers and, with the vague indication of a bow more or less in Mr. von Jassilkowski's direction, lifted it no higher than the middle button of his shirt, then immediately set it down again on the table. Henceforth, he ignored the Baron, his icy glances passing over him like the sweeping strokes of a scythe. What remained lay in pieces on the ground.

I do not know to what extent you, dear friend, have ever experienced the harrowing feeling of being exposed as a result of an abysmal humiliation. Noah cursed Canaan, when Ham derided him because of his nakedness, and this leads us to assume that Noah was hardly an introverted personality. Common experience teaches that shame never expresses itself in biblical rage, but rather in the passionate urge to subject one's wounded self-image to even more intense torment. This strange phenomenon opens up perspectives of unsuspected import, if you consider the wider possibilities. Always assuming, of course, that science is willing to focus on it as an appropriate subject. Until now, all such attempts—for instance, those aimed at dynamic exploitation of national forms of over-compensation—have failed miserably because of dilettantish bungling; and even the birth of historic greatness from the spirit of *ressentiment* has been aborted following what might be called a breech presentation. Still, it would be both conceivable and desirable to reinvigorate stunted erotic instincts with new impulses—perhaps through the planned use on a broad popular basis of the psyche's masochistic urge, which might alleviate at least for a while the catastrophic impotence afflicting manhood today.

Be that as it may: Baron Traugott felt compelled to act. The dinner drew to a close. Mrs. Oppenheimer's grandson, his forehead lightly pearled with sweat, was bending in fang-toothed and bug-eyed expectation over his *riz à la Trauttmannsdorff*, while the hired waiter was busy refilling the glasses. Directing a final cursory glance at him, the Baron turned to his hostess, remarking that he found it incomprehensible why so many Jews, who in any case had now been excluded from the leading professions, refused to apply their innate shiftiness to solve the vexing problem of good domestic help. He spoke clearly and could be readily heard by all present. But before anyone could reply, the hired waiter slammed a bottle of Madeira on the table and declared emphatically that he, as a member of a security squadron with the rank of skirmish leader (or whatever) and as the steward of the professional guild of National Socialist domestic servants, occupational group so-and-so, Greater Berlin chapter, felt compelled to protest categorically against such a presumption. Not only—the elaboration was well schooled—was such an arrogant view of the profession of domestic servant ill placed, since in the new order the relationship between employer and employee in no way corresponded to a proportional disparity in personal worth, but, in addition, he considered the potential infiltration of Jews into German homes highly dangerous, since they, as proven fomenters of degeneracy as shown in the *Protocols of the Elders of Zion*, would not hesitate to disrupt the *völkisch*-ethical bases of such households. In the case of male servants, he stressed in conclusion, there would also be the alarming exposure of German women to the danger of racial taint.

Paralyzed silence spread after these words. But the thoroughbred soon found her composure and nonchalantly told the steward and skirmish leader to refill her glass. He obeyed without demur. Afterward, the conversation, though at first somewhat haltingly, rekindled with almost fiery animation. Baron Traugott sat ramrod straight and concentrated on the disgrace simmering behind his temples. He was left ample opportunity to do so. And because he proceeded to view what had occurred according, so to speak, to the Kierkegaardean maxim that the true epicurean first personally enjoys the aesthetic and then draws aesthetic enjoyment from his own personality, his inner torment was intensified until it turned into corporeal pain, something similar to the tickling uneasiness in your lower abdomen when you're riding downward on a swing or a roller coaster—a sensation that causes both kitchen maids and chief accountants alike to squeak uncontrollably. Mr. von Jassilkowski, you understand, suppressed the urge to do so. He closed his eyes briefly and this doubly painful sensitivity, accompanied by a slight perspiration, surprisingly dissolved into a vague all-embracing and all-coveting lust.

The seating order was such that he had been placed to the left of his hostess and kitty-corner from the blond thoroughbred. The round table was not large. Without lifting his glance for preliminary direction finding, but simply following a sudden urge, he cautiously extended his right leg, blindly angling for the thoroughbred's, and soon was rewarded by both resistance and a slight counterpressure. As if coincidentally, he bent forward, letting one hand slide below the tablecloth, and grasped a silk-sheathed calf, which immediately withdrew. Quickly, though, he found a small hand, a hand that at first tried to repel the transgressor. Soon, however, it entangled his own hand in a finger teasing game, finally surrendering in a passionately sucking grasp. Without freeing his prey, the Baron leaned back and looked over at the blond thoroughbred. She sat across from him, relaxed and unchallenged, her flawless elbows leaning on the table and her ambrosial chin gracefully resting between the blossom cups of her hands. The old lady on his left, however, cowered in a strangely distorted crouch and snuffled audibly through her nostrils. Mr. von Jassilkowski abruptly recoiled but cowardice held him back. Sick with disgust and self-loathing, he continued to milk at the fingers under the table, allowing sharp nails to dig painfully into his wrists, even going so far as to impart a saucy significance to every squeeze.

Meanwhile the exaggerated nonchalance that had greeted the incident with the skirmish leader and steward had become strenuous gaiety. Cheese, fruit, dessert wines, sweets, and nuts had been consumed, with coffee and cognac, and they eventually came full circle back to champagne. It goes without saying that Mama and Papa were already very much the worse for wear, and even the bon vivant was fairly well lit. Rather unexpectedly, the latter now tapped on his glass and rose for the customary after-dinner speech. Faces empty with anticipation were turned toward him. Gratefully Baron Traugott withdrew his hand from under the table and drained his glass. The steward and skirmish leader filled it once more. Mama leaned back majestically and pressed her Messalinian head firmly into the folds of her double chin, awaiting whatever was to come. The bon vivant artfully cleared his throat. He was no longer steady on his legs, but nonetheless he started with the brash self-confidence of someone whom a long chain of successfully completed fraternity dinners, commemorative evenings, big-game suppers in East Pomerania, and Parisian bordello visits has endowed with the cosmopolitan skill of concealing utter emptiness behind jocularity.

"Honored hoshtessh and dear young couple!" (Startled, the old lady came alive and cast about glances of frigid astonishment, which the thoroughbred greeted with defiant amusement; Baron Traugott thought it best to keep his eyes cast down. But Papa started up in some confusion, babbled a request for a moment's delay, motioned for the servant and ordered him in a loud whisper to bring him his hearing aid. With the help of the experienced maid, Elfriede, the instrument was brought out and, laboriously, installed. The microphone was positioned in the immediate proximity of the speaker, among the glasses, ashtrays, and already slightly disheveled flowers, while the host, his earphones in place, regulated the volume by means of two buttons on an amplifier box. The blond thoroughbred cracked open some almonds, and Baron Traugott, who had had one too many—his soul had undergone great strain during the evening, and he was trapped in that special clear-eyed state between the first and second waves of intoxication—busily fought off incipient heartburn and kneaded breadcrumbs into little balls.)

"Dear hoshtesh and friensh!" the bon vivant started out anew under the hypnotic gaze of the hostess. "Wonsh again shle gatesh of thish hoshpiltable housh have been opelned tlo ush . . ." And so on following the usual text: the traditional way in which the friends had been welcomed, with nothing but the best that Horcher's wine cellar and kitchen could provide, concluding with the jubilantly crowning toast: "Anld now wonsch again let shle bubblesh of the widlow Cliquot play merrily in ourl glasshesh. Hoshanna!"

The outward forms of the genus toastmaster have been manifold since the days of Luther. The most common is surely he who knows how to mix humorous and serious elements so that the former induce gloom and the latter merriment. As far as the bon vivant went, he could, at least in formal terms, shoot off at the mouth in the classical style: fed by an inexhaustible cartridge strip of superficial puns and dreary banalities, he fired away relentlessly, with a hard precision to the rattling discharge and in a vaguely wavelike sweeping pattern that ensured his projectiles would land in frightening proximity to the most sensitive nerves of his captive audience. Thematically, his style was more difficult to delineate. Warned by the basilisk gaze of the old lady, he seemed to shy away from a certain point, yet, magnetically attracted to it, circled around it in ever closer orbits. He first spoke of the *pleasures of the table* in general and then specifically, since it is well known that the way to a man's heart is through his stomach, passed on to *love* and its special motivating force for *engagement*, then went on to *marriage in general*, dug deeper and mined diluvial layers of venerable European jokes—even the line about the man who wanted his wife to be a lady in his parlor, a cook in his kitchen, and a whore in his bed, but who instead found she was a whore in his parlor, a lady in his kitchen, and a cook in his bed. Having gone so far, he seemed to think he had reached the subject of *the specifics of marriage*, for he then landed with a brisk leap on truly slippery ground and broadly indulged in allusions to what the old lady occasionally may have enjoyed in private, while he waved his heavy Havana like a conductor's baton between his thumb and index finger in fantastically descriptive gestures in front of his starched shirt. Finally arriving at the subject of *the specifics of cuckoldry*, he delivered his punch line with a sweeping and suggestive glance at the host: "whoever among ush ish withshout hornsh, let him casht thshe firsht shtlone . . ."

Well now. "The knights all boldly looked about and in their laps the fair ones . . ." But then a stroke of genius on the part of the old host saved the situation—also following a classical precept, since what he did is mentioned in the conversations between Privy Counselor Goethe and Mr. Eckermann—in the anecdote of the quick-witted gentleman who silences the painful incivilities of a churlish table companion with an obscenity that drowns out everything else. One cannot assume that Papa consciously intended to follow this homeopathic precept, since he had fallen asleep a good while before, and this particular feculence escaped him unintentionally. That notwithstanding, the effect was the same: the bon vivant brought his speech to a hasty conclusion and drained his glass. Everybody rose from the table, and the children went for a last whiskey at Charley's Bar.

It might be said that their actual engagement was concluded on the way. You see, it was one of those warm summer Berlin nights, and you must yourself try to piece together the old scenery: Berlin . . . prewar Berlin on a night in June filled with magic big-city smells, darkly mysterious in the halo of seething life, crisscrossed by black waters, in which its still lights sparkled, faintly alive in the night breezes, the western parts humming with the sound of thousands of rubber tires spinning, lightbulbs glittering, and neon signs sputtering . . . Amidst all this, our two, ever so slightly and sweetly drunk, breathed deeply, holding hands, as they wandered from the shore of the Lützow canal to Budapesterstrasse. And she, the blond thoroughbred, that sleek bird, found herself floating in such fond and deep thoughts, for—you see—she loved him, loved him with all her heart: oh, she knew him, knew him by heart, all his mannerisms and crotchets, his conservative editorials and "From Society" columns and all that had been fashionable in Queen Victoria's time. She loved it all with warm, maternal love—for the sake of her own shy love for his great and pure soul.

Yes—please don't smirk!—there was something in him that

touched and affected the deepest core of her. How shall I put it? His grief, perhaps? A hint of melancholy he had about him, a demure, boyish pride, which could be felt even in the ultimate expressions of love, an unintentional reserve, a reticence in the face of her glaring forwardness, a shy holding back from the sweeping grasp of her own maelstrom: the magnificent aboriginal chastity of a real man. Purity.

Prior to that, you see, nothing of the kind had ever come into her sights, yet she recognized it. Her feminine intuition told her, the secret longing of someone who has been too often disillusioned. There were moments when, quite contrary to her usual habit, she actually felt bashful in front of him. There she was, full of wistful and emotional self-consciousness in front of this late revelation of subtle male tenderness, which protects the woman in love from herself and watches over her dignity. For the first time in her life, she felt ashamed of her past, ashamed of the succession of callow experiences, ashamed of all those despicable brutes with whom she had come together in hard-boiled lasciviousness. How different, how very different he was! How beautiful and deeply moving the old myth of Eros placing his hand over Psyche's eyes to protect them as they fly together through the high-vaulted night . . . *Hélas!*—it was not exactly her eyes that Eros Jassilkowski was shielding, for he was the one being blindfolded, as it were—but what of it!

She loved him! He was different from the others, and in that difference he was unfathomable and even mysterious; secretly, she respected him.

She held his hand and he held hers—he was lulled and enveloped in satisfied well-being and relished his bodily comfort. All the pain and anguish had been melted away in the gentle warmth of this June night. Even his humiliation by Mrs. Oppenheimer's grandson (who had not exactly covered himself with glory, the loathsome toad!), even the fingering with the old lady (that moorhen!)—it had happened, but now it was over, endured and forgiven. How happy above all others is he who does not have to discard his whole past in order to be reconciled with fate! Peace had come to his heart. Forgotten was Potsdam, forgotten the festering wound of poverty in his breast, forgotten cousin Zapieha and Allenstein, the Lower Silesians and the torment of being forever misunderstood on this earth. Everything was forgiven, and nothing remained but sheer warmth and deep emotion and gratitude: for did he not come straight from the lap of a *family?* Had he not finally returned to a mother's womb? At *home,* do you understand? That kind old dotard of a father and dear old mother in mink stole and pearl necklace: wasn't that his true home from now on, with silver and lobster and hired man and silk curtains?! Oh, how grateful he was to the girl at his side and how he would forever uphold her honor—mother and wife, in spite of everything! . . .

He held her hand and she held his—they were still holding on to each other tight when they landed at Charley's. They sat in a corner, away from everyone else, and he was kind to her and caressed her gently; and she was utterly happy and in a blissfully soft mood. She would mend her ways—what am I saying?!—she sensed how much she had already bettered herself on his account: not a glance at another man since she had met him. Dear God, I saw her sitting there with my own eyes, in the corner across from the portrait gallery of the grand old playboys (it was Charley himself who drew my attention to the two of them): thick shimmering tears ran down from beneath her eyeglasses. You have to admit: she was an enchanting person, the blond thoroughbred, she gave us nothing but the most delightful memories . . .

*What are we then if we are always
obliged to make ourselves into what
we are, and if we are in the way of
being-obliged-to-be that which we
are. Take, for example, that
waiter . . .*
     JEAN-PAUL SARTRE,
     BEING AND NOTHINGNESS

PLENDID FRIEND AND PATRON, NO NEED TO
abandon the sumptuous aftertaste of silence for a
mood of soulful confession: my conclusion wasn't
meant that way. It was merely an artful trick: surely
you, too, felt at that point that our story required
a slight ritardando to catch its breath. Something
in us hesitates to release so quickly what we have
conjured up, to abandon ourselves again to the
white-water rapids of events. So be it! This is simply because we
have encountered an instant of happiness and exclaim sympathetically: "Stay awhile, you are so fair . . ." But allow me a banal
question: what actually is happiness? No doubt you'll hit me in the
face with the whole messy pie of the usual philosophical observations
on the subject—ethically fortified and morally well kneaded, meta-
physically brought to heat and raised with some cheap baking powder provided by cynical false humility, then larded with platonic
raisins about the good and the beautiful, further frosted with epicurean desire, free of subsequent disenchantment and, last but not
least, drenched in the stoic vanilla sauce of the *vita beata*. For the
heartburn of hubris, a pinch of bicarbonate of soda, brand Schopenhauer, happiness as maximal freedom from aversion. No chance,
my friend! I won't take it anymore. Thanks but no thanks, as
well, to all chocolate-covered aphoristic snacks. Since philosophical
doubters now doubt even doubt itself, all systems have been stood
on their heads, and philosophical definitions have become threadbare. The charming audacity of aphorisms has consequently been
lost. And the illustrious scientific disciplines only do ostrich politics
and, for lack of golden sand, stick their heads in thermal mud.

No, my distinguished reader: keep away from me with the whole tradition from Euclid to Einstein, from Aristotle to Rosenberg. This midsummer night's dream has turned out to be a cheap burlesque, with causality as the stage that supposedly is the world on which the backdrops of time and space are pushed around. Now that this venerable dump is falling apart, am I to rush around the corner to a fortune-teller to learn the meaning of the play? Or should I allow myself to be seduced by block-and-tackle orthodoxy and pulled up into the stage rigging of theology? The results of three thousand years of Western endeavors boil down to either tea leaves or a short yelp for God's help.

Strange—I don't know whether you can still feel that summer of 1938 so deeply in your bones; as for myself, I can't help it. It is still in my marrow, and all the talk of collective guilt can't rid me of it. Say what you will, it was something new, something that defied all previous experience: the days, each limpid and clear as glass, building one on top of the other to form an epoch, and yet time also seeming to stand still, giving no impression of running its course or representing a succession of moments. There was nothing but a certain special kind of light: each time I try to recall something from that summer, it occurs to me as a specific degree of luminescence, abstract and ungraspable like a dream memory, like an underwater view in an absolutely transparent aquarium, in which events and occurrences float weightlessly and in no apparent order like a school of fantail fish. Never before had the amply denounced unreliability of the senses been so painfully evident as then—except one, namely the literary sense. That—no surprise—caught on right away and saw through the whole sham, and what do you know: it turned out that our modes of perception had not been ours at all; once again, we had taken for granted what many eminent authors had long ago shown to be true. My friend! If only what we call our apperception were something other than the product of incestuous literati! The filiation of all the sins of the intellect, the eternal bastard offspring of vision and ratio! Where, then, are the bold ones who will finally say: We don't want to *know* anything more! We want only *form*! Take, for instance, those old playboys at Charley's Bar: in the midst of the chaos of systems coming to a halt, after the general philosophical Black Friday, in the midst of a relentless conveyor belt of mass psychoses, they, the last knights of King Arthur's Round Table of ever-circling flips and cobblers, they truly *led* their grand lives, so that in the jousts of dice tumblers the hazy dawn of helpless mass-produced lemurs blurred into a sublimely beautiful dusk, into an evening song of a gloriously declining world's *heure bleue*, a world of feudal gentlemen. Dame Maya awarded them her own veil in honor of their chivalrous *mâsze*.

I must now call your attention to an event that may cause some surprise about the character of our hero and the historical moment when it occurred. I emphasize the historical moment since what occurred would in our day no longer be considered out of the ordinary. I'm sure it has not escaped your keen eye that the community of upright and self-effacing citizens has grown, of late, enormously in number. I'm talking about those who meekly fold their hands and say: We don't know everything, therefore we cannot know everything and neither therefore are we supposed to know everything. After solemn intellectual delights a spiritual frugality gains ground, contenting itself with approximate values, piously and modestly, and subsuming the irrational rest under the name "God's inscrutability" for simplicity's sake. Very well, then! HE was never any closer to mankind than in that ominous summer of 1938 of which we speak. Allow me to point out: HE was so close that in fact no one could see HIM, for we were so wrapped in the folds of HIS mantle that it was all but impossible to raise our eyes to HIS countenance. People who relied primarily on their olfactory sense for perception might have sniffed out HIS corporeal proximity in the folds, and then they drew their own shaken conclusions from the experience. But seeing HIM, truly perceiving HIM was impossible because of HIS all too great presence—and precisely that is the vexing aspect of our relationship with HIM.

Thus we see that to keep his relationship to man harmonious, God has to stay within his appointed boundaries. He remains—if I may put it like this—the great universal peg on which the whole is hung, but in a loose sense, in the same way that he is the great peg over the gallows at Nuremberg. To that extent, he is indeed fully comprehensible and acceptable. But as the terrifying, all-devouring, unforgiving God of the Apocalypse from whose all-seeing eyes not even a louse can hide, he is not available to us, precisely because of his exaggerated omnipresence—unless he be believed to be present in absolutely everything, in the intestines of the above-mentioned louse, as well as in the city's electrical power plant, in a bride's kiss, as well as in an SS man's pistol shot—and he would also then have to accept the consequences, his retroactive, all-encompassing culpability. As I said, I am talking about 1938. Today, this problem is already obsolete, since the God of vengeance obligingly has assumed a handy, plastic egglike form, easily portable and readily comprehensible to everyone. We are greatly indebted to much-maligned modern technology for having simplified the Lord of the Final Judgment into the encapsulated form of a hydrogen bomb, ready for everyday use.

But in the summer of 1938, if you will, this was, as I said, not yet the case. On the contrary, the weather was fine and almost eerily constant, exemplary order and cleanliness everywhere, roads in spotless condition, and the transportation system hitting new heights. Only eggs and butter had become scarce, if memory serves, but it would have been quibbling to see in this insignificant bottleneck an early vision of the seven angels threatening, their cups overflowing in divine wrath. Berlin then seemed to be rising in the air like a magic carpet—borne by breezes from a great new and ever-expanding horizon, thrilling to the possibilities that were opening up, and animated by a white-hot energy—all of this, if I may express it thus, under a silky-smooth, glibly polished surface: moments of the highest expectation, such as you experience at gaming tables or under the auspices of so-called *great* music, both of which with their almost unbearable emotional surcharge induce a kind of clear-sighted lethargy wherein your nerves and senses seem to be wound tight—such moments stretched out over days, weeks, and moons and were spread so uniformly over everything and among everyone that they filled the whole city, as if dispersed into the particles of the atmosphere. That was what caused this dazed weightlessness, like that associated with very thin air or very high speeds—and a simultaneous sensation of almost voluptuous helplessness . . . But why go on with all that since we are both, so to speak, pastor's daughters?! After all: if you're already living on a volcano, you might as well dance.

But it turned out that our two protagonists had bigger things in mind.

The blond thoroughbred, as you must have guessed, was of the Catholic faith. And even though she had certainly attached little significance to this for at least the last decade and a half of her gregarious life, she had been overwhelmed during the recent weeks by a strangely blissful uneasiness: her heart melting in suppressed gratitude, saturated with mildness, humility, and *gloria*. As Mr. von Crusenstolpe asserts in some of his comments concerning Mrs. von Krüdener, noble and sublime souls, even if otherwise quite unsophisticated, turn, as a rule, from sensual intoxication to divine beatitude in order to compensate for the loss of their earthly paradise. I will abstain from drawing any inference about Baron Traugott's virility from this statement; rather let us direct our attention to the mystical consecration of betrothal. The dear scamp was suddenly and painfully reminded of the lost intimacy of her childhood faith, the irretrievably vanished blissfulness of a child's unshakable trust in the forgiving power of the Virgin Mother to intercede on her behalf: being in love herself, she felt a deep and, so to speak, collegial bond with all the prophets of love. And so she was determined to seek lasting blessing for her endeavor from those holy symbolic figures and to purify her bridal condition through the sacrament of *confession*.

It was a quiet afternoon without appointments or things to do when she retired to her freshly waxed teenager's room with her old dolls, the fairy-tale pictures on the wall, Huysmans' *A rebours* and all of Elizabeth Arden's beauty tonics. After locking the door, she sat down with an ample supply of paper at her small mahogany writing desk to draw up a list of her sins. As she sat there, chewing on the end of her pen and looking out the window above the crowns of the trees in the Tiergarten—it was already September but a summer sky was still spread over the world as bright and clear as glass—as she sat there and thought about herself, the fount of memory suddenly became a gusher, and she swam along with it, writing swiftly and easily, at times laughing out loud and adding supplements between the lines she had already written. Her tall firm pen strokes filled page after page—the document swelled to a truly impressive length—and her mood, so recently close to penitent, improved with each new item. The afternoon passed, the maid timidly knocked on the door to ask where Mademoiselle would like to take her tea, but the thoroughbred gave no answer. She wrote, made corrections, then set about organizing the confused mass of material more systematically. She smoked innumerable cigarettes, lost in thought, and extinguished them half smoked in the ashtray. From a drawer, she dug out an album of photographs and examined the pictures with great amusement, recorded some fresh entries on her list, found a bundle of old letters, quickly went through them, carefully tore them up into small fragments, and continued her notations. Finally, she numbered the individual items and concluded with a deep sigh that the register was still incomplete and full of holes. With an energetic final stroke, she decided to make her confession *summa summarum*, wholesale, as you say. She also thought of tearing up the whole inventory but changed her mind and locked it in her drawer together with the photo album. Then she rose, spread wide the lily-white stems of her arms, and sensuously stretched her limbs. Relaxed, she fell back on her four-poster. Then she picked up the telephone and dialed the number of the Pension Bunsen. But Baron Jassilkowski could not come to the phone.

When you had wrestled with death,
Yes, with death!
When you more fervently prayed!
When your sweat and your blood
saturated the earth . . .

KLOPSTOCK, ODES

NBEKNOWNST TO HER, AT THE VERY SAME
hour the Baron was engaged in a similar endeavor.
He, too, sat deep in thought, sucking at his fountain
pen, tasting weakly of celluloid, in front of a sheet
of paper, which, however, was thus far as blank
and free of blemish as the blond thoroughbred's
throat. It is true that what he was about to inscribe
on it, in his legible if perhaps somewhat primitive
handwriting, was not a register of his sins, but merely his regular
contribution to Baron von Aalquist's *Gentleman's Monthly*, and so
he was not about to seek indulgence for past sins through a penitent
confession. For one thing, his family tradition, especially on his
mother's side, was firmly Protestant, banishing any thought of
confession; and for another, the past seemed, if sinful at all, like a
series of sins committed against him, against the ur-person identified as Traugott Jassilkowski, sins which sprang from a fateful
underlying constellation and which had developed inexorably over
time. It is not easy to interpret the deeper meaning of providence
unless you are prepared to rely on the somewhat simplistic, if gran-
diose, scaffolding of patriarchal faith and to posit therein a proof
of divine grace. Admittedly, this worldview has a lot to recommend
it. For even though—indeed, because—it presupposes that the mere
fact of being born already entails guilt, life itself appears as *felix
culpa*, so to speak, and this alone makes eventual redemption possible. Given this possibility, the concept of the tragic is abolished,
although some deeper knowledge warns us that this cannot be the
whole truth.

Anyway, Baron Traugott would have swapped with a glad heart
this harsh concept of grace, with all its prospects for joyful reward
in the hereafter, for the callous indifference of the thief on the left

and a castle in Pomerania. Yet strangely it happened on recent occasions that he would perceive in a sudden and shattering flash—experienced by his senses, not merely his cold intellect—that each and every earthly endeavor is directed toward a single moment of reckoning.

I don't know to what extent you yourself care to dwell on the thought of death—I mean you yourself dying. Mr. Toynbee, if I'm not mistaken, says somewhere that although we all realize in the middle of our lives that everyone must die one day, only later do we know: *I* shall have to die. Nonetheless, even when we're not so far along in years, we experience moments when that knowledge abruptly comes over us, not merely as an idle bedtime musing prior to falling asleep after a healthy, well-spent day ("and one fine day like this you will lie here dead") but as a startling illumination, a sudden terror grasping all our senses, like a fall into an abyss. In dreams where we imagine ourselves falling, the horror of long-suspected certainty coincides with a rapid intensification—or better still condensation—of being (and of being as we are), which persists as actual panic even after we wake up. Likewise, the terrible aspects of confronting our own mortality remain the stuff of such fleeting moments and can never be consciously reconstructed.

It came to pass—or better yet, it had come to pass that Baron Traugott sat pondering his regular contribution to Baron von Aalquist's *Gentleman's Monthly*, staring at the virgin pages of his notebook with that tense absence of thought which anyone with a literary gift must be able to produce in order to tease from the depths of his muse the first melodious syllable of the decisive opening sentences. This is, as you surely know, a condition of total self-surrender, similar to the preparatory phases of a trance or a yoga meditation: a forcing-inside-out-and-back-again of the sensoria, a process you may imagine pictorially as the expansion of the personality into a tender-fleshed cavity in which the senses, wary and aroused, probe in all directions like the feelers of a snail on the move. Through the gaping wants and needs of this vaguely defined interior space, visions drift, dreamlike and melodiously enticing, like Rhine maidens on an opera stage, while beneath them the words, melted into raw bell metal, are rolled about by slowly undulating, constantly groping and testing tentacles, continuously sifted and separated, assessed and rejected. The author himself is totally immersed and commingled in all this like a fermenting agent, and he is, without any will on his part, put at the disposal of the work that is coming into being.

Thus it was for the Baron at that instant. But you'll fully grasp the ticklishness of his situation only when you know what it was all about: the October issue of *Gentleman's Monthly* was to feature fashion accents for that very autumn! And even though the season, with its changeable weather and all its *indoor* and *outdoor* sporting and social events, allowed and even cried out for great variation in wardrobe, the possibilities that suggested themselves had been worn-out and obsolete for decades, their permutations utterly exhausted. Whatever combinations you chose, however you sought to transform, embroider, or hem them, the outcome remained dully the same and—in the full sense of the expression—cut from the same old cloth. Here, too, you were confined to the classics. Yet it is painful and deeply discouraging to imagine a world where personal initiative is condemned and limited to mere imitation of the ossified lines of the past masters, especially if you're a poet, and especially if you're endowed with a penetrating vision that can spot the plaster in among the marble in the museum gallery obstructing your view of the landscape of the imagination. This deadly edifice, which casts a hard shadow on everything around it, cypress-dark and animated by a hollow sadness, creates an overall effect of graveyardlike emptiness, and once you start looking around in earnest, scorning easy optimism or cheap words, you will find that only a few of the edges around what we call intellectual life have not fully putrefied.

Baron Traugott, as he sat there and eavesdropped on his own self, was thus confronted by an empty desert of frailty. True, the world of fashion, this least conscious and most impulsive expression of man's play drive, had been stagnating for some time—this observation was itself already an old chestnut. Even Mr. Schopenhauer had noted, resignedly, that while the eighteenth century had at least had the spirit to invent the tailcoat, since then nothing worth mentioning had appeared. Life in this sector, too, was frozen along lines based on classical concepts, from homespun textiles to chalk stripes, from trouser cuffs to rounded lapels. And therefore, everything we suffered for our attire, all our hope and faith in the redeeming power of dress and our rapture in cherishing its nuances, was becoming abstract and bloodless: the bright longing for perfection to be stilled only with submission; discipline the highest commandment; correctness instead of genius. But wasn't this precisely what defined the heart of *elegance*? Even though our image of perfection may very well be the gentleman correctly tailored from head to toe in the classic mode, umbrella in hand, topped by an Anthony Eden hat, who, wings broken, does no more than deposit a wreath at the feet of inventing genius, precisely this situation betrays subtle distinction and patrician irony: the ability, so to speak, to dance in chains, as Nietzsche put it, a privilege reserved only for the elected, who naturally preferred mirror-polished *chevreaux* to patent-leather shoes, who were cool enough to wear their black jackets with discreet herringbone trousers, and who prided themselves on the noble constraint of a well-knotted silver-gray tie. Here barbaric uniformity crystallized into a style purified of both dull submission and the impulse to rebel, the will cleansed of impurities, ennobled by service, and exclusively directed into the channels of the most supreme human taste. Baron Traugott sensed—bodily, almost painfully—this deep knowledge of the essence of fashionable perfection. The inner emptiness where he sought verbal expression vibrated with the passionate choired voices of the daughters of the Rhine. Strangely enough, in this arch-maternal moment, with this sensation of musical fulfillment, the thought of his dying suddenly overcame him.

It was, as we already know, a summery September afternoon, which arched high and clear as glass above the roofs of Knesebeckstrasse, visible from the windows of the Pension Bunsen, a little piece of sky composed entirely of air, wide, free, deliciously windswept air—remember?—and the room where the Baron sat was dipped in its usual dusky shadows; the rather musty afternoon silence of the rooming house, maintained by repeated admonitions and restrictions, almost palpably enveloped the solitary tinkling of Czerny piano exercises coming from one of the cheap neighboring flats on the courtyard. Lukewarm kitchen smells from the eating places on the Kurfürstendamm drifted in and nested, along with similar airborne fumes, in the folds of the net curtains and in the seams of the upholstery. It was a summery September afternoon, shining and blue, reminding us that somewhere out there, far away, in the luminous distance, there were pastures and fields, rust-red forests, perhaps mountains, too, and perhaps the sea with its glittering swells and wonderful white mussels in the moist sand—and it reminded us that we were living as if partaking of all these marvels of the world, as if we were actually familiar with shimmering coastlines and vanilla-scented isles, at home in a thousand cities and palaces, worldly, expert, and wise—oh, magnificence of life!—one of those equestrian days that, in a red coat and spit-polished hunting boots, flawless and lean-faced, vaults on a big horse over hedges; one of the ones whose full-blooded laughter detonates over its pleated shirtfront, white in the black severity of evening wear; one of the slim, sporty, tan ones, who stands unchallenged like a stag amidst a herd of casually grouped beauties, on intimate terms with the world's big shots, blood brother to nabobs, movie stars, and prime ministers (Say when, sir!), reminding us that if only the proper occasion arose, we, too, might confidently clap life on the back, sleep with Ingrid Bergman, play polo with the Mdivanis, bridge with Lady Mendl, and shuffleboard with the Windsors, and go surfing with the Munn sisters, reminding us that we carry within us the expectation of all this like a certainty, steadfast in our conceited idea of equal standing—though meanwhile we live as a lodger in rented rooms in Berlin, can fit all of our belongings in two suitcases, don't even have a cottage or a garden but, instead, forsaken wishes and worn-out longings, salesclerk's ideals and motion-picture dreams—that we live a window-shopper's existence, barred from the delights this grand rich life offers, worldly only because we read magazines, experts only through the advertisements, wise only by grace of the Maughams, Bromfields, Edschmids, and Hollanders, do-nothings and loiterers, nameless as spores in the breeze—reminding us that the expectation nonetheless remains alive, a promise of all and everything, of an overflowing horn of plenty held in uncertain balance over our chosen heads: a tiny hitch, a minute accident, a minuscule stroke of luck and those gifts would be poured out, would be squandered on us.

The blue afternoon was a reminder of all that, and Baron Traugott, sitting in the quiet of his boarder's room in the Pension Bunsen, slurped it in to the depths of his soul—that high Attic September sky above the city of Berlin—and his senses, in a sentimental gush, surged through him, sucked on his brightness, unchallenged, and gorged on his claims and demands. Suddenly, just as a spark is emitted from opposing poles and bridges them with a fiery tongue, the thought ran through him: I SHALL HAVE TO DIE.

In the abrupt illumination of his terror, it was given to him to see himself truly.

You realize, I trust, esteemed reader, the full weight of this crisis —no? In all probability you, too, live with the common delusion that you are equipped with an unambiguous, ever-ready concept of your own ego, which you treat just as you do another part of your anatomy: as something familiar from daily use but embarrassing when called by name, albeit something which can hold its own among its brethren and for which, therefore, you are not without affection. You, too, posit your so-called individuality in the mishmash of pretensions and anxieties filling your esteemed insides, identifying as your most singular possession precisely that which in truth is your most general attribute, that which makes you the same as everybody else. I tell you truly: once you are granted the ability to think *I—I*, pared of those human-all-too-human gonads and their urges and fears, freed from the delusionary visions that dapple the housing of your being—once you share the dismaying idea that you *are*, a being, equal in standing to those exalted desert prophets, only undiscovered, undiscoverably buried under the sands of a second- or third-hand life, lost in the fun-house mirrors of your window-shopper's existence—yet still present, being, actual, awaiting redemption, though ephemeral, ready to dissolve with each fleeting instant— once you realize you are *mortal*, then, dear friend, the path of light shall be revealed to you, rich with connections leading up and down, the path that is commonly called *religio*.

Freely admitted, here the difficulty begins. For instance, nothing is harder to harmonize with the concept of divine order and immanent justice than the clear preferential treatment in the words: MANY ARE CALLED, BUT FEW ARE CHOSEN. You certainly can't ignore how closed and exclusive the coterie of the chosen few has remained to this very day. Jesus Christ, though born in a stable, was nevertheless of royal blood, and even the most cursory glance at the lives of the saints should convince you that it contains a disproportionate number of aristocrats as well as members of the higher patriciate (particularly Roman) compared to those from the lower classes. Yes, even in Dostoyevsky, whom certainly no one would accuse of being a snob, the only surely blessed person is a prince, while the others, of more modest birth, pursued by all the devils of hell, puff their way through the mazes of a mostly unsuccessful search for God. The clearly feudal character of such lofty parables raises complex questions that cannot be fobbed off with the stereotypical command to keep the faith, come what may and however you look at the matter: the fate of Christendom depends upon answers that truly show the way to a new humility.

It will probably be useless to point out to you that even the first touch of God's hand is rich with pain—by that I mean the very confrontation with one's own self, the terrifying duel with a stranger, whose entire tormenting appearance calls out: THIS IS YOU!—the one who, naked and with no excuses whatsoever, reveals all that is most hidden in us, and the one who nevertheless, despite everything, is a being in the ranks of God's children, suffering on the cross of who he is, wounded, crowned with thorns, and his thirst slaked by only the vinegar of earthly nonfulfillment.

And the Baron recognized in him that same angel who had spoken to him—once in the imperious whisper of an incorruptible spirit to reveal his delusion and once in the grieving tone of an initiate to forgive him. And behold: he saw now that the angel had become powerless, no longer scornfully demanding and urging defiance, nor soothing in lofty melancholy—mute and blind with tears, thus the angel stood before him, and his powerlessness was that of a dream betrayed.

Oh, purity! Oh, would that none of us were betrayers of our dreams! Oh, would that we had the strength to be steadfast and faithful in the pursuit of our secret ideals! Would that we had the courage of the true confessor not to deny that we are still children at heart—even long after we've crossed the threshold between the expectation and the reality of life, and come to realize that the former is to the latter as an English waltz danced with eyes sentimentally closed is to a wild *Raspa* on white-hot coals, even long after, when the window-shopping before the delights this life offers has become ruthless consumerism, we realize that they all come from the ready-made department of creation! For truly there is no possible ransom from ourselves, not even our dreams; and never and never can we be redeemed from ourselves except in our dreams—*and in death.*

And so the Baron recognized himself in the angel, and he knew his name and named him for his own sake and did not know whether he spoke the truth or spoke the truth and preferred not to acknowledge it. He was somehow compelled to reveal himself: he needed an ear to pour himself out to, an echo that would answer his anxious question: *Who am I?*

And soon enough, an occasion for this arose, when Mrs. von Schrader called for him by prearranged bell signal, bidding him as usual to have tea with her.

Hope is faith in the future, as
likewise faith, as it were, is a
hope for the past.

LEIBNIZ

EA TOOK PLACE AS USUAL IN HER SO-CALLED boudoir, located in the rear part of the Pension Bunsen and separated by a curtain from the Schraders' conjugal bedchamber, furnished with loving care with the feminine attributes its owner had by no means forfeited. The renunciation of a proper aristocratic existence in favor of wage-earning had greatly reduced the space of the Schraders' living quarters, so that the room no longer was exclusively devoted to its original purpose, but served both as the focal point of their social life and as an office where the pension's paperwork was done. On the large ivory-inlaid secretary, an ancestral heirloom, lay a guest book and registration forms mixed in with playing cards, coffee cups, a few issues of *The Journal of German Nobility*, hairbrushes, cosmetic jars, and other paraphernalia. A dear little hat, over whose acquisition Baron Traugott had stood as an expert godfather, hung above the mirror, its surface slightly dusted with facial powder; and an autumnally nostalgic scent of asters leaking from a bottle of Houbigant, its contents already somewhat thickened with age, mixed with the fusty smell of the playing cards and more delicate kitchen aromas. Mr. von Schrader—did I forget him, dear friend?—he was employed as an accountant in the Reich's ministry for food supply, so far as I know, but this is neither the place nor the time to go into greater detail about him; you ran into him now and again in the lobby of the pension or at meetings of aristocratic societies on whose many committees his wife was laudably active—but please spare me the task of any further description; you can rest assured he's not worth your attention, a truth Mrs. von Schrader would be only too glad to confirm if you'd like . . . As I said, Mr. von Schrader was not at home (though he might well have been—maybe he was hiding somewhere, let's say in the bedroom behind the curtain, working on his collection of cigarette coupons . . . incidentally he already owned a sizable series of children's books and illustrated documentaries about recent political history—but let's drop him). As usual, Mrs. von Schrader had had tea for two served, and Baron Traugott, summoned from his writing desk to make his decision like Cincinnatus from his plow, walked through the silent corridor (exceptionally discreet silence was a prized aspect of the Pension Bunsen), not having quite found his way back into the sensible world. Entering the boudoir, he was met by the tepid vapors of femininity soaked in Houbigant and soup greens, and Mrs. von Schrader, after he had taken his seat, pushed a cup toward him and instructed him in her full, rather nasal voice: "Help yourself to sugar."

The Baron did so, sipped the tea, and remarked: "Dear old Elsie! She will never get it. We won't live to see the day she makes the water hot enough."

If this were meant to be a mere genre picture, I would have nothing further to add to this little dialogue. An ear like yours, attuned to the finest tonal *valeurs*, would find that any elucidation would coarsen the scene. You can visualize it yourself: over here Mrs. von Schrader, born Countess Rumpfburg-Schottenfels, youthful in her late thirties, a true lady in the glory of her now-passed better days, musical, aesthetically inclined, mistress of a prestigious establishment, and chairwoman of numerous social groups and clubs, who now, in the early afternoon, was wearing a robe of heavy peacock-blue silk, richly embroidered with butterflies, pavilions, and blossoms, the Seven Gates of Peking and considerable parts of the Great Wall; resplendently feminine thanks to a mighty bosom, which from a rather weathered chest became sadly alabaster-pale toward the depths of her décolletage; beside her, on the narrow side of the mahogany tea table, with a view out the window (she liked to show her profile in silhouette, for it had been called Renaissance-like by members of her bridge circle; this was also why she wore her thick hair bound in a gold mesh net that lifted it from her neck)—beside her, as I said, with his back to the curtain separating the boudoir from the bedroom—behind which, if you insist, Mr. von Schrader was busy with his cigarette coupons—beside her, damn it all for the last time, sat young Mr. von Jassilkowski, impeccably elegant, albeit dressed simply in a soft sport jacket, which he often wore when working at home, his dark hair cut soberly short and straight across, his nice eyes grave and dreamy. You can visualize it—right?—you can also hear the intimacy of their conversation, and you can recognize the harmony of a certain age-old sort of domestic arrangement, which still happily respects the rules of decorum (as is only possible among social equals); you can appreciate that special candor which results from small favors granted to a preferred tenant who has long since come to expect them (those afternoon teas, for instance, which hardly ever appeared on his bills, and if so, only because Mr. von Schrader checked and added them on when he audited the books, a privilege Mrs. von Schrader allowed him from time to time for psychotherapeutic reasons)—you can sense, as I said, the atmosphere of protective apprenticeship requited by trust; but you can also probably sniff out the odors of musically inclined and soup-greens-saturated femininity, the delicate balance between daily physical proximity and occasional delays in rent payments— in short, all the tension of an amply polished intimacy beginning to ooze, so to speak, at the points of abrasion. And therefore it is with an uneasy heart that you will hear the Baron add: "But there are reasons why in all probability we shall no longer share this pleasant occasion in the future. I intend to . . ." And interrupting himself pensively, with a glance at Mrs. von Schrader: "How long is it now that we've been living under the same roof? A good six years. Wasn't it 1932 that I moved in?"

"Quite right," said Mrs. von Schrader with her nasal Austrian drawl, to which she could lay some claim through an aunt whose second marriage had been to a Count Schönbrunn, "1932. I remember it very well."

Baron Traugott fell silent. He likewise recalled only too well that far-off Cuban-mustache period when he met his cousin Zapieha. He smiled meditatively, as people do at thoughts of youth and its follies. A feeling of gratitude toward Mrs. von Schrader blossomed in him. Not without a hint of tenderness, his glance came to rest on her Renaissance profile and the mighty maternal swelling beneath her peacock-colored house robe.

The good simple things of life—how one takes them for granted! The beloved daily bread of habit—how much we miss it after it has been lost: smells of hay and the humming of bees from our childhood, quiet evenings at home under the cozy glow of a lamp, a pair of kind hands, and the bittersweet arpeggios of Sinding's "Rustles of Spring" . . . Baron Traugott looked at Mrs. von Schrader, and the tenderness he felt for her at that moment contained an impulsive, somewhat guilt-ridden warmth of the sort which may, on occasion, move us to slap an old cart horse on the rump and exclaim: "Good old thing!" But a slight aversion was also intermingled with it, and this made him shrink from the thought of physical contact with her, as well as feel ashamed of suspecting that she longed for it on her part. Good-humored and jocular, he asked her: "If you had a daughter, and I were to ask for her hand in marriage—what would you say?"

It was now Mrs. von Schrader's turn to fall silent. Her silence then gave way to action. With motions that did not lack a certain majesty, for her arms had to circumvent the full scope of her Brunhilde bosom, she stirred the tea in the pot, so as to make it draw stronger. Her Renaissance profile was set off nobly against the light from the window. "Well, go on," she finally said in a nasal whisper, "go on with what you were saying. Your compliments have been quite singular of late."

The Baron was startled. Spiritually, he bit his tongue, so to speak, and waited.

"Go on with what you were saying," Mrs. von Schrader encouraged him with a dry smile. "Yesterday you told me that my hat was too young for me, today you've given me a daughter old enough to marry. I wonder what tomorrow will bring."

Baron Traugott looked at her and considered his situation. There she sat before him with her ponderous breasts and Renaissance profile, his maternal friend, the sensitive mentor of his developmental years, and he had now come to her to learn who he really was—at a moment when delusion and perception had become dissociated and had opened up a terrifying abyss within him, at the bottom of which it had been given to him to see the countenance of death. He had come to her as though entering a confessional, with the humility of someone who knows he has only to acknowledge his guilt with a whisper and it will be safeguarded in silence, and who now trustingly expects the *"absolvo te!"*—absolution from his own self, a liberating acquittal from the terror of recognition and the promise that his delusion was real; he had come to her like a child asking his mother to tell him the secret of his birth, full of trust in the good, which, regardless of all the things he had heard whispered on school benches and in the bushes, would permit him to prolong his belief in the friendly stork and the cabbage patch where little ones dwell under the protection of kindly angels. And here she answered him. She answered sitting in front of him with all the majesty of a fortune-teller, the wide sleeve of her peacock-blue bathrobe pulled back to her elbow, her muscular white arm stretched out, pathetically graceful, her callused hand busy with the family silver. Just as sure as she sat before him, she had made him into what he had now become: the transformation from Cuban mustache to the fresh cheeks of a candidate officer, the promotion from Mouson's hair oil to Atkinson's aftershave, from the *Illustrated Weekly* to the *Calendar of Nobility*, from timid cowering under the eyes of the maître d' to easy bantering with titled greats. That was her work—and she knew it. She knew it and knew that he knew she knew it, and thus she sat before him, silent and magnificent in the fullness of her power.

He was in her debt. He had taken and eaten what she had proffered, just as one eats bread as nourishment, without too much thought or concern—but it had been borrowed bread, bread from a usurer's hands for which he now would have to pay with body and soul, all the more severely for the innocence with which he had taken it from her. For she would exact revenge on that innocence, which she knew had not been genuine: just as she had power over him because she knew his great lie, he had power over her because he knew hers. For indeed he had always known what was behind her motherly friendship, and he had accepted what he had from her like a blackmailer who had no intention of handing over the goods.

He looked at her and felt a lump of revulsion in his throat. This is really her, he thought, the eternal enemy. An abysmal corporeality, ever in heat, a black womb, not merely the essence of selflessly granted haven but first and foremost a cesspool of moaning violence, blood, and defilement, poised to devour you at every instant. And that is what you are, born of such a womb and forever drawn to it, a creature marked by original sin, a deformity. And you will wallow your life away in such filth, and everything, everything, begins here, your delusion and even your dreams. There is no escaping it, no escaping it—*save in death.*

She waited for his answer. And he leaned back in his chair, lit a cigarette with great deliberation, and took a deep drag. "We are friends, aren't we?" he asked, slowly and tenderly. (Evil had risen up in him and he relished it.) "But friendship should be a matter of free will on both sides . . ." Another drag on his cigarette, and then quietly and with some hesitation: "As things stand now between us, we should try at least to maintain appearances." He didn't lower his voice on those last words, and they were left dangling, like a partial question. He avoided looking at her as he said this, instead gazing straight ahead at some indefinite distant point beyond the faded acanthus tapestry.

Mrs. von Schrader gave him a look of brittle artificial superiority. "You are under no obligation whatsoever, my dear." She spoke nasally.

He leaned forward, coming so close that he almost touched her. "You don't understand," he said with a grave smile. "Or rather, you don't want to understand. What I meant to say was that circumstances require us to maintain certain appearances, specifically the appearance of being *just* friends." He paused briefly to let the word "just" sink in, a word to which he had given a precise emphasis, not one iota too much or too little. Catching his breath as if suppressing a sigh (the kind of breath you take before reaching a feigned moral conclusion), he continued: "I greatly regret that appearances demand forms of decorum that at times may seem strenuous. But, after all, this is the typical tone of a friendship, the evidence of it, so to speak. Just as love is often revealed by the fact that lovers quarrel . . ."

Mrs. von Schrader continued to stir the tea in her stately way.

"Or should we admit to ourselves"—here he looked directly at her—"that things are mixed up in our friendship which don't sit well with the idea of free will."

"If you are referring to your late payments," Mrs. von Schrader replied sardonically (her cheeks, however, had reddened), "you shouldn't let them trouble you."

"Daisy"—he smiled with the good-humored derision of someone on all too familiar terms—"I know full well without your kind reminder that it behooves me to remember these regrettable facts—they are proof of the great indulgence you have always shown me, all the more so because they sometimes exposed you to exchanges with your esteemed husband that can hardly have been pleasant." He sharpened the jocular taunt conveyed by his smile, and then altered it again to one of warm seriousness. "I am well aware of all this, and I am deeply grateful to you. But you know that wasn't what I meant."

"What do you mean, then?" asked Mrs. von Schrader, struggling to keep her composure. (However, a cross of large amethyst beads hanging on her generous décolletage now started to pulsate on that steep embankment under the influence of an involuntarily accelerated heartbeat.)

What would her boobs look like if they burst those restraints? the Baron wondered to himself. Maybe they're a true wonder? Her teeth are all right. Why don't I simply throw her down on the couch over there and end this boring charade? Does it really make sense what I'm doing here?

Tenderly he said, "Why does everything always have to be put into words? Don't you know what happens when things are called by their true names? Should we really risk confronting each other with labels—love, passion? . . ."

The amethyst cross in Mrs. von Schrader's décolletage was hopping around like a mountain goat.

"What happens between two human beings," the Baron philosophized as he blew cigarette smoke toward the ceiling, "can, so long as it remains unspoken, remain full of potential. But labels are like rigid masks, behind which lurk either lies or the Medusa head of truth. Shouldn't we keep things between us as they are now, with all the magic of unexplored possibilities, the play of fantasy's reflections? . . ."

Mrs. von Schrader was sitting ramrod straight. The amethyst cross in her bosom had, with a last desperate leap, gotten stuck, half hidden in the cleft, a lopsided mark of aesthetical nobility of soul. "You're wrong, my dear," she said finally in a hoarse voice. "I see no magic in fantasy's reflections, and I know nothing of unexplored possibilities—quite apart from the fact that, try as I may, I can't understand what you mean by all this. You come to have tea with me, and you start the conversation with a pointed remark that's supposed to be part of some strenuous form of decorum or whatever, and this is how you show your friendship and gratitude! And why should our friendship oblige us to beat around the bush about anything? For my part, I don't fear the Medusa head of truth, as you so poetically put it—nor do I feel the need to lie. But if I've given you the impression that you are not entirely free to do as you like, I'm very sorry. In no way can you accuse me of ever having tried to influence your feelings."

So the point has now been reached, thought the Baron to himself (evil glowing triumphantly within him), where she has her hormones in her head and her logic in her ovaries. Now she's getting dangerous—but she's also at her most vulnerable. Now let her choke on her own venom.

"We are talking past each other," he said, and with brutal relish he stubbed out his cigarette. "And it's probably better that way. Let's end this conversation. Allow me to take my leave. I must finish writing my article." He was about to get up.

"Wait!" said Mrs. von Schrader hastily. "I want you to explain what you mean."

Once again he looked right at her. The amethyst cross still peeked up at an angle from her décolletage, but the flesh surrounding it had begun to seethe and swell against the Great Wall so that the silk rustled.

"Oh, my dear, forget it," he said mildly. "All of this is poor compensation."

"Compensation—for what?" she asked breathlessly.

Baron Traugott waved the question off. "It's late," he said. "Thanks so much for the delicious tea." Then he arose.

"No," cried Mrs. von Schrader desperately, and she reached out to restrain him. He withdrew his arm as she got hold of his jacket pocket. There was an abrupt tearing sound. "Dear heavens!" she exclaimed, and jumped up. "That beautiful jacket! I never wanted that to happen!"

He looked down at her pitilessly.

"Thank God, it's only the seam," she said as she leaned toward his pocket, blushing all over with shame, a Lady Potiphar caught in the act. "Come on, I'll mend it right away. The needle and thread are right here."

He didn't move and went on looking at her right in the eye. Slowly he said, "Daisy, what a big baby you are!"

With that she could no longer contain herself. Impetuously she clasped him to her heaving bosom.

He was submerged in the plush, Houbigant-drenched flesh. The amethyst cross dug painfully into his cheek, but he, gasping for fresh air, dared not raise his head and expose his lips. So he pressed his nose deep into the cleavage between those fleshy mounds. Meanwhile her lips were straying over his neck, tickling him moistly behind the ear and ruffling his hair. Finally he was able to grasp her and push her away. She stood, distraught, before him. Her rather weather-beaten chest had turned deep purple, and her lips twitched pathetically.

"Daisy," he told her brutally, "I intend to get married—next week, as a matter of fact. No one you know—that is, of course you know who it is." He mentioned the name of the thoroughbred.

"Oh—I see," was all she said. Above the inflamed rash on her cheeks, a basilisk's glare pinned him.

"Do you have anything to say?" he asked, more sharply than he had intended—and immediately regretted both the question itself and his tone of voice.

"Not at all," she answered nasally.

He felt her stare depriving him of assurance just as the legendary magnetic mountain is said to draw nails from the planks of passing ships.

He said, "It would grieve me deeply to lose your friendship. You don't know how valuable it is to me."

And not waiting for an answer, he took her hands in his, in order to keep her safely at a distance, bent down, closed his eyes tightly, and, with wooden lips, kissed her smack on the mouth, which remained cold and lifeless. Then he turned and went—no, fled—back to his room.

There, after locking the door, he stood motionless for a while, leaning against the wall. Then he stepped in front of the washbasin, pulled the light cord, and gazed into the mirror.

"So that is who I am," he said to himself.

I should have done her, he thought. That wasn't smart.

Oh, purity! . . .

And later that same evening when he happened to run into Mr. von Schrader in the lobby of the pension, he realized from the latter's surprisingly frosty behavior that she had become his enemy.

His maternal guardian, the thoughtful mentor of his developmental years, had withdrawn her hand from his—what did it matter? What did it concern him really? But alas, we know that this occurred in the summer of 1938, in a convergence of luminosity, color, and light in which time, space, and sequence melted into a state in which the days floated by like loose balloons in the oh so blue sky. And it took place in Berlin, floating in a state of expectancy like a magic carpet—windswept by the breath of promise, trembling with the pathos of unknown possibilities: where, then, was the border between delusion and reality? The present came without continuing on into the future and without following from the past—in a word, it was all of a sudden simply there, as it always had been in its innermost essence—as everything is prescribed in our conscience. And since it was so securely embedded, enveloped, and covered by great delusion, it was wholly lacking in effect or consequence, meant nothing at all, and when on the following day Baron Traugott found his perspicacity confirmed by a ruthlessly calculated rent bill, which the maid presented to him with an affronted look on behalf of Mrs. von Schrader, he prepared to leave the Pension Bunsen without regret or contrition—as indeed our generation usually leaves behind its past and its houses and homes: with anticipatory unrest, which today is like a residence permit for their endless makeshifts. He packed his belongings in a few suitcases and settled the spiritual balance with a generous tip for the maid.

It was the year of our Lord 1938, and the Lord was close at hand,

and great things were under way—already Mr. von Schrader was able to report in the strictest confidence from his collectors' club that the album entitled *Back Home to the Empire* was no longer considered the *ne plus ultra* of bold dreams. There may have been a slight bottleneck in the supply of eggs and butter, as we already know, but the weather remained as clear and bright as glass, and constant despite the calendar—true Hitler weather, you could say. Who, I ask you, was capable of feeling anything like regret, let alone contrition? For whatever was happening then strangely seemed as if it never actually happened; it occurred, no doubt about that, but it was so fragile compared to what was waiting in the wings; it all seemed so weightless, trivial, and spectral when measured against the all-eclipsing *anticipation.*

The Lord was at hand, and anticipation cast a huge shadow over every moment, and it was also present when Baron Traugott made the thoroughbred his wife.

For a day and a night and a morrow
that his strength might endure for a span
with travail and heavy sorrow
the holy spirit of man.
ALGERNON CHARLES SWINBURNE

AIDS OF HONOR AND MYRTLE WREATHS WERE not in evidence: the wedding was kept small. (Anyway, several days before the event itself, the witty doctor had already exhausted his supply of puns about myrtle-shaped protuberances.) Everything very English and sporty: a short civil ceremony at the registry office, followed by lunch at Horcher's only for close friends and family members. The bon vivant was not included. Nor was worthy Mamá Bremse. Strangely enough, the telegram that Mr. von Jassilkowski clearly recalled having sent in plenty of time reached her too late, so that only a generously tearstained letter arrived, weeks later, in her place, with a thousand heartfelt wishes for their happiness and bliss and words of comfort for the chaste bride: "woman to woman, married life is like a rose bush that has not only blossoms but also thorns . . ."

Worthy Bremse! Later a crate arrived, in which the good homemaker had packed the dowry of our knight-in-arms—bed linen and her best kitchen utensils, Papá's Iron Cross First Class, as well as something to make their new home more cozy: the night-table lamp whose pink silk shade was decorated with a silhouette ring of chubby-cheeked children in Biedermeier costume, the boys in droll outfits with starched collars and curved top hats and the girls in sweet little crinolines and poke bonnets.

Tender, loving Mamá Bremse! And while Baron Traugott sat in front of his baked Alaska at Horcher's, in the glassy stupor typical of a bridegroom and very drunk, memories arose (unwittingly and with no connection to anything, coming out of nowhere and disappearing into nowhere like bubbles rising randomly here and there in a champagne glass), images—so far, far away suddenly!—of Mamá's touching modest wire-rimmed spectacles beside her darning egg and a few old issues of the *Illustrated Weekly* in her little room in Allenstein. And mark it well: it was the only thing that seemed to challenge him, that felt like an accusation. And even though the bow of those glasses had been wrapped in a bit of chamois so that it wouldn't cut the bridge of her nose, it nonetheless greatly pained the Baron's soul—the yoke of a dimly understood, melancholic, fateful burden on his conscience.

Very well! Here he sat next to the bride—oh, cherished moment! oh, the twists and turns of life—here he sat, and with him Mama, Papa, and the whole circle of friends and family, and the meal was excellent and the wines superlative. Around four o'clock, the little wedding party, with one more exchange of best wishes, went outside into the brazen daylight and dispersed. Mama-in-law in full regalia, with her mink stole and clinking jewels, like Judith standing before Holofernes, propped up Papa, who, being quite drunk, was blissfully out of it. When he grasped his young son-in-law's hand to say good-bye, he cackled: "Tell me, what's your name again?"

"Traugott!" roared the Baron, deeply touched, into his ear.

"No—I meant your family name," said Papa, rather startled, and he rubbed his still-throbbing ear (he had taken to wearing one of those excellent invisible gadgets that go directly in the auditory canal). Mama pulled the floundering fellow into their car.

And in the evening, the newlyweds went to Charley's, where they were celebrated in grand style with a sea of flowers and champagne. Charley Schulz presented them with a magnum of Rémy-Martin, which was drained right then and there, and it was quite late when the overheated couple finally took leave of their friends, who sent them on their way with many a humorous innuendo.

I've always regretted, my good man, what to me seems a lacuna in world literature—namely, the lack of a first-rate description of the wedding night of a couple who have had long, animated sexual relations. The human soul, you see, is much older than the age of emancipation. An inherent and profound reverence for the *mysterium* and its rites is still deeply rooted, and to to elevate what has long since become a routine daily procedure into a *hieros gamos* is a challenge worthy of a true poet.

Since their own small apartment had not yet been furnished, they alighted for the night at the Eden Hotel. The blond thoroughbred, who knew the reception manager better than Baron Traugott did, had reserved a suite with a sitting room, bedroom, and bath. Without telling him, she had also ordered a little collation: two dozen oysters arranged around a jewel of a lobster, toast, and a bottle of chilled vodka. A taxi had brought them, and the short stretch between Charley's and the Eden had been a voyage of love, silent and hand in hand; the car with its rattling windows, enameled sheet metal, and worn upholstery, in which they had crossed from the late-night lightbulb glitter of the Kurfürstendamm into the shadows of the Gedächtniskirche (even the Traube's luminous blaze was extinguished at that hour) and then on to the Bengal-blue pendant shimmer of Budapesterstrasse, the driver's bullish neck comfortingly solid in front, had become a two-person protective shell, a respite after the hectic cheerful noise, a calm after so much hyperactive rush. They were tired and drained, but still tense from the exertion. The winning charm they had taken pains to exhibit for so many hours as *"the young couple at the center of it all,"* the masks they had donned to cover an awkward, overheated vacancy of mind, were still frozen on their faces, but now they could allow them to melt. During this long falsely busy day, they had striven for an air of debonair and detached sobriety, an enlightened irony about their relationship: now they discovered with vague astonishment that the warmth which this shared nonchalance was supposed to camouflage (and thereby also demonstrate) had indeed become real, as if their pretensions had had magic power. They had playacted so much for themselves and others that now they no longer needed to pretend, and they confused their gratitude with something which an ancient, inborn longing within them wanted to call *love*. But since at the same time they both knew perfectly well it wasn't that, they grew sad and, each of them sensing that sadness in the other, became mutually forbearing. They were a twosome, shoulder to shoulder, hand in hand—and thus they would behave toward each other from now on in their shared loneliness—oh, my friend! . . . But what do you expect? They had come from Horcher's and Charley's Bar, they both were doubtlessly upper-class and wore spanking new clothes

—in this regard they could trust each other totally—and so I ask you: what more could you expect? They were a twosome, an elegant young couple, and as such, they would cut a dashing figure at all the cocktail parties given by the Moldovlachian embassy, they would travel and go shopping, attend fashionable sports events and have friends who were as international as was possible at that time— what in heaven could you want? To be sure, in their innermost hearts, an age-old dream still lived on—searching and melancholic in his and maternally tender in hers, as it should be—a dream— what more can I say?: a dream of another, purer existence, a king's mantle of human dignity; it was love that gave this dream its regal purple, and purity was its ermine trim. But that old dream had been dreamed and longed for so often, and the steadfast ancient effort from childhood to see in every reality nothing but signs of sublime promise, symbols of vouchsafed fulfillment, had been hung on every- thing and everyone; and the bulkier and more unwieldy reality was, the more threadbare and faded the dream became, worn-out at the seams, as it were—and yet that was just what made it so comfortable. You wore it when you were alone with yourself, just as you convert last year's carnival domino into this year's housecoat; it became old and shabby, the purple shiny and the fur mangy—but the ermine tips served all the better to give everyday things a certain polish and sparkle. Oh, ancient king's mantle, you who have become the pol- ishing rag of banal reality! Fool's robe for the poet and the in- nocent—a coronation gown of purity and love!

Warm and soft and tenderly alive, the thoroughbred's hand nestled in his, and Baron Traugott held it tight until the taxi had reached the Eden. Budapesterstrasse was empty, elevated out of the darkness by the ghostly blue streetlights; suddenly from the zoo a few screeches were heard, wild and hollow and passionate, from apes or some kind of strange giant birds; a grievous angry snarling came as a reply, and for a few moments the night breeze carried over the biting stench of the cages. Baron Traugott had helped his wife from the taxi and was preparing to pay the driver, when he noticed that he didn't have any change on him, and since by then she was already standing under the scalloped canvas canopy of the Eden's entrance, he had to call her back and ask whether she had any, and she rummaged in her handbag and together they paid off the driver, who drove away with no special expression of gratitude, and now here they stood, the newlywed couple, alone in front of the locked and darkened Eden Hotel, on a night when suddenly the smells of carnivorous animals and screams from primeval forests mingled with the restless silence of Berlin, and they waited until a sleepy night porter, fussing with his clanking key ring, opened the entrance to their bridal chamber.

They entered the lobby. It was empty and only sparsely lit, the corners dark, the swanky luxury of restaurant establishments transformed into a charwomen's domain. The night porter (who because of chronic gastritis erupted in sour belches that he either suppressed against his gums and swallowed or let escape like a whistle through his gray lips) handed over their key and then took them up in the elevator, which ascended softly and soundlessly like a bit of consciousness under an anesthetic mask, opened the sliding door at the third floor and released them into the dimly lit corridor, wishing his honored guests a truly pleasant night. And while Baron Traugott (having decided from the minute he entered the hotel to rebuff energetically any such hint of wedding-night innuendo) remained distrustfully silent, the thoroughbred thanked him warmly in a tone that showed both practice and routine. They reviewed a parade of shameful second-class footwear left outside the doors, a cynical display of the officious atmosphere of discreet servility, and then arrived at their suite. Baron Traugott busied himself with the key, whose green rubber ball felt hard and unpleasantly sanitary in his hand. Surreptitiously he took advantage of the moment to yawn behind his elegantly closed, gloved left hand, almost deeply enough to unhinge his jaw and bring tears to his eyes.

They entered. The suite smelled of upholstery and respectable disinfectants and detergents. The furnishings, in the style of a department-store window, with the accent on solid gentility, had about as much character as the thread of a bolt. But as you well know, a woman's hand can, by arranging a few odds and ends (some photographs, toiletries, a colored scarf), give a place a personal note. Unfortunately—through either oversight or sheer carelessness—the young couple's luggage had not been sent up, even though it had been delivered that morning. And the buffet in the sitting room had obviously been prepared many hours earlier: the lobster, basking cinnamon-red on the silver platter, claws fantastically brandished, lay among wilted salad leaves and pads of mayonnaise with brownish crusts growing around the edges; the ice surrounding the dish had melted, half drowning the oysters, and slices of lemon swam anemically above a foundation of butter scrolls, sunken like the legendary city of Vineta. And crowning this example of negligence, the vodka was missing!

You, my esteemed friend, are acquainted with the blond thoroughbred's good qualities and charm—but you really have no idea of her overpowering temper. This was the direct and unmediated product of her freshly waxed and dividend-papered teenager's room, where she had been the terror of many a lavender-starched nanny and the helpless distress of her senile parents—the only change being that the blond tomboy with bows in her hair had sprouted into the splendor of an Ingres concubine; if you met the legendary playboys from Charley's Bar in the flesh, you might have been shown many honorable scars they bore from broken bottles or red-enameled claws that attested to her tantrums.

Baron Traugott, you see, also knew nothing of this side of her personality, but it now revealed itself to him with such natural force, so far beyond anything conceivable, that he didn't even have the chance to be taken aback. What really makes us lose our composure are experiences that somehow exceed the confines of our imagination—isn't that so?—it's said that in Hiroshima, after the unthinkable had occurred, not a single child's cry could be heard. Thus Baron von Jassilkowski was given neither the time to reflect nor the chance to collect himself and realize what had happened. As the thoroughbred blew through the rooms like a hurricane, tearing open all the closet doors and slamming them shut again with a crash, angrily pressing every call button and hammering on the telephone receiver, he stumbled along behind her making halfhearted motions of appeasement, culminating in a lame beseeching gesture, and it was only minutes later, after he found himself back on the staircase again, having been screamed at and expelled with the command to summon the night porter, that it began to dawn on him what had really occurred. But after all it was five o'clock in the morning, you understand, and he had his wedding behind him, if you know what that's like—and what's more, he had in him the cocktails and sherry, the Chablis and Bordeaux, Heidsieck, Cognac, and Grand Marnier from lunch, half a dozen randomly consumed liqueurs and two or three Pernods during the afternoon, many sorts of wine, port and Médoc, during dinner, and finally a few whiskeys, topped off by the lion's share of the magnum of Rémy-Martin from Charley; his feet hurt like hell in his brand-new shoes and the only thing he wanted to do or even hear about in this heartrending surfeit was *sleep*, nothing but SLEEP—to drift off heavy and darkly sweet into the lap of great oblivion, to be whisked away, to be released and to withdraw from the hustle and bustle—clanking jewelry, mink stole, wire-rimmed glasses, and hearing aid, Charley's Bar and boozing and females, the more the merrier. And thus did he stumble into the lobby, which had been inundated suddenly with a glare like daylight (the charwomen—a piece of unexpectedly hard, broom-rigid reality!—had invaded the shadowy realms and flooded them with naked light and slop-bucket water, so that the entire luxurious caravanserai was displayed, stripped of its cabin-trunk grandeur, like dentures in a glass of water); and he walked through the lobby with painfully cramped toes (also both wings of the front door had been opened wide out into the gray dawn mist, so that the hollow screeching of birds that arose from those alien nocturnal life forms over there, eerily scurrying about in their ammonia-drenched cages, wafted under the stiff canvas of the canopy like admonitions from another, powerful reality, lurking furtively, certain of its eventual triumph); and he reached the registration desk and unloaded and relieved himself—vomited out, as it were, everything responsible for his exhaustion, his painful toes and alcoholic excesses, his desire to sleep and excruciating sensitivity to noise, his suppressed childish whining and longing for a "there, there, it's all better," he vomited it all out in a flood all over the bilious night porter. Where was their luggage? Where the vodka?

Thereupon the unheard-of happened: the night porter rebelled—what am I saying?—he, too, unloaded, relieved himself, vomiting everything back, as it were. Just as a swell breaking against a pier and then receding will smash everything that opposes it with a hidden, secret, and thus all the more devastating force, the violence of unleashed displeasure ricocheted against the Baron and struck him will-less and speechless for a moment. This was indeed unheard of. What was happening? Unheard of, the attack on him. The haggard face in front of him—that neutral, formless gray blotch—suddenly took on features, all too closely proximate, importunately human, obtrusively alive features, the embarrassing glyphs of a tortured, insulted, and humiliated human creature. From the braided and fringed porter's uniform, the cut of which was meant to emphasize the solemnity of the servant's clumsy bows, there suddenly wheezed warm, sour, fermented human breath, far more eloquent than all the left-wing editorials and sociocritical essays in the world: "You think you can treat me like a clown, sir?!" Thus the foul breath of this man assailed the Baron. "Why, you're young enough to be my son, sir! And you come here at five o'clock in the morning with your little lady, and reeking like a still, while my son may have to stop a few Czech bullets in the next few hours! You think he risks his bones, sir, just so that you can raise a racket in the middle of the night?! The lady may be glad she hasn't unpacked her bags yet, when the planes may be overhead this very morning. The lady won't be too eager to help in the hospitals, sir. A lady like that, she's got connections, the lady's made sure of that. And you talk to me like I was a clown, sir! I was on the front for four years the last time around, sir, and you think you can talk to me like a clown! Just so that you can drink more vodka at five o'clock in the morning! You want to complain, sir? Go right ahead! I could be your father. But to let others get shot while you stand there reeking like a still, well, the Führer will take care of you, sir! He'll get you your vodka all right!"

What was this? Unheard of, confusing, and confused. What was he talking about? Painful nonsense. Monstrous, unjust accusation. Revolting revolt! The charwomen closest to the devastation put down their buckets with a clang in order to join the party. Through the cold mist at the entrance the hollow screeches of the apes drifted in. But then, as if materialized out of thin air, a young man stood between them. He had a smoothly parted perfection about him.

"What's going on, Schmidt?" he asked in the tone of the unconditional master of the situation. And turning to Baron Traugott: "How can I be of service, sir?"

He was smoothly parted, impeccably groomed, spotless, urbanely pale, obviously a trainee, destined for a future executive assignment in the hotel industry. For a fragile moment the two took the measure of each other.

A most significant moment! But I can see you don't grasp its deep symbolic import. So, at the risk of again taxing your generous indulgence with one of my digressions, let me insert one last theoretical observation, namely about the essence of *authority*. You're acquainted with various forms of inspiring awe, from the Olympian robes of a Goethe to the paralyzing, roaring, thunderbolt-wielding omnipotence of your average drill sergeant, but what we have here is more than a step from the trivial to the sublime. Wherever an aura surrounds a personality and endows its remarks with special importance because of an office held (providing a claim to legitimacy, which the aura personifies in the name and on behalf of power itself), it is subject to a strange set of laws that we commonly divide into: (a) *the rule of proportional increase of dignity in relation to the decrease in spiritual content*; and (b) *the law of reciprocity between shit and nimbus*: from its center, which will always be abstract in nature, all the way to its most remote periphery, the exercise of power becomes increasingly concrete, so that its claim to legitimacy grows in proportion to its effect.

The dapper trainee in hotel management, future administrator of both material and physical power (who, I ask you, has not at times submitted to the double sovereignty of the maître d', that fodder steward and bailiff of manners?), this dapper trainee, called to the scene by an unwelcome disturbance, stood there in an expertly controlled state of readiness. The expectant sweep of his lacquer-black eyebrows, which looked as though they were drawn in Chinese ink above his world-weary eyes, as well as his polite manner of command, betrayed the doubly powerful privilege of his position. The atmosphere of a gambling casino cloaked him, anchored by the weight of sound-absorbing velvet carpets, yet he was assiduously prepared to move on cue and steeled by the unswerving spirit of a waiter's discipline, ready to stop any disturbance that threatened the smooth and discreet course of established routine. Only he had not yet fully grown into this professional mask. He was young, so a provocative personal engagement still peeked through in places, where the seams had not yet quite closed, as it were. He was young, the picture of the *adolescent*—oh, bear with me, my dear friend, to contemplate his splendid appearance for a moment longer (ever since Winckelmann, the German mind has seen the young man as the ideal human being, the clear expression of a joyous and faithful beginning, of desire in its purest form, isn't that true?)—I want to say the picture of humanity on the threshold of life: he was a street-smart cellar rat with a passionate aristocratic bent, the hard-boiled *nil admirari* of a basement flat still in his features (though these boyhood hardships had been somewhat assuaged and softened by the ingestion of gourmet leftovers), the recently discovered weapon of social degradation held loosely in his hand like a hoodlum's knife. He stood turned half toward the Baron, half toward the bilious night porter, as if equally prepared to enforce the wishes of the former on the latter and to make uncompromising common cause with the latter against the former. Like a fencer during the opening salute, he kept the heels of his spit-polished shoes closed (shoes that had obviously not been designed for very demanding service); his left foot, turned outward, supported the weight of his dainty wiry body (as yet showing only hints of an aspiring gastronome's plumpness to come), while his right one pointed at the Baron. His arms hung loosely from his shoulders, slightly angled at the elbow, as if he were about to march away in double time, if so required, and unwittingly (a secret expression of the sublime) the tips of his thumbs and middle fingers were closed in a circle like those of a glowingly elegant wax figure.

Thus he faced off against Baron Traugott, as Goethe would say, and what he faced in him was a cherry blossom in hoarfrost: the glory and tragedy of the Occident; it was—kindly rise from your barstool—the ethos of Christian nobility.

Lord! Would that we all grew in the cellar, deep behind the mushrooms! Would that we had been given the Brothers Sass as role models for humanity instead of the Bamberg Rider and Frau Uta of the Naumberg cathedral! Zille as our educator! How I envy those kids from low-rent barracks who have been forged in the furnace of black-market deals in the slums, hardened by the discipline of loan-sharking! What high hopes I nurture for people from city shelters, destined for a better future, who spice their street games with the risk of faulty brake shoes, who treat gonococci and cobalt bombs as they do traffic accidents—soberly and with no immanent idea of guilt—who experience objectivity on fairgrounds and transcendence in movie theaters! But alas, we are missing our chance this time around, too! Oh, miracle of postwar reconstruction, oh, Deutschewirtschaftswunder, apotheosis of the middle class! . . .

Baron Traugott and the dapper trainee were facing off, as I said, with the bilious night porter between them. They took the measure of each other: the revealing power of the human glance—a reflex motion of the ciliary muscles, a subtle curvature of the ocular lens, a minute narrowing of a pair of pupils—and the imperceptible is communicated, grasped, and interpreted! Instantaneous evaluation, abrupt decision. It's a moment of ultimate intensity in human communication: two essences, two modes of being collide at the point of reckoning—a moment of totality, utmost accountability (oh, the complex balance of collar height and jacket cut, the subtle harmony of shoulder rounding and lapel shape, the telltale number of buttons, the revealing waistline!). B.T. and the d.t., facing off, recognized each other as chips off the same block: nobility! A conception of life, precious as stones of jasper and sardonyx, as rare and fabulous as a unicorn in the forest, appearing in the wink of an eye, a vision of beauty above all else, an aesthetic level to which the ethical is a correlative: what else, if not the four-star hotel industry, can produce this? Enlighten me, if you will: what religious orders have devoted themselves with a stricter conception of duty and more severe self-discipline to the ideals of noble probity, refinement, reputation, and hieratic classification? Who else today would commit themselves with greater selflessness to the service of their neighbors, in hopes of establishing more refined and gentlemanly manners, a higher readiness for self-sacrifice and engagement? Measure that, my good man, against the hotel-management trade: can't you see the ravishing court pages, bold and high-spirited adolescent profiles, nobly spiritual characters, tastefully gray-haired from their years of service? What else is still capable of all that? I ask you. The Association for the Welfare of Exiled Estate Owners?

On the other side, Traugott von Jassilkowski, as we know only too well, one of the most thin-skinned and painfully impassioned representatives of nobility's ethic, a martyr, even, for whom any other path than fair humility was blocked by thornbushes, and who had understandably rejected those very qualities that make successful people successful: a façade like a snowplow, an impudence of mind that knows only the anatomical meaning of the term "private," chariot-race tactics that involve robust, pointed elbows. No! His way—the real *Baron* von Jassilkowski's way—was the decency of the true sovereign noble (though right now this was deformed by his desire to sleep and his perplexed indignation); his was the tact of someone so aware of his own position in the hierarchy of human dignity that he could not but respect others (although he sensed from the night porter's enigmatic accusations that, as a result of a certain laxity—perhaps pardonable, given the overtaxed state of his soul— he might have unwittingly committed offense in this regard); his, finally, was also noble humility, the true aristocrat's sublime re- nunciation (and you know only too well how far that will get you nowadays, especially when this sort of noble self-control gets mixed up with the attitude of someone who had been shat upon). And, moreover, it was, as we know, five o'clock in the morning, and he had just endured his trusted wife's first unblunted display of tem- perament, and he was carrying around in him all the stopped-up abomination by which our civilization celebrates life's special oc- casions: heartburn, disgusting cocktails by the gallon, sticky Grand Marnier and revolting Pernod, blocked circulation in his patent- leather-tormented toes, his choking shirtfront, and his displeasure at the bilious night porter's dark accusations and threats (what had he been trying to say, the good man?), and before him, finally, was the prospect of a wedding night's worth of tiresome intimacy with an ambitious bride; he would have given his life to put it off until tomorrow . . . And because of all this, when the Baron gathered his remaining energy and spoke, his words issued not directly from the exquisite essence of his own soul, but instead simply recapitulated what the thoroughbred had hurled at him and what, a few minutes before, had sounded so convincing: after all, they had taken one of the most expensive suites in the hotel, with bedroom, sitting room, and bath (he now said loudly), and they had a right to expect more attentive service. And where was the luggage, which had been delivered yesterday morning? And where the hell was the vodka that had been ordered with the lobster and the oysters? A Polack establishment, damn it all.

He repeated these last words without thinking, but as he spoke them, something in his unconscious rebelled, and they sounded especially hollow.

The dapper trainee merely raised his eyebrows. He waited until the Baron had come to an end and then requested, with effortlessly well-chosen words and yet most decisively, that the gentleman please show a little more consideration for the other guests, some of whom also had taken suites with sitting room, bedroom, and bath, and then expressed his regret at the oversight—though still with superciliously raised eyebrows. If the gentleman would kindly be patient for a moment longer, he would arrange whatever was desired. His hand, thumb and index finger closed gracefully like those of a wax figure, executed an elegant loop.

He swooped away in an arc and disappeared, followed by the bilious night porter, obeying his discreet gesture, and Mr. von Jassilkowski was left alone, shivering slightly amidst the expressive clanking of the charwomen's buckets in the gray dawn.

Shortly thereafter, the dapper trainee appeared, two splits of champagne under his arm, the bilious night porter behind him, gasping for breath under the luggage. Most unfortunately, the younger man said in a practiced and perfunctory tone, he had no access to the bar at this hour and was therefore unable to provide the vodka. Instead he was taking the liberty of offering two splits of champagne from his own personal stock as temporary and perhaps more appropriate compensation.

Baron Traugott thanked him curtly.

The bilious night porter, assisted by the trainee, stuffed the suitcases into the elevator. Shaken to the core, Baron Traugott was eager to show that he was not who he seemed to be, and he tried to lend a hand. But the trainee rebuffed him with a superciliously polite gesture of denial, and instead lifted the heaviest suitcase with casual ease—this demonstration of muscular strength crowning his triumph.

One small victory was left to the Baron, though: it turned out that the elevator was too small to hold the trainee, the luggage, the night porter, and himself. So before the dapper and graceful young man was able to restrain him, the Baron paid him back in kind and, with an equally supercilious expression, ascended the staircase.

He intentionally took his time—he didn't want to encounter the pair again—and when he entered his suite, the luggage had been delivered. The thoroughbred had taken the necessities into the bedroom, and he found himself alone in the sitting room. Exhausted, he opened one of his suitcases, removed his pajamas, his robe, and his toilet kit, took off his clothes, and, blinded with fatigue, proceeded toward the bathroom. As he was about to open the door to the bedroom, he was scared back by a flustered "Don't come in!" Vexation seized him; what in God's name could this mean? he asked himself, but was too tired to search for an answer. He suddenly felt hungry and thought of having a go at the lobster, but the platter had disappeared: the thoroughbred had taken it with her. Now he understood: she, too, was tired and had found it tasteless to celebrate the traditional wedding-night ceremony. And he was very grateful to her for her delicacy (still, she could have left him a bit of lobster!). He was grateful to the point of tears, for, by the grace of God, it was now five-thirty, and the day—praise the Lord and all the saints—was over, that long, long day—oh, the twists and turns of life!—and life itself would take care of everything else, damn it! In any case, life would begin tomorrow—no, damn it, today—but in any case not before noon. (Was there a sign at the door of this hole that said: *"Conference—don't disturb"*?) Well, whatever, his new life would not begin before noon. And until then he would sleep: *sleep!* And so he set about arranging the narrow sofa into a scanty bed with a pillow and a traveling plaid—Polack service, the hell with it! . . . Yet: hail to thee, Polack hotel, dear sofa-bed-in-need, all mine, mine alone! Blessed be the divine heartrending Polack service—oh, the joy of his liberated toes against the rough wool of the Scottish plaid, the manly delight of the hard pillow—most blessed among all beds, you meager Polack sofa, all mine, mine alone.

So there he lay finally—finally!—stretched out—oh, the grati-tude!—s-t-r-e-t-c-h-e-d o-u-t—ah—eyes closed, lids shut over his tired, tired eyes (soon he would turn the light off!), his forehead exposed to the night (would he still have the strength to open the window?—breeze, cool, delicious, fresh, nocturnal breeze—oh no, damn it, the morning breeze full of scavengers' stenches from the zoo, and in a half hour it would bring in the whole racket from Budapesterstrasse!)—never mind, there he lay (at least until noon!)—removed, removed at last from all the hustle and bustle—mink stole and registry office, cocktails, luxury caravanserai and wire-rimmed glasses, patent-leather pumps, Charley's Bar and boozing and females, the more the merrier. They swirled, they swirled all around him like snow flurries; now they began to fall—white against a black background (soon—soon—he would turn the light off!), then black on a white background—ermine—no, the reverse!—heraldic ermine—where did that come from?—where on earth did that come from? . . . A man at the window—a solitary man—hysterical—tortured—vomits over a cup of tea—phooey, shit!—puke, *puke*, PUKE—no, *no*, NO—the lamp!—where on earth did that come from?—pull yourself together, control yourself, *control*, CONTROL—*A rebours!*—that was it—finally!—Against the grain—grain—thoroughbred—nobility—redemption: *A rebours*—sinks—sinks—down—to the bottom—the problems of life—soon—he—would—turn—it—off . . .

At that moment the thoroughbred tore open the door and stuck her head out. She had taken off her makeup and put on her night-gown. Her blond mane was pinned up with a pink ribbon (oh, the fatal vitality of her hair!): what was he thinking of? she called out with a whine (oh, hateful vitality of all that cuteness!)—what was he thinking of lying down like that?—he wasn't perhaps thinking of going to sleep?! She had now finished getting ready and he could come in!

Slobbering with sleepiness, the Baron arose. But with a quick "Just a moment!" she once more slammed the door in his face. He waited with mounting impatience—(oh, Polack bed, all mine!)—finally he had had enough: he knocked on the door. She called out: "Come in!" (horrifying marrow-sucking energy!), and he opened the door.

There she lay in the wide double bed, wearing her billowing whore's nightgown, blond hair gathered in the pink velvet ribbon, her lascivious lips naked and ready to be kissed. With the touchingly roguish gesture of a Savoyard peasant girl offering a basket of figs, she held out the artfully garnished platter with the lobster, oysters, toast, and mayonnaise. Her head was a bit aslant, and her myopic violet eyes (without glasses) looked at him expectantly.

It was six o'clock and he was unarmed. He went over and kissed her. She lifted the platter and waited until he had slipped under the covers and then set it down again carefully. She dripped some lemon juice on the largest of the oysters and put it in his mouth. He slurped it down (good God-given vital energy!), and then she took one for herself. "Didn't you bring something to drink?" she asked with an accusing pout. Once more he had to get out of bed and go to the sitting room, where the dapper trainee had left the two splits of champagne, only to find that they had nothing but shot glasses on hand. So he went to the bathroom, sniffed at the toothbrush glasses, and found them suitable as they were. Then he crawled back into bed. They began to gorge themselves, and it was snug and cozy in their two-person gluttony (blessed vitality!). The champagne was dreadful and tepid. One of the corks slipped through his fingers and exploded with a bang from the neck of the bottle, so that some of the yellow liquid foamed down on the pillows. Finally, when nothing remained of the oysters but the shells and nothing of the lobster but the ruins of its armor and already siphoned legs, they pushed the platter aside; the thoroughbred lay back in the cushions, voluptuously stretched her limbs, raised her arms over her head so that her prime bosom was lifted in all its perfection out of its lacy covering. She smiled at him from under half-shut eyelids with her moistly gleaming pearly teeth and extinguished the bed lamps over their heads.

Now it had gotten serious. And the Baron—despite his great exhaustion—mobilized all the internal emotion he could muster.

This is simpler than you might suppose. You merely recall everything you have carried around in life expecting the *one great love* that is bound to come someday, and this sentimental predisposition

147

proves so powerful that even after you subtract all the experiences that lacked perfection, there still remains a sizable quantity of emotional intensity. You have to be careful, though, that in so doing, all the sweetness doesn't simply dissolve into a blissful lullaby, which would all too rapidly induce deep slumber. For a world woven from external appearance is not to be satisfied with mere sensitivity: it demands action as proof.

Very well! But just as the Baron was about to tackle the task at hand, there was a knock at the door. With the tiger-spring of an experienced bachelor, he swept out of bed and donned his robe. Determined to take the most extreme steps, if necessary, he went to the door.

The dapper hotel trainee bowed before him, appropriately reserved: he was determined to convince Mr. Jassilkowski-without-a-von (did he say that on purpose or out of genuine ignorance?) —Mr. Jassilkowski—that the management of the Eden Hotel considered it its paramount duty to satisfy all the wishes of its guests at any time and to the fullest extent, and especially when some oversight had given legitimate reason for complaint, no effort would be spared to rectify the mistake. He—the dapper trainee, that is— had therefore taken the liberty, regardless of the perhaps somewhat advanced hour, of procuring and presenting the vodka, which had been regrettably overlooked. Mr. Jassilkowski (!) might be kind enough to appreciate his special effort—the dapper trainee's, that is. He bowed once again with his ironically raised eyebrows (expressing ironic servility) and departed.

Baron Traugott held the ice-cold decanter, lifted it to his lips, and took a deep swig. He then returned to the wedding chamber.

There she lay in the shadowy half-light, the billowing nightgown stripped from her gloriously warm-blooded limbs: a houri of paradise, a partridge in the garden of lust, a cypresslike growth in voluptuous abandon, her moon-shaped forehead encircled by silver tresses, half covered as if in pain by her blossom hands with their sharp, blood-colored, almond-shaped nails, pearly teeth gleaming between luscious fruit-lips split like overripe pomegranates in the expectation of sweet-drunken joys, her jasmine bosom, those magnificent twin mounds crowned by rosebuds, the amber skin of her stomach, that silky-smooth, cool, flat hillock in the evening shadows surrounding the dainty snail shell of her fragrant navel, the closely locked gazelle thighs, between which that purple mussel shell of bliss lay hidden beneath tufts of down—both bride and wife—oh, was she not worthy of his ultimate wonderment, this girl with a bad reputation! . . .

There she lay waiting for him—divinely and affirmatively primeval, so far, oh, so far removed from complex, intricate self-reflection! She let those blossom hands glide down from her forehead and opened her arms, lowered her eyelids with their thin lashes over her myopic eyes, and a gasp escaped her lips, curved tensely like a Japanese bow, a lacquer-red bow, from which her teeth shone, sharp and cruel. She licked her lips with the moist tip of her tongue, broadly and slowly, thoroughly like a gorgeous and pure animal, with trembling nostrils. She exhaled loudly and air rasped through the sharp glitter of her pearly teeth. And when she felt him next to her, she clasped her arms around him with tensile strength and drew him down toward her, for she actually loved this guy, and she intended to prove it through her actions! She was still a bit shy in front of him, true, but did not her love command her to overcome this unfamiliar constraint—today of all days; damn it all, this was her wedding night! And therefore the tenderness with which she held him had an epic scope, something like a battle of embraces (be embraced, thee millions!), intended to kindle a very special sort of fire. *The desire of the man is for the woman*, so writes Coleridge, *but the desire of the woman*, on the other hand, says he, *is rarely other than for the desire of the man.* Well, that's exactly how it was meant, so a little interruption—damn it all—could only intensify her excitement!

As is well known, a slug of alcohol noticeably raises the adrenaline level, the combustion of sugar in the body is accelerated, and the good old pituitary gland steps up the rate at which it functions. But that was one thing, you would think, that the Baron hardly lacked.

There was a smell of lobster shells and stale champagne, of upholstery and respectable disinfectants and detergents, and Baron Traugott suffered. He suffered, but from much more than an affront to his senses: it was something meta-sensual, something deeply fundamental, and its secret was concealed in the *kiss*.

Strange to think that the most chaste form of contact of which two human beings in love are capable (oh, the preliminary moment when they drink in each other's breath) can become the very essence of obscenity as well! For the blond thoroughbred was now kissing him, you understand, kissing him, while her perfect limbs enveloped him, encompassed every inch of his body—she kissed him (oh, she was letter-perfect in that art!), kissed him tenderly with chaste lips, as light as butterfly wings, as delicate as cherry blossom leaves, as sweet as the darling smile of a child.

If only she had made the calyx of her lips into the avidly sucking maw of a carnivorous beast! But *that*, that was too much! And all the while, he was clasped by her limbs, enveloped by her hips, enlaced by the lianas of her arms, and enclosed by the reptilian smoothness of her thighs—she ingested him, so to speak, flesh to flesh, in snail-like swells of greedy desire, with the slowly stretching, skin-abrading writhing of a boa constrictor, while her chaste kisses continued to dribble on his mouth like a mild evening shower.

He suffered. But suffering makes you patient. Suffering makes you clearheaded and sympathetic. Together with her, he suffered the tragedy of her tenderness, and so as to atone for his primeval guilt about it, he invested his own tenderness with an artificial pathos (all the more so, as he hoped that this would cover up the consequences of the interrupted beginning).

Now, the musician, as we know, knows that in his art there is no rigid measure of time, but that instead the fascination of rhythm is to be found in expressiveness, animated by an accelerando, a crescendo, and a rubato in succession. By then, it had become—thanks to God's inscrutable ways—six-thirty in the morning, and whenever intended expressiveness lacks immediate spontaneity, it won't find the echo it seeks, even if you intensify it into a panting furioso.

These, my esteemed friend, are the moments when you fully comprehend the concept of eternity. These are the moments when you learn how to pray. The day dawned over the great, the well-loved city of Berlin, the clear day of September 14, 1938: sunlight swept away the delicate morning mist, rising like thin smoke between the trees in the zoo, cut into towering walls by the shadows of the trunks, flowing together like green water among their leafy tops only to be absorbed into and made to vanish by the victoriously hard blue of the late-summer sky, burning out in a thousand cold fires into transparently dry luminosity—glowing in the prematurely yellow foliage, glimmering in the fine silver strands in the bark of the beech trees, and gliding over the waters of the Landwehrkanal. Around the Victory Column, whose fool's-gold statue of Nike floated unreachably high in the atmosphere, the morning traffic of diligent cabs had begun to circle. The linden trees were being sprayed, and on Friedrichstrasse the roll fronts of the Aryanized and thereby impoverished department stores were raised with noisy rumblings. Wilhelmine cornices stood out sharply against an immaculate Prussian-blue sky. Buses rolled along, trains whirred, and briefcase carriers packed away their sandwiches—the great, the well-loved city of Berlin had come alive and began to rise like a magic carpet above reality (the reality of a mere city, a streets-houses-squares city of burgeoning morning, as it appears to commuters on early trains, still blinded by sleep, and late homecomers from diving-bell-shaped all-night pubs: the charnelhouse city shedding the swampy darkness of night)—and now it floated in white-hot industriousness through the fleeting passages of time, glowing and pulsing in the light of high noon, as finally and at long last, the two lovers in their suite at the Eden Hotel, weary of the dead sprint in which they had been engaged, let go of each other and sank into unconscious exhaustion.

And it was late afternoon when Baron Traugott, bathed and impeccably and carefully turned out, went down to the lobby (now brimming with brisk, newly arrived life, cruise-ship elegance, and Lufthansa wide-worldliness. The bilious night porter had been reprimanded and relieved by freshly starched and richly braided dignitaries, the dapper trainee engagingly upgraded into a sleek Andalusian reception manager)—I declare, it was late afternoon when Baron Traugott, his mind blank and going through the automatic gestures of reestablishing connection with the world at large, opened a newspaper and learned to his enormous surprise—and probably also retarded relief—what great and momentous events had taken place during the previous memorable night. Peace had broken out over the great, the well-loved city of Berlin, dew-fresh, brand-new peace, cellophane-wrapped, so to speak—and glory over the crusty present of a freshly baked past.

But upstairs, in their suite, the blond thoroughbred slept on, her chin resting on her milky-golden arm and her fine blond hair spilling over her temples. And so happily invincible was the disposition of this extraordinary young lady that, despite everything, a glad smile nestled in the curve of her much-kissed, pouting, upturned child's lips.

Mr. Chamberlain, dressed a little old-fashionedly but with a perfectly rolled umbrella under his arm, had met our friend the Duce and the Führer in Munich.

EAR READER, VENERABLE READER, KINDLY let me in on what happened! Can you please tell me? Did we sleep through it, frivolous and triumphant like the thoroughbred, or scatterbrained and dim-witted like the Baron—or did the twilight of those days simply spirit it away—you remember it: that strange aquarium luminosity we lived in and yet did not live in, where time existed but not our time, merely time as such without our own worthy participation? Or was it simply because nothing happened—because time, operating independently of us, did not allow anything to happen? Sure, you're ready to give me the condensed summary—world history in time-line form: the Czech crisis, Munich, and so on. But I don't buy it. That's not how it was. Could it be, after all, that the LORD was at hand?

No, please, brother Cain, don't invoke GOD's name just because you worry about your Porsche, because your going to the next Cannes film festival is in jeopardy, or because next quarter's textile output is in doubt. I know that in between export deals and tax-deductible business lunches you sneak a peek into the *Daytime and Nighttime Diaries* of Mr. Theodor Haecker. But in 1938, in those days, my friend, insofar as you could tear your eyes away from your girlfriend's groin, you couldn't see beyond the stock reports. And while the decisive and great events that were occurring then may have found their way onto those pages with some degree of accuracy, apart from that, they meant absolutely nothing to either you or me or anyone like us. Plain zero. As for Mr. and Mrs. von Jassilkowski, with untroubled spirits they went about furnishing their small apartment.

Did I say "small apartment"? Quite true.

153

A delicate sensitivity, esteemed friend, has heretofore kept me from touching on financial matters. But these days—of course, you know only too well how things are now, and you surely recall what it was like not so long ago. But we mustn't forget that at the time we're talking about, 1938, things were totally different—that strangely slick surface was false, false, and supported that false, glorious confidence which allowed us to stroll like sleepwalkers on the knife-sharp edge of material existence. Nowadays—dear heavens!—the acrobatic deftness with which we've managed to hoist ourselves up again to that knife-sharp edge is called (not without a subtle irony) the miracle of postwar reconstruction and its aftermath. But the wonderful self-assurance of yore is gone, that sleepwalking lack of inhibition which gave us a dancer's balance has unfortunately been lost, disappeared forever through some kind of trick—and that makes a whole lot of difference. For that's what is so damn dubious about everything now sprouting up under our reconstruction-obsessed hands like a demented phoenix salvaged from the rubble. For in between now and then lies the confusing, never fully acknowledged experience of how pleasurable it was to fall off the edge—how pure and free the air was when no longer and not yet again polluted by the fumes of the crap which is really at the heart of everything. But where would one be if one were to ponder that, too—where would one be!?

Blessed are the poor in memory! Even more blessed are those who are able to remember at their own sweet pleasure! For ultimately, what is truth? I ask you. Let this life, in fact, be nothing but a dream, a dream in which each of us spins his *own* truth into a cocoon, a crunchy cotton armor of self-justification. Of course, as long as you keep an eye on the risk coefficient while you're doing so . . . !

To make a long story short: although the blond thoroughbred de facto and de jure was an outstanding match and her Papa a decrepit mummy, there was the old lady, still full of juice, as we know. And she didn't have the slightest intention, not even in her wildest dreams, of allowing her feckless rascal of a daughter and this windbag son-in-law any leeway for whatever shenanigans they might have had in mind. On the contrary, their comical marriage gave her a welcome opportunity to grab all the elbowroom she needed—let both of them take heed, that insolent brat and her Stritzelbitzki or whatever his name was, both still wet behind the ears. Mama, closely advised by the bon vivant and the careful counsel of one of his fraternity brothers, who was an excellent notary and attorney familiar with the management of large holdings, kept a firm right hand on the ammunition shares, while her left hand, knowing perfectly well what the other was up to, wallowed happily in fat dividends.

Hence, a small apartment, for the time being. (Needless to say, the blond thoroughbred howled and swore that Mama shouldn't think she could get away with it; her legal adviser, a good friend from Charley's Bar, had always warned her what the old bird was up to but she hadn't wanted to believe him. Now that both the front and back wagon wheels were deeply mired in shit, it wouldn't be easy to pull it out, but he would see what could be done, he would handle it . . .) Hence, a small apartment, as I said.

The beautiful dream image of jodhpurs, a castle staircase, and stud pens—where had it gone? I beg you: it had been fantasized and dreamed with such inner logic and tangibility that its actual materialization seemed almost superfluous. Mr. von Jassilkowski had so fully ingested it that it had actually come into being—for, once more, what is reality? What do you call it when the apparent truth produces the illusion of reality? Truly, I tell you: I'd like to see the man who, after meeting the Baron, did not immediately envision a scene of autumnal leaves, red coats, and double posts, who did not automatically sniff saddle soap, aged port, and registered cow herds. Therefore, naturally, a small apartment, just a pied-à-terre in jolly Berlin (you know how burdensome a large household can be in uncertain economic times): two rooms, kitchen, and bath, on the third floor of one of those clinker buildings from the reform-happy 1920s, which look so strangely antiquated when found between the magnificent edifices of the forever stylish nineteenth century, kittycorner from Charley's Bar. And naturally, despite the excessive central heating, a rustic brick fireplace had been installed in one of those tiny rooms (on account of which there had been an awful row with the building management), bookshelves to the right and left of it (books, especially those old leather-bound editions, instantly make any room cozy), and in front of it a low coffee table, a miniature refectory table with a specially added shelf between its cross-braced legs for Gotha's *Calendar of Nobility*, on top of which there were always a few issues of *Esquire*, a Kirghizian dagger, and Peter's tobacco and pipes. Peter? Well, you couldn't very well call someone Traugott for long, now could you? Peter, of course, had his own leather club chair with a Scottish plaid laid over the back. Lots of well-polished leather everywhere, chintz on the walls, and cast iron. (As a special treat for her little Peter, the thoroughbred had insisted on a polar-bear-skin rug, but it had turned out to be too big for the room, and so, after violent altercations with her old lady, she had swapped it for a Persian carpet.) The rest of the furniture was Biedermeier, a painted peasant wardrobe, a rather dubious Old German chest, and a mahogany secretary. And some tin, as goes without saying, a brass mortar as an ashtray, two Delft tiles, three flowerpot mats of antique velvet with gold braid, a petit-point cover for the telephone directory, and a few more of the precious little knick-knacks that always make a place look so lived in. Their friends from Charley's Bar—who followed and commented on every phase of the hard-fought battle with building management for the rustic fireplace, comparing it to similar instances of obstinacy they knew and offering moral and legal support to the couple—contributed communally an enormous matchbox holding foot-long matches, decorated with the groom's coat of arms and mounted in a cast-iron frame. (The witty doctor, who always had to do things his own way, did not participate, but instead gave the thoroughbred—and her alone—a rare private printing of *Forbidden Fruit*, purchased long ago in Port Said.) For the long wall in the sitting room, Baron Peter would very much have liked one or two ancestral portraits, and Mama in Allenstein would have been only too happy to offer the two framed pictures of Grandpapa and Grandmama Bremse, but he did not want to deprive her of such cherished mementos. Instead Grandpapa's Iron Cross of 1870 and Papa's First Class from the Great War were displayed in open cases on top of the bookshelves, and for the wall space they purchased two colored prints from the *Paul et Virginie* series, between which they hung (ah, the liberating air of the city) a print of Marc Chagall's *Circus Rider*.

Very well: the apartment not only was sweetly done but also

mirrored the personalities of its inhabitants and decorators. (In the sitting room, the blond thoroughbred had left most of it up to her Peter, merely adding a few things here and there, whereas the bedroom was largely her doing, patterned after her freshly waxed teenager's room at home and containing the very same furniture—the four-poster, the lacquer vanity, the Schnorr von Carolsfeld pictures, the phonograph, the dolls, the beauty tonics, and all the junk, though, of course, here more crowded together.) As I said, the small apartment expressed the character and lifestyle of its occupants, especially in the evening with the lights on. (It is well known that the choice of lighting fixtures is one of the most difficult in interior design: when the Hanseatic cog ship, which hung from the ceiling, shot forth light from its cannon hatches, when the fox-hunting scenes shimmered on the big parchment shades of the table lamps, and the rococo wall sconces were ablaze, when the fireplace was going and the masculine scent of Peter's Capstan tobacco pervaded the room, their new home felt cozy and charming. Thanks to a surreptitious tapping of her parents' wine cellar, there was also no lack of superior liquid refreshment.) The small apartment was a gift of good fortune—what the hell!—a hospitable shelter and a Fort Nobility, a bastion against life's daily skirmishes. And even though Mrs. von Schrader's bridge circle had closed ranks rather too easily over the gap left by Mr. von Jassilkowski's sudden departure, so that in the beginning, the young couple was more or less restricted to the company of casual acquaintances and friends from Charley's Bar, who were hard to classify socially, they did not have to wait long for society to acknowledge their new status as full members of the propertied classes. By the end of October, they had already been invited to a rabbit shoot at Klekow.

 LEKOW, DEAR FRIEND, WAS THE HOMESTEAD of Count Friedrich Wilhelm Klützow-Klekow in the Brandenburg March, twelve-hundred-something sandy acres with some pine groves—all right? —shot through with rabbit burrows like a Swiss cheese, but unfortunately not so creamy, with a great many different types of potatoes, and an ancestral castle not far from the scabby heath. Fritze Klützow had married a cousin of the blond thoroughbred with a firmer handhold on the munitions shares, and they had grown close discussing the family finances.

When the Baron and Baroness Jassilkowski of Fort Nobility arrived at Castle Klekow on the evening prior to the shoot—a tilbury carriage had picked them up at the Lower Kummerfeld train station—two of the expected guests were already there, Kreuzwendedich von Bobzien and his sister Erdmute.

Erdmute was about twenty-two, tall, very girlish in figure, and redheaded, self-conscious to the point of having nervous tics, though her typical utterances, breaching the walls of her inhibitions like gunshots with inaudible concussions, revealed surprising determination and stubborn judgment. Once she had managed to blurt out one of her apodictic pronouncements, she would quickly fall silent again and lower her long red lashes, as if to fend off all possible disagreement. "Isolde had to be slaughtered," she would insist abruptly. "I knew all along the bull didn't cover her well." And her flame-colored lashes would fall guiltily over her pale eyes, as if she had given alms to a shameful beggar and feared he might try to repay her.

There was something oddly fascinating, touching, in her manner,

158

simultaneously pushing forward and compulsively pulling back, and this was also expressed by her virginally lissome and still somewhat childlike, undeveloped body, which in no way bespoke asceticism (among her peers she enjoyed an almost legendary reputation as a horsewoman), and Baron Traugott—pardon me: Peter—a connoisseur of women to his fingertips, made her the object of his surreptitious interest. In this he was aided by the easy and emphatically informal atmosphere of the small circle which, for now, did not require him to be on guard and watch out for himself in his usual torturous way. Fritze Klützow-Klekow (the Baron was secretly waiting to be addressed by name, so that he could decide accordingly whether to reply with the formal "Count Klützow" or the familiar "Fritze," but somehow the conversation didn't provide any opportunity; Sabine, Fritze's wife, referred to him in the way of a family relation as "Peter," but only when speaking to the blond thoroughbred)—Fritze Klützow was the gracious head of the household, identifiable as such by his casual patent-leather pumps, which he wore with gray cotton socks and a loose flannel suit, the jacket cut perhaps a bit short. He and Sabine (she was medium blond, chatty, and prone to plumpness) lived in obvious harmony unencumbered by prudery, for they laughed heartily at the naively earthy remarks made by the thoroughbred which had at first caused Baron Peter to wince. But much of the success of the evening's easy and relaxed atmosphere was due to Kreuzwendedich. (He had been born during the battle of the Marne, hence his rather unusual name, which means loosely "God smile upon us" and expressed the fervent hope of the nation for a victorious outcome.)

Kreuzwendedich was a second son and of course therefore destined for a military career, but here and now (against all regulations) he was not in uniform. He, too, wore his lieutenant's braids in good venerable style, which meant that he would join the Golden Horde but soon after quit the service (if nothing intervened), for he expected an inheritance from an unmarried and thus childless uncle. This uncle's Pomeranian estate was known as a center of the arts and cultivated life, for said uncle, a Mr. von Bobzien-Wellentin, now in his late seventies and known among his former regimental comrades as "Natasha," was a generous sponsor of young male actors and art students, a great conversationalist in his own right, and an aristocrat of the old school, famous for his love of music. Castle Wellentin had more to offer than its renowned park, designed and planted by the owner to resemble older models. (The ephebes at Charley's Bar cooed with envy at the mention of his so-called fox hunts, nocturnal games of chase through the yew mazes, in which a valuable gold watch carried by Mr. von Bobzien as the "fox" was presented to the eventual winner.) In addition to a comprehensive family archive, the entire series of Gotha's *Calendar of Nobility* beginning with the very first issue and missing none, and a gallery of ancestral portraits touched up and completed by local artists, the castle boasted a collection of military decorations and medals famous throughout the province, which had on more than one occasion attracted the attention of the older students from the high school in the nearby county seat when they went on field trips.

The future administration of these prestigious cultural artifacts cast a presumptive aura of responsibility on the nephew Kreuzwendedich. He had been to Austria with the annexation troops, knew Vienna, and behaved accordingly. In contrast to his sister, he was dark and had what is popularly understood as an aristocratic physiognomy, to wit: a noble hawk nose, large jet-black eyes with transparently thin lids, and a well-formed, very red mouth, which naturally, with no intent on his part, wore a somewhat pained smile. His hair, wetly combed back close to his narrow head like a striated cap, ending at the temples in two pointed Spanish sideburns, the chalky pallor of his skin, the languidly arched eyebrows, and the lost smile of his blood-red mouth—all this reminded you of those cloth dolls you find underneath the sofa cushions in petit bourgeois homes, the ones with moonlike lonesome heads lolling over their neck ruffs—the main difference being that Mr. von Bobzien's eyes were hardly the dull black of a *Pierrot lunaire*, but sparkled with an enticing, lively, almost lusty curiosity.

As soon as Mr. and Mrs. von Jassilkowski entered the drawing room—in exact terms, Castle Klekow was only the master's house in a former annex, for the original ancestral home had fallen into ruin after the main estate had to be given up; you entered directly from the outside stairs into a hall that served as the dining room and where the table was already set; to the left was the red drawing room, called that not so as to differentiate it from some other blue, green, or yellow drawing room, but because the window curtains were cut from the same wine-red velvet with which the chairs for the round Berlin-style table were upholstered—when Peter and the blond thoroughbred, still in their overcoats (they had no chance to take them off in the dining room), entered the red drawing room, Kreuzwendedich von Bobzien took in both elegant apparitions with his pained smile and the approving eyes of an expert, especially Baron Peter's mouse-gray glen-check suit, comparing it with his own with respect to number of buttons and width of trouser cuffs. He himself wore a coffee-brown, loosely fitted, and exceptionally long belted wool jacket over his regulation gray officer's trousers and (as a familiar of the house and a remote relative of the Klützows) the obligatory patent-leather pumps. A red-and-blue-striped tie, adorned only with a discreet pearl stickpin, swelled out lushly from his low swallowtail shirt collar in a loose knot.

"Cavalry at Ludwigslust?" he asked as they were introduced, rolling his shoulders so as to straighten his jacket collar. And as the Baron assented: "Served myself for some time with that old crowd." A short nod, and the contact was made.

Dinner was served in the hall, with the coachman who had brought the guests from the station functioning as footman. But first the Countess Mother had to be brought down, and this gave rise to some awkwardness. Neither Traugott (sorry—I can't help it)—neither Peter nor the blond thoroughbred had been told that the Countess was deprived, as a result of a longtime nervous ailment (temporarily, it was still hoped), of the use of her legs. Nevertheless, she was most amiable and still possessed her faculties, so that she was in no way troublesome. When the footman-cum-coachman Wilhelm opened the door to announce dinner (and let in a pungent wave of stable odors) and Fritze turned to Kreuzwendedich, saying, "Come help me in handling Mama," the thoroughbred burst out into bell-ringing laughter and roguishly asked for an explanation of this suggestive request. Sabine quickly apprised her, and the blond thoroughbred, still greatly amused, said: "Oh, I see, I thought something quite different was meant." Everyone laughed (except Baron

Peter, for whom the incident was most painful), Fritze Klützow even pinched her arm, and thus any misapprehension dissolved in the general merriment. They all stood at the table until the old Countess, her arms around the shoulders of the two men and held in a belted seat contraption, was brought down from her living quarters and put in her seat at the head of the table; then Sabine introduced the thoroughbred and Peter (with horror, he noted that Erdmute, very much in contrast to the thoroughbred's casual "good evening," had bowed and kissed the old lady's hand), whereupon the Countess quickly resolved the little issue of seating arrangement by ordering Traugott to her left and Kreuzwendedich to her right. Sabine and Erdmute had to sit together, that couldn't be helped—but no: in that case Sabine and Fritze would be together—so it had to be the other way around: the thoroughbred next to Mr. von Jassilkowski; no, they were also a couple: ergo Sabine, then Erdmute, Fritze, and then the blond thoroughbred—that worked, the puzzle was finally solved and they could all sit down—but wait, not yet. Sabine, Erdmute, Fritze, and Kreuzwendedich remained standing behind their chairs, their hands piously folded over the high backs, eyes lowered, while the Countess Mother in severe devotion declaimed the simple, childlike words: "Come, O Lord, be our guest and bless all that you have given us. Amen." Only then could they sit down. Wilhelm brought around the first course, as well as his characteristic stable odors.

There was another small incident during the meal, which was very simple (the big dishes being reserved for the dinner after the shoot on the morrow). This time it was caused by Baron Traugott—I mean Peter—himself: after the Countess, who—as mentioned—was most gracious and in full possession of her faculties, had exchanged a few noncommittal remarks with him, he raised his glass to drink to her health. Although she acknowledged this politely, he could sense a certain astonishment among the other guests, and there was even an exchange of looks at the far end of the table. But Sabine saved the situation by remarking that in Scandinavia it was also the custom to raise one's glass to a lady, that in Sweden, indeed, a lady wasn't even supposed to touch her glass unless her dinner partner to the left had first toasted her. The Countess Mother, on her part, declared that the gesture, doubtless one of civil and gracious intent, required no excuse, and with a delicate smile, conscious of her social sovereignty, she raised her glass to the Baron. Erdmute agreed with Sabine's comment and declared abruptly, "Something different for a change," then lowered her long eyelashes and fell haughtily silent. And now it was Fritze Klützow's turn, and he raised his glass with a smile to the blond thoroughbred. Kreuzwendedich seemed truly to enjoy the whole incident. Bending elegantly forward, past the Countess Mother, he asked in a tone of shared understanding: "You know Vienna, naturally . . . ?"

Fortunately Baron Peter was spared the need to reply (it would have grieved him to disappoint this most genial man), since at that very moment the door suddenly opened and another guest in a loden coat came up to the table—Willhardt von Lassow, known as Pinne, Fritze's cousin. He was slightly under average height, dressed like a gamekeeper, highly self-assured, obviously very much at home in Klekow. After greeting the Countess, Sabine, Fritze, Erdmute, and Kreuzwendedich, he explained that he had come a little earlier than planned but you always had to lead the target a bit—wasn't that so?—and, as it happened, he'd already eaten. Questioned as to where he had left Armgard (this turned out to be his wife, although it was difficult to imagine such a country yokel having any civilized relations with a woman—even if it were just a girl doing her compulsory year of rural service—let alone being a husband and head of household), he replied firmly that she had "breeding problems" and could not go out but sent her regards. "Is it bad?" asked Sabine compassionately. Pinne made little of it: "No, no, nothing serious, just a little displacement; it'll work itself out all right." He then greeted the thoroughbred and, after having inspected him sharply, introduced himself to Mr. von Jassilkowski with a loud and explicitly distinct "Lllassow," briefly grasping the Baron's hand and, as his glance shifted away, adding, as if to himself, a strangely Austrian-sounding "Kissyerhand!" He then drew a chair up to the table and joined the circle.

Fritze Klützow could not get over his regret that Armgard had not come: "That means we'll have too many men tomorrow," he said. "Happens everywhere," said Willhardt von Lassow, called

Pinne. "Hinds and does in the minority." And after a glance at the circle: "Quite a herd of stray stags." Smiles all around. "Quite a herd of stray stags," agreed Fritze Klützow, "migratory game, the whole lot." As if obeying a telepathic command, they both raised their glasses, Wilhelm the coachman having placed one in front of Lassow. "High time to arrange a proper shoot," concluded Pinne Lassow, putting down his glass. "The Führer will see to that," said Fritze. "You can count on it," agreed Pinne Lassow. "He already has it in hand."

The meal over, they rose once more and took their places behind their chairs, and the Countess Mother folded her hands and with lowered eyes said grace: "Thanks be to God, for he is merciful and his goodness is everlasting. Amen." Then they all joined hands, right and left, and intoned: "*Gesegnete Mahlzeit!*" The Countess Mother retired—that is, she was carried back upstairs in her belted seat, this time with Pinne von Lassow replacing Kreuzwendedich von Bobzien.

The rest of the company retired to the red drawing room, and some time was taken up with more details of the Countess Mother's afflictions and general expressions of marveling that, in spite of everything, she had retained her faculties. Fritze returned and was much taken with the idea of a glass of punch, but everyone agreed they shouldn't drink tonight since they had to get up so early in the morning. And anyway drinks would taste all the better after a jolly hunt. So everybody went to bed. Sabine showed the Jassilkowskis to their room.

The Baron was, however, too excited to go to bed. Excited? Did I say excited? Yes, quite right, he was excited. He paced back and forth in his dressing gown, talking at the thoroughbred, while she tried to make herself comfortable in one of those very high, hard, and narrow beds, intending to read *Master Percy's Progress* as much as the dim bed lamp would allow it. Yes, he was excited. He had been so oddly affected by everything here: childhood memories, you understand. All of it, the specific way of life, the land, the house: the house especially reminded him of home because it wasn't too big or pompous like one of those baroque imitations of a princely court palace, as you might imagine a Prussian nobleman's house. A gentleman's mansion, that's what it was. Country aristocracy, gentry folk. With their beautiful tradition of self-esteem! Rough and unpolished on the outside, admittedly, but that's the country way. The country's like that, after all. But underneath, the genuine pure core. The delicate respect, for instance, with which Fritze and this Lassow, this Pinne, had carried the Countess upstairs, did you notice that? And she herself, the Countess! She was really and truly a grand lady in the old style, of the old school. Grand and simple, she's probably never been farther away than Stolp or Berlin in her life, and yet: what style! And how astonishing that, in spite of everything, she has retained her faculties! This Erdmute, by the way, was made of the same stuff. One day she too would be the same: grand and simple. That was the stuff from which such mothers are fashioned. What matter that they didn't have their own bathroom! Sabine wanted to renovate the castle—fine, but Sabine . . . "Excuse me, she's charming, of course, but let me tell you, so you don't misunderstand, she's different. You notice it right off. Certainly, these people have accepted her as one of their own, and very quickly, too, because they are much too polite to let anyone notice something like that. Not that she's in any way inferior, by no means, why should she be? After all, doesn't industry boast many families of the highest culture? Different, that's all. An outsider wouldn't notice this right away. Yet it can never be covered up entirely. And these people here, as I said: they're basically polite, despite their rough core—no, wait, I mean despite their rough exterior. We're not as uncouth and backwoods, we country folk, as we might seem to others. Take this charming Kreuzwendedich, for instance; granted, he dresses like a scarecrow, but clothes can be learned in no time." Good Lord, when he, Traugott, thought of what he looked like when he came from East Prussia many years ago—but what cannot be learned is the inner culture, the mature form—how shall I put it?—the heritage which has to be handed down to you from past generations—it's blood, race. He would be master of Wellentin one day, this young Bobzien, one of the most beautiful and cultured houses in Pomerania. (Erdmute would certainly get something of it, too.) And he, wasn't he charming? That look of recognition that knows how to spot what is genuine, regardless of how different it may seem on the surface! Or the delightful gesture with which Fritze had raised his glass to her, the blond thoroughbred, after he, Traugott, had taken that small liberty with the old Countess? How graciously this extraordinary woman had accepted his gallant break with convention! What was Sabine thinking? Was it not a sign of refined piety that Fritze left the house exactly as it was, with no changes, just as his mother had set it up fifty years ago? This washbasin over here with the water lilies—I don't care if you call it kitsch! It resonates of a simple and devout life, rich in tradition. The beds in which she gave birth to her children (to this the thoroughbred objected, without looking up from her book, that she was astounded it had ever gotten that far, considering how hard the mattresses were) . . . Baron Peter fell silent as he paced across the room. These may also have been the beds in which her husband, the old Count, had died, he commented crisply. (Why did he need more than one? the thoroughbred wanted to know.) Baron Peter ignored her frivolous question. He still remembered with acute pain the death of his own father, so he said. ("Once in the lap of the beloved, loving father," sings our friend Hölderlin, isn't that right?—"but the Grim Reaper arrived and swung his cruel scythe . . .") Yes, the death of Papa: he had died right after a hunt. He had been outside all day in the fields and hedges without anyone suspecting that something was wrong, and then he had come home, lain down, and died . . . And that's what it was: the memory, which had been summoned up so vividly, so tangibly, by everything he was experiencing here now, as if he, who had been away from home for so long, alienated from so much, had found his way back. Like the prodigal son—didn't she understand what this meant?

Tomorrow, for instance, there would be a shoot. His first shoot after so and so many years! His first shoot since childhood, to be exact. ("In East Prussia, we start young . . .") Oh, she had no way of knowing what this all meant to him, after all those years in Berlin, that oppressive big city. She had never known anything else.

He went to the table and inspected the obsolete gun they had unearthed for him in one of his doddering father-in-law's closets. From the outside it still looked passable—just an old gun. But the barrels, the barrels were rusted inside, so as to break your heart! ("Such a thing could never have happened in our home. Strange that there are people in the world who have no relationship with firearms.

A gun like this is a living thing . . .") By the way, shouldn't he confess to the master of the hunt that he didn't have a license? It would be very awkward if the ranger came around to check . . .

"Then you just say you've forgotten it at home and slip the guy five marks if he makes a fuss," the blond thoroughbred said, and turned a page.

No, no . . . Peter dismissed the suggestion with a forgiving smile. That's what he had been talking about earlier—that's what it was, the difference, the different worlds. Here (and at home) you didn't bribe officials. People here didn't think that everything could be bought and sold, as people in industry did. Here there still prevailed what used to be called the *good old Prussian spirit*, yes, precisely, and it still held sway in houses like this one, in fine old country families . . .

"All right, get in bed and let's go to sleep," said the thoroughbred, closing her book and snuggling as comfortably as possible into the hard and slightly moist pillows. "Tomorrow we have to rise and shine with the roosters."

True, tomorrow meant early rising . . . he looked once again down the barrels of the old blunderbuss, drew a bead once or twice on the elaborate wood ornaments of the wardrobe, and prepared some shells for tomorrow. Then, at last, he took off his dressing gown and got into bed.

Could she understand this? he asked, looking dreamily at the ceiling, his arms crossed behind his head. Could she understand the feeling of homecoming—that it was like the prodigal son returning home . . . ?

Certainly, she said, already half asleep. She understood him only too well.

With that, she drew his head to hers and kissed him tenderly and maternally.

Baron Peter turned off the bed lamp, lay motionless, and sighed deeply from his troubled heart toward the ceiling.

And then someone knocked on the door, and it was darkest morning—what am I saying, it was still night, bone-shivering, eerie night (ooh, the loon! how he hoots, how he screeches his fearsome call); someone—you couldn't make out whom in the dark—brought in a small pitcher of hot water covered with a towel and lit the ceiling light (a tulip shade of opaque glass), and now everyone had to get up, up and out into the cold darkness, into the dead forest, rustling under swiftly moving clouds. (The murderous gang, he hears them, hears them, hears them in his dream: sleep, Reaper, go to sleep . . .) Steps could be heard throughout the house, doors banging, and a dog barking outside in the yard—short, dampened noises falling into the dark silence like stones in a brackish pond, but they signaled that things were in motion, preparations were being made, boots laced, belts tightened—soon they would all assemble, armed and determined, as the stars slowly faded and the fleeting clouds slackened under the wan moon, as the darkness imperceptibly lifted and morning broke over the jagged black line of far-off trees, becoming leafless, losing the veils of darkness one after another until the landscape rose up, cleansed of darkness, into the pure, still-sunless brightness . . . and then, arising in this light, a threat would spread over the fields and strips of trees, over the bushes and bracken, unnamable but clearly demarked—as if it had grown spontaneously from the new day (oh, eternally new condition!), there suddenly would be a pole to which a whisk of straw had been tied—an eerie bewitching fetish—and then, within view of the first, a second and third . . . and over there, across the plowed fields, suddenly a sparse row of young scrub pines . . . here and there and yonder near the groves and higher up by the logging trail, the ground would be marked off in this manner, and the threat weighed namelessly over these designated areas.

Then they would drive to these plots marked off with murderous intent ("come, nearby Reaper, come"). They would peel off one by one from the quiet group, grinning with determination, and one by one, each would take a place by one of the markers. They would press the locks of their rifles sideways, open the barrels, and fill the cavities with easily gliding shells; then they would close the weapons, now dangerously armed (barrels snapping into their locks with a soft irrevocable click), and they would lower the muzzles to wait for whatever appeared in front of them: the sun would now be picking off the pure blossoms of morning—the sun, pure and hugely bright, carrying death within.

But right now, it was still dark and bone-chilling cold. (The threat still had to be woven together: the gang snored all around, the murderous gang—but the first light coming from the castle, suddenly glimmering in the dark landscape, was it not the star of death? Others were lit by the first one, here in the castle and over there in the gamekeeper's house and in the beaters' cottages—an evil constellation began to shine on earth, while the stars gradually faded away in the sky, as if they wanted to have nothing to do with it.)

And he did not hesitate at the call to make himself ready for the kill. He woke the blond thoroughbred, who pouted sleepily, then sprang out of bed, washed hastily in ice-cold water (considerately leaving the hot water for her), and began to gird himself: oh, the voluptuousness of rough, masculine, coarse cloth, thick footwear, tight, cold-resistant wraps at the neck, wrist, and knee! Oh, the firm belting, the reassuring cohesion! The deliciously cold and steely weight of the iron weapon in my hand! —Forward, forward! Come forth, ye children of Teut, come, ye children of Teut to the valley of battle!

Since the thoroughbred was dawdling, he went ahead, for he felt a hearty hunger—a very different hunger, oh yes! from the one he felt on late, morose, and leisurely mornings in the city (Kranzler, Mampe, movies, Charley's Bar—where have you gone? Spook caverns—smoked out, wiped off, swept away like so many night spirits by the sharp freshness of this morning—"many, oh, many are my days profaned by sin, sunken down: oh, lofty judge, don't ask how, but let merciful oblivion be their tomb . . ."). Fritze, Sabine, Erdmute, and Pinne were already at breakfast, and Kreuzwendedich had finished his and left to see after his dog; Fritze wore a sleeveless shooting vest, which set off his well-bred horseman's head on his narrow shoulders to great advantage; Sabine was in a Tyrolean costume, and Erdmute, wearing ski pants and a monogrammed windbreaker, had obviously just extruded one of her apodictic declarations, for her eyes were lowered. And Baron Peter joined them with a brisk greeting, fetched his coffee from the sideboard, and cheerfully sat down to eggs, country sausage, and fresh bread. (This fellow Pinne had once more added quite distinctly to his greeting the mysterious phrase "Kissyerhand"—what was that supposed to mean?) When the thoroughbred finally made her appearance, in a Scottish plaid skirt, a cashmere sweater, and a snazzy fox-fur jacket, something of a general conversation began to flow, and he was no longer alone and exposed (this Pinne—this Mr. von Lassow—had begun to get on his nerves). He was prepared for action, and it was a fine morning on a high-spirited day.

The arrival of two more guns was still expected, Fritze's uncle Count Klützow-Ödemark (who surely would have breakfasted already, for he was a bit touchy and peculiar and not always easy to handle) and a neighbor, the lease-tenant of a state-owned estate, Grotkopf (he would get breakfast himself; he was used to that and was certain to bring sandwiches with him in a paper bag). Together with the gamekeeper, that made seven guns, with the first shot to be fired at daybreak. So they had to hurry, for the sky had already begun to turn gray and the cold stars were receding into the vast emptiness. And we—oh, sing, sing a jubilee, you far-off glittering constellations of Uranus! Bend down, Orion! Bend down!—we are the sons of the Sublime . . .

They grabbed their weapons. But then Baron Traugott—Peter, damn it all!—remembered again that he didn't have a hunting license. And as it was too late to admit that, he was the last one to step out on the stairs leading to the courtyard, his anxious glance checking for the authorities.

Thank God, no ranger in sight. Two large horse-drawn carriages with rubber tires stood ready, one covered inside with straw and equipped with makeshift racks for the guns, and many ragged muffled figures could be seen milling around, leaning on sticks and cudgels. In front the tenant farmer Grotkopf, lumpy and angularly polite, conversed with the gamekeeper Engelhardt. Off to one side next to the car in which he had just arrived stood Count Klützow-Ödemark, tall and gaunt like a ghost, snugly buttoned up in a yellow coachman's coat that reached almost to the ground; he snarled at the host in a caustic voice and without any preliminary greeting: "I've been standing around here for almost half an hour while you've had your breakfast—when are we going to start?" Greetings were exchanged, and he was introduced to the thoroughbred and Baron Peter; "Klützow," he barked, and stretched out at chin level a dismayingly large, bony, wine-red hand that emerged from his coat sleeve and squeezed their fingers with painful force.

And then there was the amiable Kreuzwendedich. How strange, how very changed he now seemed, that winning young man! He was wearing wide army-issue riding breeches, reinforced on the inside from the knees up and along the thighs and halfway over the buttocks with heavy gray, greasy, shiny leather; rough oiled boots, quite wrinkled in the shaft with leather marching laces and wheelless spurs; and over it all a loden coat, buttoned up to the neck, with a shoulder cape, which he had girded with an army belt: the belt buckle featured a swastika entwined by two ears of wheat and the motto "God with us!" His chest was crisscrossed by thongs and cords, to which were attached, among other paraphernalia, a heavy triple-barreled shotgun-rifle (there might be boar about), a pair of binoculars, a field canteen and a shell case, a Voigtländer camera and a little horn. Suspended from his belt and swinging against his legs were a hunting knife, a map case, and a collapsible stool. A flashlight, a silent dog whistle, and a wound-up trace leash also hung from the buttons of his jacket pockets. ("So where have you put the tent and the stewpot?" asked the blond thoroughbred.) From his left arm hung a gnarled oak stick, while his right hand barely managed to keep control of a stubbly-haired boarhound on a short chain ending in a spiked collar, who panted and wagged his tail in tremulous excitement, plagued by flea bites and crouching in murderous anticipation.

Although his outfit alone more than sufficed to transform him into a menace, an even more vital change had occurred on his head: over his wet-smooth hair, combed back in scraggly strands with Spanish sideburns, which had given him the puppetlike, sentimentally romantic look of a pierrot, he had slapped on a gray conical headpiece with a narrow brim bent down almost vertically to the very edge of his eyes; a small badger beard was stuck arrogantly in its band. ("Do you also have an elephant tusk as a stickpin?" asked the blond thoroughbred.) Yet his face remained the same, though its milk-white pallor now began to shimmer in the gray light of dawn—his hawk nose jutting out directly under the brim of his hat, his eyes riveted below the horizon, the pained smile, a face still full of curiosity and tempting sensuality—all this transformed the former black, white, and red pierrot into a girded angel of death—and oh! his slim hand held not a mandolin but, rather, firmly and tenderly, the cold triple-barreled weapon.

Fritze quickly discussed a few organizational details with the gamekeeper Engelhardt. In the short wait that ensued, Pinne Lassow (could it be that he wasn't that bad after all?) turned to Baron Peter and, pointing to his rifle, asked, "What kind of a thing is that?" Everybody gathered around the firearm. Just a very old gun, Baron Peter admitted, but he happened to like such antiquated things, for they often shot better and were more reliable than modern, hammerless ones. ("Old guns scatter," interjected the thoroughbred, "said the pastor when he baptized the dotard's twins." General laughter.) Of course, the handling of such a weapon was rather more complicated, Baron Peter went on, but if you were used to it, it presented no serious problems. After all, our ancestors managed to shoot with them. With models as old as this one, you had to take care when using smokeless shells, and actually you should only use black powder. "When Papa shot it last time," the thoroughbred confirmed, "he looked like a Moor because of all the powder smoke." "So it isn't your gun, then?" Pinne asked the Baron, looking him square in the eye. No, admitted the Baron, to be absolutely precise, it belonged to his father-in-law.

As if the weapon itself had lost value because of this admission, the general interest in it dissipated and everyone turned away. The impatient voice of Count Klützow-Ödemark made itself heard again: "How much longer are we going to stand around here?" he snarled. (The cold morning mist made his breath condense into a small gray cloud in front of his mouth, rather like the ones you see in pictures of bellowing stags.) "Are we going to hunt or just sit here and chat? I can pass the day better at home." Fritze gave the signal to get under way.

They all pulled themselves together—that is, they climbed into the carriage and sat as best they could. Kreuzwendedich's impetuous stubbly-haired hound jumped in, too, howling, crowded and pushed everyone, stepped on everyone's feet, and tried to climb into Count Klützow-Ödemark's lap, but was yanked back, shouted at, and kicked under the bench. ("Why don't you make that mutt run next to the carriage? This is intolerable: I'd like to shoot him in the head right here and now!") At the same time, the ragged, cudgel-bearing troop of beaters, who until then had been immobile, raptly observing the scene, suddenly showed some life: following a rough command from somewhere, they divided into groups, erupted in sudden explosions of bucolic mirth, and as one assaulted the second wagon and climbed into it, scrabbling awkwardly over the wheels and side panels, stumbling and pushing and tumbling together in a dense human tangle; then, just as suddenly, they once again were motionless, mute, their eyes fixed unswervingly on the aristocrats in front. The coachmen cracked their whips, the heavy horses started up with a ponderous jerk, and thus they rolled out of the yard, swaying and jolting over frozen, stiff ribs of mud and into the open fields.

And then the sun rose, bloody and frosty—cloud masses brushing fiery skies, heralds rising silently—and there it was, reality, for so long dreamt and longed for: real life, the life of *the great world*—a carriage filled with nobles, a lofty breed of men come together for the gentlemanly sport of the hunt: time-honored practice of knights, caste ritual. (When Kreuzwendedich asked whether the start of the shoot would be sounded, Fritze replied easily that he might blow on the mouth of his gun barrel to alert the beaters, but Kreuzwendedich only flashed a pained smile and said he'd sound his horn—blowing the horn was essential to any kind of hunt, after all. "I guess you learned that from your uncle in Wellentin," commented the blond thoroughbred.) But wait a second! What was that? What was missing in this reality? Why is the singing in my heart so heavy with melancholy gloom? Fulfillment! Fulfillment! O sacred goal of all the holy spirits! When shall I embrace you, drunk with the wine of victory, and be at rest forever more? . . . was it the land, sparse and exhausted, so unlike the glorious autumnal park in the advertisements, where the red coats shine like berries in the bushes? Was it the flippant jargon, the vulgar voices of these aristocrats? Had the dream been too fair, his desires too grand, too broad, too insatiable, so that no reality could do them justice? Well then! A carriage full of gentry, charming people about to pursue their rural pastime—wasn't that enough, wouldn't it make a nice picture series for Baron

von Aalquist's *Gentleman's Monthly?* The elegance of Aristona cigarettes, the pure-blooded manliness of Henkel champagne: what did
they have over this incontestable reality? What was wrong with this
backdrop? (Granted, Erdmute's ski pants and windbreaker from the
German Young Women's Association and this boorish farmer Grotkopf with his bristly little mustache and bulbous nose did not add
much to the overall atmosphere; but on the other hand, weren't
Fritze's and Sabine's Tyrolean hats the real McCoy, properly shabby
and adorned with pins from the most famous ski resorts—Zürs,
Sestriere, Cortina d'Ampezzo—"and only those where we've actually skied!"; and Count Klützow-Ödemark in his long yellow
coachman's coat, didn't he look as though he'd just arisen from an
ancestral tomb?) What, then, was wrong with this picture? Everything certainly looked genuine enough, a roundabout open-air stag-
ing, so to speak: the woods weren't made of balsa (of course, they
weren't exactly the oak groves of Dodona either, but only a meager
copse of scrub pine)—but what do you want? The trees were real
trees, the shoot was a real shoot (wasn't that the first row of poles
over there, with straw whisks marking the stations, stretched out
menacingly over the fields?); and the nobles were real nobles—no
theater in the world could have costumed them any truer to life. (It
was said that the first Klützow was cited around A.D. 800—probably
in the runic memorandum of some shaman who pierced his nose
with an amber peg in order to ward off thunder.) What was it, then?
Am I totally mad? Isn't the battle of passions over by now? Friend!
If only we never fraternized with the actors! If only we never pushed
onto the stage and saw that the miracle world is made of ropes,
glue, and gauze! Consider the happy spectators: from the beaters'
wagon, the ragged pile of cudgel-bearing bodies stared at them,
spellbound by the spectacle, sucking it in, missing not a single gesture. Ah, reality!

They had reached the beginning of the first drive (away with you,
you desires, you tormentors of folly!), and everyone dismounted—
the beaters' wagon had branched off and disappeared behind the
lisière of the woods—and silently they walked to the marker poles.
Fritze, as master of the hunt, assigned everyone a station: first, the
tenant farmer Grotkopf to the unpromising side position, then Pinne

on the corner (a fox might appear here!), and then Baron Peter. The thoroughbred wanted to share Fritze's station, Sabine accompanied Uncle Ödemark, and Erdmute stayed with Kreuzwendedich. Hats were waved and "happy hunting" (begun by the tenant Grotkopf) was wished, and then the others went on their way. He watched them go until the next post had been positioned—hand signals to avoid dangerous shooting—and then he was alone.

Autumnland! In front of him, a grove of young pines slanted slightly upward, a pair of chickadees scurried in the branches, the treetops rustled in the wind. And then a dissonant, wavering sound wafted over from where Kreuzwendedich was stationed, stopped, then started up again and echoed in tortured ululations through the woods. And—"thou drawest near, oh, battle: down they come, the brave youths from the hills, down into the valley below"—a remote howl of voices could be heard, bucolic yet intense, coming closer and closer and suddenly rising to a breathless screaming pitch on one wing of the advancing beaters' line, where you could barely make out: "Hare! Hare! Hare!" then waning for a while before flaring up again in a long-drawn-out "Hare to the rear!" Thus it ate its way like a forest fire forward into the high silence of the morning landscape in order to devour it. The chickadees in the bushes fluttered this way and that and whirred away. And suddenly a shot to the right, from Grotkopf's station, and then a second. And then to the left in the underbrush, a breathless panting drew closer—closer— closer—and Kreuzwendedich's boarhound, who had torn free, burst from the brush, dragging his leash behind him. And to his right, from Pinne Lassow's station: "Hare! Man, look out!" and the stubbly-haired hound was yanked backward and disappeared yowl- ing behind the row of guns going after the hare that had broken through. The shrieking beaters came closer and closer, and two shots came from the left and then another, and then another, and the first beaters came into view among the sparse trees, their eyes on the Baron, swinging their cudgels and beating them fiercely against the trunks and branches of the brush, they advanced, the black caverns of their mouths gaping open as they yelled, their rags tied with string, stomping around, savagely alive in rude, joyless merriment—the merriment of unconstrained thrashing and screaming, the merriment of marauding, scorching, beating things to death and trampling them in the mud: a peasant revolt, the mob surging toward him, cudgels swinging, eyes glued on him with unholy curiosity and anticipation, on him, their true prey.

And then they were through and they stopped, rested on their sticks and gaped. (Seen up close, their eyes were full, sated, and gorged on what they had seen, as if there were no room left in them for desire or expectation or hope.)

The drive was over and—oh!—for the short while it had lasted, he had been quite lost to himself, quite spellbound by what was happening around him, unconscious of his own being.

The first drive was over, and he had missed his chance and come away empty-handed. (Where had that hare come from? And why couldn't Kreuzwendedich keep his dog on his leash?) But Kreuzwendedich was getting what for from Uncle Ödemark because up in front they hadn't gotten anything either. Fritze too (probably distracted by the blond thoroughbred) had not been paying enough attention, and the gamekeeper had missed twice when the hare was already much too far away. But Grotkopf the tenant approached in triumph from behind, chewing his slice of buttered bread, followed by a beater with a hare. So, all right. Four hares had broken through to the rear—"I'm telling you, the whole drive was set up wrong," lectured Uncle Ödemark. "Hares run uphill, uphill, not downhill!" Two had been missed in front, and one had been shot—that made a total of seven. Proof at least that there was something out there, that was the main thing. On with the next drive!

Autumnland! Colorful splendor of the bushes and groves, luminous clarity of birches and ruddy Scotch pines, good fallow earth, delicate scent of faded leaves, silky blue sky, cool glittering sun! Once more Kreuzwendedich's magic horn sounded, once more the bucolic howling of the beaters was heard, and once more he stood and waited, his eyes fixed tensely ahead. The chickadees chirped, and from the right and left abrupt and frightening shots assaulted his senses and then there was suddenly a rustling and darting in front of him, and there—there it was all of a sudden—THE HARE—a big gray hare—precipitous reality! And all his aroused senses functioned independently of his will: somehow he pressed the blunderbuss to his cheek, somehow he aimed the barrel at his prey, somehow his finger found the trigger—there was a crack, a painfully loud bang, woolly fur rose like dust, and the hare, in full course, sat down broadly on its haunches. But an incredible power of will, which made its round eyes protrude from its head, drove it on. With a rowing motion, dragging its paralyzed hindquarters, it came straight toward Baron Traugott, and this tremendous effort made the animal seem almost supernatural. The extraordinary willpower in its tortured eyes was horrible. The Baron's second shot went astray, and only when the hare was right in front of him, when Baron Peter had reloaded in a frenzy of trembling and horrified impatience, did he finally manage to finish him off with a shot in the back. The hare's loose limbs, barely holding together at the torn midsection, continued to twitch, one leg vainly bobbing, trying to jump, in motions of helpless protest on the brown carpet of pine needles. Then this being was finally extinguished, remaining in death as in life the very essence of flight, of senseless flight from death. The beaters arrived soon thereafter, picked up the piece of naked bloody raw meat with its four dangling legs and a playboy's grin on the bloodstained face and carried it to the carriage.

Be that as it may: Baron Peter had made his mark, he had stood the test and had not been found wanting, for Uncle Ödemark and Kreuzwendedich had each shot a hare, as had Pinne Lassow, who had also bagged a rabbit. Thus, only the master of the hunt remained without game, and that was as it should be, for good manners dictate that the host show polite reserve. It was time to go on.

Another hare, which in the next drive ran alone along the row of guns and was shot at and missed by all, came into Baron Peter's range, but he followed suit and emptied both barrels into the moist earth. And then, during the following drive, he was joined at his post by Erdmute.

She announced her intention as they chanced to walk next to each other among the beaters. Abruptly she said in her low voice: "I will be joining you now!" After which she lowered her eyes arrogantly and blushed.

They halted at one of the poles marked with a straw whisk. Baron Peter tried to make whispered small talk, but she said severely: "We must keep silent!" So they stood side by side, listening to the chickadees and then Kreuzwendedich's horn, setting off the wild howling of the beaters. And then—oh, gracious fate!—a hare came hopping along into his range, and the Baron dropped him cleanly with a single shot. And then they continued to wait, and then this drive, too, came to an end, and they silently joined the others.

A great to-do was under way because the gamekeeper claimed to have sighted a fox—it sounded incredible, but why not? Uncle Ödemark questioned him sharply and then turned to Fritze: "The whole thing was set up wrong, of course. If you knew there was fox about, you bloody well should have put me at that station instead of your employee, and if you didn't, you bloody well should prepare the next hunt better. Please remember that next time! And incidentally, these endless wood drives make no sense at all. Now all the hares are out in the furrows, not in the woods."

Nevertheless, everybody now had his two hares, even Fritze, and Pinne Lassow had an additional rabbit. Not much time was spent on lunch—sandwiches and hot punch had been brought out in the second wagon—and then they got on with it. This time the drive was out in the open fields, but when Baron Peter looked around for Erdmute, she had joined Pinne Lassow at his station.

He now became aware that the thoroughbred had been with Fritze Klützow all day: her lively chatter and silver-tinkling laugh echoed through wood and valley. Once more, Kreuzwendedich's magic horn sounded, and once more he stared ahead in hypnotic expectancy, forgetting himself and the world, and again shots were fired. And, in fact, he shot another hare (after having missed two more, unfortunately, but they had been quite fast and far away, and, after all, he didn't know the gun very well as yet, that rusty old thing, which he thought strayed somewhat to the left, certainly the right barrel at least) . . . Now he was in the lead with his bag, for three hares was more than Pinne's two and a rabbit, and he began to rehearse his speech as king of the hunt.

But this was not to be, for Pinne shot another two, and Uncle Ödemark suddenly boasted a total of seven, although only twenty-one pieces of game—including one jay shot by Kreuzwendedich—had been laid out for the count, instead of twenty-three. (Grotkopf the tenant had also, as he liked to say, blown out the candle of another Master Rabbit.) "This mutt of yours is totally worthless," remarked Uncle Ödemark to the angel of death, "absolutely good for nothing. Entirely incomprehensible that he couldn't find the last two hares, both marked quite unmistakably, I saw them without a doubt. The dog is worthless. What's more, I'm not sure but that this"—as he turned, his sharp eye spotted the tenant Grotkopf and he corrected himself—"that these beaters didn't pocket one . . ." And thus the exalted day ended—oh, happy day of self-forgetting! —and the sky once more grew pale and dull, shadows thickened across the landscape, the chickadees in the bushes fell silent, and only the song of a thrush could be heard here and there. And the earth, the good earth willingly drank the glittering red blood of its murdered creatures, but the poles with straw whisks stood for a long time afterward as memorials to the terrible threat . . .

Once more, they climbed into the carriage. The heavy horses plodded clumsily homeward, clanking their chains, and they jolted through the late-afternoon sunset, suddenly very tired but satisfied, as after a day of hard work, their rifles smelling pleasantly of burnt powder, shot, the dog, and hallooing; Kreuzwendedich's stubbly-haired hound sat trembling among their legs, shivering with excitement and itching from flea bites, and eagerly sniffed the dark air. And then they were back at the castle, and the tenant Grotkopf took his leave with angular politeness, clicking his heels and saying "Heil Hitler," "Happy hunting," and a plain old German "Auf Wiedersehen"—and they were once more among themselves, thank God.

INNER WAS AT SEVEN O'CLOCK IN THE RED drawing room. Sabine in a short silk gown and Fritze in a dark blue suit with a gray waistcoat bridged the distance between the perfection of Baron Peter's dinner jacket and the Prince Albert worn by Count Klützow-Ödemark. Kreuzwende-dich was in uniform (at the sight of which the Baron shivered, for in his subconscious he still feared that an official might come to check his hunting license), and the amiable angel of death flashed his usual pained smile with his sparkling eyes above his silver lieutenant's collar. And then there was Erdmute in a sky-blue dress with a gold brocade sash. Only Pinne Lassow refused to submit to the custom of the festive hour and continued to wear his gamekeeper's coat, though now at least with long trousers. And then the blond thoroughbred made her appearance in a grand evening gown, a wrap of seven silver foxes, a diamond star in the ash-blond mass of her hair that curled down on her glossy naked shoulders. Some gallant shuffling, self-conscious blushing. The smell of roasted meat. It wouldn't be long before they could sit down.

In a moth-eaten livery of Frederician cut, adding the penetrating odor of mothballs to the stable scent, the coachman-cum-footman Wilhelm opened the door to the dining room and announced dinner, whereupon Baron Peter asked Fritze Klützow, "May I help you?" Fritze took his arm. "Why not—but to do what?" "I meant handling the Countess." Fritze declined with thanks: his mother would not dine with them tonight—the strain of a hunt dinner was beyond her strength.

They went to the table. Baron Peter was placed to the left of Sabine and on her right Uncle Ödemark (though a relative, he was the most advanced in age and rank, in addition to being the king of the hunt); next to him was the blond thoroughbred and to the left of Baron Peter, Erdmute. At the lower end of the table, the three remaining men, Fritze, Pinne, and Kreuzwendedich, had to sit together—that couldn't be helped. And: "Never mind, we'll manage to have fun on our own, right, Pinne?" and "Why, yes, Fritze!" and "Won't we, Kreuzwendedich?" Baron Peter piously folded his hands, but tonight there was no prayer, tonight was formal: the chairs were pushed in against the backs of the ladies' knees, and everyone could sit down. Sherry was served with the first course, and then Fritze requested a moment's attention. Unfortunately the bag for the day couldn't be properly displayed since it already had been sent to the butcher shop, but he wanted at least to read off the results, to wit: Count Klützow-Ödemark, seven hares, five recovered (loud bravos from all sides); Mr. von Lassow, four hares and a rabbit; Mr. von Jassilkowski, three hares; Mr. von Bobzien: two and a jay; and he himself had bagged two hares. He wanted to thank his guests for their patience and their excellent aim and now furthermore *bon appétit*. There followed the customary roast with vegetables draped like hay on a harvest wagon along with a thick brown gravy and mashed potatoes. They drank Moselle. The conversation was dominated by Count Klützow-Ödemark, who, having peeled off his oversized yellow coat like an antler shedding its velvet, seemed even taller and craggier than before. His angular head was almost totally bald; ten strands of white hair were glued in painstaking symmetry onto his glistening bare skin. He had no lips whatsoever, and his sentences were crushed flat between his dentures and his constricted larynx and then snarled out from his broadly stretched mouth, cut into his face like a firing slot in a gun turret. His eyes were bright and piercing, encircled by bushy eyebrows and crinkly brownish bags. He conversed mostly with the blond thoroughbred but spoke occasionally to Fritze, Pinne, and Kreuzwendedich, and it seemed to Baron Peter that his remarks were loaded with obscure double meanings.

In fact, the laconic concurrence from the rest of the table, the only thing Count Klützow-Ödemark allowed by way of response, was oddly rigid and self-conscious, as if the conversation were only being kept up for the sake of appearances, followed with half an ear and half a mind. Baron Peter felt as if the company were waiting for something, *awaiting* something, he alone knew not what—indeed, as if everyone were awaiting this unknown, enigmatic something from him. Sabine, the hostess, gave Wilhelm an awkward sign. The great platter with the roast, already once plundered and devastated, was passed around again, while the conversational exchanges became ever more lame and indecipherable. Finally, they congealed into orphic fragments of a strangely nebulous sort offered by Uncle Ödemark and Pinne Lassow, which the others seemed to follow with a certain spiteful glee, but also as if embarrassed at their keen hearing. When the plates had been cleaned for the second time, a rather lengthy pause of collective uneasiness ensued. But even before Sabine could signal Wilhelm to clear the table, the Count resumed the game with Pinne, this time proceeding as in bank-shot billiards, where the cue ball has to carom off two rails before striking any others. He raised his glass to his host and rasped: "I wish to thank you for a most successful shoot, my dear nephew!"

"May I remain seated?" asked Fritze, bowing and raising his own glass to him. Another small pause.

The Count, raising his glass to Baron Peter: "Cheers, Mr. von— eh—"

"Jassilkowski," Pinne helped him out.

"Why, yes, cheers, to Mr. von Jassilkowski!" the Count finished.

Baron Peter replied correctly: "I thank you most humbly, Count Klützow!"

The Count, with a glance at Fritze: "I'm delighted you seem to feel at home in our northerly provinces."

Baron Peter: "I come from East Prussia myself, Count."

The Count, with a surprised look all around: "Oh, I thought you were from Vienna."

"No, district of Pillkallen, Count Klützow."

The Count, this time glancing at Pinne: "Why, in East Prussia you must do a lot of hunting, no?"

Baron Peter: "Indeed, Count Klützow."

The Count: "Oh, well. We here are not exactly South Prussians either."

Pinne Lassow: "Thank God, no. For my part, I'd find it exceedingly painful."

The Count: "Blood is thicker than water . . . Cheers, my good Pinne!"

Pinne Lassow: "Kissyerhand!"

Kreuzwendedich cleared his throat; it sounded artificial. Fritze Klützow pulled himself together and said: "Well, yes . . . then let's go on to dessert. Sabine."

Sabine gave a sign to the coachman. Dinner ended, quickly and silently.

When they were back in the red drawing room for coffee, the general mood once again became halfway relaxed and cheerful. Fritze had some punch served; Kreuzwendedich searched for dance music on the radio and, when he couldn't find any, made do with the phonograph. Wilhelm meanwhile cleared the dining room, and Pinne asked Erdmute to dance. Baron Peter danced with Sabine, and Count Klützow-Ödemark with the blond thoroughbred, whom he held terrifyingly close, his hulking bluish-red murderer's hand cupping her naked armpit, pressing her to him with lewd strength. Gliding past, she directed an amused glance at Peter. "I especially love the world," Count Ödemark could be heard croaking in her ear. "I mean *le grand monde*, of course. I've always felt very much at ease in it . . ." Sabine said: "Uncle Ödemark is charming. A great ladies' man. But don't be alarmed. It's been a long time since he was able."

Later, Peter danced with Erdmute. They danced in silence, but to his astonishment, the girl spit out the following sentence: "I found it quite right that you didn't make a speech." Baron Peter was startled. "Was it expected?" he asked. "I had that feeling but I wasn't king of the hunt." "You sat to the left of the hostess," said Erdmute. "But the international protocol," he defended himself, "gives the guest to the right the place of honor." "Even so," she said implacably, "I myself found it great. Something different for a change." They were silent for a while. "Do you ever come to Berlin?" Baron Peter asked, strangely moved. "No," she said. "In January I am going to Paris to be a fashion designer."

It was getting late and Pinne Lassow was noisily drunk. When told that his coach had arrived (it turned out he was hardly an apprentice gamekeeper but, rather, the well-heeled owner of one of the largest estates in the district), he said grandly, "Let the coachman park in the shade." Then he turned to Baron Peter: "The company was in exceptionally high spirits, wouldn't you say? Your kind would probably think: The swine were stinking drunk, right?" The Baron puffed himself up (Erdmute stood close by) and replied coldly: "It cannot be denied." Pinne exploded with laughter. "It cannot be denied, Fritze, can it?" he shouted, fully satisfied, and briskly smacked Klützow-Klekow's narrow shoulder. "No, it's undeniable! Cheers, Mr. von Jassilkowski! To the district of Pillkallen! Kissyerhand!"

Kreuzwendedich interposed himself skillfully. "Maybe we'll see each other in Berlin," he said. "I'm often in one of those nightspots, the Owl. Two charming Viennese sisters run it."

Uncle Klützow-Ödemark also took his leave (he had meanwhile been dancing the whole time with the blond thoroughbred)—took his leave with unpleasant curtness. Everyone went out to the front stairs with the departing guests and waved goodbye. Count Klützow-Ödemark's car was the last to leave. "That's one horny old geezer," said the thoroughbred, wrapping her silver foxes more tightly around her naked shoulders. "But his day is long gone," repeated Sabine pensively. "Really?" said the thoroughbred. "Then it must have been Kreuzwendedich's flashlight in his pocket."

They went back inside, drank the rest of the punch, and soon said good night and thank you very much. And the next morning, Baron Peter and spouse returned to Berlin.

Only a few know the nature of virtue.
CONFUCIUS, ANALECTS

 O THAT HAD BEEN THE SHOOT AT KLEKOW, and Baron Traugott talked all winter about having to go and finally take the hunting test, as soon as he had a free moment, in order to get back his license. But unfortunately, this was unnecessary because no further invitation to Klekow was forthcoming, even though they had sent their hosts, as thanks for the delightful time, Count Ledebur's *Hunter's Primer* with a poetic inscription in it. It is true that Sabine had written that they should come all by themselves in the spring for a less hectic snipe shoot ("Peter would certainly enjoy it, for it only happens once in a blue moon"), but spring refused to come that year. There was snow in March, and in addition political developments were once more rather worrisome—so their visit was postponed until summer.

That Baron Peter was not involved in those political events, as so many others were, was the result of a circumstance he was never quite able to explain. At the end of February, he was notified that he had been transferred from the cavalry at Ludwigslust to the 9th Infantry Regiment in Potsdam, with which, when notified by its command, he would perform his next exercises. Secretly he suspected cheap revenge on the part of Mrs. von Schrader, who, with her connections, had first opened the ranks of the exclusive 14th Cavalry Regiment to him. But, then, why the 9th, which after all was quite la-de-da, too, and brought him even closer to the Potsdam circle? In any case, the call-up never materialized, so he was still not even a noncommissioned officer and was missing out on the flower war in the Sudetenland. It was some consolation that the charming Kreuz-wendedich also served with the 9th in Potsdam, and together with the blond thoroughbred, the Baron had twice gone to the Owl in

hopes of running into him. He was well known there, of course—
Kreuzwendedich von Bobzien! Oh yes, he came frequently, a loyal
regular, but today of all days he had gone to Küstrin, what a pity,
surely he'd regret it very much. Would they like Mr. Vogel from
Vienna, the Owl's lone entertainer (albeit with vocal assistance from
Irmi), to sing Kreuzwendedich's favorite tune, "The Old Chancery
Clerk"?

Thus, March and April had passed and May begun when one day,
Baron Traugott—I mean, Peter—set out to visit Mrs. von Schrader.

Not only on account of the 14th Cavalry (though he certainly
meant to have a word with her on that) but also because spring had
finally arrived, and the heart simply thaws, you know, at the sound
of thrushes warbling on those first warm evenings—there's nothing,
not a sound on earth more moving, I'm telling you, than the foolish
sweet song of this bird suddenly dripping in through the windows,
open for the first time in the year, above the hum of the big city on
a pigeon-colored evening! . . . And then there's the scent of the
streets on those evenings, the scorched smell of tires on asphalt, the
moistness of a bit of earth around a tree that has grown right there
in an iron basket in the sidewalk; those sweet smooth twigs: Knut
Hamsun's Pan would moan! And that soft air in which noises seem
to hover (even big-city noises are suddenly soft and conciliatory: a
voice rises, words spoken as if in a dream—a human voice!), and
the lights dissolving in the gentle pigeon-blue air and rising like
gossamer toward the heavens, and the mild shadows—shadows in
all the colors of flowers, violet shadows, nightshade shadows . . .
So primarily, as I said, it was spring, and the winter had been so
long, so long and lonely—friends, oh yes, all kinds of friends and
noise and gay turmoil and boozing and Charley's Bar, but alien,
alien—how shall I put it?—a world that wasn't his own, a reality
he had never wished for—ah, your dreams! . . . And now it was
spring, and he was in a tender mood and very much himself, not
Peter with his pipe and capstan, but simply Traugott, Herzeloyde's
son (who knew of this secret nobility?) . . . and then, secondarily,
there was the matter of small arrears in past rent, which had to be
cleared up—enough: Baron Traugott set out to visit Mrs. von
Schrader.

It was teatime—a familiar hour—and when he rang the bell, it was good old Else who opened the door, saw him standing there, and said pointedly (already anticipating her mistress's possible reaction): "Oh, it's you! But Mrs. von Schrader has visitors."

"Tell her I won't disturb her long," said Baron Traugott with a smile. She retreated hesitantly, and he entered.

"One moment, please!" she said, still of two minds (after all, two rooms were vacant just then). She left him waiting and went back to announce him.

Strange to find himself waiting there, where he had once gone around with the heedlessness of someone in his own home or, better still, like a paying tenant whose rights supersede the owner's. The ever thick, musty air and enforced quiet of the boardinghouse were no longer maintained for his well-being but now seemed like a bulwark of silence directed against him. (How often had he, as carefree tenant, cast an indifferent yet curious glance at someone standing there, someone who was not yet or no longer in his position. Anyone coming out of a nearby room and walking through the corridor would look him over, Baron Traugott Jassilkowski, with the same assessing detachment and move on with the same unabashed lassitude, while he waited there, not daring to advance to the center of the room.)

Else—she didn't need to say a word to let him know that Mrs. von Schrader, with a tone of astonishment tinged with irony (a barely perceptible raising of the eyebrows) and the haughty pathos of a fortune-teller, had said in her nasal voice: "Why, show him in!"; he could see it in the old servant's stiff offended expression, the look of someone compelled to follow an order running counter to all sound reason. And since the order had been issued contrary to her expectations, she now hoped to be proven correct that he was up to no good, an outcome she tried to bring about by her sullen demeanor.

"But Their Highnesses are here for tea," she said in admonishment, her tone betraying something of the reluctant protective feeling, the old-maid, mother-hen affection that long-serving domestics in boardinghouses often develop for some of their younger tenants.

"What highnesses?" asked Baron Traugott.

"Prince and Princess Hohenheim-Ambach and their niece, Countess Schlierstedt," replied Else with the fluency of someone on intimate terms with well-known persons of high rank. She went ahead and opened the door to the boudoir. Baron Traugott entered.

Alienation! The old boudoir to which he had been so accustomed was no more. The curtain separating it from the Schraders' nuptial chamber had disappeared, as had the beds themselves: there before him was a freshly painted and papered, somewhat sketchily furnished, proper drawing room, in which the princely personages and their niece sat at the tea table and, with them, clearly demonstrating her equal rank, Mrs. von Schrader herself.

"What a rare honor!" she said in nasally ringing tones, offering him her hand to be kissed. "May I introduce you: Mr. von Jassilkowski—Prince and Princess Hohenheim-Ambach, Countess Schlierstedt. Else, bring a cup for the Baron." (Was this ironic? Or had she used the title accidentally, subconsciously influenced by the loftiness of her present company? Or had she simply found it awkward to introduce Their Highnesses to a mere "von," a member of such low petty nobility, as it was called?)

The Prince got up and almost upset his teacup in the process. He was small and very dainty, dressed with the utmost modesty, even shabbiness, and had the overeager politeness of the very shy. He shook hands with Baron Traugott and bowed several times, then hastily withdrew his hand as if fearing he had gone too far, sat down, and greedily began to eat as if starving. Little could be made of the Princess's expression, for her face was concealed by a broad-brimmed hat, a towering structure with ribbons and swatches, extravagantly old-fashioned and yet persuasively idiosyncratic; it sat on her head like a confectioner's cake. She, too, was small, dainty, and the gracefulness of her gestures was all the more remarkable because her quick, delicate movements with their ferretlike, restless animation seemed to occur independently of her will: while her body sat in cake-crowned immobility, her hands scurried about like a swarm of playful mice.

Countess Schlierstedt was a true beauty, of Parisian elegance. She couldn't be much older than twenty-four, and her black eyes, knowing and cool, took in Baron Traugott with lazy indifference, as he bowed over her hand.

He drew up a chair, and a place was made for his plate and cup. They spoke with elegant, nasal Austrian drawls, the *s*'s very sharp. (Even Mrs. von Schrader's accent, inherited from her mother, Countess Rumpfburg-Schottenfels, had become more pronounced, the Baron noticed.) With the appropriate courtesy, the Princess turned to the newly arrived guest and said, "We were jusst sspeaking of Princess Schönstein-Hohenschönstein, the former Duchess of Branca—you know her, I suppose."

Baron Traugott said he did not.

"A mosst elegant persson," said the Princess, as if recommending the aforementioned in the highest terms.

The Prince looked up nervously from his plate. "I tidn't think so," he said. "She wore exactly the ssame hat you tid." Hastily, he resumed eating.

"Iss she really a Branca?" asked Mrs. von Schrader. "Issn't she the sisster of Izabel Schönbrunn, the sisster-in-law of my Aunt Lentschi, who iss a Montezuccoli."

"No, no, my tear!" said the Princess, her hands dancing like jolly elves. "The sisster-in-law of Lentschi, that iss the wife of her brother. She iss a Caccio-Cavallo."

"Sso she can't be a real Branca," said the Prince, "if she iss a Caccio-Cavallo."

"We can alwayss look it up in the *Court Calendar*," suggested Mrs. von Schrader with impartial assurance.

"But, my dear Max," said the Princess, "Bubi attended the wedding himsself."

"Pubi lies," said His Highness sharply. "He wrote me the other tay that he wass ssenting me ssome sstamps, but he never tid."

"Well, be that ass it may, she'ss a Branca," said the Princess, nodding at Baron Traugott with a smile and winking conspiratorially, as if to assure him that he needn't worry, he could trust her absolutely, without minding anyone else.

"We can look it up," Countess Schlierstedt said, and stood up.

"The Gothas are right over there, Melanie," said Mrs. von Schrader with the comfortable composure of an elder relative who needn't bother to move when young women are around.

Baron Traugott had also jumped up. But Melanie was already at the bookshelf and returned with the *Court Calendar*. Standing, she

189

was disappointingly short and stocky. The beauty of her upper body, which had made her look like a queen when she was seated, was canceled out by disproportionately broad hips and short legs. Yet her feet, in very narrow small shoes, had a fascinating elegance. "Here, look it up," she said to Baron Traugott, and gave him the book.

He began to turn pages, and the Countess came to his aid. "No, you have do look in the third ssection." She took the book from Baron Traugott and leafed through it. Then the Princess grasped for the book without looking at her; as if her index finger were equipped with an eye, like the arm of a starfish, it riffled through the pages, then pointed to the relevant paragraph. "Here you'll find what we're looking for. It's the second paragraph. Read what it ssays!"

Baron Traugott read: "Pr. + Duke (H.H.) Eberhard Engelbert Ferdinand Maria Anton Eusebius Johann Baptist Joseph Friedrich Leopold Bonaventura, * Lemberg (Lvov), 14 Feb. 1887, R'l & Imp'l Cpt. (Ret.), High Knight o. Malt., Kn. o. Bav., O. St. George; × Piacenza, 4 July 1912, Giuseppina Marcella Giovanna Francisca Anna Alessandra Adelaide Maria Tommasina Maddalena"—"Dat's her, our Lentschi," the Prince interjected happily—"Paola Angela Pia Pallavicini, house o. Marchesi Pallavicini . . ."

"There you have it," said the Princess triumphantly. "She iss a Pallavicini, and not a Branca and not a Montezuccoli and not a Caccio-Cavallo." She nodded again to Baron Traugott from under the cake brim in conspiratorial accord, as if this had been settled between the two of them. "Thankss sso much. Thankss sso much."

"Sso she can't be a sisster of Lentschi Schönbrunn either, this Lentschi," the Prince concluded stubbornly, "if that one wass indeed a Branca."

"And by the way, what iss Mutzi up do?" asked Mrs. von Schrader with suggestive emphasis, or so it seemed to Baron Traugott, who also caught the more than casual glance directed at Countess Schlier-stedt. "Sstill the ssame?"

Countess Schlierstedt remained silent.

"Aunt Lentschi wass a bit worried when I lasst ssaw her," continued Mrs. von Schrader, cutting through the thickening silence.

"Dear Got," said the Princess with almost youthful grace, *"elle n'a pas le talent de conserver les affections* and hass fallen in with a rather fasst crowd."

"Incidentally," said Countess Schlierstedt, "the other day in Frankfurt at the Hohenburgers' I med a man, ssimply the funniesst thing: a perfect Count Bobby. Actually he wass called Mr. Gruber or ssomething of that ssort, but a perfect Bobby, right down to the way he talked, everything, totally backwardss . . ."

"What? A con man?" asked the Prince, looking up from his plate with militant suspicion.

"Nod ad all," said Countess Schlierstedt, "just a Mr. Gruber from Vienna."

A brief sticky pause ensued. The subject was changed. Baron Traugott turned to Mrs. von Schrader and complimented her on the Pension Bunsen's redecoration. She acknowledged him with a stiff haughtiness that scarcely concealed an underlying satisfaction, as if to suggest that quite a few things had changed since his departure. Out loud, she merely said: "We have more space now. Cerdain developmentss have daughd uss that it is better not to have long-derm denandss, so we changed Number Five into our private bedroom."

The Princess sought Mrs. von Schrader's hand with one of her own elfin ones, patted it, and said, "She'ss a courageouss liddle one, I ssay!"

Baron Traugott made further inquiries, and Mrs. von Schrader's brusque answers clearly meant to imply that he enjoyed this courtesy only in consideration of the presence of Their Highnesses and the exalted atmosphere emanating from them. Meanwhile the Princess was talking to her niece. The Baron heard Countess Schlierstedt say to her aunt in a slightly subdued voice (as if what she was telling her, although she was much too self-assured for secrets, was not meant for everyone's ears): "Believe me, tear Aunt Ada, you'll find it incredible but many people have dold me, and it wass confirmed by almosst everyone I assked—and I've assked almosst everyone— thad thesse dayss in ssociety, thad iss even in our circles, there'ss hartly a young lady who iss faithful to her hussband. It'ss a fact. Everyone sayss sso. I could name namess, my tear Aunt Ada, you'd be aghasst. And only the other tay, a certain well-known persson told me in Munich it'ss ssaid that in ssociety, that iss in our circles, there iss only one young couple who are an exception, and that'ss Engi and I. And then the ssame well-known persson told me—and thiss will interesst you—that it's ssaid thiss iss only tue to my having had ssuch a sstrict Catholic upbringing."

"Ssee, there you go," said the Princess energetically.

They turned once more to the others. Mrs. von Schrader offered cake to the Prince, who accepted it with thanks and devoured it hungrily, as they continued to chat about this and that. Finally, after an appropriate interval, the Baron gave Mrs. von Schrader to understand that he wished to settle a small business matter pending with her and needed a moment of her time before taking his leave. Mrs. von Schrader asked to be excused for a moment to attend to the Baron. "But of coursse, my tear, ton't let uss tedain you," said the Princess. "I undersstand: bussiness, bussiness affairs—who doesn't have them these dayss." She patted Mrs. von Schrader's hand again and murmured: "She'ss a courageouss liddle one!" She nodded approvingly, giving Mrs. von Schrader to understand that she could always count on her appreciation of that courage and that she should carry on as before.

When Traugott bowed to her, she took his hand and covered it: "Goodbye, my dear Baron Jaschczinsky!" she said, raising her head and allowing him for the first time to see her eyes under the brim of the cake hat. These eyes were stunningly beautiful, of a radiant sapphire blue. But it was not only their color and sheen that made such an impression on him: they were filled with GOODNESS.

That almost bowled him over. He was still somewhat in a trance when he stood with Mrs. von Schrader in the hallway and tried with some composure, under her cold stare, to explain the long delay in payment. And behold: simply and from his heart, without forethought, he managed it all very well, and then he kissed her hand quickly and said, "Thank you so much, thank you so much."

She looked at him, and suddenly there were tears in her eyes.

Outside, spring was in the evening air, and he could have bawled like a baby—*goodness*, man!—so it still existed, existed in spite of everything, a loftier form of humanity—*nobility!*—so he hadn't dreamed in vain, only dreamed mistakenly, dreamed too small—oh, the errors! The horrible blindness of our window-shopping existence, the corruption of our indoctrination by advertising, the devilish bane of class differences! *Goodness*, man! . . .

Spring was in the evening air—rustles of spring—and a secret lurked in the hydrangea-colored lights on the Kurfürstendamm, Easter promise in the provincial side streets, and he might have continued strolling for hours, out into the violet-blue dusk, out into the hidden buds and rising sap of the Grunewald, and farther on into the darkening countryside (to Potsdam, who knows, perhaps all the way to the Neue Garten!)—but he wanted to preserve all that was in him like a pearl in the shell of his heart instead of letting it seep out into the shoreless sea of emotion—wanted to let the overpowering revelation grow quietly like a seed corn within himself. *Goodness*, man!

So he went home without any detours and found the little apartment empty; a slip of paper on the bureau in the hallway told him that the blond thoroughbred had dropped in on a girlfriend and expected to be home around seven. So he sat down at his desk and did nothing but look through the window at the spring sky, pondering, thinking. The thoroughbred came home, he heard her opening the front door with her key, then she came in, stopped, and turned on the ceiling light. "You're here?!" she said. "Why don't you turn on the lamp, Sweet Pete?"

She came over and kissed him, and he closed his eyes and let himself enjoy the feminine Chanel scents, the soft tickle of her fur stole, the cool smoothness of her cheek.

"Are you unhappy?" she asked. He shook his head and said, "No, on the contrary"—but did happiness and sadness really ever occur one without the other? And she said: "Come on! I'll make something extra-tasty for dinner" (dear terrible vital force!). And then she stormed through the two small rooms, strewing about her fur and handbag, her gloves and hat, then put everything quickly and efficiently back in place, returned in a snow-white lab coat and showed him all the delicacies she had purchased on impulse and brought back with her. "Look! Lobster mayonnaise! I know what my Sweet Pete likes!" And a bottle of wine to chill, that was his task as the master of the house. "But why won't you turn on your desk lamp? You're ruining your eyes!"

(Oh, is that the only thing that ruins our eyes?)

He let her turn on the desk lamp—ever since Castle Klekow it had been put there, the old night-table lamp of good Miss Bremse with the pink silk shade, decorated with a ring of glued-on puffy-cheeked children in Biedermeier costume. (Why not show some piety for his dear old childhood horrors, too? Were they not also the residue of a simple, devout, and dutiful life?) He remained seated and pretended to prepare to write but merely stared past the lampshade at the nighttime spring sky, which had darkened to the hue of a nocturnal flower.

"Do you still have work to do, Sweet Pete?" asked the thoroughbred. (Horrendous old proximity of life!) And he said, "Yes," and she said "What on?" and he said, "An article about shoes. The leather industry has taken out two pages of ads . . ." And then he faltered, for it suddenly occurred to him that it is industry which creates our ideals. "Write it quickly and then we'll make ourselves really comfortable, okay?" said the blond thoroughbred, kissing him again as she stormed out. (Dreadful, yet captivating existential joy!) And there he sat and thought. What was he thinking? Alas, I don't know. Maybe nothing other than: *The pink light that appears and then fades over and over in the sky there above the rooftops is surely the Sarotti mooring sign. You can also see it glowing from Knese-beckstrasse. I'm glad our apartment gives out on the courtyard and not on the street. There's something so deeply moving about an empty, neglected courtyard on a spring evening in the middle of a big city. But Knesebeckstrasse was also nice. The thrushes used to warble under the windows there, the narrow alley was quiet, and yet an excited hum came over from the Kurfürstendamm. How very much alone you were there!* —And maybe he thought: *When one is alone, one is filled with dreams.* —Or maybe he thought: *I should just start writing my article on shoes, just begin it. Never think about* that, *but simply carry on, "a courageouss liddle persson," and let everything develop from there. Never lose it! But carry on in the meantime! Shoes, for instance. What elegant shoes that Melanie Schlierstedt had on her dachshund legs!* —But it may well be that he was thinking of something altogether different, of anything whatsoever—I wouldn't know, as I said. What does someone think who has been suddenly confronted by sheer goodness? How the devil should I know?

And then the thoroughbred stormed back in, having quickly and efficiently prepared a succulent dinner, and he followed her silver-belled call; they sat down and spread napkins over their knees. The windows were wide open, the spring evening was warm and mild, they ate lobster mayonnaise and a small steak each with wine, the thoroughbred nattered on about her girlfriend and peeled an orange and, much as he resisted, insisted on popping the tart slices one by one into his mouth, and the evening, darkening outside to a deep lilac, carried over to them the sound of steps from the courtyard and a soft human voice. And then he sat down once more at his desk and prepared paper, pen, pipe, tobacco, and ashtray, together with the latest issues of *Esquire* and *Gentleman's Monthly* and *Adam*, placed his pocket Knaur dictionary within easy reach next to his Duden Unabridged, and doodled and shilly-shallied around until it got too cool to keep the window open, and so he shut it, nodded to the thoroughbred in an encouraging and reassuring way, as if to intimate that she was to go on as before and that she was a courageous little person—all the while being close to tears, overcome by emotion at the thought of so much goodness in the world. Then he sat down again and painstakingly lit his pipe.

The thoroughbred, too, was seated—no, rather, she lay, hung, nestled, creeperlike, her luxurious limbs relaxed with snaky flexibility in the chintz armchair before the fireplace. She hung there like an anaconda from a branch. As usual on intimate evenings at home, undisturbed by visitors or entertainment plans, she wore a spare, airy two-piece outfit, appropriate for the always overheated rooms, abbreviated shorts and a striped tank top. She dangled her naked thighs over the armrest and crossed and intertwined her legs. Her soft, dyed-red Moroccan-leather house slippers contrasted sharply with the luminous shimmer of her silken skin. Her torso, her deluxe bosom, and her hips were hidden, for she had twisted her upper body around so that she could bury her chin in her arms on the backrest. Her head, crowned by that shower of blond hair, seemed to lack a corresponding body, like that of the snake lady in the sideshow booth at last year's fair. She held her head still, and her violet eyes stared at him through her horn-rimmed glasses, her eyebrows raised enigmatically, with a Giocondan smile on her lips. From time to time, she freed one arm from this position with a lazy slithery movement and let it fall and swing over a box of chocolates at her feet. Her long fingers with their sharp scarlet nails searched idly among the frilly paper cornets in the box until they found a filled one; then her arm lazily withdrew, looking boneless, and transferred the sweet to her mouth, which then chewed it with pouting enjoyment: *she was bored.* She had a few books from the lending library lying next to the chocolates, but she was in no mood to read. Outside, spring had arrived, the evening was mild, and the overheated radiators brought the temperature in the room to that of a greenhouse, which made her skin prickle. She lay, hung, nestled in animal wellbeing, her tendons and joints voluptuously relaxed, thoughtless and satisfied. Her boredom was saturated by the pleasantly regular rhythm of her healthy breathing, her powerful circulation, and her perfectly maintained glandular functions.

"Would you like a chocolate?" asked the mouth in the middle of this motionless head, violet eyes looking at him from beneath the twin arches of eyebrows and spectacle frames. She had a child's soft voice (Mrs. von Schrader's voice was lush and rich like a tropical sunset)—a little child's voice which, in tender moments, she diligently cultivated and which, at present, eerily heightened the sideshow magic of her snake lady's head.

"No, thank you," he said, with melancholy patience.

She continued to chew and pout for a while, not taking her eyes from him. She then changed positions—her naked thighs rubbed audibly and suggestively together, while she freed and then once more entwined her legs; her arms lifted her head slightly and placed it farther up on the chair.

Baron Traugott was growing irritated by her steady gaze.

"Why would the leather industry still buy full-page ads?" asked the mouth with the Giocondan smile. "Don't they already have enough orders for army boots?" (She was indulging her boredom.)

"Maybe they have to," Baron Traugott said, with brisk patience. "As a diversion."

(Thereby giving us a few more ideals, he thought.)

She felt around in the box of sweets and licked and sucked her chocolate-smeared fingers. "Is it really hard to write something snappy about footwear?" asked the mouth.

"Yes. No. Not particularly," he said, drawing patience from his immense reserve of human goodness.

(The sky was hyacinth blue. What captivating elegant feet this little Schlierstedt girl had!)

"But you haven't even started," said the mouth.

"I'm thinking of something else at the moment," said the Baron. *(Didn't she know that at that instant he felt like the virgin Mettelil, playing her golden harp, breasts swollen with milk?)*

"You're boring," came the child's voice from her mouth.

He did not answer.

"Am I your little birdie?" asked the mouth.

"Yes, you're my little birdie," he answered, with terrifying patience.

"And are you my puma?" asked the mouth.

He did not answer.

"You're boring," said the mouth with its Giocondan smile. "Come on: I'll tell you a riddle. What is it that growls and grumbles, loves to be petted, has pointy ears and a small . . . tail?"

"Your puma," he said with eerie patience, gazing into the hyacinth blue beyond the windowpanes.

All of a sudden, she let herself fall from the backrest. The head with the Giocondan smile disappeared. Her folded arms had disappeared, too, and she had drawn her thighs under herself. She was so tightly balled up that he could no longer see her.

"You're boring," she sulked from within the chair. "Give me a piece of paper, and I'll show you how to write an article in no time."

He threw her paper and pencil and then bent over his work. He heard her rustling and shuffling but he didn't turn around; he pretended he was writing himself and secretly dreaded her sudden laughter, for he was sure she wasn't doing anything sensible but was merely inspired to doodle something, some sort of grotesque animal, a rutting unicorn with seven eyes and steaming nostrils, which she would then show to him with a jubilant cry: "Look, there you are!" . . . Still, when he stole a glance at her after a while, she was sitting upright, chewing on a pencil and looking pensively into the fireplace, then in fact she put pencil to paper and started to write with her rapid and bold strokes.

"Peter," she said after a good half hour (outside, the night had turned deep indigo), "look what I've written."

She came over and placed a sheet of paper in front of him. He read:

"It's not only the clothes that make the man but also the shoes. Ever since the Greeks strutted about in high-laced buskin sandals across open-air stages, the shoe has been more than a necessary and effective protection on life's thorny paths. The shoe is the crowning touch on the overall impression made by elegant people everywhere—even though this crown must be trod on by delicate feet. It is the infallible identifying mark of its wearer's character and social station. It supplies the rhythm for the melody of everyday life. For the easy tempo of morning, a crepe sole floats over city pavements, and in the evening, the stiletto heels of beautiful women beat out a staccato like castanets on the dance floor. It was from the shoe of his mistress that the playboy of yore drank his champagne. And the otherwise almost completely nude beauty queen would be less assured of exciting the desired response without her graceful five-inch heels, which make her legs appear so long and flawless. The shoe is like the picture of Dorian Gray. The sins of its wearer leave wrinkles in the glossy finish of its smooth leather, each false step bends it out of shape. Show me your shoe, and I'll tell you who you are!"

Oh well. *Mulier taceat in ecclesia.*

"Let's go to bed," said Baron Traugott. "I don't know what's the matter with me today. Spring fatigue, I suppose."

She looked at him. Her maternal instinct told her that somehow he was suffering. "It was just a joke, Sweet Pete," she said. And then she added in a low voice, "Would you like to pop by Charley's?"

"No," he said, "not tonight."

"Well, then, let's go beddy-bye!" she exclaimed cheerfully, confident of her powers of consolation.

And then they went to bed and—behold: this, after all, was the best she had to give, and give it she did—dear heaven, of course, she loved to give it to him, in fact she was delighted (the air was so warm and mild and, anyway, she had been looking forward to it all evening long)—she gave it to him lovingly, as I said, and quite differently than she had to anyone before. For she truly loved him, her Sweet Pete, and she was happy in his arms and much too natural and uninhibited, too confident in the blissful awareness of her own magnificently robust carnality, ever to suppose that he was not equally happy in her arms. This made her tender ministrations powerfully despotic.

And he was defenseless. He shrank from the naked brutality and offensive intimacy of her loving embrace, but the sweetness of the resplendent darkness, of intoxicating self-oblivion, lured him on (was she not like a bit of death?) and so he abandoned himself—kindly wipe that smirk off your face!—yes, he abandoned himself to her, to her and to the blissful feeling of being extinguished in her maternal womb.

Thus have I had thee, as a dream doth flatter,
In sleep a king, but waking no such matter.
SHAKESPEARE, SONNET

 UDDENLY IN THE MIDDLE OF THE NIGHT IT
happened that he woke up. He had dreamed, and
that's what woke him. His dream was horrible
and at the same time tormentingly lustful. In the
darkness he could hear the even breathing of the
thoroughbred next to him. He turned on the bed
lamp and looked at her, lying lovely in her sleep,
one cheek cupped in her hand. Her loosened hair
foamed out over the crumpled pillows in devastating silky blond
fullness, windswept like the locks of Botticelli's Venus. Her red-
enameled nails stood out against the whiteness of her hands. Her
lips, bare of lipstick and softened by kisses and touchingly pale, were
slightly parted. She was breathing lightly and regularly, like a child.

What he had dreamed was this: He had woken beside her, as was
now actually the case. But she had not been alone: a man lay next
to her, some male. His hair was cut short, and he had knotted muscles
with the oiled sheen and good proportions of a circus athlete. His
thick black mustache, waxed and brushed into two spikes like a
sergeant major's, together with the seed-pale whiteness of his skin,
gave him the repulsive masculinity of pornographic photos. She, too,
had been naked, warmly full-blooded, her bodily cavities giving off
their scents, and she had laughed at him, Baron Traugott—her
husband!—with the baby-toothed grin of a whore; they had both
laughed, as they lay there sinfully close, mute and unmoving like
puppets, their scorn shaking the dead dream air. And he had been
powerless against them.

Powerless from weakness and from lust. For it had been lust to
see her thus, as nothing but body, coupling, sex: nothing but sin.
And there had been lust in the humiliation he felt from the whore's
laughter, paralyzing, marrow-sucking lust in impotence when con-

fronted by the coldhearted vengeance of her eyes. Lust was his weakness. He had tried, neurasthenically, to drive them apart, but they had simply wiped him away with their laughter—what cheek!—nipping his effort in the bud, merciless in their twosomeness: powerful, indomitable, sovereign in sin, elevated in their laughter high above his little shit fit and wormlike wriggling. And he still felt this degradation as blissful lassitude in his limbs and joints. His heart was beating in anxious hard strokes.

So there he lay, half upright, and looked down on her. She was wearing a nightgown of fragrant linen, its gathered bodice decorated with a border of harmless white embroidered blossoms (oh, he had cured her of her taste for movie-star negligees!). A strap had slid from her shoulder, her skin was smooth and still tan from last summer. She slept soundly and healthily, her face glistening with fresh night cream. Her pale lips turned up slightly at the corners in the beginning of that cute, pouting smile he knew so well: all her cheerfully insolent lightheartedness, her roguish and playful tenderness, her droll and childishly headstrong temperament lay in it. Under the covers the contours of her body were clearly visible, large format, well proportioned, luxurious, radiating health and life, suntanned and well aired by Berlin breezes—golf-links limbs, a Lido beach goddess. And sleep, the deep unencumbered sleep of a child (the highest mark of genius, according to Kierkegaard, isn't that right?) spread over her like innocence, clothing her in innocence as the fine white linen of her maiden nightgown did her voluptuous body. A hint of British steel lingered over her, fresh as pine needles, pure as malted milk, the scent of spacious and well-waxed nurseries, dried-lavender nannies, big bright hygienically shining rubber balls, pale milk-and-roses playmates and golden childhood tresses, well brushed twice a day.

And he passionately hated the deceit in this naive, nursery-rhyme innocence, this fake purity; hated the saucy, ribbon-wearing, pony-coach-driving carelessness that let such sinless indulgence of her every carnal appetite develop; hated, with a zealot's venom and with the dark misery of the damned glowering in his heart, her deluxe soapy-fresh childhood that had never ever been dimmed by the dull vapors of servile moralism.

At the same time he desired her with an intensity he had never before known or experienced. As if suddenly the most secret dungeons of his soul were torn open (those subterranean chambers into which we force our abominations, the sediments of our lowest impulses and most sinful insinuations, locking them up behind bulkheads, rat cellars of the soul), as if they suddenly opened, the flood of irrepressible, self-destructive lust for the vulgar and the obscene and the filthy that swelled over him only intensified his desire. He had to stop from throwing himself on her as she lay there sleeping (perhaps she wouldn't even wake up, would just writhe lazily and voluptuously under his greedy hands, panting with her eyes closed while she took him within her, not even recognizing him, would go on dreaming, uninhibited, experiencing everything she, too, had repressed and sealed away—and what was it in her case?—and never ever would he possess her entirely, would always be only a mediator, devil's pimp, witch's incubus . . .).

There she lay breathing like a child. And he gazed on her innocence, the absence of sinfulness typical of well-brought-up people, that golden derision, which makes the trouble of virtue seem pointless, negates the prize of effort and denies achievement—which invalidates the sweat of the ascetic and makes the flagellant's blood flow in vain. What was it: *purity?* The sharp spurt of cold water from a faucet on a frosty September morning—or a bubble bath, frosted-glass lamps, heated Turkish towels, perfume of hard-currency munificence? Behold her bloody fingernails, as they bear witness against it, the claws of Astaroth: they tear the flesh from the bones of the righteous and, like daggers, penetrate their hearts! Fear them, hate them, persecute them, trample their unconscionable glory to a pulp, crush their bright-eyed guilelessness! For they are the *evil ones*, they who are the masters of themselves from the start, who clothe their shameless nudity in white linen, fine and soft as down, while beneath they rut like sleek beasts, beautiful and well fed, sinfully corrupt, their limbs wrought of gold, contracting and relaxing in indolent enjoyment.

He hated her. But even more so he hated himself, hated his flesh and its impetuous desire, this feverish, sweat-soaked lust which shook him, this wasting hollow pull in the pit of his stomach, this marrowless fluttering in his joints. He lay quite still so as not to rouse her, snake that she was; so as not to incite her limbs to the typically slow, slithery, slippery, fleshly envelopment, which he feared like nettles and fire on his skin but also desired—with the ardor of fear and raging need, screaming for it with the mute cry of someone tortured by lust. He lay motionless and stared down at her.

A gnawing, piercing pressure in his lower abdomen alerted him that he desperately needed to piss. This discomfort may also have entered his dream. He recollected another image (*recollected*, indeed: the other image *collected* from some realm within him and now paralyzed his normal senses): how the tormenting, lustful plight of his powerlessness had lent him (unforseeably and to his own dismay) a terrifying strength, how—as if an evil, ghostly hand were directing his arm—he had struck out blindly and repeatedly with his fist, which suddenly was holding the estate manager's rod, and how he hammered on the bristly head of the circus-booth athlete, while the naked thoroughbred kept smiling her whore's smile, until the head caved in with a muffled crack and exploded, bursting like a ripe pumpkin. Blood had squirted up, drenching the rod, his fist, and his arm; it had streamed over the thoroughbred, puddled up around the two of them, a pool, a pond, and then a shoreless lake cornering him, rising higher and higher . . . shame overwhelmed and annihilated him, shame at an outrage that could not even be endorsed as his own (it had occurred against his will and contrary to any of his intentions when he was trapped in humiliation and degradation— it wasn't *his* deed). The water rose, and as he realized with terror and horror (against his will, but yet with guilt, primal guilt) that he had murdered his father, it seemed that the promise of ineffable and unearthly bliss, transfigured redemption, ultimate liberation was sinking, foundering, dissolving in those dark, abysmal, and shoreless waters, to become one with them. And only one final insurmountable inhibition saved him from slipping in with them.

Murdered his father. Yes, indeed. For that disgusting, gnarled, whitish, pornographic-postcard model with the sergeant major's mustache (horrible how the wormlike folds of the bristly skin on his head had burst under his relentless blows!), that randy circus

athlete: that had been Papá. And at the same time in this terrible
dream, the blond thoroughbred had merged and become inter-
changeable with another being (which had given her that iridescent
inscrutability and oppressive familiarity, the familiarity of a close
intimate, of someone completely on to him: the accusation of silent
comprehension): *with Mamá.*

There he lay, and it was night. Silence. The light breathing of the
thoroughbred. Lust, weakness, anguish. He got up in awkward silence and went to the bathroom. When he returned the blond whore
had rolled over; with an animal's infallible instinct, her body, accustomed to comfort, had sensed the cozy prewarmed space in the
bed, and a shimmer of happy satisfaction could be detected on her
face, glimmering with night cream. He nudged her back over to her
own side without waking her (it was easier for him now to touch
her, although her childlike innocence was more tempting than that
of the lightly clothed, sleeping St. Lidoire, who was got with child
from an evil-minded passerby; nonetheless, his feeling of weakness
only increased as his shame grew, for his weakness was the weakness
of shame)—and he lay down cautiously next to her and turned off
the bed light.

And there he lay, and it was night. Silence, but for the light innocent breathing of the thoroughbred. Painful incomplete voiding,
remnants of anguish, weakness, anxiety: it was night, and demons
were on the loose, the slavering nightmares and raging banshees,
and the vampires descending like shadows and rising heavy and
plump with blood, and the ones with no names that press down and
melt away, that sprawl across you and suffocate you, and the ones
that scornfully surround you, and the ones that admonish you in
toneless blind words like bell strokes under water, and the ones that
have already passed a judgment on you that cannot be appealed. It
was night, and the roofs pressed heavily down on the confused tangle
of boxy houses, so crammed together, the heavy ceilings of rooms
sank on people sleeping within—night, filled with moans and groans,
unconscious helpless snores, children's whimpers; darkness pierced
by glances that suck at you—quick thieves' glances, slow burning
glances of people overcome by envy, demented glances of murderers
and pale terror-struck glances from their victims. Night. Silence. The

soft, provocatively innocent, mockingly pure breathing of the thoroughbred. Her scent of night cream, hair, and woman. And weakness and exhaustion. And anguish, and shame and lust (the lust of shame). Sweat beaded on his forehead and hands, and humiliation gaped in his heart. He knew what had happened to him in his dream (it had been with him from the beginning). And he also knew how all at once it had become so huge and overwhelming. He had known this, too, from the beginning—truly, I tell you: no man lies to himself in his heart of hearts.

And it surrounded him ("for the night gave me a name"—right?—"which would be greatly feared by anyone who chanced by day to learn it")—it stood around him and named itself, admonishing him in toneless blind words like bell strokes under water (the bells of Vineta that call up the dead)—it stood around him and had passed a judgment that could not be appealed. He knew that he bore the mark of a mysterious curse, a divine curse, ignominious and horrible, like the plague or leprosy; that he was stricken with something unspeakable, contemptible, with a destiny that came from primal guilt and at the same time clothed him in a new, most deplorable innocence: the innocence of not-being-able-to-do-otherwise. And he knew there would be no redemption for him—*save in death*.

But when he woke again (for he had finally fallen asleep, crushed, probably, overwhelmed by that huge darkness—he knew not when and how; only his exhaustion and the heavy sluggishness of his limbs made him realize that it was quite late)—when he woke again, it was morning and rain was streaming down the windowpanes. The thoroughbred had been up and about for a long time and was bustling in the next room with the cleaning lady. He rose wearily and went to the bathroom. She joined him there as he stood idly watching the water run ("lacking in deeds and heavy with thought," as my colleague Hölderlin says); he endured her cheerfully fresh morning tenderness with both genuine and pretended fogginess, and she laughed at him and called him her old sleepy Peter and brought him his breakfast while he was in the tub, buttering his rolls and popping little honey-dripping pieces into his mouth—wholly absorbed in this quintessential maternal act of feeding, her much-kissed, heavily lipsticked, pouting mouth pantomiming how to chew and then bravely swallow, as one does instinctively with small children. This tortured him horribly, and he would have loved to bite her finger, but even that was too much for him. He understood what it was that had made her intertwine and flow together with his mother in his dream: the craftiest and most secret of all sins, the preservation of evil by means of guilty love.

To escape her and be alone for the day, he pretended to have business downtown that would keep him busy until evening. Because she insisted, he finally agreed to meet her at seven o'clock in Charley's Bar. Moved by a deep innate knowledge of the magic power of attire, he dressed with special care and studied elegance. But there, too, something had changed, something was new: what motivated him was not merely the ancient secret urge to transform the self, to disguise oneself so as to fool the demons; it was a need for solemnity. His dressing routine was sublimated into a cultish act: he wore his gray chalk-striped worsted as if it were an insignia of man's way on earth, a suit of armor, a coronation robe, or a hair shirt. Then he went out. As he left, the thoroughbred kissed him heartily right on the mouth.

ENSE, LIGHT RAIN HAD FALLEN ALL NIGHT—
relentlessly, with springtime intensity, in watery
veils that seemed to rise and fall at the same time
(you can see this in sudden showers at sea)—and
finally petered out toward morning, though the
sky was still overcast with gray mist, moisture was
in the air, and all of yesterday's earthy, seed-
plumping, thick-gushing and sticky-swelling, sap-
drawing, or otherwise spring-signaling scents were now drowned;
it smelled of rainwater and nothing else, which proved once again
that the weather in our climes only rarely produces atmospheric
effects suitable for emphasizing or contradicting exceptional states
of the human soul; that's why I recommend that, save as further
evidence of our general unconnectedness in this as in other respects,
weather be used only sparingly as an artistic device.

I regret this all the more because my concern for decency forbids
me to describe Mr. von Jassilkowski's tender psychic condition other
than indirectly, through delicately chosen pictorial metaphors—
rather like Maupassant's technique of displacing the emotional curve
of a suburban, Sunday-afternoon outdoor coitus to the sobbing of
a nightingale. But, as far as birds and bees go, a Berlin morning in
the spring of 1939 doesn't offer much that can poetically transfigure
a complex process on the borderline between body and soul (except
perhaps its thrushes, which have already been used elsewhere more
appropriately and which, by the way, were now silent).

It happens that this was nothing more than a normal, wet, overcast, early-spring morning—if only you'd refrain from attaching the
usual lyrical associations to this circumstance, which I mention here
just as a seasonal indicator—a banal, gray big-city morning, not

exactly bitter cold, but not nearly so mild as the previous evening —a morning, in short, when you take three steps outside, glance up at the clouds settling in, sniff the air, and ask yourself whether you should have worn the mackintosh instead of the ulster or, conversely, the ulster if you chose the mackintosh. On the borderline between body and soul, however, this unanswerable question is of greater sartorial than medical import and is thus likely to intensify our subject's existing sense of inner fragmentation. For the sartorial is usually thought to create an equilibrium between psychological and physical components of sensation, and its disturbance results—as I'm sure you already know—in discomfort of both types. Your blushing pleasure at these dubious cultural-critical witticisms won't tempt me to borrow metaphors from the picture spread of technical civilization for the emptiness of the *noche oscura del alma* and its negligent beneficiaries—and not only because their frequent and amateurish use will gradually turn all stomachs of any sensitivity. As a means of scaring children they may be well intentioned, but even little Johnny quickly sees how threadbare they are.

Do not, esteemed one, speak against the solid calming influence exerted by orderly images of cogent, planned action and well-regulated proceedings, such as a big-city morning provides. Take the Baron, for example: he went out into the new, yet already so gray day, and as the aforementioned question about the choice of overcoat intensified the conflict in his night-fogged mind and fractured its remaining shadows, he felt his way, fussy and restless, along various paths in order to choose a fitting backdrop to his desperate mood. He thought about the good old hike from Halensee out to Grunewald, but he shied away from the dignified, bourgeois-groomed quiet of the suburbs, the narrow-minded presumption of newly white-washed, space-economizing architectural achievements, standing next to naive Wagnerian façades from the boom years of the last century, both of which lined the streets; it was painful to think of the tin-can-strewn misery to which these streets led, the paltry rust of pine logs, which even the most unshakable faith in God and fatherland could only praise by asking who had put them there. He felt a revulsion for their artificial stillness, the stillness of a vacuum in the midst of busy, humming activity, audible and discernible from the vibrations in the air and in the moist soil—doings, affirmative activities, adding up to a great remote roar, the collective effort of millions of the faithful: how cheap, in contrast, the precious sweet note of a raindrop falling from a wet branch on the lawn of one of those villas . . . No! What Baron Traugott craved right now was *bustle*—the salutary effect of actions unfolding—and precisely without the *idée fixe* of purposeful direction, just activity as an end in itself, the annihilation of the present through the denial of the future and the past, the pure happiness of being withdrawn from one's own self in performance, performance itself as the immediate, sole recognized, sole known objective before one's eyes. He stared under the hat brims of the people coming toward him, and in so doing became aware of the heresy in his refusing to believe truly in what they believed: the undeniable autocracy, purposefully regulated down to the smallest and ultimately most senseless elements, of BUSTLE as the supreme law of heaven and earth. And as if to atone for this sinful offense, he wished fervently to surpass the average by being supremely average, if possible. So he walked along the rails of quotidian habit to the Kurfürstendamm and took his place there—solely because of an inner need to conform—with the others waiting at the bus stop, willingly inserting himself into the order of activity so as to be absorbed by God's Grace into the bliss of self-forgetting. He had no aim. If only to steady the listing vessel of his lie with the ballast of a half-truth (because at home he had pretended to have business appointments), he decided to go in to the offices of *Gentleman's Monthly* sometime that day. (By the by: why in God's holy name, do you say in German "in to" the office instead of just "to"? What is being distinguished here, that one should go *in to* the office but only *to* the theater, *to* a whorehouse, *to* church?)

Be that as it may: the bus was overcrowded, and he squeezed himself, not without some secret enjoyment, into the living mass of his countrymen and contemporaries, letting himself be pushed and pulled, as if by the peristaltic contractions of a digestive tract, toward the front, toward the glass partition separating the light and spacious driver's cabin from the pen of the lay herd. There he stood, stabilized by an arm firmly hooked into a leather strap, submerged in a primal state of vacant round-eyed gazing, facing the driver's broad back and ingeniously operational limbs, immobile, as the film of street images rolled by, now curving, now spurting, on the transparent screen of the windshield. Something unusually soothing emanated from that affable slovenly uniformed back; it sat, massive, losing none of its humanity between the overly large collar and the homey rough cloth of the cap, well seated at the solid, centered core of diligent motion, arms and legs busily pressing levers and releasing them, pulling and pushing, sliding, nudging, and turning things; and the ease with which the ponderous vehicle responded to this intense activity was like a miraculous—I would even say artistic—sublimation of will, which you would have never suspected given the driver's bulk. And just as an unexpected and easy trick performed by our fathers may have excited a sudden surge of tenderness in us when we were boys, even though we knew how ordinary it was, so this driver's will and skill, born of his professional obligation to meet the bus schedule, evoked a sense of pleasurable gratitude in the Baron and thereby soothed him. This same broad troglodytic back was also the solid, centered core of the street scenes, the ever-swerving panorama that streamed by the windshield. And as though its aura of tobacco fumes and uniformed sourness had become a part of this panorama, the swift sober procession of cityscapes also took on a motley folksiness, the fresh colors and shapely joy of a market fair. The confused choreography of the crazy crowds in the streets became like life, whirling, gushing, pushing forward, pushing forward—life, so confusing in the exuberance of its images and yet so simple in the uniformity of birth and death, laughter and tears, love and hate—oh, life! Healing through God's multicolored masses! Benevolent fleeting time, which makes life bubble up and sink back, bubble up and sink back, oh, you sweet consolation!

He got off the bus at Unter den Linden and went on foot to Friedrichstrasse. He let himself be driven by the tempestuous crowd; gone was the need for isolation, which restlessly urges one on to the moment of truth, and he felt buoyed by something close to pious submission, as if subjugating himself to the secret magic rhythm of the city had brought him into a mystic union with its elements and now carried him floating high above the earth. The swarm of vehicles and people around him seemed to dance as if animated by the horn of Oberon, and a luminous joyfulness spread over them, the joy-fulness of St. Theresa, in whose company people laughed on their way to the heretic's stake. Berlin, greatest of great cities! Your clear generous sobriety, your bygone wit and your street-smarts—oh, the ballast of half-truth in the swaying vessel of your lies! Like a magic carpet, your boastful snobbery has lifted you above all reality, you, most German of German cities, exceeding all of them in your self-intoxication. Thus you flew through the air, a magic vehicle, shout-ing: look, look, I'm flying!

And so it happened that on his walk the Baron encountered First Lieutenant Kreuzwendedich von Bobzien.

He was walking along in full uniform, a cherub of a more severe order amidst the frivolous crush of civilians, his dark eyes—focused on the edge of the horizon by the edge of the visor on his eagle-decorated cap—tempting in their jet-sparkling sensuality, his usual pained smile on his handsome red lips. When he recognized his hunting companion, his smile widened, two sharp lines cut across his thin cheeks, and his lips parted to bare an even row of teeth that appeared strangely dead and yet voraciously greedy against the ex-treme pallor of his face. Making an ironically wide arch with his angled arm, he brought his right hand, palm turned outward, like a marionette's, to the polished visor of his cap and said with dashing nonchalance, the usual melancholy irony in his voice: "*Heil*, my dear fellow! Where from, where to?"

They shook hands. "I caught your scent once at the Owl," said Baron Traugott, "but you had just left for Küstrin."

"Küstrin? Possible, quite possible," said the angel of death, in-souciant and indifferent. Then, with an encouraging glance: "Shall we lunch together?"

The Baron—what do you want, human beings do require nour-ishment after all—assented. "But only if you'll give me the pleasure of being my guest," said the Baron (so that his truancy could be excused as social obligation).

"But please," Kreuzwendedich said firmly, and in a paternal ges-ture took the Baron's arm at the elbow. "You will be my guest, of course."

"All right then, but provided there's a rematch."

Great satisfaction with this theatrical exchange of courtesies was clearly painted on the melancholy ironic face of the angel of death. He examined Baron Traugott out of the corner of his eye to assure himself that his own spurred boots were no less polished than his companion's narrow oxfords and then fussed over the buttons of his coat, which he adjusted by rolling his shoulders.

"Well, shall we?"

"Yes, let's."

"Do you have any suggestions?"

"None whatsoever. You decide."

As it turned out, the angel of death had a very specific suggestion: quite close by, a small tavern known only to insiders—"the cellarmaster of my Uncle Wellentin," Mr. von Bobzien explained, hitting a solid note, his chin pressed comfortably into his collar, as if to dismiss any doubts about the quality of the recommended establishment. "I mean, my uncle takes his wines from him, you know? Extraordinary type—I mean the proprietor. A perfect gentleman. Himself the owner of some big vineyards in the Rhinegau. Only runs this pub as a hobby. Passionate gourmet and whatnot—you know? Huge collector."

Once more he glanced over sympathetically at the Baron. "You yourself must also have—how shall I put it?—interests . . ." He nodded shrewdly, "I noticed right away . . ."

They turned onto Französische Strasse. The tavern was called Fritzsche-Duroche's Gentleman's Retreat (even though it turned out that the owner was a Mr. Eberlein) and was furnished in Old German style. The walls, where they weren't paneled in black wood, were covered with drinking toasts inscribed in fancy red Gothic script. Carved vine tendrils and bunches of bursting grapes held by bacchanalian cherubs adorned the partitions between booths. There was a smell of casks, boiled crustaceans, and cold cigarette smoke. A gray-haired waiter with the coal-black eyebrows of a magician and tails whose blackness had taken on a greenish hue from the sour flat fumes of wine-cooked food, the worn spots in his striped shirt carefully camouflaged with starch, leaned against a center table covered by a white cloth on which a display had been mounted of various English sauces, pepper mills, mustard jars, two platters of somewhat dubious-looking oysters and lobsters, and, as the crowning show-piece, a fruit compotier topped by a pineapple. As the two gentlemen entered, the waiter pushed himself off with an experienced if ponderous turn of the hips, waved the rust-spotted napkin under his left arm, and greeted them with patronizing devotion, in his glance the slyly assessing smile of an expert trapper. At the same time, an assistant with the mien of a pallbearer materialized from the shabby background and, in a well-exercised maneuver, tried to steer the two young clients into a side alcove. But Kreuzwendedich shooed them off and proceeded into the nether regions of the Gentleman's Retreat. The waiter stepped aside and bowed knowingly, with the satisfaction of profound accord, and then collapsed again against the resplendent center table with the exhausted self-absorption of a man with sore feet. The woeful assistant meanwhile turned away indifferently toward the blackish-red curtains that concealed a window giving out on the courtyard. The angel of death, followed by the Baron, walked past them into what proved to be Mr. Eberlein's office, which doubled as a private dining room for specially favored guests.

It was a small room at the end of a short, unlit corridor off which doors led to the kitchen and the rest rooms. Mr. Eberlein rose, a heavy, block-shaped man, from behind his Gothic desk. He was of barely average height and apoplectic stoutness; his burly, bullish frame seemed about to burst the seams of his tight, square-padded black suit. In his small eyes was cunning, the keenness and tough patience of a tradesman. But under a tiny straw-colored mustache his lips protruded sensually, never entirely closed, downturned bitterly at the corners and revealing very small teeth with wide gaps, reminiscent of the yellowish pale bellies of two coupling snails. Kreuzwendedich faced him and affably offered his hand. "Mr. von Bobzien!" Mr. Eberlein said with a gummy Rhenish accent and a toneless croaking voice while tucking his head into his steer's neck in military fashion.

"This is my friend, Baron Jassilkowski," said Kreuzwendedich, gesturing toward Traugott, whereupon Mr. Eberlein came out from behind his desk and repeated the sharp snap of his neck, hoarsely croaking, "Baron, sir!" and taking Baron Traugott's congenially outstretched hand into his own fatly upholstered yet surprisingly strong one. His eyes were full of the suppressed contempt of a money-bags for high-sounding, titled, but usually unprofitable and merely sporadic customers, but this in turn was overruled by the self-imposed discipline of the penny-saver; lots of pennies together can add up to a round figure with plenty of zeros. "Do you gentlemen wish lunch, or does Mr. von Bobzien require something special?" he asked with insinuating tonelessness.

Baron Traugott's frayed nerves sensed a subtle rebuke directing them back to the dining room, but Kreuzwendedich countered with his pained and knowing smile and said: "I wanted to introduce Baron Jassilkowski to you and have a little luncheon to celebrate the occasion." Mr. Eberlein's head bent once more to his shirtfront. With a nonchalant gesture like that of sowing seed, Kreuzwendedich added: "Baron von Jassilkowski is the brother-in-law of my cousin Klützow from Klekow, married to the daughter of so-and-so" (here he gave the family name of the thoroughbred). "Baron, sir!" Mr. Eberlein puffed up from his waistcoat. He raised his eyes again, but they remained veiled, the eyes of someone who is not easily fooled and who has his own sources of information. "May I ask the gentlemen to be seated," he croaked, indicating a table in the corner, on which stood glasses and sample bottles. "The office is rather cramped, but on the other hand, the gentlemen will be quite undisturbed. I will call the headwaiter right away—or may I take the liberty of arranging the menu myself?" Kreuzwendedich and Baron Traugott exchanged sybaritic glances. "You arrange it, Mr. Eberlein," Kreuzwendedich replied cheerfully. "You arrange it. We'll see whether you treat us as well as you do my Uncle Wellentin."

Mr. Eberlein smiled reassuringly and dispelled these facetious doubts, shaking his short fingers in front of his stoutly stretched waistcoat: "With me, Mr. von Bobzien," he croaked, "youth comes first. Be young with the young, and let age pay the bill, I say." He laughed silently, in a terrifying sudden display of jocularity that ended with equal abruptness. This unanticipated outburst made him indeed look like a boar (which his name means in German), a mean old one. His bright little sparkling eyes opened wide so that their irises and pupils looked nailed to the middle of his protruding white eyeballs, his shoulders heaved, his head sank way into his neck, and in panting bursts a toneless "ha, ha!" issued from his gaping snout.

"So what shall it be, gentlemen?" he croaked, suddenly as serious as ever, even rather bitter. "A nice cold cherry soup to start, yes? A nice Rhine sturgeon with hollandaise, very fresh, came this morning." (His thumb and index finger formed a circle in front of his vest.) "Then a nice rump steak with lots of onions, that's just the thing for you gentlemen, to give you vigor, to put a bounce in your step." (Again a frightening outbreak of laughter.) "Peas, green beans? Pommes frites? And afterward, gentlemen, perhaps a peach melba or nice crêpes suzette?"

"Ah—the—the melba," Kreuzwendedich decided after a short pause in which he realized that this was a question directed at him. He looked at the Baron with a radiant face. "Cheese?" asked Mr. Eberlein. "Yes," said Kreuzwendedich, "with some of those apples I saw out there." "And a nice little coffee afterward," said Mr. Eberlein, crowning the menu and pirouetting toward the door. "I'll order it right now. But first, Mr. von Bobzien, Baron, I want to give you gentlemen a little taste of something from my vault." He opened the door; his lips closed, fat and bitter, over his gap teeth. "Möller!" he called out into the unlit corridor with a toneless croak of terrifying authority. Since there was no answer, he turned around: "The gentlemen will excuse me for a moment!" He was about to leave, but then a door opened outside. "Mr. Eberlein?" "Bring me up a number two seventy-four right away," croaked Mr. Eberlein. "And then, Möller . . ." He stepped into the corridor and closed the door behind him.

"Well?" Kreuzwendedich said, and leaned back comfortably, crossing his legs. The Baron did likewise and said: "Tops!" They both took out their cigarette cases and offered them to each other. "Splendid fellow," said Kreuzwendedich, "from an old patrician family in Trier. Must ask him later about his collections."

Mr. Eberlein returned with number two seventy-four. He handled the slim bottle with expert, spare motions. The minute nails on his small, skillful hands were deeply ingrown in the plump fingertips. Using the corkscrew hanging from a thick watch chain on his waistcoat, he opened the bottle with a pop, smelled the long cork, with great concentration poured some wine into a glass, sniffed it, tasted a sip, sucked it against his gums with his little eyes closed and raised to the ceiling, swallowed, and then smacked his lips apart, so as to inhale the remaining aroma of the wine deeply through his nostrils. Then he reopened his eyes (involuntarily you expected them to make a smacking sound, as his snail's lips had) and for a moment or two gazed into the glass. With a swift, brutal motion he threw the remaining bit of wine into the corner of the room, smiled bitterly at the two young gentlemen, and, carefully filling their glasses, puffed the incantatory formula: "Nineteen twenty-one Nöllenheimer Freudenstück, gentlemen, Riesling Select, estate-bottled by Gymnich."

"Do you know the 'twenty-one Rüsselslaarer Veltscher and Sack?" asked Baron Traugott archly, hoping to dispel what seemed to him the oppressive solemnity of the moment. Mr. Eberlein straightened, holding the bottle in front of him as if presenting arms. "Baron, I have been in this trade for forty years. I may say in all modesty that there is no great wine in Germany I do not know—I may say so, Mr. von Bobzien, may I not? It's no accident that your uncle, the gentleman from Wellentin, takes all his wines from me—true, or am I right?" (Abrupt laughter, then once again serious.) "Nowadays, 'twenty-ones are practically all sold out or gone. Such vintages are reserved for only the best of clients, Baron, Mr. von Bobzien. If I guess correctly, the Baron's esteemed parents-in-law still have a few bottles of it in their cellar." (His eyes peered coldly and objectively at the Baron from behind their fat lids.) "But if the gentlemen will now be so kind, please taste this wine. I have held back this vintage for years because it is only now that it has reached its absolute peak. The body, gentlemen, the noble ripeness, the flowery aroma, you won't soon find them in any other wine. This is a *ne plus ultra*, gentlemen. Some years ago you would easily have paid twenty marks for such a wine; now I'm giving it to you gentlemen for a mere seven-fifty, simply because I don't have any space left in my cellars. All today's clientele wants, Baron, Mr. von Bobzien, are potable table wines, you know? For such an exceptional vintage as this one here, there are but few connoisseurs left. And I'd rather give away such a wine below cost to true connoisseurs like yourselves than have it overage in my cellar—true, or am I right? Baron, Mr. von Bobzien—to your health!"

They drank devoutly. "Well?" Kreuzwendedich asked, looking over the lip of his glass into Baron Traugott's eyes and taking another sip. "Perfect!" the Baron said, nodding in Mr. Eberlein's direction, and carefully set his glass down on the table. "Finish your glasses, gentlemen," croaked Mr. Eberlein. "The bottle must be emptied. It will only spoil now that it's open." He laughed his horrible, eruptive, obscenely fat, toneless laughter.

"Won't you drink with us?" asked the Baron.

"Thank you, gentlemen," Mr. Eberlein declined respectfully, "thank you but I still have sampling to do later, and I mustn't spoil my palate."

They drained their glasses, and Mr. Eberlein filled them anew. "In the past," he croaked, "in the good old days before the last war, gentlemen, we had young officers from the guard regiments in here every day. The gentlemen sometimes used to stay until five or six and then went directly to the dance halls. The Count Klützow-Ödemark, Mr. von Bobzien-Wellentin—why, I knew those gentlemen when they were still lieutenants. Those were the days, gentlemen! There was no one who hadn't been to Fritzsche-Duroche's . . . The Gentleman's Retreat, gentlemen, that was a symbol, nothing like it exists today. I'm going to show you something, gentlemen!" He went over to his desk and took down a framed sheet hanging from a nail in the wall. Cautiously and solemnly he brought it to the table like a reliquary. It was covered with an already somewhat yellowed Gothic script, its characters pointedly upright, closely spaced, and swiftly written. Baron Traugott and Kreuzwendedich put their heads together and read: *If a German is truly to know his strength, he first must have a half bottle of wine in him—or better yet a whole one. v.B.*"

"Bobzien?" asked Kreuzwendedich, but Mr. Eberlein shook his head with bitter amusement. "Below? Bülow? Bredow?" Mr. Eberlein still shook his head. "Blücher?" suggested Baron Traugott. "You're getting warmer," croaked Mr. Eberlein. "Hindenburg?" jested Kreuzwendedich. Mr. Eberlein looked offended. "I should say not! Come now, gentlemen, why not Hugenberg? *B*, gentlemen, it begins with *B*!" "Well, yes," said Kreuzwendedich, "Hindenburg was also called von Beneckendorff." A perplexed pause of some length ensued.

"Gentlemen, do you no longer recognize the hand of the Iron Chancellor?" puffed Mr. Eberlein. Baron Traugott and Kreuzwendedich exchanged an embarrassed glance. "What?" said Kreuzwendedich. "Bismarck? He was here?" "More than once," puffed Mr. Eberlein. "As a lieutenant?" "I should say not!" said Mr. Eberlein, offended. "You should be able to discern that from the handwriting! The strength and maturity of it! No, he was already well into his nineties, but still sprightly, I can assure you. His eyes, gentlemen, his powerful straight bearing!"

They had their fill of the handwriting. "A great man!" said Kreuzwendedich finally. "Fantastic man!" added Baron Traugott. Mr. Eberlein's lips turned down bitterly and, dissatisfied, he carried the autograph back to its place above his Gothic desk.

"Incidentally," said Baron Traugott, while Mr. Eberlein stretched for the nail, "I've been transferred from the Fourteenth Cavalry to your regiment."

"What? You don't say!" said Kreuzwendedich. "The Ninth Infantry? By Jove! That's terrific!" He raised his glass. "Shall we drop the formalities?" "I'd be honored," Baron Traugott responded. "I find it more proper anyway with him here," said Kreuzwendedich, nodding toward Mr. Eberlein at the back of the room, "since I introduced you, so to speak, as family." Once more, they toasted each other.

Soon the bottle of Nöllenheimer was empty, and the meal was served. Mr. Eberlein took the liberty of suggesting a sequence of beverages: "The cold soup unaccompanied—or would the gentlemen fancy a glass of Amontillado? No, I agree, that would only spoil the aftertaste of the Nöllenheimer. With the sturgeon, a lovely Moselle, number two eighteen, a very pithy vintage. Then a nice full Bordeaux with the rump steak, yes, number three twenty-four—or would the gentlemen prefer a porter ale?—I still happen to have a few genuine English bottles—but then again you gentlemen probably want to stay with German grapes . . . Afterward, I would suggest another two seventy-four . . ."

The last of these was consumed by all three of them, for Mr. Eberlein finally allowed himself a glass. "It is my misfortune that I always let myself get talked into it in the end," he puffed, and sat down with them in an impressive illustration of his undoing. "But when I look at you gentlemen sitting there, it is almost as if the good old days were back. In the past that's the way it was every day in the Gentleman's Retreat, and what eccentrics, what unique personalities there were among our guests! Count Klützow, your uncle the gentleman from Ödemark, you know, at one time made a hobby of collecting ladies' shoes. How crazy he became whenever he was on the trail of a pair of those smart little half boots! All the rest, I mean, everything from the boots on up, never interested him! Quite out of the question, gentlemen! The half boots were the thing!" Mr. Eberlein's terrible laughter broke out suddenly and then turned off.

"Shoes?" exclaimed Kreuzwendedich, looking Baron Traugott in the eye. "Not me!"

"I wouldn't say that, Mr. von Bobzien," croaked Mr. Eberlein. "It's more widespread than you gentlemen might think. These days, gentlemen keep their little fancies better concealed, what with the laws and all. But in those days, personal idiosyncrasy was more in fashion. And in those days, all the ladies wore half boots . . . !"

"Yes, yes indeed, I can well imagine," said Baron Traugott entirely against his will, the wine and the exuberant atmosphere having loosened his tongue. "Only yesterday I saw Milly Schlierstedt—you know her," he said to Kreuzwendedich (hating himself for it), "the niece of the Princess Hohenheim-Ambach—and she was wearing a pair of shoes you could truly become enamored of."

Proud acknowledgment was reflected in Kreuzwendedich's dark eyes.

"Yes, you see, gentlemen," croaked Mr. Eberlein, "it's especially in the highest circles of society that such things are most common, more so indeed than you gentlemen might suppose. You say that tastes vary, Mr. von Bobzien—*de gustibus non est disputandum*, right?—and I say: 'Thank God!' " He let loose with his eruptive laughter and then cut it short. "The gentleman your uncle from Wellentin, well, it's all well known. But you see, science has examined these things and come to its conclusions. If you believe the scientific journals on these things, they are all dormant in childhood, and the gentleman, the Count from Ödemark, told me once personally that as a child he was truly enamored—as the Baron so beautifully put it—of the patent-leather half boots of his French governess. So what can you do about it? You gentlemen will admit there's a certain style in such fancies. Something original, as it were. But nowadays, who can afford a French governess?" Mr. Eberlein laughed horribly. "You may not believe me, but we had here a gentleman from a top-notch family, old nobility, big fortune, *et cetera censeo*—I'm not going to name names, gentlemen, but I'm sure you've heard of him—this gentleman, incidentally one of my most regular customers, had a sister, a few years older, a charming girl but as a child extremely temperamental, who frequently pushed him to the ground, as children do, and stepped on him. What can I tell you, gentlemen? That was enough for this fellow to develop into a regular Sacher-Masoch!"

"What?" asked Kreuzwendedich, puzzled. "Cakes?"

"Why not?!" croaked Mr. Eberlein, shaking his index finger at him. "You certainly have a sense of humor! Sacher-Masoch, not the Sacher torte! Sacher-Masoch, the man who discovered masochism, Mr. von Bobzien. Anyway, this customer of mine was one of that school's most illustrious representatives. Appears by name in numerous scientific works—of course, only by his initial. It's says here: *Patient Baron F. corporis superiorem partem nudavit et puellas trans pectus suum et collum et os vadere iubit et possit ut transgredientes summa vi calcibus carnem premerent.*"

"Latin!" said Kreuzwendedich with a happy glance at Baron Traugott. "*Corporis superiorem partem nudavit* . . . Crazy bloke! I didn't catch the rest of it. What did he do with it?"

"Now then: *puellas*, the girls," croaked Mr. Eberlein, accompanying his words with appropriate gestures, "*puellas*, the girls, right?—*trans pectus*, across his chest, as it were—*et collum*—and collar, right?—*et os*, the bone—*vadere iubit*, liked to walk—*et possit*, and could—*ut transgredientes summa*, until an excessive amount, that is: innumerable times—*vi calcibus*, when the half boots—*carnem premerent, premerent*: pierced; *carnem*: the flesh. Well, when the heels of those little half boots pierced his flesh. Crazy bloke, as you quite rightly said, Mr. von Bobzien, and anyone who heard or read about it would say so—not to mention actually witnessing it"—Mr. Eberlein laughed—"but I knew the Baron personally. Grand seigneur of the old school, gentlemen, education, culture, lineage, charisma: in one word, personality, a real original. *Amico pectus, hosti frontem!*" More dreadful laughter issued from Mr. Eberlein's snout. "Of course, it should be *amica* to agree," he puffed. "If you still had as good a grasp on your Latin as I do on mine, you would have corrected me right away, gentlemen: not *amico*, but *amica*. Fortunately, tastes vary—right, Mr. von Bobzien?" He slapped Kreuzwendedich on the thigh, and Baron Traugott, deeply mortified, turned away, while Kreuzwendedich cautiously drew back.

"Surely you gentlemen know the lovely verse," Mr. Eberlein went on, high-spirited. "The innkeeper's wife kept by her side / A burly groom hermaphrodite . . ."

He indulged himself without restraint. He was going full speed ahead, the hoarse Mr. Eberlein, so that the two young gentlemen had no need to keep up a conversation and could drain a third bottle of number two seventy-four in silence. Baron Traugott, however, had for some time felt an urgent need to be by himself for a little while, and when Mr. Eberlein finally paused, he rose. And to his great dismay, Kreuzwendedich did, too, commending the idea and joining him on his excursion. "Don't be bashful, gentlemen," snorted Mr. Eberlein cheerfully. "No compunctions about that, of all things. *Navigare necesse est*, gentlemen, there's a place for it in even the smallest hut. First door to the left, gentlemen."

The unease that had gripped the Baron became anguished nervousness in the tight quarters of the little room. But, to his great relief, the angel of death's finely chiseled profile on the other side of the partition remained grave and downcast, with the usual dreamy, slightly pained smile. "Nice pub, no?" he finally asked. "Very nice," Baron Traugott concurred. "Extraordinary man, this Eberlein." "Extraordinary man," Kreuzwendedich agreed, "talks a bit too much at times. Have to think about getting on with it soon." "As soon as you like," said the Baron, "I still have some things to do in the city. But it was a delightful lunch. One of these days we'll have to get together at the Owl." " 'The Old Chancery Clerk,' right?" smiled Kreuzwendedich over the panel, essaying his best Viennese accent. He combined the rolling motion with which he habitually straightened his collar and shoulder pads with a slight bending at the knees and a bit of shaking. "Have to do it again soon. I expect we'll be seeing more and more of each other."

They returned to Eberlein. "What is it that he collects, that man?" asked Baron Traugott in the corridor. "Half boots?" "Not at all! Old music," said Kreuzwendedich. "Scores from the Middle Ages and things like that. Famous for it throughout Europe. Great organ player himself. Fabulous culture, that chap. Rhineland. Trier. Old Roman colony. Fluent Latin. A bit too much at times."

As they took their leave from Mr. Eberlein, Kreuzwendedich took him aside and said sotto voce: "You'll send me the bill, as usual?"

"Can't I . . . ?" said the Baron, reaching in his breast pocket.

"Out of the question," said Kreuzwendedich. And with a pained smile, he added to Mr. Eberlein: "As usual, right?"

"As usual," croaked Mr. Eberlein, his eyes hooded, his head tucked into his shirtfront.

Then they were standing in front of the Gentleman's Retreat, and the Baron realized that he was drunk. "A most delightful luncheon," he said. "What time is it, by the way?" The day seemed to have become abnormally bright.

"Four," said Kreuzwendedich, swinging his angled left arm to produce a wristwatch from under his stiff uniform sleeve. "I have to hurry off to Potsdam. Still have to attend a little meeting with some of my officers there."

"We'll see each other soon," said Baron Traugott. "You have our address. It would make my wife very happy."

"Kiss her hand for me," said Kreuzwendedich with Viennese elegance. "And as for your military exercise," he added generously, "I'll fix that. Can't go on like that. Will be taken care of promptly." Then he raised his hand in an ironically wide arc to the polished visor of his eagle-decorated cap, his palm turned outward, like a marionette's, and said with melancholy derision: "*Heil*, my dear fellow!" Straightening his collar and the shoulders of his uniform with the rolling motion, he walked off, turned around at the corner of the street, and waved back. Baron Traugott waved, too, and was still smiling after he had gone, breathing heavily from the Nöllenheimer simmering in his blood, blinded by the bright light of the afternoon, happiness in his heart. *He had found a friend.*

> *This enormous desire lifts our*
> *spirits but painfully so: alas,*
> *lying here below, we are propelled*
> *up to lofty heights only as*
> *epileptics.*
>
> JEAN PAUL, HESPERUS

E HAD FOUND A FRIEND—WHAT AM I SAY-
ing!—he had earned him and fought for him, lured
him from the clutches of treacherous existence,
wrested him from fate: he had suffered.

Mademoiselle de l'Espinasse once wrote to
Count Hippolyte Guibert (you know, Julie l'Espinasse, the one who was linked with Shani d'Alem-
bert and Ratty Walpole and Sepi Mora of the
Pignatelli-Aragon—my God, *elle n'avait pas le talent de conserver
les affections* and had fallen in with a rather fast crowd)—she wrote
to Hippy Guibert that only unhappy people deserve to have friends.
What a fine aphorism! What a subtly expressed and sublime conception of friendship! I tell you, if you need advice on the subject,
throw away your Montaigne. The man may have had an excellent
head for psychology (but what, after all, is psychology if it is not
learned through suffering? Nothing more than a room-service science, a night porter's empiricism), but he failed to penetrate the
spiritual profundities of the matter.

In our soul, dreams are so very close to love! A friend! A friend
—is not just one of those chance companions, washed up at random
by the brackish water of everyday life, not just an incidental and
indifferently tolerated mate in the same harness moving at the same
equally idle trot, not just a drinking and whoring and money-
borrowing buddy, not of those low-life allies from Kranzler and
Mampe, the regiment or the movies, the whorehouse or Charley's
Bar. A friend, my friend, is a prince of life: one of the watchful
guardians at the gates leading to the seven inner courtyards that gird
the mystic prize of time; the sword-bearing protector of the fortified
rings we must penetrate, one after another, if we are to approach
the meaning of this empty passage; the one who, strict and strong,
bars us from entering so long as we have not been purified by the

grief of time unfulfilled—but also the one who welcomes us with a smile once he recognizes us as an initiate, who greets and anoints us with nard, clothes us in precious garments and bestows on us the insignia of the chosen few, and thus introduces us into the renewed circle of life. Proudest of all moments (oh, humble moment!), when a newly attained secret rank, like a silent magic formula, opens the gate to a realm where you find new challenges and prove yourself worthy, when your sword-bearing guardian is transformed into your friend and host, henceforth marching at your side to herald your name, to praise and protect you—chivalrous servant in the service of life!

Oh, strange, wondrous structure, this world that each and every one of us erects within our innermost selves—fortress, Grail castle, and den of thieves, a thousand projections of self, defended and blocked by a thousand obstructions, walls, ditches, barriers, and relays that we must storm and overrun to reach our own true selves—wise Uncle Toby Shandy! Utopia of the inner empire, mirror image within us of the world, of whose overwhelming actuality everything actually tangible is but a symbol, every sensual experience but a metaphoric adventure on the treacherous path toward conquering and winning ourselves!

Thus had he been won, his friend Kreuzwendedich, and Baron Traugott, striding aimlessly along (he was walking but didn't know where, walking out into the twilit overcast afternoon, now once again alive with springlike, earthy-scented gusts of wind, walking and letting the earth roll along under his feet, that never-ceasing rolling of the earth)—Baron Traugott praised him to the skies, his friend Kreuzwendedich, and praised himself for his new rank and praised life, this period in time so filled to the brim, grief-stricken and malevolent, always thrilling life, foaming, bubbling up and sinking down, bubbling up and sinking down, this triumphant life that seethed in his veins—sweet, wine-given sense of concord with the world!—drunkenly he praised this swirling, picturesque, iconoclastic, constantly regenerating life, surging toward form, toward *form*, toward FORM—life, which constantly needs and stamps out new forms, detaches them and sweeps them away, swells up again and lets new forms appear. He praised it drunkenly and drunkenly walked into its midst, and the picturesque city unfolded before his wine-flickering eyes . . . would anyone say he was unhappy?

Goodness—how am I to know what you'd call it? You with your hands in your pockets every time something frightens you—for it's there that a handhold, a firm place can still be found, isn't that right?—contentment with quality work, continuity, stability—now that we have hard currency again, thank God, you might even find an extra five marks in them, which would give you a really tangible and concrete hold on happiness: what do I know about your *mneme*?

Behold: here is someone strolling through the city—the city of Berlin in the spring of 1939, as I've said. He passes the castle. He walks along the right-angled streets leading to the canals, which can almost pass for Dutch *grachten* yet are not true *grachten* but merely canals (in these parts water is not a natural innate element of life—right?—but rather an element of nature conceived as an adversary to be mastered, that is, overpowered and subdued). Still: small, well-proportioned houses here, well-run-kingdom houses, so to speak, soothing and orderly in comparison with the aberrations of the industrial barons' boastful palaces, so typical of the power-hungry, breast-beating Wilhelmine period (as if a delicate sense of aesthetic form could be better satisfied in Mycenae than on Friedrich-strasse!)—though, on the whole, also somewhat empty and glassy: the horse painter Krüger with a tinge of Caspar David Friedrich's ghostly midsummer-night stillness and a good dose of Hosemann, you can be sure) . . . And so he continues and comes to squares surrounded by pathetically purposeful high-rise cathedrals of the textile-producing *Horla* that will succeed mankind, as the clairvoyant mad Maupassant predicted—an extraordinary artistic achievement—no? The building itself as icon, more than mere space to attract believers in the creed (and creditors), for we know that it was not the experience of inner space, as with the French, but rather physical design itself that led us early on to organize mass without splitting it up: thus not Gothic, but rather Neo-Hohenstaufic: the image of all-beneficent EFFICIENCY, the phoenix of our miraculous postwar reconstruction tame at its feet, and on appropriate steps to the right and left according to rank, the representatives and executives of its power, its saints and martyrs—imports in their ring-wearing hands, export contracts in their pockets, the seal of a general power of attorney imprinted on their youthful foreheads. It is there perhaps—gloriously vanquished and relegated to the domain of olms and lemurs, subsisting in caves and under damp stones, crushed by the collapse of their own powerful visions—that George Grosz cowers . . . And so the lonesome walker goes farther and farther on and comes to a market—oh, just some wholesalers' loading ramp with thundering elevated trains speeding over sooty vaults—yet nonetheless a scene full of color and plenitude, what do you want? Potatoes, leached-out cabbages, frozen and then thawed (you can take Liebermann to heart on that subject: a well-painted turnip is better than a poorly painted Madonna!): fresh earth and rotting compost, seeping juices, a patina of fertile spoilage, of deterioration in the recesses of musty walls . . . And he walks past it all, right across it, until he comes upon long rows of empty houses built of yellowish-gray clinker bricks, washed to a metallic gleam by rivulets dripping from leaky drainpipes—not Zille, hell no! Käthe Kollwitz even less—and don't forget the social aspect: secular happiness in window boxes and kitchen nooks; shirt-sleeved, card-playing lust for life; stale office air and briefcase virility; bed-warm, shopping-net, worn-out-abdominal-pregnant womanhood; silver runic primers, house culture, Dürer's hare on the wall and Rilke's *Cornet* on the bookshelf.

And so he rides on—pardon me—strides on, strides on, and carries through it all the poverty of his happiness, the wealth of his grief, through, along, and past it all, past bridges and canals, downward-sucking subway tunnels (not the experience of inner space . . .), past sky-high rows of windows and along rails and still more rails, bundles of rails branching out in all directions, spliced glimmering steel ribbons that drag you along with them into the far-off, pigeon-blue nothingness, mighty overpasses like the temple of Judea sumptuously bejeweled with red, yellow, and green traffic lights, and then, over there, sooty-black churches, extinguished, petrified, and skeletal like burned corpses. And then suddenly there's a wide, glassy open space in the twilit early spring evening, swept by earthy-scented gusts of wind, with the empty construction scaffolding and blank firewalls pushed deep into the background, the fragments of half-finished imperial administrative fortresses rising among them, raised by raging petit bourgeois monumentality, set down on efficiently cleared sites.

And he strides past and across and along all of it—drunk with nameless grief, silently celebrating the prize of existential grief in his breast: a divine minnesinger, anointed with nard, clothed in precious garments, in blossomy delicate linen, matte shimmering silks, sinfully expensive cashmere—the insignia of the chosen few among mortals! He strides along in spit-polished custom-made oxfords, the seven-fifty Nöllenheimer roaring in his temples, moved, urged on, driven by the tension of blissful unhappiness in his heart, celebrating the prize of time fulfilled . . . And now would you kindly tell me, esteemed reader, why you always smirk at such descriptions? Don't try to fool me! You in particular, your head filled up with Sartre and his chums, you more than anyone carry with you the spirit of the horse trader who, when kicked by a horse, exclaims: "How charming! What a fiery temperament! It wants to play, this friendly spirited creature!" Or do you believe that I am only here for your amusement? What a mistake, my good man! In an era that amuses itself with Mr. Högfeld and Eugen Roth, I've no desire whatsoever to be part of the nation's treasure trove of humor. Behold: how he strides along in the spring of 1939, the son of Herzeloyde, through the still-undamaged Berlin of '39—behold him and weep!

Yes, weep! For he walks on, forsaken and alone through Necropolis and thinks, thinks, thinks . . . why not weep? Well, let me tell you: I like that. You're a man after my own heart.

Go ahead, you eternal youths, tip the Nöllenheimer (sale-priced at seven-fifty) into the green pressed-glass goblets and let us rejoice. Let us lead a life of breeding and composure (breeding: the loose rolling of the shoulders to give collar and jacket padding a better fit; composure: a nonchalant hand gesture like sowing seed and a horseman's chin comfortably pressed into your shirtfront), let us, from a cool distance, with subtle worldly skepticism, gaze into the cloudy eyes of existence below cost. There goes Someone (capitalized) strolling alone through the day, thinking, thinking, thinking —but what is it that he thinks so hard about? What is it flaying around in his poor foolish head—*thinks, thinks, thinks*—repeat after me: *thinks, thinks*—what is it that beats between his palate and tongue against his cranium like one of those sticks you tie to the forelegs of a stray dog? . . . I'll whisper something into your soul, good friend, it's truly no easy matter to endure this life. Do you still expect us to be taken seriously while we're at it?

You know—often, or at least on occasion, I've thought about the phenomenon of *lying*: not philosophically, of course, not in any basic terms, but quite literally; after all, one does have something like imagination . . . And admit it: what would life be like, this one-times-one, without the differentials and integrals of the lies we tell? What would it come to, this world, this marvelous misunderstanding—this adventure—without them? It occurs to me that we exist in an entirely different environment than we think. Not one of the creatures that crawl here on earth nor even the ones that fly in the air resemble in any way the images of our inner world; that leaves the ones that swim in water. The artworks created by our lies, aren't they surprisingly like the skeletons of radiolarians, for instance, the filigrees of *Hexacontium dryomedes*, interlocking like Chinese ivory carvings—like the tales of *A Thousand and One Nights*, one enveloping the other in arabesque embroideries; or the enchantingly elegant bells of *Clathrocyclas ionis*, which resemble women's skirts of the finest lace (the spellbinding fraud of fashion!)? Indeed, I say: join with me and bow down in awe at the fabulous spectrum of color and the multitude of forms among the polyps and medusas, the shellfish and sea cups, the coronatae and sea roses, the forests of corals, the worm bundles and snail lappets, the jellyfish cloud of lies with which we transform the cold, unlit deep-sea landscape of naked truth into the incredible realms of inner life . . . But what were we talking about? About Mr. von Jassilkowski, of course.

He had reached the Jannowitz Bridge, and just then those earthy fresh gusts of spring wind had wiped away all the slate-gray cloud veils from the sky, so that it looked sparkling clean and turquoise blue; over there beyond the delicately scaly waters, the sharply contrasting green of a copper roof could be made out, and in the rows of house windows to his right, the watery gold of the setting sun coagulated in huge drops. It was captured there—*aurum potabile*, Berlin Select, Vintage 1939—for one pregnant, incredible moment.

Then it was suddenly swallowed up, vanished, withdrawn from the world. The turquoise-blue sky retreated into an inconceivable clarity (a sea of non-light, if this makes any sense to you, a dead luminosity, bereft of all brilliance, an anti-light, the antithesis of light)—suddenly there were no longer shadows and therefore also no depth, no space; and as if this loss of dimensionality had also suspended the sequence of events and with it the law of gravity here on earth, everything appeared to be in a state of timeless suspension, devoid of motion and sound (even sound became incorporeal as the sights lost their specificity and, floating there, merged into everything else that was floating). There above the rose-bug-colored roof, a plane climbed slowly, large and nearby, separated from its sonorous drone, which was absorbed in the dull turquoise waters of the evening sky, and ascended unencumbered over the hard jagged skyline and glided away slowly, nearby and large. Between the boxed-in chasms of the houses, however, in those non-spaces entirely filled with motionless, clotted matter, woven from soundless sound and unlit light, strange and wonderful shapes coalesced, welled up like jellyfish, bubbling and veiled, rising up from the core of the shadowy cubistic boxes and animated by the rapt rigidity of the swimming contours of ghostly transparent life, a life that seemed salvaged from the very depths of dreams: astonishingly giant, inflated, delicate and luminous in watercolor hues, heraldic images, structures of textile patterns, forms and colors from the fields of gynecology and dermatology— pale fiery reds or yellowish exploding aureoles puffed up like infectious boils, and aquamarine, pink, and pearly violet bundles of feathers, thrown higher, yet held back from the point of overturning like the traditional three ostrich plumes of the Prince of Wales (the lily as symbol of purity); fluttering, waving flowers in umber, purple, and crimson, the lobes of their leaves swaying limply and dreamily as if in slow motion; weightlessly pendulous bells in transparent aquamarine, smoky blue, and opal hues, darkened by other inky influences; garlands arranged in loosely overlapping, floating, indescribably delicate rows, like the hairs on the tip of brushed heraldic fur; soft, trembling spiny spheres and erratically gliding stars; and alternately fleshy and compressed or stumpy and inflated slabs, whose blubbery edges protruded like lips. The slimy, coarsely skinned backs of these indistinct shapes were marbleized, spackled, covered with pustules, deceased and corroded, their surfaces like ribbed carpets, shags, and *frottes*: matted, furry, velvety, and silky internal tissue, turned nakedly inside out, slitted and tucked in pleats. Veils and gauzes, foamy laces, waving strands and luminous whip-tails, rocking and blown back and forth like the hair of a drowned man; moistly bloated, lazy, cantankerously creeping maggots like cucumbers in rich frog-green and glowing orange colors, checkered, banded, and lozenged, tiger-striped, piebald or batik-patterned, strewn with flowers and pocked with spindly stars. Suction cups like the hard craters symptomatic of syphilis in its early stages, colorless clouds of mucus, horrifyingly alive with jet-black buttons for eyes, abruptly contracting and then just as suddenly thrusting upward in spasms, only to spread and slowly sink down again, either black and ocher in ringing, wriggling turmoil or pallid like hortensias and reddishly veined like entrails. Monsters all, seemingly spun in soft glass, weightlessly dragging themselves along or stalking on spidery legs, tapping and groping, expanding and contracting, rigidly stretching their feelers, blindly swinging their tentacles, pushing and climbing relentlessly upward—gelatinous clumps that were tenderly alive, adhering and hanging by means of their innumerable angled and fragile legs while their shapeless bodies revealed the delicate tracing of their sublimely primitive vital organs, as in an X ray. All of it.

And the Baron was struck to the core with astonishment. For he recognized in the swelling tropics of this swaying and florid stillness THE PLAYBOYS IN CHARLEY'S PORTRAIT GALLERY.

Yes, in truth! Just think! That's where they had gone off to—while we had all been racking our brains over their spooky disappearance—here was where they had been interred: in fear. In the liquid spirit of good old Jakob Böhme, who first drew the linguistic connection between the words "quality" and "*Quallen*" (or "jellyfish") and, in turn, "*Quallen*" and "qualm." That's where they reside now—in this linguistic connection. So they had received their divine reward, after all, as I always knew they would, as spiritual sources of primeval nature, taken up within God himself. There they now float with the multicolored flora from their buttonholes, ties, and handkerchiefs through the seminal waters of *philosophus teu-*

tonicus, scurrilous octopedal contortions of their dwarfish bodies keeping their spidery legs attached to their usual barstools. And with their characteristic bubbly, inflated, translucent, bon vivant faces and unremitting vitality in their jet-black button eyes, they are waving the transparent bells of their cocktail glasses in cheerful greeting. And that latecomer Traugott Jassilkowski, of all of Charley's fellows, was the one chosen to rediscover them—*sancta simplicitas!* As if every one of us poor unfortunates, even without a crystal ball, had not been fascinated at one time or another, inspired to mystic reflection by the alabaster bosom of the blond thoroughbred!

And now I once more ask you to join me in a respectful bow—not a sharp snap of the neck à la Eberlein, but rather the deep and reverential bow of Starets Zosima before Ivan Karamazov: for Baron von Jassilkowski, you understand, gazed knowingly into their terrifyingly lively button eyes and neither flinched nor tried to escape. No, he strode down into the depths of this arrested and clotted world of Böhme's third quality—he descended like the German Simplicius to the sylphs at the bottom of the Mummelsee: in order to reach the center of the world. He went down into the abyss of the subway, down into that glimmering, shimmering magic underworld and took the next ghostly train to Charley's Bar. And what he sought there was the *truth*.

T'S OFTEN SAID THAT WHAT MAKES HUMANS
human is looking into the depths of truth. Truth,
it is said in turn, is available to us and within us
at all times through language, however crude and
obscure it may be. Even Pontius Pilate knew what
to think of that. But you see, strangely enough, I
don't have much use for that man. I have no use
for chubby-cheeked, nattered-out common sense,
especially when it takes on a worldly judicious mien. The question
mark here comes not after the statement that *truth is relative*, but
rather after the statement that we are condemned to *establish* the
truth. "The time is out of joint: O cursed spite, that ever I was born
to set it right": surely you don't believe that Hamlet's cry of distress
refers only to the difficulties he encountered as a criminal investi-
gator! To find oneself condemned to establish the truth: O cursed
spite! And on the other hand, while we're quoting literature: "What
need Man fear"—thus Jocasta asks, isn't that right?—"what need
Man fear, slave to incertitude, without a light safely to foretell the
future?" To exist as best one can out of harm's way, that's the best
course. Isn't that the real wisdom of the world? That's the wisdom
of a lady, worthy friend! What a truly elegant aristocratic way to
lead your life: what indeed need Man fear as the slave of incertitude?
When Duke Maximilian of Bavaria had finished roaming through
Nubia, getting as far as the Second Cataract of the Nile, he had his
guide, Aloys Petzmacher, play the mountain zither atop the Cheops
Pyramid . . . And yet people still go there searching for truth! Maybe,
after all, Mother Bremse's genes . . . what am I saying?!

But no, good sir, as far as that goes you're on entirely the wrong
track. Bremse, really! Yet who would not want to admit publicly
what extraordinary strength the aristocracy has gained through the

influx of bourgeois blood, particularly patrician blood! Who was Bismarck's mother? I ask you. Who was Moltke's? William the Conqueror's? Who would not gladly have people of industry, science, altruism, general philanthropy, love of all creation (even kindness to animals) on the spindle side? Who can be sure how many of those forebears, from pure bourgeois pride, may have rejected or renounced a patent of nobility: Kohn, for instance (the Aryan ones, naturally, East Prussian with a *K*), couldn't that be related to Kuno or Kunz, the names of knights whose great blossoming lineages even today bestow upon their offspring the proud identity of noble birth?

Again—no, dear friend! Your view of the matter is totally false! I know perfectly well that self-exposure and confession are two passions of our age, but that's no reason for you to point your militantly ungloved finger at everyone and everything. The science of looking through the keyholes and rummaging in the dirty linen of the soul is not appropriate here. What makes all our lives so especially exciting is their fantastic unreality. It's really nothing short of quixotic to try to wring out the truth from abstractions that make life into a cheerful "as if" between "thou would like" and "thou shalt." But the high art of the asymptote, Lord, is not only a direct path to transcendence but also an immediate revelation of the spiciest existential possibilities.

Take the following as an example: Plato says that the good men are those who content themselves with merely dreaming about what evil ones actually do. Well, isn't that just typical? Like a rude official, this dictum forces you to decide on short notice whether you wish to belong to the infamous evil group or displace the lion's share of your existence into the dream realm. Let's put it in concrete terms: just for fun, let's say an Oedipus complex. Mamá in Allenstein would no doubt protest vehemently against a vote for the first alternative —if not with conscious indignation, then certainly with great alarm. On the other hand, the latter alternative would expose you to the worrisome consequences, which in extreme cases might even undermine your physical health, of inadequate repression and neurotic substitute formations. If you went to a psychologist, he might be able to cure you of your disorder in a clinical sense—but never in a moral-ethical one. Truly, one could become very jealous, if one wasn't already: what appears to the entrepreneurial spirit in its boldest imaginative flights as the philosopher's stone, the alchemist's *perpetuum mobile*—a hair remover that simultaneously works as a hair tonic—this is something that today's medicine, especially psychotherapy, has easily developed for itself.

I'll repeat it once more for you: the solution lies in asymptote. The ability to approach the always antagonistic hyperboles of thesis and antithesis without identifying oneself with either, to transfer evidence to the realm of infinity, to assign your meager *ratio* the a priori logic of associations, and to condense logical abstraction into analogy—and you will suddenly see how from an approximate value, compressed within the smallest space, *elegance* all at once arises.

Elegance, my friend—and nothing but elegance. And just consider it for a moment: ultimately we deal in the moral-ethical realm with nothing but our baser instincts, the dirty old mutt within us, right? Even with the best of intentions you can't deal with this ravenous beast the way Uncle Ödemark dealt with Kreuzwendedich's boarhound—a sharp yank on its collar and a few firm kicks in the ribs—please, our entire humanistic enlightenment legacy would object to such conduct, not to mention how aesthetically unappealing it would be. So, since we have to carry this cur within us like a spiritual gene, the only thing to do is to see how to make the best of it—who knows? Maybe it won't look so bad trimmed as a Kerry Blue. Truly, I'm telling you once again: elegance! The saint's hand gesture, as the great masters rendered it: the thumb and index finger describing a circle and the three others pointing rigidly conveys both admonition and celestial promise simultaneously. Thus will they sit in a circle on the Day of Judgment, their eyes raised heavenward, and as the roll is called they will kiss their fingertips whenever they see exquisite elegance.

But what's the use of talking about it: Baron von Jassilkowski descended undaunted into the subway station and made for Charley's Bar. The ghost train of the underworld glided on its rails through dark tunnels that pierced earth and rock, that opened up onto brilliantly lit caverns and then once more narrowed into black siphoning tubes, whose walls reverberated from the thunder of his vehicle. Then it rose in abrupt silence to plunge through the smoky-blue lake of the spring evening, at the base of which a myriad lights, on richly strewn glittering expanses, suddenly swam—secret lights hardly ever seen by ordinary mortals, the lights of caves and mines, dwarves' lamps, perhaps reflected and multiplied in the sparkle of nameless treasures—yet always ready in the wink of an eye to be shrouded, to vanish, to disappear (whereupon this lake bottom would be left black, lifeless, jagged, ripped and riven in the unlit waters, with torn silhouettes of shipwrecks bearded with seaweed hanging over the cliffs): right now, their glimmering, for some unfathomable reason, seemed almost homey, a part of his own inner being, richer, closer than the thin cold remote stars of the world above . . . Well then! His train passed for a while through the flat blueness above all this and then dove down again, roaring and thundering, into the black maw of night, where here and there, from alcoves and passages, glowing steam gushed, sparks showered, restless hammering knocked and banged. And finally—who can measure time on a voyage to the center of the earth?—the ghost vehicle stopped at the Uhlandstrasse station, and he found himself at the stairs that brought him step by step up to the rushing, glittering magnificence of the Kurfürstendamm: a fabulous immense grotto of giants in the glare of thousands and thousands of sparkling, flickering lightbulbs, in the deadened sound of the city's roar! And he swam through the darkly shimmering water and the veils of cascading light that fell upon him, crossed the black, perilous stream of automotive gondolas, when a red light stopped it for him, drifted with the crowd like a wave past the dream-ships Kranzler, Mampe, Gloria Palace and Café Trumpf, until he saw that signature magically written in the night above Charley's door. There stood the doorman, strangely detached and glazed with crocus blue from the dense material glow of the neon tubes, an oversized sea-blue admiral. Amidst the glitter of his braids, lacings, and epaulets, his vulgar, street-wise face was stretched in a welcoming grin, and his lips parted on teeth shining as through a veil; he raised his right hand to the brim of his cap, in the violet shadow of which his eyes seemed to be as cavernous as a skull's, clicked his heels together under the wide soft fall of his sailor's trousers, and with a mighty gesture of his massive gloved left hand held the door wide open. And Baron Traugott went past him through the magic shower of neon lights, penetrated the yielding resistance of velvet curtains keeping out the drafts, and found himself in the narrow cabin of the cloakroom, where in passing he threw his overcoat on the table, from which octopus arms retrieved and stored it away in the back, then descended the three backlit steps of opaque glass and arrived in Charley's.

And there sat all of them together in dense clouds of cigarette smoke like the crew of a ghost ship: Charley with the glassy stare of a habitual drunk and Tom the Mixer in his white steward's jacket; the tough gang of squires at the brass rail; the gobbling and cooing ephebes with their parrot voices, always a bit hoarse, making a din, and then in the back, at the corner table in front of the sofa, the witty doctor, a bit seedy, graying, nailed through his forehead to the mast of his own debasement; and finally the blond thoroughbred in a cloud of peroxide with her quizzical sylphlike smile and her violet mermaid's eyes behind thick glasses—and then on the wall the portrait gallery of the Great Gentlemen, distended like bubbles, tinted like jellyfish with watercolor hues, wondrously giant, swelling up out of the multicolored flora of their buttonhole flowers and ties—now admit, don't we live in an aquarium!? Put your stethoscope for a moment on the terminology we use to analyze people —*neurosis*: doesn't that just explode like some fiery-red radiolarian? Or *psychotherapeutics*: isn't it flagellant and telescope-eyed, a transparent yolk sac hanging from the warm, teeming *eu*? *Libido*: a swaying bell with a mild flute tone, rocking at the delicate impact of its soft consonants. *Oedipus complex*: why, that's dark and shimmering gold, purple, and radiant, it's larval, coiling, bushy like the crest of a helmet, spiky like the point of a lance, and at the same time fluid like ink—and what bizarre offshoots blossom from it, the most drastic perversions, the gloomy *noblesse* of the Satanist and the sumptuous blood orgies of a Gilles de Rais, who stilled his rutting in the steaming entrails of freshly slaughtered children, on down to less prosecutable urges like ordinary masochism and sadism, the interesting collector's zeal of the fetishist, or the scurrilous drolleries of the transsexual. Admit it: all this has a certain style, character, playboy originality; it's gentlemanly and racy compared to the petit bourgeois homebodiness of regular Saturday-evening coitus; it's tart, full-bodied, pithy—it's wine, in a word (oh, the lively splendor of the great names: folksy strength in NÖLLENHEIMER FREUDENSTÜCK, sturdy patrician pride in GRAACHER RUPP, golden guild mastery in ÜLZINGSLEUER MÜNZBECHER, rough-and-tumble, provincial jolliness in RÜSSELSLAARER VETSCHER UND SACK, the courtly fairy tale that is UNDINGSBERGER ADLEY!). Wine, I declare, wine—compared to the tepid raspberry juice of Christian moral discourse. It goes from mouth to mouth in the cigar-scented twilight of the Gentleman's Retreat, invoked whenever great names are called up and noble vintages are drunk, whispered with a ring of true conviction wherever quality is praised: *"See that chap over there? Don't look too obviously! Elegant fellow, don't you think? Great friend of mine, Pole, Baron, brother-in-law of my cousin Klützow at Klekow. Huge degenerate, Oedipus complex, the works. And you should see his wife! Most delicious blonde, steel industry—unlimited possibilities, just between the two of us. No Wednesday's child, no sir! Smart couple, the two of them!"*

But once again I digress, damn it all, my flights of fancy using you as a plaything—what did I mean to say? Alas, I belong to that group Voltaire singled out as the only truly evil one: the bores! You want to hear the story of Mr. von Jassilkowski, isn't that right, and here I am splashing around in the bottomless depths of associative onomatopoetics: *the trees were hissing like green geese* . . . But look: the lion's share of our experience derives, after all, from HEARSAY. We think we are creatures of sight and probably don't realize how hopelessly trapped and forsaken we are in the thousandfold echoes of our labyrinthine auditory sense. "What we have seen with our sunlike eyes . . ." Well, all right, but think of everything we've *heard*! I'm telling you: that good old cobbler Böhme! That other quality: SOUND—reverberation, tone, word—the spiritual source of life, believe him, for he learned it directly on his cobbler's ball (what is that but a piece of silence, captured by a ghost's hand!)—he overheard it in its compressed core of silence. The tropics of our underwater landscape have their origins in hearing—oh, beware the wasteland of eyewitnesses!

But why am I still gabbing and gabbing? Ask Baron von Jassilkowski himself.

As he descended into Charley's Bar that evening, everything immersed in the mysterious sylphlike smile of the blond thoroughbred; as he approached her, sapphire-eyed mermaid, born of foam in the moon glow of her peroxide mane; as he waved to her and she rose slowly, her gorgeous limbs in lazy voluptuous play like a canephora, round yet slim in luxurious physicality, and came toward him, stretched out her arm and placed her mother-of-pearl hand with its red dominatrix's nails on his shoulder and followed him—followed him somnambulistically past the mute carplike stares of the squires and ephebes, Charley, the gray-haired doctor, and Tom the Mixer, on out of Charley's Bar; as they then stepped out the door and into the street, and the crocus-blue powder from the neon lights showered their faces and transformed them into moon-solitary clowns, Pierrot and Columbine in mask-petrified melancholy, their mouths like gaping wounds under spellbound eyes; as the doorman in his admiral's uniform snapped his massive gloved right hand to his cap, awkward and dainty like the Frog King, to salute them, and they pushed themselves off like two swimmers into the undertow current of the night's darkness, gushing, sucking, pulling at them: all of this and everything else around them was nothing but sound, reverberation, tone—the sensory world of fishes, motionless in water, avidly listening fishes so sensitive to sound that their eyes protruded from their heads.

Only many years later (only after I had learned a lot I didn't know then—be kind enough to excuse me from revealing how and from whom)—only many years later did it come to me that this sound, reverberation, tone, and so on, whatever the hell you want to call it, had taken the form of a conversation (behind language, remember), a perfectly ordinary everyday conversation remarkable only for its beautiful faith, which took place that evening behind my back—or, God knows, perhaps some other evening—as I sat as usual at the bar. I heard a voice saying:

"I say, listen here!" (The arrogant penetrating intonation alone, sharp as a cheese knife, would have caught my ear.) "You're a doctor, aren't you, or at least you call yourself one? I just happened to run into an acquaintance of mine, aristocrat, old name and so on, though himself quite young—anyway, out of curiosity: you know the sexual bond people supposedly share with the parent of the opposite gender? I mean, the early pleasure derived from suckling . . . breast-feeding, and naturally the corresponding feelings of jealousy and hatred toward the father, who of course also seeks his place in the sun from time to time, you know?—the relations between father and daughter, mother and son, you'd know better than I: all of that is repressed by the conscious mind in later stages of childhood, right? But nevertheless, it remains stuck in the unconscious and may re-surface any day in the form of what you'd call substitute formations or symbolic compensation or something like that—a Jewish theory, isn't that true?"

I'd have given anything to have been able to turn around and find out who was asking this question, but the squires at the brass rail blocked my view. And I could only hear the answering voice say perfidiously, "Yes?" And from this drawn-out, halfhearted, hypo-critically encouraging expression of assent, I immediately recognized the witty doctor and could imagine him lying in wait for the next question, ready to shoot it down from behind his façade of callous cynicism as Pinne Lassow did the hares at Klekow. I stared up at the gallery of playboys on the wall and kept listening:

"I mean," continued the first voice, "someone who was a bit overattached to his mother in early youth and quite naturally de-veloped feelings of envy and hatred toward his father might, in his later years—how shall I put it?—confuse these latent impressions, isn't that right? So that, for example, he not only does not fear, but plainly wishes that the present object of his erotic desire—let's say, for fun, his wife, okay?—that he's not only not afraid, or better yet, he's so afraid his wife may sleep with other men that he actually wishes it would happen—I mean, that just imagining it gives him pleasure . . . ?"

"Yes?" came the voice of the dissolute doctor with the same in-tonation as before, and in my mind's eye, I could see the friendly basilisk's smile with which he would be staring at his victim. How-ever, he didn't seem to be in the best of form that evening (inciden-tally, this had been happening increasingly as of late, for the signs of general social decay could no longer be ignored and they distracted his grimly self-ironic attention from his own condition: a hint of negligence, disintegration had crept into his cynicism)—to make a long story short, he wasn't in his usual form, and so his routine wit short-circuited and made him say: "Interesting acquaintance of yours, that. Let me have his address one of these days."

But the answer—or rather, the next question—came promptly and unaffected by that dreary joke: "I merely wanted to know: *what do you call that?*"

You're astounded, aren't you? Exactly as I was at the time: what a touching faith in the exorcising power of the word! *What do you call that*—as if perhaps some answer like "suppurating psychic ichthyosis" would have brought immediate relief. The man who knows the secrets of the body becomes a father confessor; that's what it means, isn't it? But only the one who knows the secrets of the word can administer the blessing of absolution. Anyway, the witty doctor, in worse form than ever, failed to grasp the deeper significance of the question. He replied with his usual sarcasm and rattling emphysema: "What do you call it? All depends on how sophisticated you are: either loving thy neighbor or being a pig motherfucker."

At which there sounded, in ghastly keeping with the overall program, the silver bell laughter of the blond thoroughbred, and its ascending harmonic scale carried away all the nonsense, as well as the underlying sense, of this brief conversation.

"Must he always crash the party, good old King Kandaules?" she exclaimed, as a postscript to her foamy cascades of laughter, her pleasant feminine charm transforming the unseemly gravity of the exchange into a graceful, spirited conversation.

And since at that moment a squadron of squires detached themselves from the brass rail, rumbling down from their barstools like boulders from a mountain scree, shoving aside everyone behind them, and departing to the hearty greetings of their drinking companions, the field behind me was cleared and I could see the reflection of the regulars' table in the corner with the sofa. And there to my surprise I saw the Baron.

You have to remember that at the time I didn't have the privilege and great pleasure of knowing Mr. von Jassilkowski as intimately as I do now, my slight acquaintance with him (only by sight) having been much fortified since then with confidential information. I didn't know whether it was he who had been asking the questions, nor did it cross my mind, since his speech didn't usually have the sharpness of a cheese knife, being—if aristocratically curt—melodious and supple. But what does it matter? I ask you. I saw only his serious expression (sensitively closed lips, yes?—brows—how did Victor Hugo put it?—brows like two bulls butting heads—no, not the Baron's; his, rather, resembled two of those slim Nubian mountain goats with smooth necks and elegantly curved, sickle-shaped horns; his glance, downcast into the unfathomable depths of his cocktail glass)—as I said, I saw only his expression reflected in the mirror and interpreted it—how interesting it was!—as concentrated thoughtfulness (you should have seen his suit: the finest *fil-à-fil*, mouse gray like Molossian caviar, cut like a torpedo)—interpreted it, damn it all, as introspective musing, and indeed, wasn't there a deeper meaning hidden in even the witty doctor's most insipid jokes? You see, it's truly a question of how sophisticated you are. Erotic emancipation is and will always remain a prerogative of the upper classes. There's no room for sexuality in an eat-in kitchen—try as you might, you can't change this fact. The frumpy housewife who runs from her gas ring and Mason jars into the arms of a lover truly deserves social disgrace, while the elegant leisure of a *lady* would hardly be complete without the excitement of some erotic philandering. On the forehead of some lout (admit it!) the cuckold's horns are little more than an excrescence emphasizing his innately unappetizing features; King Arthur, on the other hand, can carry them like crown antlers on the lead stag. Truly, I tell you: the German language wouldn't be among the world's most profound if the similar sound and nearly identical spelling of "*Hahnrei*" (cuckold) and "*Ahnenreihe*" (lineage) were only an accident. Take a stroll through the gallery of noble horn-wearers, from Potiphar's husband to Napoleon: across the aisle are the likenesses of the corresponding females in onyx, marble, and jade, in oils painted by the gifted hands of Botticelli, Watteau, Gainsborough, and Romney—and not a single Philipp Otto Runge among them, dear friend! Believe me, the matter deserves deeper thought. There's something to it, and that's why I wasn't surprised (on the contrary, I would have been rather disappointed if it had been otherwise) when the Baron said after a short pause: "You're right. In the eighteenth century, when taste still counted for something, that was just part of aristocratic manners. Coincidentally, the man I was referring to belongs to such circles."

That's how it was then. But today I know that this sentence was spoken quite automatically—not after deliberation, not as a *conclusio*, you understand ("the quickly seized prey of the eagle's flight of thought," as Kleist puts it)—today I know that Mr. von Jassilkowski wasn't thinking of anything at all, but was merely listening. That he was listening to *what was uttered*.

But at this point, we must distinguish one last time among certain basic concepts, dearest friend. You will frequently encounter the term "utterance" in today's highbrow journals. You should resist pleasant shivers of awe, triggered by the putative proximity of the divine; it doesn't amount to anything more than what someone meant to say—don't ask me why people choose such a complicated way of communicating, so that the "utterance" has to be discovered before what was really said can be understood. That's not at all what I'm talking about. What I mean by the phrase "what was uttered" is the new reality that is created by the mystical act of speaking, which doesn't have to relate to the rational meaning of what is said. "Why does everything have to be put into words?" the Baron had plaintively asked Mrs. von Schrader when—as you may still recall—he had called on her seeking tea and absolution and had found himself compelled by that arch-motherly high priestess to unbutton his lips. What is said can at most be cognition. What is uttered can approach revelation.

But who still has ears to hear it? Alas, we whisper our revelations into hollows just as King Midas' barber did the secret of donkeys' ears, and the marsh reed scatters them idly into the four winds!

Well. Anyway, the Baron listened. And then—whether it was reverberation, sound, tone, silence (or the reverberation of silence) —whether it happened that evening or before or after or simultaneously—who can tell in a world where dimension has been abolished?—this is what happened: the moonbeam-blond thoroughbred got up from the circle she held spellbound with her sylphlike smile, unfolded the full sumptuousness of her luxurious frame, came toward him, placed her hand on his shoulder, and followed him somnambulistically—one of the dancers from the nut-harvesting village of Karyas, who, with heavy wicker baskets on their heads, stride through the silvery ecstasy of moonlight, one of the caryatids, with maternal power, whose love Baudelaire craved so—followed him floating, enraptured, and yet with a heightened consciousness brought on by the astonished carplike stares of the squires at the bar, the ephebes, Charley the drunk, the dissolute doctor, and Tom the Mixer; she stepped out with him into the shower of crocus-blue neon light which shed its powder in front of the door to Charley's, and there the two of them pushed themselves off into the high tide of night, diving into it while holding each other's hands like lost children, until they once more felt solid ground under their feet, the threshold of their clinker-brick palace from the dynamic-modernizing twenties. Together they entered the elevator gondola and a ghostly hand lifted them to the third floor and their small apartment. And then—but how shall I make you understand what happened next in that world without dimension, where time and space and context had fallen apart so indescribably and then been knit back together in a way that contradicted everything up until then? Isn't it something worthy of Don Quixote that I'm still trying to *tell* you a story, even though we all know how arbitrary in our age any juxtaposition of words has become? Apollo, engraver of syllables . . . oh, please! Just look at the gang that still plays the lottery of sentence combos, those pompous knights of postwar reconstruction in their dusty literary robes! And the Forty Thieves from the word jungle of *littérature engagée*! As if the obligation to be "the conscience of one's race" could be fulfilled by applying literature as our orderly Neumann does disinfecting ointment! No, dear friend! Let us, without further ado, go to the movies. For the future belongs to the comic-strip spread. The ultimate objective is the technically perfected psychoplastic film.

SETTING
The small apartment
(*Fort Nobility*)
Decorator furniture, chintz, lamp-
shades, forged iron, rustic fireplace,
the Bremse night-table lamp

CLOSE-UP
an armchair

Think of the set as having been constructed in your own mind.
IMAGES and SOUND are projected against the walls of your soul,
which serve as screens. The LASER BEAM illuminates targeted sensory spheres, selected and scanned in each shot. You can provide
your own plot synopsis.

And now:
Set empty.

SOUND on.

Clapper. Camera rolls:
Enter HE and SHE:
SHE cheerful, relaxed;
HE visibly agitated, self-conscious.

SOUND
Dialogue.
HE: Christ, it's hot in here! Did you
leave the heat on?
SHE: But, Peter baby, the windows
are wide open.

LASER BEAM darts over nervous
sphere:
Resistance against "Peter baby"
SOUND
A child's voice sings:
Don't forget your bathing suit!
Meanwhile HE says:
That's nonsense of course! Exactly
the other way around!

IMAGE
HE goes to the radiator and turns
it off.

LASER BEAM is set briefly in
motion:
Resistance vaguely coupled with lust-
ful tickling
Associative sequence, subconscious:
Key concept: "Other way around"
Voice dissimulation
Female impersonation
Statute against homosexuality

Janus head
Transvestite
A man mistakenly lost in a ladies'
room
The Legless Lady
IMAGE (following shot)
HE goes to the window.

    Meanwhile:
    HER voice: I'll just fix us something
    quick to eat.
LASER BEAM vaguely sweeps over
the edge of heightened consciousness:
Basic sensation: revulsion
Associative sequence:
Pan
Bedpan
Casserole
Outcast
Socrates
Hemlock
Nightshade
Night commode

    Meanwhile:
    SOUND
    Dialogue
    HE: Don't bother! I don't feel like
    eating anything.

Simultaneous:
IMAGE
HE, turning his back, closes the
window.

    HER voice: Just something cold.
    Steps.
    Door.

HE looks at HER over HIS shoulder.
    Conscious associative sequence:
    Key concept: Naive
    Statue of Schiller
    Apollo of Belvedere
    SOUND
    A *man's voice* calls:
    Retournons à la nature!
Rousseau in housecoat and turban,
quill in hand, sitting at desk, his right
leg extended gracefully.

(*fade*)
Countess Schlierstedt
Bucolic shepherd scene
Fragonard
Boucher

SOUND
Minuet.
The *man's voice*, admonishing:
Retournons à la nature!

Summery meadow
Flight of pollen
Insect fertilization
Honey
Seed
Urine

Simultaneous:
IMAGE
HE very carefully draws the curtains
shut over the closed window.
Fade to: Windowpanes crowded with
hordes of large-eyed lemurs (*Tarsius
tarsius*), long-fingered lemuridae (pla-
centa diffuse!). The animals keep
trying to get a look into the room.
Small hands glued to the panes.

Associative sequence:
Key concept: Good neighbor
Walt Whitman
Democracy
Statue of Liberty
(*Backfire:* McCarthy hearings—
Socrates) American family scene
around TV set: daughter reading Kin-
sey Report, older son fiddling with
klystron tube

SOUND
Trumpet solo:
"Postilion of Longjumeau."

Simultaneous:
IMAGE
HE has closed the curtains tightly,
turns around.
Cross-cut: Interior
The walls recede and reveal tropically
luxuriant flora.

LASER BEAM intensified:
Heat
Associative sequence, willfully
capricious:
Tropics
Tropic of Capricorn

SOUND
Student Choir singing: "Miller's
daughter, you dainty thing, doesn't
your fanny bloom in the spring . . ."

All jumbled together:
Klystron
Python, Pythia
Delphi
Tube

SOUND
A voice says: *Ad usum delphini.*

LASER BEAM intensely focused on
the nervous sphere of consciousness:
Nonsense
Fleeting memory of feverish condition
in childhood. A uvula glued like a
sprig of mistletoe at the back of his
cranium between his neck and the
roof of his mouth cannot be removed
despite all the efforts of his tongue.
Associative sequence:
Measles
Masereel/The Sun
Nettles
Wetness
Urine

Meanwhile:
IMAGE
On a sudden impulse, HE starts to
undress.
Cross-cut: The door opens. SHE en-
ters, carrying a platter of cold cuts.
Sees HIM. Expression: surprised and
amused.

SOUND
SHE says cutely: Well, well!

Cross-cut: HE stands stark naked
over his desk, intently busy with
papers.

Meanwhile:
SOUND
HE: I was simply too hot. Don't understand how you can stand it. (*nervously, in passing*) Why don't you take your clothes off, too?

IMAGE
Cross-cut: SHE, at the coffee table in front of the rustic fireplace, about to put down the platter. Looks up from HER half-bent position.
Between HER and the camera: the armchair.
(*Camera rapidly focuses on chair*): HER head squinting over the back-rest. Expression: slyly teasing!

SHE says: But we'll catch our death, all naked like that.
HIS voice (*with studied indifference*): I can always turn the heat back on again.

IMAGE
SHE straightens up slowly. The sly teasing dissolves into a slightly puffy expression of erotic expectation.

SHE says: Don't you want to eat anything first?
LASER BEAM focused on the affective sphere: *Rage*
Disenchantment
Associative sequence:
Key concept: Before
Rapidly leafed through:
Advertising material
(Brochures, inserts, etc.):
Text: "Before and After"
French weave
Hair growth prescriptions
Breast enhancement pills
Strength tonic
Dietetic teas
Penetrating the sphere of consciousness: Sharp urge to urinate. Mingled with the lustful sensation of "letting go"

Striking out
Broken dishes
Lampshade
Pots and pans hanging (chamber pot)
Furniture movers (grasp heavy cum-
bersome things, move ponderously)
Box with a woman sawed in two at a
circus

    Meanwhile:
    SOUND
    HIS voice (brutally): I'll give you
    something warm for your stomach
    soon enough!

IMAGE
SHE suddenly cheerful, humorous,
radiant.

    HER voice: Ooh! I'm looking for-
    ward to that.

Swiftly begins to undress, energetic,
zestful: dress, shirt, bra, stockings,
garter belt.
Fade to: Nimble, sticky, small monkey hands, fiddling with buttons,
loosening ribbons.
Lemur eyes.

    Associative sequence in the intellec-
    tual sphere:
    Contrasting pairs: Nature-art
    Nature as individuality, art as its
    contradiction. Art as an act of hesita-
    tion: the lowering of panties and a
    striptease.
    (gliding away into the subconscious)
    Brueghel
    Boorish peasant scenes
    Ruffianism
    The Mad Bomberg
    Blomberg
    The National Seal
    SA marching
    Nuremberg
    Veit Stoss
    Krakow
    Poles
    Ghetto at Kazimierz

Smashing/slamming/ramming
Sharply increasing urge to urinate

IMAGE
SHE, naked, perfectly formed, standing straight and looking at HIM with
anticipatory pleasure.

*Associative sequences (simultaneously
in separate groups)*

Pastoral Venus	Padua (Paul)	Wet tea leaves
Milkmaid	St. John	Camomile
Milking stool	Francis of Assisi	Lingerie
Udder	Sermon to the Birds	Pubic beard
Euterpe	The Birds and the Bees	Shorn beard (Paul)
Muse	Sweets	Paulus
Mush	Confections	Epistle to the Corinthians
Uncleanliness	Condor Legion	Currants
Professor Unrath	Condom	Nipples
Heinrich Mann	Spanish Fly	Chest medicine
Masculinity	Spanish collar	Tuberculosis
	foreskin)	

Merging into: *weakness, impairment.*
Urge to urinate becomes unbearable.

Meanwhile:
SOUND
HIS voice (*commanding*): Stay where
you are! Sit down in that chair over
there!

IMAGE
SHE, at a loss, sits down rigidly pos-
tured in the armchair.

LASER BEAM focused on the sensation of *impatience*, which merges
with the distress caused by his urge
to urinate.

Meanwhile:
SOUND
HIS voice: No, exactly as you sat
over there yesterday, with your legs
over the armrest—no, turn toward
me, more toward me . . .

Meanwhile:
Memories of fever intensified.
Inability to dislodge slimy nodule
glued to the base of his cranium despite tongue acrobatics, clearing his

throat and croaking. Dimly grasped
possibility of salvation by wetting the
bed.
Alarm. Revolt of the masses
Caesarian gesture

> Meanwhile:
> SOUND
> HIS voice: More toward me! Yes,
> like that! Now put your arms on the
> backrest and put your head on them!

Associative sequence:
Max Reinhardt the Jew at the Riding
Academy in Salzburg
The Jews' yellow star
The bon vivant
Oppenheimer
Jew Süss

IMAGE	SOUND
SHE has followed his stage directions and now hangs like an anaconda in the branches of the armchair. *Fade to:* A thick, pale-fleshed snake coils itself around the armchair in lasciviously slow and slithering motions and ultimately envelops HER head.	A VOICE speaks: Quo vadis?

> *Associative sequence:*
> Franz von Stuck's painting *Sin* with a
> wigged blonde, a python wound be-
> tween her thighs and around her
> plump body
> *Jugendstil*
> Max Klinger engraving: a naked man
> in a primeval landscape, gnarled,
> muscular, with a Pilsudski mustache,
> and holding a cavalry saber, stands
> protecting a half-naked governess
> with a wasp waist and Cléo de Mér-
> ode hairdo, who lies crumpled up on
> the ground.
> Friedrich Nietzsche
> Mrs. Förster-Nietzsche
> Frau Professor
> Mamá
> Wire-rimmed glasses

Meanwhile:
SOUND
HIS voice (*throaty, raw*): Take off
your glasses!

IMAGE
SHE obediently takes off her glasses.
Expression: Intrigued
but already unconsciously occupied
with thoughts of the room temperature and dinner.

HIS voice (*as before*): Stay behind
the chair! Leave your legs where they
are!
SHE (*with growing impatience*): But
this way you can't even get at it,
Peter baby!

All LASER BEAMS in violent
motion:
Repulsion
Associative sequence, rapidly, dissolved by panic into separate groups
simultaneously
Key concept: SEX

Visconti coat of arms: an enormous snake in the process of swallowing a man; genealogical trees growing from the groins of reclining knights, their escutcheon shields hanging down like two cherries; Colleoni coat of arms—he had three; equestrian statue of Bartolomeo; children of Haimon on horseback; shield of Wimmersal; the Salburg; castle of the Counts von Eltz; counts; cunts	Prehistoric Venus, hypertrophied hip area, obscenely enlarged vagina; the Arch-Mother: Gaia, Rhea; Uranus devours his children; a sliced-off male genital plunges hissing in a wide curve into the sea; Aphrodite Anadyomene; shells, grottoes, inner sancta, wine cellars, trays of boiled crustaceans, mollusks (*Brechites vaginiferum*), shiny things, smoothness, fish-bodied, fish line, slime	Bad, battle, bed, riverbed: deep, depths, abyss, plunge into it, Grand Canyon, cannon, erect penis, peninsula, island, isle: the *Ile de France*, Ile de Paris, Parisians, Mistinguette; fashion plate: the flapper look of the twenties, bowler hat, raised hemlines, low waistlines, cigarette holders; French bull terrier with hog's-bristle collar and leash; women's emancipation; a man's man, Scheidemann, Stresemann, a man on the move, Mensa, men's club initiation, menstruation

Merging into:
Intercourse, conception, motherhood,
Mamá
*Sliding across as a superimposed cen-
soring symbol:*
PAPÁ'S ESTATE MANAGER'S
CANE
Piercing urge to urinate
ALL LASER BEAMS focused on:
Release

SOUND
Full orchestral section of the Berlin
Philharmonic playing the fourth
movement of Brahms's Freedom
Symphony.
Voice-over:
HIS voice (*suddenly booming,
inhuman-superhuman, as over a
railway-station loudspeaker*): TELL
ME NOW! TELL ME EVERY-
THING! I WANT TO HEAR ALL
OF IT!

IMAGE
HER head, separate from her body,
placed on the snake coils of her arms
resting on the back of the chair.
Expression: trite, posterlike, set off by
the banality of her cascading peroxide locks.

With a clear voice and the labori-
ously precise enunciation of the
Snake Girl at the carnival. The head
says:
What is it you want to hear, my
Sweet Pete?
HIS voice (*booming as before*):
EVERYTHING! AFTER ALL, I
WASN'T YOUR FIRST ONE!

Rapid associative sequence:
Key concept: The first
A group of sprinters during the final
spurt of a dash: the winner, his face
painfully contorted and his head
thrown back, breaks the tape with a
forward thrust of his chest. Winkel

253

ried throwing himself into a bundle
of lances.

SOUND

A VOICE calls out: An alley to
freedom!

Spears. Spikes. Hedgehogs. Sea ur-
chins; rising cow fish exploding because of excessive internal pressure;
cracked-open roasted chestnut—the
fresh brown polish of its core visible
through the slit in its green skin; a
moss pillow; exploding spore cap-
sules, powdery willow catkins.
Pentecost: on a flowery meadow, a
ladies' man, dressed to the nines, bur-
rows under the skirts of underaged
girls, while smiling absently and
encouragingly.
Sharp, explosive pain in the lower
abdomen: blood drips, damp, heavy,
warm; proximity of death; a priest
bends murmuring over the scene.

Meanwhile
SOUND

HIS voice (*now cottony*): Why,
you've whored around like a Carme-
lite nun, don't lie to me. So tell me
how it was. Tell me all the things you
did with the others.

IMAGE

HER face, at first merely puzzled, is
transformed, turns serious, small,
stricken: a frightened child's face.

SOUND

SHE fearfully: Peter baby—come to
me!

HIS voice brutally: Come on, tell
me! Neither of us is exactly Peter
Rabbit when it comes to sex.

Short associative insert:
The hare shot at Klekow, mangled,
dangling from a pole with a grinning
playboy head, smashed to bits by one
of the beaters
Painful burning urge to urinate

SOUND
HER voice (*piteously*): Come to me,
Peter baby!

IMAGE
HER face, close to tears.
A ribbon in child's hair.

SOUND
SHE (*whispering*): Come to me, Peter
baby!

Cross-cut
He approaches her reluctantly.
(*Tracking shot*):
As HE stands in front of HER, SHE
gets up from the armchair, wraps
HER arms around HIS neck and
draws HIM down to HER.
Close-up: THEIR heads pressed to-
gether, HIS half hidden by HER
hair.

SOUND
SHE whispers in HIS ear (*over
echo*): But I love only you. Really no
one else but you, Peter baby. After
all, we're husband and wife now,
aren't we?

LASER BEAM focusing alternately
on *sensations of rage and shame*
Associative sequence:
Wishful fantasy—HE grabs HER by
the hair, pulls HER to the ground
and beats HER with a stick (the estate manager's cane). Bremse's night-
table lamp falls over. SHE slithers
onto the floor, rises, and returns the
blows, begins to gain the upper hand.
Upper body
Shirt
Child in a nightshirt
Chamber pot
Spankings on the bare bottom of a
three-year old; an exchange of blows
between two boxers
(*straying off*) Boxer Rebellion
Peking 1900
Count Waldersee in tropical uniform,

255

a helmet with a pointed spike and a
khaki neck flap turned up against the
sun

> SOUND
> A VOICE calls out: *Germans to the
> front!*

Entrance of Emperor Wilhelm II to
Jerusalem; H.M. on a white mount,
clad in a flowery silk coat (a gift
from H.M. the Empress, with embroideries by H.M. and her ladies-in-
waiting); Garde du Corps helmet;
Mamelukes from the embassy form-
ing a row of honor; intimidated Ar-
abs in the background
The Wailing Wall
Wall-mounted urinal

IMAGE
SHE abruptly pulls HER head back
from HIS and looks into HIS eyes,
stricken.

> Meanwhile
> SOUND
> Do you really love me, Peter baby?

Scared, SHE climbs off the armchair
and kneels in front of HIM, forcing
HIM down with HER to the ground.
Their naked bodies, sharply defined
in the harsh light, pale and haggard,
are entangled in a contorted position,
reminiscent of Egon Schiele's *The
Lovers.*

> Meanwhile
> SOUND
> HIS voice, hoarse: It's precisely be-
> cause you love me that you have to
> tell me. Everything, you hear! All the
> sordid details!

IMAGE
HE pulls HER head to HIS own and
buries HIS teeth in HER mouth;
HER nipples become erect. A deep
probing kiss.

Obsessive image: Uremia

When THEIR lips finally part, the
camera closes in on HER face until
Close-up: SHE struggles for air. HER
eyes: sly, myopic, blinking.

SOUND
SHE (*breathless*): So you're one of
those!

SHE licks HER lips as SHE looks at
HIM.

SHE: Now it comes out. (*Pause for
breath.*) You're a fine one, all right!
Trying to dig up dirt—that's how
you get your kicks!
HIS voice (*panting*): Tell me! Everything, you understand!

IMAGE
SHE presses up against HIM.

SHE: All right, then listen (*teasingly,
in the cadence of a nanny telling a
fairy tale*): Once upon a time, there
was a man, a very, very big man with
black hair all over . . . (*interrupts
herself*).

SHE stares at HIM piteously.

Says (*guilelessly pouting*): My knees
hurt. Couldn't we do this in bed?

HE pulls HER up brutally.

HE: All right then, let's get into bed.
But there you're going to tell me
everything!

SHE (*relieved*): Yes, in bed I'll tell
you fantastic things.

HE squeezes her wrists together.

HE: And no fairy tales, you hear?
SHE: Ouch!

As SHE leaves, SHE snatches a bit of
meat from the platter.

SHE: No fairy tales. All the sordid
details.

257

SHE laughs at HIM like a slut over
her shoulder and takes a big bite out
of the meat. HIS face, in extreme
tension, is thrust forward and follows
HER along with the camera.

> *Rapid fade-out and slow fade-in
> again*

TRANSITION SOUND
Smetana: The Moldau, first at full
volume, then receding in waves and
once again returning.

IMAGE
Their bedroom: four-poster bed, mahogany wardrobe, lacquered table (on
it Huysmans' *A rebours, Les Fleurs
du mal,* and Dickens' *Christmas
Carol*), dolls, fairy-tale pictures on
the walls (Schnorr von Carolsfeld).
Among the pillows on the bed, below
a canopy of floral chintz: HE and
SHE (*dialogue inaudible*). HE talks
to HER insistently. SHE appears to
balk but responds from time to time
with a sphinxlike expression and a
coquettish whorish smile.

LASER BEAMS focused in rapid
succession on:
Impatience
Rage
Lust
Bitterness
Erotic excitement
Abdominal pain subsides; in its place,
a feeling of emptiness, of having been
drained, of lassitude

Meanwhile:
Sexual tremors in the subphrenic region, accelerated cardiac activity,
shortness of breath

SOUND
remains wavelike as before, at times
synchronized with heightened cardiac
activity, building to an overly loud,
thunderous volume: *The Moldau.*

IMAGE
He grabs Her arm brutally and
bends over Her, threatening.
She throws Her arms around His
neck.
They embrace.
Close-up: Her head close to His,
Her lips at His ear. She begins
Her tale.

> There appear in increasingly rapid
> succession, each one shown with
> Her in alternating suggestive or ex-
> plicitly sexual situations:
>
> THE PLAYBOYS FROM
> CHARLEY'S BAR

Final fade-out
END

 O THAT WAS THAT. WHAT ELSE DO YOU WANT to know? Maybe how "it" all ended? Right? I trust that your interest in the fate of Mr. von Jassil-kowski and his blond spouse doesn't go beyond the literary. You want to hear their story, nothing more. But nothing less either. So I ask *you*: what is this "it," the conclusion, *the end of the story*? Faced with such a question, the personalities of the main characters evaporate into abstraction, their fate subjected to aesthetic rules. Anything still worth being recorded must be evaluated on artistic scales of value. So what is the end of a story? It must fulfill the relevant criteria—but what criteria? You're placing me on the horns of a deep dilemma of conscience. My unease is twofold, as befits a democrat: I'm appointed master where I'm prohibited to rule. You understand: who in today's artistic circles, if only because of our rent-control aspirations to the sovereign authority of a Goethe, can avoid evaluation, or avoid thinking that if only it were acknowledged that he had created his own world, he'd be granted the right to create the laws governing it? If this were true, my story would indeed come to an end right here and now. Can it continue at all? *How* should it continue, pray tell! For I am forbidden to create *my own* world. All I'm allowed to do is report faithfully, nothing else. You see me in the calamitous but inevitable situation of the Realist, my esteemed reader. For as I said, the matter is out of our hands. We are not Olympians, not even Private Prometheans. We live among our own kind, self-skeptical, modest, and conscientious. And in light of our skepticism, even our most subjective perceptions prove to be identical to most other people's—which is commonly known as objectivity. Conscientiousness keeps us from seeking another reality besides *this one*. Our artistic conscience turns us into

260

reporters. And thus the faithfulness of accurate reporting once again imposes upon us forms which—pure and simple—mean the end of storytelling itself.

Scheherazade, you see, thought the end of a story was nothing more than the beginning of a new one. Likewise the blond thoroughbred did not finish her stories that first night. It soon became evident that she had no real objection to this rather melodramatic form of seeking pleasure. Not only was Baron Peter-Traugott spurred on to hitherto unsuspected heights of achievement; she herself, in the course of the storytelling, began to lose that strange shyness she had always felt in the face of his chaste reserve. Finally she was able to show her true self, all the magnificent licentiousness of the frolicsome slut she was, and although this may have meant a certain loss of sweet intensity between them, she got her money's worth in other areas.

No, her storytelling was certainly not confined to that first night. Although the munitions heiress was nowhere near as blessed with sweet verbal gifts as the vizier's daughter or Schahriah's sly wife, she had no fear of running out of material for the next thousand nights, for she found in a drawer of her desk—call it accident, if you will—the register of past sins that she had remorsefully drawn up a few weeks before her wedding and had lazily never consulted. Now it came into its own. And where it failed, there was always the portrait gallery at Charley's Bar to jog her memory: often, when Baron von Jassilkowski sat at the regulars' table in the sofa corner, lost in deep brooding, he stared up at that opulent parade of long-lost playboy grandeur, searching in vain among those hypertrophied heads, cocktail glasses raised in snappy toasts, successfully and unsuccessfully depicted round shoulders, collars, silk breast-pocket handkerchiefs, carnation boutonnieres, and stickpins for a key that would unlock the secret of their legendary existence—for glyphs of a reality that could not be grasped and that, despite its overpowering dreamlike presence, remained remote from the realm of actuality. As wonderfully lively and convincing as his Scheherazade's tales were (and he could not have experienced them with any greater sensitivity had they been engraved on his eyelids with needles), he was in the dark as to what they were to him and what they meant for him;

they were a dense and substantial reality, which might have finally —finally!—confirmed his own reality if he confronted them. But no, they were specters, again only specters and nothing but specters, conjured up by his bold selfless spot checks on the existence of truth—*truth*, that's what I said—he was looking for genuineness, totality, identity.

You may not want to believe, venerable friend, in the heroic qualities of Mr. von Jassilkowski—that's your mistake, and I'm sorry for you. It is not granted to your petty soul to follow the heroic path of someone like him! And yet this path stretches so long and clear before us, phase after phase according to the myths containing the ur-knowledge of the human mysteries: of the calling, the setting out, the initiation, and then the descent into the terrors of the underworld. Every savior, my good man, must survive his own harrowing descent into hell so as to achieve the ultimate objective, imposed on him by fate, of this adventure. The elixir of life, the source of redemptive wisdom, the fountain of youth and eternal rebirth lies concealed in the underworld—*below the waters*: the way to it is the way of suffering and temptation, and the most terrifying of the perils lying in wait along the way is *metamorphosis*.

Sir, if you still don't believe in the heroism of Mr. von Jassilkowski, at least try to sympathize with the torments he endured. There he sat under those pale watercolored revelations of the great playboys of Charley's Bar and stared at their racy, divinely assured, and indisputable presences, felt himself called, tempted, tried by the magic of their high-spirited cup-swinging *haecceitas*—and yet he was aware of being mocked by their unattainable, never-to-be-achieved existence, forever being withdrawn into an unreachable beyond: he recognized himself in them and vice versa; he was one of them but then again not. For nightly, you see, as his timidly aroused Scheherazade whispered her abominable confessions in his ear with bated breath and apprehension, the flesh he held in his arms bore overwhelming witness to the truth of her stories, and he would metamorphose so fully into one of them that he lent the heat of his own body and the sweet torment of his own lust to their ghostly shades; and, conversely, he derived lust from them while at the same time becoming the lust of the woman in his arms, the blond thoroughbred, the lust they had excited in her, and he received the lust she gave him as a gift intended for them and also coming from them: and thus did he remain simultaneously blessed and betrayed, made richer by one great poverty and poorer by one great source of wealth, a king without a country.

And it also came to pass in those summer days of 1939 (in addition to everything else) that the thoroughbred, sitting next to him at the regulars' table in the sofa corner (we had noticed that she was quiet and pale and complained of occasional headaches and inexplicable fatigue, but we attributed it to the climate), would covertly slide her big bold hand with its ox-blood enameled nails into the Baron's, his stare meanwhile affixed to the portraits above the bar, and would say, low and tender, grieving with unavailing regret: "If only I had known you back then, my Sweet Pete . . ."

Back then—what mockery! Silk shirts and Cuban mustache—happiness, innocence of ignorance! Zoppot and cousin Zapieha—youth: "For they are purer than the purest stone and, like a blind animal just starting out in life, they are yours alone, wanting nothing and needing only one thing: to be allowed to be as poor as they truly are . . ." Ah, youth and its dear *Jugendstil*!

And so what had to happen in the end did happen: the thousand nights came to term, and one morning the blond thoroughbred's confessional register was exhausted. She had nothing more to tell and could respond to his panting questions ("What would you do if you met *him* again and he were lying here next to you where I am now?") only with a simple "Sleep, Peter" (whereupon she would do just that). The last, most perfidious effort of the duplicitous specters to withdraw without revealing their secret! But the hero will capture them and force them to reveal their true selves—he will make them real . . . And thus it was Baron Traugott himself who hit on the clever ruse of taking up a phrase she had used time and time again to silence him, namely: "But I never loved anyone except you!"

"What exactly did you mean by that?" he asked her. "Before you knew me, you couldn't possibly have loved me, could you? And ever since you've known and loved me, as you say, nothing else has occurred *despite which* you love me—OR AM I WRONG?"

Of course she tried to explain how she had meant it, but he drove her into a semantic corner, insisting on a literal interpretation of her words, and since his impatient heightened urgency again stirred up the fires they had both come to find so satisfying, she soon gave in and adapted to this development: mightn't he be very angry, she asked with ravishing playacting timidity, mightn't he even beat her, perhaps? And when he left this question entirely open, she begged: "But not too hard, Peter baby!" And when he caught her wrists in a brutal grip and ordered her finally to come clean, she confessed haltingly: no, in fact (although he should by no means take it seriously at all!), no, she hadn't exactly refused her favors, as the saying goes, to every man she had met since she knew him—"but only in the very beginning, Peter baby—please don't hit me too hard. It was only for kicks . . ." That notwithstanding, she was able to recount the incident in every sordid detail, even adding a name and a final distinguishing characteristic ("*il n'y a pas de détails*," says Valéry, no?) by cautioning him: "But be careful, Peter baby. The guy is terribly strong, an amateur boxer. I wouldn't mix it up with him over this."

A woman most worthy of being adored! A true magician at conjuring up objects of desire! No, more than that: a standard-bearer for the highest ideals of femininity, arch-woman, ur-Mother, Queen of the World! For what you may overlook in all this, my esteemed friend, is the self-sacrifice of love.

There came a night in that summer of 1939 that seemed to have no end, indeed refused to end, with the bell-like tension of the glass-clear succession of transparent days, when the anticipation was almost unbearable, days almost bursting with anticipation—a night when a whisper rose from dark-lilac shadows and reached an eager ear, blew over to it as light as down, and it said the following words: "Peter? Peter, you know that great big blond guy who's been coming to Charley's lately? You know that evening when you went to see the old Schrader goat, I told you I spent the afternoon with my girlfriend? I wasn't with my girlfriend at all . . ."

Did you catch that? Isn't it just like a fairy tale? The ghosts that haunt him now relent: the past is overcome, its song no longer entices. The present approaches and, with it, the ultimate and most difficult of all tests, the seduction of reality—*ah, bel héros, si tu posais ton doigt sur mon épaule* . . . And it is love itself that sacrifices so as to provide the prince with the most tormenting of all temptations—reality! *Bel héros! La possession de la moindre place de mon corps t'emplira avec une joie plus véhémente que la conquête d'un empire! Avance tes lèvres* . . .

But anyone who ever put a cocktail glass to his lips at Charley's in those days and happened to look over the rim at the regulars' table in the sofa corner—that is, anyone who still had eyes for something other than his own expectations in this mood of general expectation—might have discovered to his surprise and dismay that Baron von Jassilkowski was glaring back at him, eyes murderously glowing under anguished pitch-dark brows; out of nowhere, it could happen that Baron Traugott's usually artfully blank countenance would fill to bursting with a Dostoyevskian, subterranean, all-consuming, mystic-holy animosity. "Does he have Party connections?" someone asked Tom the Mixer one day.

Even stranger things happened: for example, he began to talk of his mother more often, proudly, even arrogantly. Mrs. von Jassilkowski, living in great seclusion in Allenstein, East Prussia, began slowly to take on features and then definite form: where once there was nothing more than cloudy amorphous outlines, like certain hasty unfinished pieces hammered by Michelangelo from marble, increasingly precise contours now emerged of a finely chiseled bust of an untouchably pure, selfless, dutiful, tender, musically inspired widow of many years (and former intimate of the Countess Döndorff). The Baron seemed to have been carrying her in his heart as a secret treasure, a role model, anima, standard of morality and virtue; and when in conversation he alluded at times to certain moral imperatives or sensitive states of the soul, matters that seemed odd to the libertines at the regulars' table, he'd declare, not without proud stiffness: "I get that from Mamá . . ."

But that only in passing.

It was the second half of August and the crew at Charley's brass rail began noticeably to thin out. Often, one of the missing ones would suddenly appear in the doorway, no longer his former self: somehow you couldn't quite believe your eyes—until you realized that, amidst the thunderous greetings, this fellow's strange depersonalization was due to his new field-gray uniform, which magically transformed that unmistakable big blond guy or this thin dark-haired one, whomever, into an anonymous Private Nobody; and you jokingly tried on his helmet and bought him a farewell round; there were some pretty wild goings-on in Charley's back then, and yet still, in some incomprehensible way, nothing really ever happened, everything seemed distanced from reality . . . But that too just incidentally: the calendar, as I say, showed the second half of August, and although it was the only proof that time was indeed passing, each day went on emerging from the one before in miraculously timeless fashion, clear as glass and pure as a bell and filled to the brim with overwhelming anticipation—while the dark flower of Baron von Jassilkowski's suffering blossomed into its ultimate painful splendor, bearing the sweet fruit of the mystery in whose solution our salvation lay.

It happened that at the end of one of those dream days he sat in the evening light of his desk lamp and waited, waited for hours, because the blond thoroughbred was still out. He had passed the day on business in the city and returned home in a mood of subterranean depression, having been vexed at the offices of the *Gentleman's Monthly*. His already tormented soul was further inflamed by a barbed paradox: through some negligent blunder in handling his papers, the thoroughbred's playful sketch "On the Shoe" had somehow gotten mixed up with the pages of his latest contribution ("Personality—the Keynote of the Season") and had come to the attention of Baron von Aalquist. This last, irritable of late, had used it as an occasion to tell Baron Peter-Traugott some unfortunate truths—namely, that the quality of his work had fallen off and that he'd better get himself together fast, which should be easy, judging by his excellent, witty, sparkling, if fragmentary and unfinished essay on shoes. He, Baron Peter-Traugott, could not lower himself to clear up the mistake (editors are, after all, notoriously inconsistent). So it was only on his way home that the germs of self-doubt turned virulent and began to eat away at the core of his being. Thus he came home and found the small apartment empty—an inexplicably emphatic eloquent emptiness, or so it seemed to him, though there was nothing unusual about the blond thoroughbred being late. But from out of the sky, from out there beyond the window, night had begun to creep in—*night creeps over the city, the streets aglitter with kilowatt pearls, shadowy oceans sprinkled with lights, damming the tide of darkness*, doesn't it go like that?—and here was the lamp with its fringed red shade, pasted with a circle of silhouettes of chubby-cheeked children in Biedermeier costume, the boys drolly dressed up in starched collars and curved top hats and the little girls in crinolines and poke bonnets, and the dear old homey lamp cast its mild, subdued light courageously against the darkness—the dammed-up tides of darkness—oh, panic, oh, despair: "the unconscious and the miraculous and the infinitely dark, rich cycle of legends: his early years, so full of foreboding"—but the thoroughbred didn't turn up and the hours went by, one by one, falling into that great hole of the past. And so he sat and waited, and the thoroughbred did not return. She couldn't be at Charley's, for he had called and been told she had been there early in the evening but left soon after, and her girlfriend was away on vacation. And it was late—"soon the dawn patrol will come—night slowly staggers off . . ." and he was overcome by a great anxiety, a fear of primal abandonment, a humility, great and wild, and while his soul was still torn between anger and hope, between despair and damnation, his heart learned THAT IT WAS FULL OF LOVE. He knew what it had suffered and why it had been made to suffer this pain: it had been filling up with love—*eros* and *agape, amor complacientiae* and *benevolentiae* had melted into the pure bell metal of urgent profound spirituality—rejoice at the pain!—and just as a saint's dry rod, wakened by the power of divine certitude, sprouts green shoots and bears witness to the glory of the lamb, so there suddenly bloomed in the pentecostal depths of his being the *truth*. Purity! Integrity! He examined his soul all the way to the bottom, and he recognized the slag metal that had made it imperfect but that now was dissolved by the power of love. Purity! Integrity! "Here on earth I call unto Thee, as my heart is filled with love, for Thee wisheth to lead me to a high mountain . . ."

And at that instant he heard the spectral humming of the elevator echoing through the walls (the comfortably cozy purring of the big cat Homeyness—how many times already that night had it deceived him!), heard it approach, coming closer as his panic grew, and then—oh, fair terror!—it did indeed stop on his floor, and a key was indeed inserted into the entrance door, and Baron Traugott— I mean Baron Peter—he—alas, we must forgive what is all too human!—he felt both a sense of relief and a pedagogic impulse (oh, the tragic duty of an educator to be rigorous! We are handed the schoolmaster's rod along with our first primer!) and, behind them, forgiveness and reconciliation, doubly sweet . . . Enough: Baron von Jassilkowski suppressed this painfully beautiful need to reveal his love (only for the moment, only for now) and girded himself, solemnly severe. The thoroughbred entered. He turned to her.

Her entrance occurred, an event, a turning of the times: she was suddenly present, but present in a special sense, expected and yet unforeseen, unbelievably believable, as if his secret doubt that she would return (at its core a doubt about her ultimate reality) had hatched her out of nothingness. She was there as if suddenly a hole had been filled, the hole that his unmotivated consciousness of her existence had projected into insubstantiality—filled, yes, but in a manner that was surprisingly independent from him and alien: for, you see, it was she, all right, and yet not she who had returned. It was *she* who was physically present and extant, and yet she was created entirely anew by that never-before-experienced, never-before-anticipated situation, with no continuity with or logical connection to what she had been before—though still burdened by a misleading resemblance to it—and nonetheless she was still magically related to herself, unmistakably and quite obviously THE BLOND THOROUGHBRED . . . Thus she *entered* the scene, thus she struck, like a prophecy fulfilled, fate in person, with the full force of tangible reality and yet as unreal as a dream apparition.

She didn't say hello. She looked at him as at a mere object, indifferently and aimlessly, neither curious nor surprised, nor with any sign of recognition, devoid of love or hate; and then she lifted her eyes beyond him. She closed the door behind her and leaned against it. She hadn't taken off her light overcoat and wore no hat; a strand of her platinum-blond hair fell over her forehead. Her eyes with their raised brows were small and glassy, she wasn't wearing her specs and her myopic gaze was dull and expressionless. The wide guileless sulky child's mouth—lipstick smeared—cut broadly across her face: a ravaged, emptied face, her high angular cheekbones jutting out, the flat hollows of her cheeks tailing off to a greedy lower jaw, curving around to form a rather vulgar chin, the smooth, still unblemished neck skin contrasting with the darker hue of the oily-gray powdered layer above it. She breathed through her open mouth, and she reeked of alcohol.

Having stood like that for a while—no more than a few moments—she detached her deluxe body from the door with a sloppy and insouciant flinging motion of her shoulders and walked, or rather sauntered, her hips swaying automatically (oh, those hospitable hips, the high-flung basin whose true calling was that of motherhood, lazily swinging her harem's litter on its back like an arrogant indifferent camel; the fragility of those long-stemmed legs—the twin pendulums of a corolla!), thus she strode to the chintz armchair and let her handbag slide down the back, holding on to the handle, and for quite a long time looked down at it broodingly, as if she were plumbing the depths of some strange emotion she had never experienced before. Then she turned to Baron Peter-Traugott and said curtly, soberly, unemotionally: "I SLEPT WITH A GUY." With that she sat down in the armchair.

Baron Jassilkowski—how shall I tell you this? (for once again, things started to happen in a timeless and spaceless series of merger and simultaneity, but this time, for God's sake, let's stay within customary narrative boundaries!)—Baron Jassilkowski felt in the pit of his stomach the purplish darkness of a sharp pain of oddly scintillating splendor, coiled and creepy like a worm, curled and bushy like the crest of a dragon's helmet, thorny like a martyr's crown, piercing like the point of a lance and at the same time runny like ink. (Associative sequence: squid—whalebone: *Lay down your arms*—boneless—tentacle—entwining—snake—slither—sleazy— bon vivant—*sl* as a sound of sensuality, lasciviousness and lechery: *slurp, slaver, slide, slip,* SLEPT, *slouch, slough, sloth, slime*—*slit*, pain center, personality core, ego seat: ARSEHOLE)—and as the flamboyantly exploding pain melted in his body and filled him with a heavy sweetness, his spirit separated from his earthly presence in an ineffably luminous, unattainable brightness, and he knew—knew with the blissful certitude of recognition (Plato's *anamnesis*): "This is death!" Death. "The great death that everyone carries within—for we are but leaf and skin: great death is the fruit," isn't it? And he also knew at the same time that this—DEATH—was not the extinction of the flesh, for his flesh remained here on earth, rooted in it, in the earth and in its dreamlike unreal reality. He felt his shoulders straightening and he heard his voice say (it was his voice, but in spite of his purple pain, it sounded stiffly ironic and cutting): "Save it for later. You're drunk. Where have you been at this hour?"

"With a guy," replied the blond thoroughbred. Unexpectedly and to her dismay, a tear welled up under her thin eyelashes and swiftly ran down her cheek in an errant arc, curved under her nose and stuck, clear and glittering, in the corner of her lipstick-smeared, pouting child's mouth. She licked it away with her broad, carnivorous tongue and swallowed it.

"Later, I said"—the voice of the Baron could be heard. "First go brush your teeth. You're totally drunk."

The thoroughbred lifted her head with the remoteness of an animal and fixed her dull myopic eyes on him. The heavy strand of blond hair from her splendidly full peroxide mane that had fallen over her forehead now dangled in front of her nose. Strangely, it was precisely the overwhelming strength, the superabundant vitality of those Merovingian locks that now endowed her with an almost ghostly unreality, that tail of Mazeppa's stallion, that banner of sound equestrian health which flapped about her in a moonlike silvery sheen, spectral grasses swaying with the tide of supra-reality. The Baron, in his untouchable serenity, recognized that she *too belonged to the dead*: this embodiment of life itself, the flesh-powerful, magnificent, divinely assured, life-affirming blond thoroughbred, too, was just an illusion.

And this illusion spoke: "What are you turning me into?" she said heavily (the words sounding dampened like the strokes of a bell under water). "What are you turning me into?" And just as abruptly, in a headlong and quite unexpected rush, she leapt up and swung with all her might and hit him over the head with her handbag. It was a heavy, hand-sewn bag, but not even solid German crafts-

270

manship could withstand the violent impact: the handle ripped, and it glanced off the Baron's head and crashed into the silk shade of the desk lamp.

Baron Peter-Traugott grabbed the thoroughbred by the wrists.

"What are you turning me into, you fake! You miserable fraud!" she gasped at him, her breath hot and saturated with alcohol.

He flung her back into the chintz armchair.

His great cheerfulness and serenity remained as untroubled as the late summer sky, which rose from the dissolving darkness of the night, lifting its veils over the city of Berlin in the year 1939, impenetrable as he himself in his pure transparency: the most terrifying of his fears—TO KNOW HIMSELF SEEN THROUGH—had just lost its hold on him. For mark my words: our knowledge of the frauds and deceits of our own existence, which smolders underground and oscillates between dreams and waking, is part of life itself and its immanent illusion, the ambiguity of value which only gains its true significance in the thought of our mortality. This is one of the terrors and torments of consciousness itself and its self-destructive bastard offspring, conscience, which is always the conscience of being *between* realities, distorted and torn by flight and longings, fleeing and longing whose sole ultimate objective is death. It belongs to the pathetic attractions of this conscience that it can replace the optative with the present indicative tense—the "Oh, if it were only so" with "It is so"—dream activity transposed into the state of waking, born of fear . . . But the Baron now realized how invalid his fear of life —his fear of dying—actually was: he had suffered his death and yet lived on, blessed by his pure unsullied serenity. The hero, you see, had indeed won the elixir of life. He held it in his hands, and its magic power transformed reality: *he could no longer die.* No one could. For behold: they shall live and multiply and shall not be defeated by time—no longer be defeated by time—not defeated by time . . .

He looked down at the ruined lamp—it lay there destroyed, forever extinguished, the tried-and-true lamp of his childhood: a shard from the shattered bulb had torn straight through the silk shade and severed the head from the starched collar of one of those diminutive chubby-cheeked Biedermeier boys with the curved top hats; there it

271

lay and never again would its light shine mildly and cozily on an evening. He realized how useless it looked in the clear light of dawn: home—memories (Father Montesquieu had his sons woken up every day with the sound of music)—what could it all mean to him in his death-born serenity? Rejoice! For we shall not be defeated by time!

He turned around and abandoned Fort Nobility.

Oh, Oedipus! Why do we tarry still?
Let us set out! For you have already
pondered your decision far too long.
SOPHOCLES,
OEDIPUS AT COLONUS

 Y VENERABLE FRIEND, YOU WANTED TO HEAR
the end of our story, and you were right to insist
on it, for it is a heroic tale, as I've said, and a hero's
life is not fulfilled just because he triumphs over
himself: his victory is completely established only
by what the symbolism of knighthood calls the
"Joy of the Court." The vital elixir of revelation
that will cause the times to change and that he
has won from his own innermost core ("the unconscious and the
miraculous and the infinitely dark, rich cycle of legends: his early
years, so full of foreboding") needs to be validated, made general,
and this cannot be accomplished by the power of formula alone:
only by first *living* himself what for us others is to become a new
and improved model for life does he become conqueror, redeemer,
and savior.

Well then! Baron von Jassilkowski walked through the bright
morning. He wandered along the empty Kurfürstendamm, past
Kranzler and Mampe and Venezia—dream backdrops of the great
chimera that is the past!—past Bleibtreu-, Wieland-, and Wilmers-
dorferstrassen, via Halensee into Grunewald. (Already the red bar-
berries were ripening and dying asters breathed weakly in the flower
beds; "whoever is not yet rich as summer ends . . .") And it happened
that on his way he encountered a remarkable apparition:

It was a woman and yet not, for her womanhood was so exaggerated that it somehow lost its quality. She approached with her
head held confidently high. The powerful sweep of her Valkyrian
bosom swelled and creaked against the stiff canvas of her pea-
sausage-gray windbreaker; she wore a belt hung with a fire ax, an
electric torch, an alarm whistle, and a pistol holster. In the crook
of her arm, a helmet swung by its chin strap. She wore a skirt that

273

(not unlike the lobular excrescences of certain salamanders, remnants of their aviary past) flopped ludicrously around her legs like a rudiment of a former long-discarded way of life, for its once draped and subtle bell shape was now spoiled by a pair of rough trouser legs, bound at the ankles and tucked into sturdy footwear. Her thick dark hair, formerly caught in gold mesh at the back of her neck, was now tamed by the tight straps of a Scottish shawl, a strange cross between a Phrygian bonnet and a turban, rolled and knotted severely high on her forehead, which gave her head the air of both bold independence and housemotherly ingenuity. The marching tread of her sleigh boots crackled militantly on the asphalt of the still-empty Kurfürstendamm.

And the Baron recognized this Nike as Mrs. von Schrader on her way to an air-raid drill.

She greeted him with a nasal, golden-brown *"Heil!"* and invited him to accompany her part of the way. She belonged—she told him—to a group of society ladies who had been receiving instruction in emergency air-raid procedures for an unthinkably long while, i.e., ever since the days of the "Black Reichswehr," and who had now risen to appropriate positions of authority. Under martial law, her sidearm, a Walther model, would lay low anyone who dared to oppose her orders.

Nothing in her present getup recalled her former incarnation as a bleached-out, grandly offended, stiff high-society fortune-teller. The promise of great things to come, large-scale dispositions, and real decision-making surrounded her with a brisk cheerful aura: it seemed as if she were drumming out her marched steps as a kind of playful staccato to the exalted legato of the melody that carried her along the asphalt—as if she, like some daring tomboy, wanted to underline with this contrapuntal, hoydenish stepping rhythm the fact that she was really floating on air. She was humanity come into its own, freed of its shackles and liberated from all base, everyday entanglements. And Baron Traugott, himself swept along on air cheerful and serene, adjusted to her dashing cadence.

As they both kept step to the echoing rhythm on that hollow morning, she chatted about her organization: the general's widow from Potsdam was understandably in a leading position, and among its younger active members were Her Excellency's daughter, of course, also Jutta Mittwitz—surely he had met that young lady, originally from Lower Silesia, at some party given by the diplomats of a friendly power—and Erdmute von Bobzien, too—Mrs. von Schrader, who was a regular Nike, knew of course that he had been invited to Klekow: both Jutta and Erdmute were her remote nieces (her family being as extended as King Priam's).

And then there was also a young Countess Lehnhoff from the district of Pillkallen (or was it Gumbinnen?—of course, Gumbinnen; though it might also have been Eydtkuhnen), whom he surely knew, and also a considerably older but still absolutely active and lucid Döndorff, one of her close neighbors. And behold: in the course of this brisk overview, Mrs. von Schrader also included the Baron and Baroness Jassilkowski in this circle of blood relations and tight social connections. It would be a crying shame, she said bluntly, if his young wife went on being aloof from her circle; they were really counting on her participation, all the more as they had heard by way of Milly Schlierstedt, who, of course, was close to Fritze Klüt-zow, that Madame Jassilkowski would be just the person to infuse some wit and life into the whole undertaking, which until now had had a rather dry tone thanks to official Party influence. Mitzi Schön-brunn (her direct niece)—surely he was aware of the rumors concerning her, in which there was, needless to say, not the slightest grain of truth—she, Mitzi, had also been won over, and now, if the well-known Baroness Jassilkowski could also be added, it would look smashing, particularly to the younger set. For, after all, they had no intention of letting themselves be trampled by the petit bourgeoisie, *comprenez-vous?* Therefore, she (Mrs. von Schrader) had been intending for days to call the blond thoroughbred to invite her collaboration.

Sounds familiar, doesn't it? Society—the body corporate of the highest forms of being—welcomes the hero into its midst. The heroic journey approaches the point of transfiguration: the "Joy of the Court" is close at hand.

Indeed, continued Mrs. von Schrader, there was also reason to hope that Princess Hohenheim from Ambach, whom he had also met (and who, incidentally, had found many words of praise for his exemplary manners), would ultimately accept the presidency of the Ladies' Auxiliary Imperial Air Defense League, even though some of the aforementioned Party authorities (who had their eyes on Mrs. Emma Göring-Sonnemann) had voiced objections on account of her blindness.

Her blindness? Yes indeed, on account of her blindness. But she was perfectly able to read the *Almanach de Gotha*?!! No, my dear friend, that too was make-believe—or rather, one of her amazing skills: she had developed such a fine sense of touch that she could find any page with the greatest of ease—though only in the various *Calendars of Nobility*, preferably the Hofkalender, of course. A skill she had acquired in childhood. But her eyes themselves were quite blind.

Those eyes of goodness, sir!

And Baron Traugott, infinitely distanced, cheerful and serene, knew that it could not have been otherwise, and that it was good that it was so.

With that, they had reached the Pension Bunsen and smiled at each other, the hero and his Nike. From a window in the house across the street the last measures of "Eroica" could be heard—perhaps somewhat odd at so early an hour, but nonetheless in keeping with the clear hollow tension of the morning. Then there was a voice, and it was no longer the dumpling, bubbly, fawningly obsequious intonations of the announcer of earlier days: a strong voice, which carried and echoed as if calling all within earshot to judgment, filled the quiet intimidated Knesebeckstrasse with words of portent, announcing that that afternoon at fourteen hundred hours, the Führer himself would address the nation. Then it broke off, as if nothing further could be added to that threat, and with drumrolls and fife caprioles, a choir of rough and determined men's voices intoned in harshly chopped rhythms: "On the heath a tiny flower blooms . . . [kettledrums] and its name is . . . [more kettledrums] EEErica!!!" Cannon shots.

Hero Jassilkowski and Nike Schrader looked into each other's eyes and smiled. "Farewell," she said. She did not add "forever," but he knew that was what she meant and knew it was an order. His smile widened.

She let her glance merge with his one or two moments longer—golden brown with Frederician sapphire blue—and he felt the sacred shiver of consecration, of transcendent union running through him, in which she was simultaneously his lover and his mother. He was transfigured by bliss: the *hieros gamos* was complete!—then she turned on her heel so abruptly that the fire ax, electric torch, and holster lifted together horizontally with her billowing skirt: for a moment it looked as if there were indeed wings there, or at least the stumps of them, which, though anatomically out of place, were about to spread in flight. But Baron Traugott did not wait for this goddess of victory to ascend on her rudimentary wings. Unaware of the military figure he cut in his elation at such a sanctified and blissful moment, he turned smartly on his heel and raised his forehead to the cool and immensely clear morning light above the Kurfürsten-damm.

'Tis war! 'Tis war! Oh, divine angel,
raise your great voice and halt the strife.
'Tis war, alas; I wish that I would
bear no guilt through all my life.
MATTHIAS CLAUDIUS

ENDINGS! ENDINGS! DEAR FRIEND, YOU wanted an ending for our story, and here it is, effortlessly unraveled, an ending without truly being one, just as in those fairy tales that finish "And they all lived happily ever after, and if they haven't died, they are still alive today." Precisely that is the secret of our story, the cat I've kept so long and artfully in the bag, so I could let it out at the end—namely: THEY DIDN'T DIE. All of them are still alive today. And they're living well, according to the law they inherited, the one Mr. von Jassilkowski lived out for them in his own life. He alone is no longer among the living. But neither did he die. *He was taken from us.*

For what kind of criterion—I ask you again—was to be fulfilled by him, or by us, or in us for that matter? Who determines our borders? What keeps us together, so that we constitute something to be ful-filled (as Heidegger calls it)? Are we not boundless like the universe itself, only comprehensible in a state of constant expansion—wave frequencies—sound, reverberation, resonance—I'll say it again: the liquid spirit of the good old cobbler Böhme—to sum up, beings of the third quality, entities of origin and agony (or in German: *Quellen* and *Quallen*), jellyfish—shapeless, dubious, questionable in whatever form, ephemeral, insubstantial—Proteus our one true God: *what should we fear?*

Your aesthetic sadism demands tragedy, dear sir. But where do you see any possibility for it? Show me a heroic downfall! Show me an atonement! The miracle of postwar reconstruction perhaps? Where is there Nietzsche's "victory within failure," since we seem to be succeeding at everything we do? What is culpability anyway? Even that most enigmatic form of innocent complicity—the guilt of *being thus*, the contrition of consciousness faced with its own lowly condition and its rebellion, the miserably heroic defiance of our predestined inadequacy—what is that? I ask you. A psychopathic extravagance? Inner emigration? And, of course, we reject the idea of collective guilt, as everybody knows: *so what should we fear?*

Death? Don't make me laugh!

Behold: at that time, on that bright clear late-summer morning in the year 1939 (it was nearly September, you recall)—on that morning when Nike Schrader appeared to him, Baron von Jassilkowski found himself staring his corporeal death in the face as a *janua coeli*, a gateway to redemption and transfiguration. And this is how it turned out:

When he returned home sometime later that morning, he was greeted not by the blond thoroughbred, but instead first by the pungent small of carbolic acid and then by their attorney and good friend from Charley's Bar, who had so eagerly engaged himself on their behalf in legal discussions with her mother over her inheritance. His stuffy, grave, and warily condemning expression unambiguously identified him with the other party in their dispute, and he apprised the Baron of the following in curt, well-chosen words.

The fall of the blond thoroughbred into the chintz armchair, together with the presumed psychological stress preceding and subsequent to it, had placed the Baroness in considerable danger. For what Mr. von Jassilkowski had obviously failed to notice and what his spouse, presumably because of her well-known sense of camaraderie, had concealed from him was that she was seven months pregnant. Scheherazade's nights had not gone to waste: Little Jassilkowski was on his way.

Or rather, Little Jassilkowski had already arrived, the good friend and attorney from Charley's Bar went on to inform him with humanitarian solicitude (bolstered rather threateningly by a governmental-political tone of voice), before he in his untouchable serenity could show the slightest sign of shock or perplexity. There was even some hope of keeping the newborn alive, for he had been put into an incubator immediately, but the condition of the blond thoroughbred was cause for grave concern. He (the attorney and good friend from Charley's Bar) strongly advised against a visit to the clinic: that is to say, while he could not prevent such an attempt by defendant Jassilkowski, he was forced to bring to his attention that for both medical and legal/ethical reasons instructions had been issued not to admit him, this in accordance with the blond thoroughbred's express wishes.

He merely wanted to communicate this, said the attorney and good friend from Charley's Bar, and now his mission was accomplished. He would have to be excused from giving his private opinion about the events in question, which were as unfathomable as they were regrettable. He then took his hat, raincoat, and briefcase, saluted the Baron with a sharp "*Heil!*" and departed.

Let's reflect on this a moment—try to put yourself in Baron von Jassilkowski's psychological position—hadn't some sort of criterion just been fulfilled? Couldn't this be the final revelation that his senseless and grotesque secondhand existence had come to term and been rounded off? Was it not incumbent upon him now to extinguish it, erase it, this life under these humiliating conditions, which had even succeeded in propagating itself and all its shitty premises in the cause of eternal reiteration of absolute mindlessness: Kranzler, Mampe, editorial offices, movies, *Gentleman's Monthly*, 9th Infantry Regiment, boozing and females, the more the merrier.

You can rest assured, my friend, that suicide is a moral problem only insofar as it is due to a temptation, at times inseparable from human nature itself but to be resisted for various reasons and ideological considerations. According to Kant, a human being tempted by suicide should first ask himself whether the maxim of the decision can be elevated into a generally valid law. But it may be assumed that in the heat of the moment, most people would be readily inclined to answer in the affirmative. Even (indeed especially) from the Christian point of view, life is a highly dubious asset. On the other hand, there is the Thomistic argument, according to which a human being, as a creature of God, is not *sui juris* and therefore not entitled to dispose of life and death. The dominant ethical standpoint of the present day tends to treat suicide as an act of moral weakness. But isn't the testimony of a Plutarch more just and convincing than that of a materialistic bourgeoisie? Whatever. You can easily see that suicide is not simply a type of death but rather an act of high significance in the sense that by doing it you reveal what you consider sufficient cause for doing away with yourself. As far as Baron von Jassilkowski was concerned, he could have easily made a noose out of his most faithful tie—the knitted black silk one was strong and slippery enough (especially when lathered with soap) to bear the weight of a not too corpulent adult male, if it was attached to the Hanseatic cog lamp.

But, friend, friend, friend, what are we gabbing about?

He did not hesitate for a moment, untouchably cheerful and serene, this protégé and page boy of Nike Schrader; he did not tarry for a moment when faced with the temptation of tasting the sweetness of his outrage and entering the great dark womb of Mother Sleep; not for one wink of an eye did he succumb to the spiteful temptation to eradicate the deceit of life through the deceit of dying—no!

Not even a shadow of confusion or aberration fell on his luminous soul. Was he not already distanced from this earthly reality by another kind of death, having been granted another, newly won immortal life? And wasn't everything that could and did occur in those days of mystical events in a strange way not really occurring? And weren't the events that did happen occurring entirely automatically, without our lifting a finger? Didn't they occur over our heads, as it were, reaching us only as if in a dream or secondhand? For behold: the attorney and good friend from Charley's Bar had not yet reached the gates of Fort Nobility when he bent over and picked up a paper that had been slipped in through the mail slot. As a conscientious adviser in matters of marital difficulty and munitions shares, he first read the addressee's name and then handed it to the Baron.

It was an official document with a stamped seal. Baron Traugott opened it. It was his army call-up.

Much do I know, remote events I perceive,
the fate of those who counsel, the fall
of the gods of war.

EDDA

TILLNESS! SILENCE! NIGHT IS FALLING. AND our story has come to an end. *Night creeps over the city, the streets aglitter with kilowatt pearls, shadowy oceans sprinkled with lights, damming back the tide of darkness. Drunken night*—and our story has come to an end: *A bum leans over the bar of Time and stares into a black bottle full of stars, stars sparkling like the foam in beer. Soon the dawn patrol will pass by. Night slowly staggers off. And then the day* . . . Our story has come to an end. Onward with consistency and necessity to the end. You say no? Good friend! You say that our hero should be confronted with one more choice, one more decision to be made: Potsdam or Kurfürstendamm, Private Nobody or hero of the home front? My good man! What you are saying is that it would be out of character for him to accept the decisions of *moira* without protest? Indeed, my dear sir, our duty is to question the rationale behind the rules we should obey so as to gain a better understanding of what we believe. But at that time, St. Anselm's *fides quaerens intellectuum* had not yet been introduced into Prussian military service, you understand? In any case, I don't know to what extent you can project yourself back into those far-gone days. Memory is sin, goes an Arab proverb, right? And I can only figure out how it was then by looking at today, by assuming that what everybody saw coming, with ever-greater concern in those days, was brought home to our hero on all sides with such malicious assurance that, when it finally did come, it must have seemed almost liberating to him. Overriding, overpowering ANTICIPATION dominating that period: it was finally realized. All right then. I also assume that especially the elevated and therefore more conservative circles of society, in which our fable takes place, had invested their anticipation of the unavoidable with a security that also contained elements of satisfaction, if not relish. For such an attitude not only expresses the distance between the social elite and the leading political or, better yet, cultural trends of the day, but also corresponds perfectly to a certain aristocratic conception of life, in which both opposition and support express a similar passion for participation, for making common cause. IRONY alone elevates the individual above the nauseating miasmas of the collective; and what man has aspired to, as the highest goal of human wisdom, by means of arduous asceticism and isolation from the world, this—in the final analysis—can also be achieved by an ironically distanced *négligence*: the Leibnizian *émigration du monde* as a lifestyle free from plebeian intrusion, suspended, as it were, between heaven and earth like Muhammad's tomb . . . I beseech you: life and the values of life are actually overrated, and those who have enjoyed both are inclined to believe that this strange temporal existence of ours has an innate tendency to resolve contradiction on its own, given time, whether we pay any attention to it or not. You are allowed, in the spirit of equity, to give priority to the things closest to your heart, since everyone knows you are closer to your shirt than to your jacket. And people in those days who wore shirts by Jacquet and jackets by Knize had their hands full stocking up on new shirts and jackets, just as people do today whose shirts and jackets are made of the only true synthetic fiber, our miraculous postwar reconstruction. Ultimately, it doesn't matter how we spend our interim periods—why even talk about them?!

Stillness! Silence! It is night: *night creeps over the city, shadowy oceans sprinkled with lights, damming back the tide of darkness. Drunken night . . .* But enough of that, the hero: such a predestined outcome fits his basic constitution to a tee, isn't that so? For did he not live out all of our lives—did he not live *our* life in a heightened symbolic form? I tell you, he did not hesitate for a moment. He thought of Nike Schrader—if of anything at all—and chose the path of duty. The path of triumph and transfiguration.

What did you say? Oh yes, he did return. Once, in the spring. And the blond thoroughbred—she had completely recovered and was beautiful, even more than before—as the saying goes: the first child improves the mother, the second, well, you know the rest as well as I . . . Without a word, she rushed into his arms and wept tears of happiness and grief against his chest.

But that was later, as I said. First he shipped out. He shipped— he was shipped—to Poland. *Revanche pour Zapieha*—is that what you're thinking? Didn't they all live there together, those black-haired fellows with night-watchman mustaches, his archenemies, the fathers? Up and at them and let them have it! But that's wrong. It wasn't that way at all, dear friend: what had shipped him there was his cheerful serenity. Shoulder to shoulder with Kreuzwendedich, the painfully smiling angel of death, out and onward, always in the vanguard. When he returned, he had made lieutenant and wore a cross of iron: the Iron Cross First Class.

And then he was shipped to France, still shoulder to shoulder with the sensuous enticing angel of death and still cheerfully serene. Nor did it ever leave him, not even when he came home on a short furlough. He sat with his little blond son, who had outgrown his incubator in perfect health and whose baby hair growing over the soft fontanel already resembled the thoroughbred's life-affirming Merovingian locks. He sat him on his knee, paternally affectionate, and smiled down at him. And when he happened to drop by Charley's in the evening, he raised his glass in high spirits to the great playboys of the twenties—unapproachably, indisputably sovereign in his cheerful serenity, as they were themselves.

And it was night: *night creeps over the city, the streets aglitter with kilowatt pearls* . . . Did you say you've already heard that? You're bored? Well, holler "Lights out!" as loud as you want, as in those nights when bombs fell on beloved Berlin. It's totally irrelevant. I merely find it beautiful: *Drunken night. A bum leans over the bar of Time and stares into a black bottle full of stars* . . . For me, it's filled with dark beauty. But it has nothing to do with our story. Our story has come to an end, I told you. How could it not have ended? Our hero was shipped out again, First Lieutenant Baron von Jas-silkowski, 9th Infantry Regiment, this time to Russia, all the way to Stalingrad. And that's where he stayed.

He stayed there like all the others: Fritze Klützow and Pinne Lassow and Karl Mittwitz with his bold pirate's nose, and—no, not Kreuzwendedich: how could he die, being himself the angel of death?—he got out on the last plane (the crew of this last plane must have been enormous). Nor did the Moldovlachians stay, for they too turned up again. They—artillery to the right and grenades to the left and Mamá's little baby in the middle—had drawn an all too human conclusion from their quite inhumane situation and had run away, isn't that so? And if they are not yet dead, they're still living happily ever after in Munich-Bogenhausen.

HE, however, stayed there. Only, HE did not die. HE was taken from us.

You may not want to, but believe me: HE was taken from us. HE did not fall in battle nor was HE wounded. HE was not overrun or taken prisoner. HE was simply no longer there. Disappeared. Disintegrated.

Those few of his comrades who are still available for questioning report something very peculiar, namely, that HE became noticeably ethereal, almost transparent in those days. In fact, in the hideouts, they say they could see the flames of candles, or whatever they were using for light, right through HIM. And then one night—alas, not a big-city night—*streets aglitter with kilowatt pearls, shadowy oceans sprinkled with lights*—a night that was very different from this one—although also great, oh, greater and more nocturnal— Urania, that glimmering virgin, would be saying hello, holding the universe together in wild delight with her magic belt: on such a night, sprinkled with explosions, HE disappeared. HE was simply somewhere else and never again was there the slightest indication that HE was ever there. HE did not even get a mention in Plivier's book. HE was taken from us.

And now pause to consider what became of HIM. What do you think? Was HE instantaneously compressed, turned into a glimmer of earth? Did HE suckle at the breast of Mother Earth like Gregor at the stone? Will HE come back someday and become pope? Will Thomas Mann nominate HIM the next German king, as he did once for Gerhart Hauptmann? Weimar or Potsdam—Potsdam or Kurfürstendamm? Or was HE secretly called out of the world like Oedipus in the fields of the Eumenides? I'll tell you the answer: HE was transplanted into the gallery of great playboys at Charley's Bar. HE belongs to the ranks of our mythic heroes.

For, you see, HE left behind a message of redemption. HIS life has become an example: as we know, HE lived out all of our lives in heightened symbolic form—and HE *did not die*. Therefore, we won't die either, you can count on it. None of us will die—how could we? We don't even exist, my friend.

I could prove this to you very easily. But what's the use . . . *Night creeps over the city, the streets aglitter with kilowatt pearls, shadowy oceans sprinkled with lights, damming back the tide of darkness* . . . A Negro poem—did you know that? Do you know what you have to be to create a poem? A Negro? No, my esteemed friend! You have to be alive . . . *A drunken night. A bum leans over the bar of Time and stares into a black bottle filled with stars, stars sparkling like the foam in beer* . . . and hadn't Berlin, the much beloved, been erased by the tide of darkness, skeletoned by the sparkling stars of megabombs—and hasn't it resurrected, sprinkling with lights, aglitter with kilowatt pearls? . . .

And you? What do you have to fear? Truly I say to you: LET US REJOICE, FOR WE CANNOT DIE! What sort of death can you expect, after the phantasmagoric unreality of our lives, after the fraud of this third-quality and third-hand existence? Do you really believe that we can die like Pietro Aretino in that painting by Feuerbach? Oh, what's the use . . . *Soon the dawn patrol will come—night slowly staggers off. And then the day* . . .

Behold! Here you sit, like a child outside the barn door, pondering the meaning of my story. I told you all along: it has no meaning at all. What for? Why do we need one—what good would it do? You are used to having one, is that it? Everything has its purpose, right?—and after you've spent your valuable postwar reconstruction time (measured in Deutschemarks) listening to this, you'd hate to think it was wasted. You'd like a little moral to take home with you. All right, then! You shall have it. Here it is: *wait for the movie!*

You want to make your life into a work of art? From a tender age you've been told—those entrusted with your education surely did not neglect to tell you that since you unfortunately had little talent for painting watercolor caricatures or playing Sinding's "Rustles of Spring" on the piano and no aptitude whatever for verse other than reciting dirty limericks—that you should at the very least try "to make your life into a work of art"—to quote Goethe for the very last time—to give fiction a higher level of reality through appearance. Yet it is misguided—Goethe goes on—to persist in maintaining appearances until nothing remains but vulgar reality itself.

Doesn't the example of the hero Jassilkowski teach us this lesson?

So draw your own conclusions. What else do you want? Isn't it within the realm of possibility that you, in your capacity as a captain of industry with good connections in Bonn, might be invited for a small-game hunt in, not Klekow, which is now regrettably in the Eastern Zone, but let's say Bröseltorf, near Buxtehude; it may even be "in the works," as they say, that you might be a member in good standing of the Flottbeck Riding Club as early as this spring, flying high over hedgerows sprinkled with red berries, atop a bay stallion, clad in a pink coat like a real English squire. But I have to warn you about vulgar reality. The dream-come-true that Mary-Jo Smith might become a countess and travel to the Alps to shoot chamoix is already so close within her grasp that it is no longer fabulous, but rather merely trivial. And therefore, the realization of such a fantasy-dream can no longer have, either for Mary-Jo Smith or for you or anyone else, the redemptive power of a blissful miracle, the paradisiacal arbitrariness of being-in-itself. My friend, this is because you, just like Mary-Jo Smith, would find yourself, in spite of yourself, in that state of "divine absence" Monsieur Sartre cites from Valéry . . . I'll let it go at that and won't ask any more questions. For why can't we abbreviate the efforts of existential philosophy and arrive at commonplace truisms by following our own less intricate rationalizations. Buy a movie ticket and watch Errol Flynn in the role of William Tell. Abandon yourself to the magic of his great acting talent. You will discover that, as you become engrossed, you are not imagining yourself as William Tell but rather as Errol Flynn in the attractive role of William Tell. The fact that it is Flynn who has the privilege of trying on ever new and mutable fantasy guises without having to surrender the domain of unreality allows him to remain always and essentially Errol Flynn. That is the "divine presence," in a sense, which elevates him above our kind. Flynn does not even attempt to "become real." He is unreal and remains so, according to the law we have inherited. We rightly revere Flynn as a demigod, as a creature who dwells in a higher harmony of being than our kind can attain. On the other hand, you have your own cross to bear, my worthy friend, and the worm in your heart, the cause of your cheap guilty conscience, is the bastard combination of delusion *and* reality. You're a snob, my friend, a metaphysical snob, and like any snob, you try to perfect the world and your own miserable existence in it by achieving the greatest possible perfection in the backdrop of your life. This passion for perfection is nothing but a way of hating the world. Truly, I tell you: there are better ways of hating it. Wait for the movie.

Learn your lesson from hero Jassilkowski. HE raised himself high above his station. HE triumphed at Stalingrad. I don't really know what you think, but I presume that the name of the city triggers various associations for you—according to Stendhal, the art of war consists of hardly anything more complicated than seeing to it that you have two of your soldiers on the battlefield for every one of your enemy—but at Stalingrad even this simple maxim was evidently not taken into account. Sacrifices were made—surely you remember: *the fighting of the Sixth Army will one day be proudly remembered for its defiance of death at Langemarck, its tenacity at Alcazar, its bravery at Narvik, and its readiness for sacrifice at Stalingrad—* indeed, sacrifices were made there, a whole hecatomb, though I can't imagine to what deity. Perhaps to Reality? . . . Oh, why even think about it? *Stillness! Silence! It is night. Drunken night. A bum leans over the bar of Time and stares into a black bottle filled with stars, stars sparkling like the foam in beer* . . . Even when quoted over and over again, it's beautiful. A Negro poem.

And what does it mean for us? What do we care about the beautiful lamentations of those who still have to fear death because they're alive? *Night slowly staggers off. And then the day* . . . So what?! Why should we fear it, the day, we who know it will never come, for whom the succession of day and night is still proof of the *ignoratio elenchi*, we who merely know it from hearsay and expect it in the approximate, as a vague something in the vaguest of realities, one more ephemeral phenomenon in the ephemeral tropics of our underwater world? What is promise for us—the word? A *flatus vocis*, a glossolaliac undergraduate prank, misunderstanding as the only form of understanding itself. Go to the Sistine Chapel, raise your eyes to Michelangelo's ceiling, and try to resist the temptation to exclaim: "Look, honey, a Daumier!"

You still want information about the blond thoroughbred? She's living in Bavaria. She somehow made her way there when the whole business in Berlin went up in smoke—and the Americans, bewitched by her beauty like the paladins of Charlemagne by the charms of Angelica, immediately took her on. She's doing fine. The munitions shares, too, have been revalued. She's doing all right.

Her little blond boy must be close to puberty—what a darling child! But consider this: he is growing up without any tradition, young Master von Jassilkowski. The little apartment in Berlin is no more, took a direct hit, and with it the Iron Crosses of Papá and Grandpapa and Great-grandpapa—alas! The fathers ate green apples and stunted the growth of their sons . . . And all of it *pour le roi de Prusse*.

The same explosive device that fell on the good old clinker-brick palace from the dynamic modernist twenties also destroyed Charley's Bar—blown to powder, as we used to say—and thus the ancestral gallery over the bar is gone, too. However, memory is sin, as the Arab proverb goes, right? A new complement of heroes will arise to take their place.

But just so that the young gentleman doesn't have to do entirely without connection to tradition, I thought I'd give him a small present. One of those pretty framed tiles that are all the rage these days as decorations for the home, with the inscription:

IN MEMORIAM
PROFESSOR SIGMUND
FREUD